ADAM GOULD

Julia O'Faolain

Adam Gould

TELEGRAM

This first edition published by Telegram, 2009

ISBN: 978-1-84659-060-3

Copyright © Julia O'Faolain, 2009

A full CIP record for this book is available from the British Library.

Manufactured in Lebanon

TELEGRAM
26 Westbourne Grove, London W2 5RH
Tabet Building, Mneimneh Street, Hamra, Beirut
www.telegrambooks.com

I

For a long time, the former Hôtel de Lamballe retained the grace of the *ancien régime*. Even in the 1890s, when it had been a mental hospital for fifty years, its grounds could reclaim a radiance which was often at its most beguiling when one of the figures in the foreground happened to be that of Monseigneur de Belcastel. Though an inmate, he wore well-cut cassocks and moved with a courtly ease, which, if you were a Mason – many were – and disliked priests, might strike you as 'fishy' or even sinister. Yet if you were to engage him in chat, you would find him good company and refreshingly free from self-conceit. His mind was quick, his curiosity lively and his slim ankles twinkled amusingly in their violet silk socks. There was nothing slimy about him, and he had clearly not shirked life's physical risks.

Gouged into his right cheek was a scar so tender that squeamish visitors tried to stay on his left. But his friendliness could foil them, for he had a vivacious way of turning his head, and when he did, the purple scar flashed like a grin and could put off the very people he had hoped to draw close. When this happened, his cheek pulsed, and the scar leered. One of two things: the monsignor lacked vanity or – a better bet? – chose to punish it. Adam Gould, his attendant, sometimes pondered the odds, for he knew how pride disguises itself. Besides, there were rumours of a scandal.

'Not', Dr Blanche had warned when engaging Adam, 'that such tales can be trusted. When you get to know each other, Monseigneur de Belcastel may tell you his side of the story. Meanwhile, if this is to be a true asylum, we mustn't ask too many questions. I haven't asked *you* many, you'll note.' And the doctor smiled his soft, affable, fat man's smile. 'My own guess,' he confided, 'is that our noble prelate is more martyr than villain.'

'You mean he's a scapegoat?'

Blanche shrugged. 'There are two sides to his story. This one,' he handed Adam a slightly thumbed press cutting, 'is probably best taken with a pinch of salt.'

Le Journal des débats, January 1890
CLERICAL PLOT (?) COMES TO LIGHT DURING FIRE

Morbihan, Brittany. Some mornings ago house-guests in one of our more illustrious châteaux awoke to find that fire had broken out and cut off the main exit. Luckily some sportsmen, who were hunting nearby, smelled smoke, raised the alarm, broke down a side door and forced their way in. Thanks to this resolute action, lives were saved, major injuries avoided and a curious discovery made. One of the rescuers, an illiterate man, was directed by a prominent personage – we have been advised by our lawyers not to give his name – to save a box of important papers. The man obeyed, then, some time later, on failing to find its owner again, entrusted the box to the local schoolteacher who, as he put it himself, 'smelled a rat' and gave it to the police. This led to the discovery of a secret society pledged to destroy the French Republic, instigate a coup and restore the monarchy.

At first several senior army officers and churchmen were thought to be involved, but it now appears that, since the only man – a priest – against whom there is any proof is mentally unstable, the plots may prove fanciful. Trusting in such an outcome, this newspaper's editors welcome the chance to remind citizens that the present pope has warned against putting divisive politics before the unity for which true religion strives. Unlike his predecessor, Pope Leo XIII understands the world in which he lives, so there is no longer any reason why a man should not be both a good Catholic and a good Republican. If it is so in America, why not in France?

Aristotle wrote that even God cannot change the past, and it follows that old grudges should be buried sooner rather than later. The habit prevalent among reactionaries of referring to our Republic as a 'shrew', 'scold', 'harridan', 'whore' and 'witch' is a proof of political immaturity. Perhaps such people should be denied the vote?

We shall keep our readers abreast of further developments.

The suspect cleric is, we learn, to be confined in a private asylum near the village of Passy on the outskirts of Paris. It is run by the distinguished neurologist, Dr Emile Blanche, an enlightened and charitable – though some might say 'naive' – gentleman whose readiness to open his doors to the politically compromised of all persuasions has more than once earned him the nickname of '*blanchisseur*' or launderer.

If his new boarder is sane enough to do so, he should be made to answer for his activities. Democracy demands openness, and attempts to defeat the ballot box must not be tolerated.

'It follows,' said Blanche, when Adam had read this, 'that, officially, our poor friend's malady had better continue to defeat us. Do you take my point?'

'Yes.'

'He was badly burned.'

'You mean ...?' touching his own cheek.

'Oh, in every sense.'

'Poor gentleman!'

'Yes. I am relying on your sympathetic flair.' Delicately, the doctor laid a finger to his nose.

'Flair?'

'Mother wit. Trust yourself.'

This exchange took place when Adam was twenty-two years old, had just ditched a plan to become a priest, and didn't trust himself at all. Mother wit had not been valued in his seminary. Perhaps he had none? Like small animals parted too early from their mothers, and in his case from his native habitat, he might lack instinct. He certainly lacked assurance. The doctor, though, so pooh-poohed his doubts that Adam, one of whose uncles had come here twenty years before to help with another monsignor, saw that Blanche supposed him to have inherited skills as specialized as those of a Swiss Guard.

'A charming gentleman, your uncle!' Blanche enthused. 'He could soothe the most intractable hysterics.'

Notoriously, the uncle's monsignor too had been a charmer. Monsignor George Talbot had been the late pope's favourite chamberlain and adviser for years before his dementia was noticed. Indeed it might never, the uncle's letters speculated, have been noticed at all if the Vatican Council of 1870 had not brought northern churchmen to Rome. These unnerved the

papal court. Being used to living among Protestants, the north-
erners were rich, liberal with donations, fussed about gravitas
and showed such shock at the eccentricities of the *cameriere
segreto* that in the end the pope felt reluctantly obliged to have
his '*caro Giorgio*' spirited to Paris and Dr Blanche's discreet,
private establishment.

Talbot's affliction had been some sort of religious mania,
but Monseigneur de Belcastel was clearly a different sort of
man. He seemed startlingly sane. There was nothing eccentric
about him at all. Yet here he was, outside not just the circles
in which gentlemen of his extraction might expect to revolve,
but outside normal society. And so, to be sure, was Adam. A
hybrid outside this asylum, he would, he knew, be considered
a 'half-gentleman' back in Ireland and a 'spoilt priest' by his
seminary classmates, some of whom were still praying that he
might return to their fold.

His uncle, though less prone to pray, had rallied when
needed.

> '*I've sent a thumping great letter of recommendation on your
> behalf to le cher vieux Blanche,*' *he had written when Adam
> left his seminary,* '*so don't let me down any lower than I've
> done myself which, after a trip too many to the gee-gees and the
> gaming tables, is very low indeed. I hope, by the way, that you
> haven't got it in mind to turn into a 'remittance-man' – i.e.
> one who, like myself, is paid by our sainted family to keep away?
> The pay is far too meagre to be divided! As things are, I only
> keep body and soul together by wintering in cheap and chilly,
> out-of-season resorts here in Normandy. By the same token, it
> would be as well not to breathe any of this to Blanche on whom
> I seem to have made a good impression! What a lark! It tickles*

me to be asked to recommend someone. It's the first time in my life. So, you see, you've made me happy.

Talbot was a funny old fellow. To cheer him up I used to wear a white sheet and pretend to be the pope. It was like playing charades! I would regularly issue bulls and anathemas against people we disliked. Great fun! Hope your own troubles clear up.

Yours, blasphemously, in Christ,
Uncle Charles

* * *

Two years later, Adam had grown fond of Belcastel and was familiar with his tastes and character, but had still no more than a hazy notion about the predicament which had pitchforked him here.

Then Madame Blanche, when tidying an old hatbox, came upon cuttings from monarchist papers which the doctor had forgotten. These revived Adam's curiosity.

La Gazette de France, January 1890
SMELLING RATS IN MORBIHAN

Lest our readers be misled by recent reports of fire and scandal in the home of a noble Breton family, we have made our own inquiries. They reveal that the fire was almost certainly started by the 'rescuers', who were no doubt paid to discredit the gentlemen gathered inside. It follows that the 'subversive' papers were planted in the château rather than rescued from it.

Royalists should know that their withdrawal from public life leaves their friends vulnerable to such manoeuvres. It has delivered France to its present vulgarity, *ennui*, ignorance of the art of living, puerile parsimony and absence of respect.

Worse: it has led to time-servers usurping the aristocracy's role. It is now three-quarters of a century since it was first noted that men who aimed to stay in office had to vary their oath of allegiance so often, that the number of their perjuries could be reckoned by their appointments as easily as a stag's age is reckoned by counting the branches of his horns.

Paradoxically, this limpet grasp on preferment ensures stability. As regimes change, continuity is assured by renegades.

A sadder paradox is that men of honour, like the one who became a scapegoat in this story, find that confinement to a lunatic asylum may be the idealist's lot. In a democracy success is often a sign of moral weakness and failure the wages of virtue.

'Don't imagine,' said Monseigneur de Belcastel when Adam showed him this newspaper cutting, 'that the *Gazette de France* approves of failure. Those journalists think me a great fool and that it's just as well I've been put out of the way. Losers end up by fighting each other like caged beasts. No wonder they talk of smelling rats.'

II

January 1892

Passy, like its neighbouring district, Auteuil, is a leafy area full of mature trees and high-walled gardens which slope down to the River Seine, and though the doctor's establishment really is, as he claims, an asylum from the world, it is haunted too by some of the world's grimmer ghosts, being housed in what was once variously described as a château or hôtel belonging to Queen Marie Antoinette's close friend, the princesse de Lamballe. She perished almost exactly a hundred years ago, in the September massacres of 1792, when, according to some, her head along with more delicate parts of her anatomy was paraded on pikes outside the windows of the imprisoned queen. Did this really happen? How to be sure? It may well be happening now in inmates' dreams, for monarchist propaganda keeps such stories alive. After her death the princess's estate became a pleasure garden, and later a place of ill repute which had to be closed down.

Piquantly, dubious heads now hide here again, and the latest arrival is the fashionable, forty-two-year-old fiction-writer, lady-killer and journalist Guy de Maupassant, whose misfortune – he was delivered some weeks ago in a straitjacket – arouses the malign curiosity of his one-time professional colleagues. Journalists are an envious breed because their currency – fame – is one which they themselves rarely enjoy. Guy, though, did enjoy both fame and its fruits until last 2 January, when his maladies finally got the better of him. He had been baffling them for some time, growing ever more desperate as he went from doctor to doctor and from spa to spa, sampling every sort of cure while raging at his clouded vision, migraine headaches, toothaches, hallucinations, weight loss and memory lapses.

For a man who had always prided himself on being an athlete, these afflictions were painful. To the darling of Paris's racier drawing and bedrooms, they were like Samson's loss of hair. Compared, though, to his inability to write, they were less than gnat bites. For years he had swum, hiked, rowed, sailed, cuckolded and rutted with endurance and skill, but writing was what had quickened his *élan vital*. It had prolonged the fleeting moment, kept sensations quick, allowed him to relive his life and try to understand it.

Now it no longer did. His master-talent for pinning perceptions to the page was drying up! He dreamed of dried inkpots. Sticking his pen in them. Failing to. The inkpots then turned into women who – how dull the world was! – were dry too. Impenetrable! He couldn't ... *Merde*! Was the dullness the world's fault or his? His of course! His! His brain had grown sluggish, his mind – what? Babbly? Babel-y? Or did he mean 'blurry'? More and more often now, words evaded him.

And what you couldn't say, you ceased to see. Was 'blinkered' the word he wanted? 'On the blink'? Tantalizing syllables shifted shape in his fumbling brain. 'Blll … ank'? That was it! Blanked! No, *blanched* mind? Doctor Blanched? Might it be the morphine? Thoughts, jumbling like broken type, scattered and escaped his grasp. Helpless, when he needed most to take control, he heard himself, once or twice, spout rubbish.

At lunch, last New Year's Day, at his mother's villa at Nice, this happened. When it did, the shock on his relatives' faces so shocked *him* that, to spare them further pain, he jumped from his chair, tore his napkin from his neck, stuffed it in his mouth and ran from the house. The last thing he heard was his mother screaming entreaties that he stay. He doubts he'll see her again. Or write again. Ever.

He loves her more than anyone in the world. Always has. Always! Which is why he didn't turn back. It is also why, in the shuddering small hours of the next morning, he put a gun to his temple and pulled the trigger. He was a lucid pessimist who had read his Schopenhauer and took pride in confronting life's nastiness head – ha! – on. His own life had been more benign than he could have hoped it would be, but now, prematurely, at the age of forty-two, the good times were so clearly over that he pulled the trigger, felt the hot burn of gunpowder on his temple and – and that was all! Nothing more. The magazine was empty. No bullets! His valet had removed them! Baffled, then enraged, but still intent on doing what he had set out to do, Guy put his fist through a windowpane, located his carotid artery and, using a splinter from the broken pane, began to cut his throat – only to be rescued, farcically, all over again, by the kind, dim and obtusely devoted valet.

All that sangfroid for nothing! That effortful screwing up of courage! No wonder Guy went mad. He was caught in what could have been a script for a child's puppet show. 'Bang, I'm dead! No! Haha! Here I'm back. Thwack! Thump. Fizzle! Hack the artery! Ow! The splinter broke! *Merde*! Shit and re-shit!' 'Life', like puppet shows, 'consists,' as Guy himself wrote, warningly, not all that long ago, to a very young woman, 'of boredom, wretchedness and farce.' *Misère*!

Did he believe it then? No. Now he does, for all three have caught up with him! Farce first! Farce and indignity! Those are what take over when you lose control!

Crunching up and down the frost-glazed paths of Dr Blanche's gardens, he breaks ice shards under his boots. They mimic the bright splinter in his memory. In clear-eyed moments he can see his madness. When he does he is free of it: sane, distanced and in control. He can't be *sure* he is seeing it, though, or which memories to trust. Lucidity trembles. Fiction is on the loose. With any luck his worst memories may prove to have been hallucinations.

The scar on his throat, though, is real enough. And so is the warder who is keeping watch on him. So he knows that he has ended up where he had planned never to be, and wouldn't be now if that interfering fool hadn't foiled his plan. He curses wellwishers!

***

On the other hand, could the valet have been right? Might a cure be effected? Even now? It is not five years since this same man, François, was marvelling at his master's stamina in bed and at his desk. What an appetite in those days! What industry! While now ... François too is keeping watch, but furtively lest the sight of him upset poor Monsieur Guy.

'Don't let him see you,' is Dr Blanche's order. The mad, he explains, can 'associate their trouble with the very people who try hardest to help them. They don't like doctors either,' adds Blanche. 'We put up with that. It's part of our vocation.'

So François hides indoors, peering through the slats of a shutter at his frail, hoop-backed, thin and diminished master who until recently drew women the way honey draws flies. Maybe the greedy creatures did for him! Sucked the life out of him as they sucked his juices! Like ticks! Right from the start François feared just this. He'd have shoo'd them away if it had been up to him which, unfortunately, it never was. Judging by their insistence, there must have been a sad dearth of men ready and able to satisfy the harpies! Reminiscently, he shakes his head. The things they got up to! François, who is just a bit younger than Monsieur Guy, was pleasantly shocked. Some of their practices, well ... In Belgium, which is where he comes from, he doubts if anyone ever saw the like! Or heard of it! Woman after woman used to come to Monsieur Guy's door, heavily veiled, propelled by uterine ardours, sly but avid, pushful, yet always afraid to show her face! Titled ladies in some cases, and almost certainly married! Working for Monsieur Guy taught you a thing or two about human nature and the ways of our betters. Oh indeed! Some left clues: coded notes, impudent or carelessly forgotten visiting cards and gifts with indiscreet endearments. Underwear. More than once, when there was no time to lace them back into their corsets, these got left behind and had to be hidden, since it wouldn't do for one lady to find another one's under things. Not that some weren't ready to engage in *parties carrées* and the like! Foursomes! The trysts were in the *garçonnière*, in one of Monsieur Guy's yachts and in out-of-the-way hotels. François kept a half-anxious count and worried even then that his master was wearing out his health. But in the old days the writing too went ahead. Thirty-seven handwritten pages in one day! François noted those numbers approvingly. Good stuff too. That was the year Monsieur Guy published that cruel but moving novel *Pierre et Jean*, which he based on a news item he'd found in the press.

It was the press which used to provide him with raw material, with work — he often produced so much of it that he'd have to sign his stories with different names – and, of course, with fame. His novel *Bel-Ami* was about a journalist and, just as the book showed up the newspaper world, that world has now started sinking its claws into him. With his own eyes, François has seen newsmen hanging about the village of Passy, asking questions and buying drinks for locals. Vultures! He has warned Dr Blanche, who says he'll take measures. Given half a chance, François himself would like to wring their prying necks.

L'Intransigeant
12 January 1892

Is there really no better way to stop Guy de Maupassant taking ether and opium than by handing him over to the three-star doctor who is getting enormous publicity from all this? Won't any benefit the writer gains from sobering up be undone by the shock of finding himself interned in a well-known lunatic asylum?

The press went to town on the thing. Perhaps it amuses

Monsieur Guy's *confrères* to use his own weapon against him?
It is a fiction to call him a drug addict. His use of ether was
medicinal! He took it for his headaches.

***

This morning Dr Blanche called a staff meeting. It was attended
by his assistants, Drs Meuriot and Grout, along with a warder
called Baron who looked after Maupassant, and by Adam
Gould who, thanks to two years' diligence and the goodwill
inherited from Uncle Charles, was fast becoming the aging
neurologist's right-hand man.

The director was indignant. Something must be done about
the press. Here. Read that. He laid a bundle of papers on the
table: *Le Gaulois, Gil Blas, Le Figaro, L'Écho de Paris* ... Flicking
through them, he said he was less bothered by the lies than
by the accurate bits. Some unnamed doctor – who? – had
clearly discussed our new patient with unbuttoned candour
to the hacks. Here, listen to what was picked up by *L'Écho
de la semaine*. 'He keeps asking for his thoughts,' the leech
had told the *Écho*, 'and rummaging for them as one might
for a handkerchief. "My thoughts," he begs. "Has no one seen
them?" They have escaped him and fly about like butterflies
whose flight he cannot track.'

'That,' said Blanche, 'is more or less exactly what Maupassant
is saying. He talks about butterflies and the difficulty of pinning
them to the page. Someone from here must have leaked gossip.
I don't for a moment believe that it was anyone in this room.
It could be a gardener or a chambermaid or, although I hope
not, it could be one of the warders. But talking to the press has

to stop. Is that clear? Yes? Well, until further notice, nobody is to go in or out without good reason, and the gates must be kept locked. It would do our patient no good at all to read this sort of thing in the papers. And we can't refuse to let him see them. Other patients get them, so how keep them from him? I've been wondering whether we should appeal to the editors to show more discretion? And sympathy? After all Maupassant did good work for them!'

Dr Meuriot had a wry smile for this. As Dr Blanche's second-in-command, he made a point of not being a yes-man. Indeed, he exuded authority, for his face, already enlarged by a fuzz of mutton-chop whiskers, was gaining height as his hair receded. 'I,' he said, 'favour lying low. A row could bring this establishment into disrepute.' He dismissed Dr Blanche's idea of printing a statement to the effect that Maupassant was well enough to read what was written about him. 'Our good-hearted director underestimates the scribblers' venom,' he opined. 'Not everyone is as open-minded as he. We could easily get their backs up.'

'No *reproach* need be implied,' said Blanche, 'if we print it as a news item. We needn't make a direct appeal. Just say he reads the papers. You don't think they'd twig?'

'Oh, I do think they'd twig,' cried Meuriot, 'and feel challenged and reply, and what good would that do us?' He sighed, then lowered his voice to say he hoped the director would take in good part what he felt obliged to say now, which was that *friends* could be the source of the leak. Dr Blanche frequented drawing rooms, did he not, where old acquaintances of Maupassant's asked him for news? Unsuspecting as he was, he probably supplied it. 'That *could* be where the papers got their facts.'

There was an embarrassed pause.

Then Dr Blanche said, yes, he too must be more careful, and Dr Meuriot made appeasing hand gestures while the others looked at their feet and said nothing, being in doubt as to who exactly was in charge. Dr Blanche, like his father before him, was the nursing home's director. Distinguished but unworldly, he had never bothered to buy the premises in which his family and patients were housed, then one day found to his shock that, behind his back, Dr Meuriot had done so 'for a song'. That was some time ago; the shock had faded, and the two managed to jog along, collaborating more or less amicably, but moments like this put a strain on their goodwill.

Employees too felt the strain. Adam especially, since he had no particular training and knew that once the director retired there would be no place here for him. And Dr Blanche was seventy-two.

As they left the meeting Dr Blanche drew Adam aside and asked him to spend time with Maupassant, who was in a black despair and needed company.

'You're young and that's in your favour. Try your charm on him. Soothe. Joke. Tell him stories. Have you read any of his books? You have? Jolly good! Praise them. We're trying to give him fewer sedatives. Monseigneur de Belcastel is expecting a visitor this afternoon, so you'll be free. A vicomte de Sauvigny.'

***

By now Adam was used to the monsignor's ways. The prelate – lean and handsome despite his scar – must once have been gregarious. Even now he received visits, often from men who looked like ex-officers and no doubt shared a common allegiance since, when they were expected, a scatter of objects was apt to transform his room. A silken-tasselled, showily scabbarded sword, inscribed in one of the less familiar dead languages, would be lying conspicuously about, while on his prie-dieu a missal bound in blue and stamped with royal lilies invariably spilled a stream of devotional pictures no bigger than playing cards; a crown of thorns embraced the royal arms of France; the limbs of a crucifix sprouted further lilies; portraits of the last – now dead – legitimist Pretender and of the live, but less loved, Orleanist one flanked those of a weeping Virgin and bleeding Sacred Heart. Seen through the bars of a cage, the late pope, portrayed as a prisoner of the Italians, figured among the suffering. After each visit, the props would disappear.

Belcastel did not hide these, but neither did he want help with their arrangement. His ritual was private.

It interested Adam, for, in his Irish childhood, politics and religion had blended in just this way. Back then, sprigs of withered 'palm' – actually spruce – locks of hair and the like had been as apt to commemorate patriots as saints, and so the monsignor's display revived memories as cosy as old toys. Some were a touch sardonic, for Adam's papa, a pugnacious man who had sat as an MP in the Westminster Parliament, had been prone to mock the glorification of failure – and here it was again.

This father had been an impressive figure in his son's early years. He was fearless on racetrack and hunting field, and, when electioneering, could discomfit most hecklers. Inured to long odds, he tried during the land war, which broke out in 1879, to speak both for his fellow landlords and their increasingly desperate and turbulent tenants. Neither group trusted him of course. Mating nags and thoroughbreds, mocked indignant friends, might get short-term results when breeding horseflesh, but in politics it amounted to disloyalty. He remained unabashed.

Naturally the small Adam coveted his approval and tried to be like him. He inherited his bent for mockery, then – oh horrid irony! – found cause to turn it on his papa himself. Their most aching failures were with each other. Thoughts about this were unmanning, and Adam sometimes felt as if he were walking on ice, while, deep below, intractable memories lurked. He dared not confront them lest they make him want to bang his head on the ground and behave like the more hopeless inmates of this place.

So he held in his mockery when looking at Monseigneur de Belcastel's exhibits and, although his practised eye picked up the – surely spurious? – implication that the uncrowned King Henry V of France was a Catholic martyr, the sham struck him as harmless. It was certainly less harmful than the claims of samplers praising Home Sweet Home. Or so it seemed to him, given what could happen to homes and had to his. His mother had embroidered charming samplers in her day. One featured a Gaelic motto to the effect that there's no hearth like your own. Not long after she finished it, Adam's father informed her that his hearth was no longer to be hers, and a few months later, she was dead and Adam in exile.

He could see the green, silky Gaelic words in his mind's eye: *ni'l aon teinteán mar do theinteán féin.*

Best thrust that memory back under the ice.

He did not believe that the monsignor or his associates had started the fire in that château two years ago.

'Never worry,' he remembered his father saying, 'about the man who sings loudest about Ireland's ancient wrongs. Ten to one, that's *all* he'll do. It's the fellow who tips his cap to you who's apt to take a potshot from behind a hedge and agitate for the confiscation of your property.'

'Just as the affectionate father,' Adam sometimes answered in his mind, 'is the one who'll unexpectedly disinherit you.'

***

Belcastel never wanted Adam to be present when he had a visit, and today, as usual, chose to receive his guest alone. So Adam went to see the new patient.

Maupassant, a red-eyed, stubbly-bearded, wasted-looking man, was standing in front of a mirror examining a scar on his neck. He did not turn when Adam came in, but addressed their joint images in the mirror.

'Sometimes there's no reflection. Have you ever looked in a mirror and seen no one? Just emptiness. Silvery. Like a pond. I can't be sure if it's my eye trouble.' He touched a finger to the glass. 'That isn't me. *That*,' pointing to Adam's face which had appeared behind his shoulder, 'is!' He grinned, then grimaced. 'But it's defying me. See! When I laugh, it doesn't! Maybe you've taken my face. You look the way I used to: young, raw, a bit coarse, but pleasing. Women always liked my face. Give it back.'

'It's the mirror,' Adam told him. 'It's a bad mirror. We'll get

Baron to take it away. Meanwhile,' he took off his jacket and put it over the glass, 'let's cover it.'

'My moustache,' said the patient, 'used to be as light as foam on my lip. Airy as beer foam and the colour of beer! I always brushed it up and back against the grain. Women loved it. And my hair, which is now falling out in handfuls, was as thick as a hedge. Curly! Hard to get a comb through! A bit vulgar according to the Goncourt brothers, who couldn't bear my success. Do you know them?'

'I don't need to,' Adam drew the patient across the room. 'Come and sit by the fire. I know about mean remarks. I have been called a half-peasant, and my hair is like a furze bush.'

The patient pushed a finger into Adam's quiff. 'Mmm. It *is* dense. I had a she-cat once, a tabby, whose fur I used to comb backwards with a fine comb I had bought in Italy. Sometimes she would squeal and purr with pure pleasure and sometimes she would run away. Her pleasure became so acute it was like pain! She didn't know what she felt and that reminded me of me! I am a bit feline myself. Contradictory. Mixed. Like a bastard! I wrote a lot about bastards, yet, do you know, it was only quite recently that I understood why. It was because my mother kept hinting that I was one.'

'Your mother?'

'Oh most insistently. And it is not true. These things are easily checked. She is not a liar, you understand. It's more that she arranges things to look a certain way. She would like people to think I am poor Gustave Flaubert's son, but the truth is she slept with Jesus Christ. So I am his: the bastard's bastard.' Maupassant's gaze locked on to Adam's. 'God,' he told him, 'is to make an announcement about this from the top of the Eiffel

Tower. I am the only begotten son of the only begotten son!'
For moments his gaze hardened, then he burst out laughing.
'You're not sure how mad I am or if I mean it! True?'

Adam said, 'Yes, it is.'

'I'm not sure either. But what is sure and certain is that my
mama has ideas above her station. The Eiffel Tower is quite
close to here, but I haven't been out lately to look at it. Is it
still standing?'

'Yes.'

'It is a monstrosity and should be pulled down. Some of us
protested when it was put up, you know. It is like a gigantic,
rotted phallus! A dildo! Or the skeleton of a giraffe! Ugly, ugly,
ugly!' Suddenly worried, he asked, 'Did I say all that before? I
mean just now. You must stop me if I repeat things.'

'Shall I make us some tisane? To get warm?'

'No, just sit with me here. Put on another log. Stay close. If
I feel I'm losing control and ask for a strait waistcoat, you must
bring it fast. I am worried sick about my mother. Poor woman,
she has had a hard life. I was supposed to make everything up
to her and now look where I am!' He shivered. The fire didn't
seem to warm him.

Adam put on a log, blew until the flame caught, closed the
fireguard safely and asked, 'Why were you to make things up
to her?'

The sick man looked vague. 'How do ideas get going? Maybe
this one started as an excuse? A fig leaf and reason for not getting tied up with other women? Yes. Other women!' Now, as
though he had slid onto a familiar track, he was speaking in a
rush. 'It's hard to stay free, as you'll discover! Show tenderness
and you're done for. Women cling, the race works through

them, and its will to endure makes us sniff around their smelly orifices. Like dogs. The God who created sex is a cynic. Am I depressing you?'

Adam shook his head. 'My father,' he said, 'has a racing-stable, so muck doesn't disgust me the way it does you. I remember a cunning story of yours, an amazingly brilliant feat in a way, because ...' He paused with some cunning of his own, to see if the writer was enjoying this praise. But Maupassant's attention seemed to have lapsed. Best perhaps to plod on. 'The end of this story of yours had me in tears,' Adam told him hopefully, 'even though, earlier on, it had seemed icy with disgust and rage. It starts with an account of pigeons pecking seeds from dung.' He waited for a sign of pleasure, but his flattery seemed to have fallen flat. 'Do you remember,' he coaxed, 'which of your stories starts that way?'

'How?'

By now Adam too was losing the thread. 'With seeds,' he reminded them both. 'In dung.'

'Dung?'

'Yes.'

Minutes passed. The patient's breathing grew heavy. His head sank to his chest, then suddenly rose.

'Seeds in dung,' he exclaimed as if he had all along been pondering this. 'That's it. *That is* how our mothers had to take our fathers' seed, and why mine tries to pretend I'm a bastard. All our mothers – yours too, Gould, depend upon it – would like us to suppose that the Holy Spirit visited them. My mentor, Flaubert – a truly great man by the way – was the nearest mine could come to imagining a spirit. I don't blame her. Telling stories is a comfort. Did I tell you that I don't drink? Nothing but water. Thinking up stories is what I do instead. I don't read much. I look. I like to see things with my own eyes. I try to see quite small, ordinary things precisely and coldly and find a significance in them that nobody else has seen. That's the way to write.'

'Things like seeds in dung?'

'Yes. If I could still do it I might recover my wits. But François has stolen my manuscript with all my ideas, so how can I?'

'Don't you mean that he took your bullets?'

'Do I?' The patient looked puzzled. 'Maybe I do,' he admitted. 'Poor old François.'

The two stared a while into the fire's smoulder. Aerated by the bellows, it had settled to hollowing dry logs into flights of tiny, red arcades which, now and then, flared up, then collapsed in smothers of pallid ash. Adam hoped the writer wasn't seeing bad omens here.

**

Monsignor de Belcastel's mind *was* on omens. Belief in these was forbidden by the First Commandment, and very wise too! His opinion had been confirmed by seeing how fellow inmates were driven to scrutinize imaginary signs and meanings. These could be anywhere. Anywhere at all. In chicken entrails, their own shit, or the postman's failure to arrive. Faith in creation's concern for us turned the world into an animated hoarding, pulsing with tip-offs. Excess of faith was, Belcastel had come to think, the bane of our time. He fought the idea, though, for it smacked of apostasy. Words like Turncoat and Mason came to mind. Anarchist! And, to be sure, the great argument for the true faith was that it kept false ones in check. Even it, though, could become unstable.

Hope, too, could be destabilizing. Its trust in the power of human reason led to high-handedness. Look how parliament had banished God from the schools of France in just a few years! 'Laicizing'! At the same time – a mean turn of the knife – it had made attendance obligatory! This in a country which had sixty-four million Catholics and hardly two million dissidents! Mad, thought Belcastel. Parliament, in the name of progress, was trampling the sensibilities of families who saw the new measures as a theft of their children's souls. He had seen grown men shed tears of rage over this: fathers offended in their natural prerogatives, sons offended by the offence to their fathers. They felt martyred and murderous, and so did the nervously adamant deputies.

Faith and hope had turned poisonous. Charity was the rare, good virtue and, to the monsignor's surprise, Dr Blanche had it.

To his further surprise, Belcastel relished his retreat from the irksome angers outside. It was not a total retreat of course. People visited.

The *maison de santé* was run as a blend of nursing home and private house. Patients, when well enough, ate with distinguished guests, and there were some whose status shuttled between the two. It was a fashionable place. Even during Belcastel's stay, famous wits had come to dine, exchanging banter with the sick, and he had seen the verbal fireworks which can precede breakdowns dazzle visitors. This phenomenon, Dr Blanche explained, was called 'the fastigium'. The coherence of lunatics' visions could be startling.

The doctor had a wide circle of well-connected friends, and

so had his son, Jacques-Emile, a successful painter, who had a studio in the grounds. So all sorts of people visited. Gentle and simple. When not at meals, the monsignor avoided them all. He arranged for his own guests to call in the afternoon, considering them to be a liability and best kept out of sight.

Ironically, he, the asylum inmate, was level-headed, while his visitors, many of them scions of inbred families, cherished hopes as obsolete as the beasts on their escutcheons. Hopes he could handle. What worried him were plots. Taking the blame for these had landed him in here, but when he complained, the plotters' peace-offering was to elect him to be the spider at the heart of yet another web of madcap schemes.

'Mad as hares,' was what he thought of them all! 'Dreamers and botchers to a man! Brave, yes, gallant, yes, but, oh dear! *Tous des exaltés*! Oh Lord,' he prayed, when he had the heart to do so, 'deliver me from loyalty to men of too much faith.'

Yet how *could* he refuse them? If they went elsewhere for advice, who knew what harm might be done? Just now, while laying out the ritual objects he kept for visits, he didn't know whether to laugh or cry. As he unwound its white wrapping from the portrait of the uncrowned King Henry V of France, alias the comte de Chambord, now dead these dozen years, he sighed for the meanings of white flags. The comte's refusal to adulterate his notion of himself as God's appointed and swap his royal white flag for the tricolour had driven supporters crazy. In the secrecy of their dreams and in safe company they might insult the flag – '*drapeau de mon cul*' – threaten to wipe themselves on it and rage at their leader's obstinacy. Publicly, they brought their keenest eloquence to the attempt to make him budge. 'For your own sake, Sire,' they had pleaded, 'for your followers' sake, for France and for the Church, will you not sacrifice the symbol and grasp the reality? To win votes? To take power?' The word intoxicated them. 'Power,' they cajoled repetitively while imploring him to show some flexibility. 'Wisdom! Statesmanship! Remember your great predecessor and namesake, Henry IV! Was *he* wrong to compromise? He wasn't, was he? So follow his example! Help God to help us!' But no. He wouldn't – and lost at the ballot box. He, as he saw it, owed it to God not to alter one tittle of his prerogatives and was as ramrod stiff as – well, as today's visitor. Recalled to what was going on at this very moment outside the asylum gate, Belcastel laughed at the neatness with which it summed up his dilemma.

'With all due respect to the First Commandment,' he told himself, 'it is an omen!'

What had happened so far was this. His visitor, the vicomte de Sauvigny, had tried to climb the tall asylum gate and got stuck. It was a handsome, old, wrought-iron gate made up of curls and coils, and the toe of the vicomte's boot had got caught in one of them. The foot inside this boot was on the outside of the gate, and by putting his weight on it, the vicomte had managed with some difficulty – he was forty-two and stiffer than he had supposed – to swing his other leg over the top, turn it and find a toe-hold on the inside. His two feet were now pointing in opposite directions, but he could liberate neither. He hadn't the strength to swing back the foremost one, and his hind leg was held firmly in the coil of an iron curlicue. Possibly his enraged exertions had caused it to swell.

'Will you come out, Monseigneur?' The man who had come to report on all this asked Belcastel. 'To calm him down?'

'Yes, yes, of course I will!'

Belcastel had immediately gone to look for his cape. Of course he'd come! The words 'calm' and 'down' were worrying. Things could turn nasty. Balm had better be poured! Head inside his opened wardrobe, he had begun poking speedily and impatiently through a smother of cassocks and batting away assaults by increasingly lively lengths of recalcitrant black wool. They all looked the same. Back and forth he went but, to his annoyance, failed to find the cape. Adam would know where it was, but where *was* Adam? Ah, he'd sent him away. Mm. Was that the cape? No. Belcastel's irritable gesture sent something swinging, which returned and hit his nose rather hard. It was the sword which he had planned to lay casually on a side table. It was a ceremonial one which had been presented to his father in recognition of his gallantry at the battle of Castelfidardo. Fighting for the pope. 'See,' the sword was meant to have reminded the vicomte, 'I, Belcastel, son of the hero of Castelfidardo, have every right to take issue with you. My loyalty is incontrovertible.' In fact, of course, it was not – or rather, yes, it was, but subtlety, not swords, was Belcastel's weapon. If the object of one's loyalty were to split, what then? Just now there was a painful but vital matter to be addressed, which ... Never mind that. Find that cape! No point going out without it and getting pneumonia. Was his nose bleeding? God knew what was going on at the asylum gate. The monsignor was well aware how unbridled monarchist outbursts could be. Bad language would be the least of it. Seditious comments were likely, given the vicomte's rheumatism and hot temper. Both had been contracted in 1870 when he had fought with the Papal Zouaves to save the pope's territory from Garibaldi. They failed, of course! An utter débâcle! While the whole Catholic world watched! Defeat had rankled and left the vicomte thin-skinned. He wouldn't relish being made to cool his heels outside an asylum since, as he frequently put it himself, he had suffered enough affronts in his life and 'swallowed enough toads.' He'd surely have made his seditious comments by now. Insulted the French Republic and the government of the day. Annoyed the servants. Embarrassed everyone.

'Say you couldn't find me,' decided Belcastel. ' Say I've gone somewhere quiet to read my office.' He closed the wardrobe door and picked up his missal. 'By the time you say it, it will be true.' No point, he thought, in losing face – in so far as he had any left to lose.

'He's in a right stew.' The man had already explained that the vicomte had climbed the gate because the porter's delay in opening it had kept his carriage waiting. 'Would I be right in guessing,' he asked, 'that he's a military gentleman? Used to being obeyed pronto? We thought as much! Very hot under the collar he got straight off. So you can imagine what he's like now. The porter didn't have the key because Monsieur le Directeur is keeping it himself. He wants to make sure that none of those newspaper fellows sneak in. We tried to explain this, but Monsieur le Vicomte thought we were defying him. He called us Republican scum.'

'I'm sorry about that.'

'We can't open it now anyway. Not while he's stuck on top. Moving it will be a jerky business. The ground's hard, you see. Frozen hard, and he might slip and fall or end up hanging from one foot. Break a leg maybe.' Did the man's eye have a wistful glint? 'And if one of us went up to try pulling his foot out, we might get a kick. Or get stuck ourselves. Do you see, Monseigneur?'

Belcastel did. 'Ask the Irishman to deal with him,' he advised. 'Monsieur Gould. Tell him it's a delicate matter and that I'd be grateful if he could help the vicomte to climb down.'

***

A question startled Adam.

'Do you know what my name means?'

Reflections from the fire reddened Maupassant's eyeballs, and if he had seen himself he might have screamed. His skin too was red. Adam wondered about sedation, though the patient hated it and had complained just now that the place was infested by insects armed with morphine syringes. A joke? Here in the asylum jokes rarely worked. There was no norm to bounce them off. Maybe the query about his name was a joke too?

As it happened a similar one had come up earlier in connection with the reprinting by this morning's *Figaro* of one of Maupassant's stories. It had been published for the first time seven years ago and was about a killer-demon called the Horla (*hors-là*?) whose name meant 'out there'. But what did *that* signify? Coming from a monkish writer, it might have meant 'the world'. Or 'death'? Dr Blanche, though, had a more comforting suggestion. The Horla, he remembered, was the name of a gas balloon which the writer had paid for, named after his story and travelled in from Paris to the Belgian coast.

'At a height of 8,000 metres. So "Horla" just meant "up in the air". It was a publicity stunt, and Maupassant had come in for a lot of teasing. People said he was trying to raise his image!'

The reddened eyeballs were still expectantly fixed on Adam.

'What does your name *mean*?'

'Yes. "Mau" or "*mal*" means, of course, "pain" or "evil". So *Mal passant* is sinister, don't you think? A hard death perhaps? An evil passage? A bad passer-by.'

Adam managed to laugh. 'Why not "a passing trouble"?' he asked bracingly. 'Something like a cold. Or a cold sore.' 'Keep the laugh going,' he told himself and thought of the cold water one throws on hysterics.

'And would you bet I'll get over my passing ill?'

'Why not? I'm no doctor, mind.'

'But as a betting man?'

'Yes.'

'My brother died in a madhouse three years ago. Badly! Horribly! When I saw the name on his tomb stone: Maupassant ...'

'Better not think of it. You're wallowing ...'

'What?'

'In despair. They called it that in my seminary. Also "the sin against the light": the unforgivable one.' Adam shrugged. 'They saw us as an army. Despair is desertion.' I, he was thinking privately, did not despair. What I did was leave and lose all my friends. 'Priests can be tough.' For a moment his sadness was for himself, but he refused to indulge it. Perhaps *he* needed cold water thrown over him? He wished he could have supplied the man before him with even a false hope.

***

The vicomte's niece had been waiting in the cold for what seemed an age outside the asylum gate. 'Is anything happening' she felt like asking the coachman. This would have been an oblique sort of protest, but she didn't make it for she had been bred to show restraint, and, besides, it was clear that nothing *was* happening. Uncle Hubert had stepped out of the carriage, climbed the gate and got stuck. That was all. She might have giggled at his rashness if there had been anyone to giggle with her, Gisèle say, or some other friend from school. But she had seen none of them since her wedding, so she sat back in the shadows, tucked the rug around her knees and reflected on how, by rights, it should be her turn to be rash. Instead, here she was hiding in embarrassment while her uncle made an exhibition of himself and called people 'Republican scum'. She had just heard him do this.

She was not yet twenty, and her husband, whom she scarcely knew, was off in darkest Africa, trying, poor lamb, to make their fortune, which he had better do fast because his family, like her own, was penniless. This was why she was now staying with her aunt and uncle.

'Our friends' Uncle Hubert liked to explain, 'have been out of power for too long. Six decades!' Poverty, he sometimes added, became a badge of honour when you saw how many had turned their coats and joined those who controlled patronage. 'Poor France!' he would exclaim, and shake his head. Danièle always imagined a soft-fleshed lady being martyred in some bloody way: *la France*.

'I should have married a Republican,' she would tease to cheer him. He liked to be teased. 'Or a Bonapartist. Even an Orleanist would have more hopes.'

'We are all Orleanists now,' was Uncle Hubert's stock reply. 'Willy nilly! The Legitimists died out. Soon we may all have!'

Danièle wished she had brought her embroidery. Or a charcoal foot-warmer. Life was humdrum. She yearned for something unexpected – not Uncle Hubert's sort of scrape but something tenderly frivolous and – yes – rash. Perhaps she was just missing her husband? The word pleased her: 'husband'. It was still quite new. Unused. She had been married for well over a year now. But very little of that time had been spent with Philibert, whose letters from the Congo could have been from a stranger. She found it hard to reply.

'His last letter,' she had told her aunt, 'says that cannibals break their victims' legs several days before killing and eating them. It makes the flesh sweeter. They do the same thing with fowl.'

Her aunt crossed herself. She was a nun and had been granted leave by her convent to chaperone Danièle who might not otherwise be allowed to share a house with Uncle Hubert.

'Don't you miss your friends in the convent?' Danièle had worried.

But her aunt said that looking after a vulnerable young woman was a corporal work of mercy; so, while engaged in it, she was, spiritually speaking, close to her sisters in Christ.

'I don't feel vulnerable,' Danièle objected.

Her aunt agreed that she probably wasn't, but said one must avoid giving scandal.

'So it's the scandalmongers who are vulnerable?'

'Of course.'

***

'Tell me about your monsignor,' asked Maupassant. 'That is a burn-scar on his cheek, isn't it? He's been through fire! Like the demon in one of my stories whose victim becomes so terrified that he is driven to trap him in his own house then burn it down. Naturally the demon escapes. Why do you look worried? I'm talking about a *story*.' The patient's tone was ostentatiously sane. A teasing gleam flickered across his features. 'You don't *burn* a demon, but the victim had lost his head.' He cocked his own head sideways. 'Perhaps you've read it?'

'*The Horla*? I just did. I was thinking of it just now.'

'I thought you might have. It was in this morning's *Figaro*. I wrote it at a time when I could still control my demons.' Smiling. This *was* a joke. 'Perhaps your monsignor too is a demon and that's why he didn't burn, or only in one spot? You don't know what to think, do you? You think I'm odd. What about him? Is he odder than I am?'

'Who knows? He's certainly more secretive. I've learned more about you in an hour than he let out in two years.'

'So you are unable to tell me his story.'

'Afraid so.'

'Tell me something else then. Something to blot out what is in my head. What is the worst thing in yours, Gould?' The patient's smile had an airiness which might once have been second nature. Was he mimicking it now? Adam suspected that he was. Suave and amused, it might have been his drawing room smile. Quick and overly responsive, it conjured up alcoves and secrets. 'Others' troubles bring relief.' Briefly the smile slipped, revealing that Maupassant was in the grip of some sort of pain. An intimate, inner one, Adam surmised, in some private part of himself. The slippage, though, was suspect for, after all, this man had been a notorious charmer. Maybe what had softened women was that they had sensed that pain? Maybe he had learned to let them? Well, he wasn't in control of it now. As he sat, his hands kept moving from hip to knee like trapped crabs: back and forth, hip, knee, hip, as though measuring the length of his thighs. His knees too jigged. You could feel the vibration. 'The whole reading public knows my stories,' he told Adam. 'Tell me one of yours. Something private. Tell me about, oh, I don't know ... your mother.'

'My mother died when I was twelve. She wasn't yet thirty.'

'I'm sorry. Illness, was it? Or an accident?'

'It may have been suicide. Actually, it must have been.'

'Ah, I've been intrusive! Sorry! I really am. Oh lord! You mustn't think of it, Gould. Think of ... Look, I'll tell you a thing about *my* mother which I hate to tell. I've written about it, but that's different. Putting things in a story makes them seem like – well, a story. They become easier to forget. Talking is harder, but here goes. When I was ten I saw my father beat her savagely. I saw him grab hold of her neck with one hand and hit her face with the other. With all his strength. Again and again! He seemed to have gone mad. Her hat fell off. Her hair fell around her. She raised her arms to defend herself, but couldn't. And neither, to be sure, could I. There I was, ten or maybe less, maybe nine years old, watching my sweet, clever, elegant Mama be assaulted by *my father*. It made no sense. It was as if the world were coming to an end and normal expectancies had collapsed, but there we still were! What could I do?

To whom could I turn? I screamed, but he paid no attention. I rushed out and hid in the garden. I spent the whole night there in a kind of agony. The next day – this was somehow worse and more baffling than the scene itself – they behaved *just as they always did.*' The patient was panting. Saliva dripped from his chin. He didn't wipe it. His head was like an outsize but shrivelled pomegranate, ridgy and crimson with dry, bald patches. 'They went on in their ordinary way.'

'Yes,' said Adam. 'The ordinariness is what destroys you.'

'You've known that?'

'Yes.'

'Aren't you going to accuse me of wallowing?'

'But you didn't, did you? You survived and grew up and wrote and helped people survive their own horrors. You've just helped me.'

'Have you noticed how calm I am? Maybe it's done me good to tell you?' The sick man's fingers, though, were flexing and making fists.

'I suppose he wanted money from her? Scenes like that are usually about money, aren't they? A lot of your stories are about it.'

'You've read them?'

'I'm reading them now. So are the doctors. From duty, but also pleasure. Some are painfully harsh, but we admire them.'

'So tell me a story about someone you know. Not your own. My mother used to find incidents for me, kernels of narrative which I could develop. She was good at it. You find them in the oddest places.'

'Like the pigeons pecking seeds out of dung?'

'That's it! Dung, sewers and I suppose madhouses are what

people try *not* to see, but looking at them can be instructive and ...'

Adam laughed. 'I'm not flattered then that you come to me for a story!'

The sick man produced his sanest smile. 'My dear fellow ...' But before their conversation could go any further a message arrived that Adam was wanted at the gate.

'I'll stay with Monsieur,' said the man who brought it. 'You'd best hurry,' he warned Adam. 'There could be an accident.'

***

So far nothing at all had happened at the gate on which Uncle Hubert was still stuck like one of those culled animals which gamekeepers hang on fences to prove their diligence. He must be frozen! Poor, dear, foolish uncle! No doubt someone would eventually bring a ladder and get him down. Meanwhile thank goodness he was wearing gloves. Inside the carriage Danièle too was cold. She kept shaking her hands to help the circulation and occupied her mind with its best memories which, in spite of everything, were of her marriage. She had happy childhood memories too, of course, but now that she was grown up, they seemed to belong to someone else.

Her husband's name was Philibert d'Armaillé and they had met first at her mother's funeral. A bony Belgian cavalry officer with knifing eyes, he condoled with an intensity which took her aback, for she was not feeling intense. Her mother's decline had been punctuated by so many unconsummated deathbed scenes that the family's grief was depleted long before she died, and Danièle's mourning was to consist of willing herself to forget how sickness had winnowed away her mother's character, leaving her as simple as a leech.

'I am so sorry,' the tall officer had said and stabbed her with his gaze. 'I remember my own father's end vividly.'

Then he named his father whom she recognized as the subject of one of Gisèle's bits of choice gossip. He was, said Gisèle, a notorious groper and had been seen, bare bum, riding a parlour maid in a moonlit shrubbery. The inappropriate memory got in the way of Danièle's response to Philibert. So did shame. Whose? This was unclear. A mould of it furred her mind. Perhaps it made her seem deceptively docile at the receptions which her brothers, once the mourning period was over, decided to arrange. Pliant – did he think her tender? – she may have seemed to lead d'Armaillé on.

'You need taking out of yourself,' said the brothers, who were surprised to find how long they had left her alone with their mother in that mausoleum of a house. Two years? Three? 'We must make things up to you.' But they, of course, had their own lives to lead. Both were bachelors and soldiers, and neither could have her with him.

I am a mole, she told herself. Dazzled. I have been living in the shadows and mustn't leap to conclusions about anything.

'You should get married,' said the brothers. 'Order new clothes. Try rubbing geranium petals into your cheeks.'

Later there was a squabble followed by a duel. A rumpus. An enemy insulted Philibert and was challenged. The cause was complex. It involved family honour, but since parts of it were not for her ears, she never got things straight and hesitated to judge.

'Spiritually, we are all one family,' said Philibert to her on the eve of his duel. Her younger brother agreed to be his second. The other disapproved and held aloof.

She feared he might be killed. Instead he killed his opponent whom he should not – it was, she learned, widely felt – have challenged since he himself was a crack shot. The press made a scandal of the thing, describing him as a murderer and the motives as risible. He then challenged a newspaper editor, whereupon his superiors let him know that they would have to court-martial him if he didn't leave fast for the new Congo Free State where a ragtag force was fighting black Arab slave hunters. The Force Publique. No, Philibert, it was not the sort of outfit cavalry officers joined, but it was that or face a court martial. Seriously, said his well-wishers, you'd better forget horses. Sell yours. So he did and went. Frankly, he told Danièle, he wasn't sorry to be leaving for a place where a man could test himself. Saving savages from slavers was a noble cause. And so was teaching them to work, which he understood to be part of the plan. On the eve of going he asked her to marry him and she, in a confusion of feelings, encouraged, it should be said, by a belief that her brothers wanted her settled, said 'yes'. It was all very quick. The honeymoon was in France so as to get Philibert off Belgian soil.

She helped him prepare for his African journey, and together they studied maps on which vast areas were still blank. Philibert was to join an expedition which would fill in some of these. There were no roads. Only a web of rivers with great drumming names which ran through tangles of rain forest. Slidy syllables rippled on his tongue: Congo and Lualaba, Sankuru and Lomami. She came to think of her husband's penetration of her body in terms of maps showing pale, virginal spaces, thinly streaked with black. Nestling under his shoulder, she felt him ride her dark rivers. Her Congo and Lualaba, her drumming conduits.

But she did not get to know him, for they had little time, and besides, she had neither standards of comparison nor any knowledge of men. 'Teach me some bad words,' she challenged. 'When you and my brothers crack jokes, I feel a fool. Don't you want me to be able to laugh with you?'

Indulgently, he gave her lessons, *un cours de polissonnerie*, which opened up a province of the mind where she must disport herself secretly, since she was not, he warned, to let anyone know what she knew. Be sure and remember that, Danièle. It's our secret, private, just between us! Then he left.

And began sending her coltish letters. All about ambushes and skirmishes and swiftly built bridges which, as often as not, got swept away at once, toppling 'our men' into rivers from which there was no rescuing them. They were not, of course, Belgians but locally recruited tribesmen who fell like ninepins. Arms and legs could be seen swirling past in the boiling current. Enemies' heads were delivered in baskets. Bodies with 'steaks cut from their thighs and upper arms' strewed pathways and Philibert's prose. She guessed that he was using her as a witness and his letters as a diary. She must not, he admonished, throw them away. They were also, she understood, an effort to continue their bedroom intimacies, a purging of his own horror, an attempt to keep her close. He was expanding the *cours de polissonnerie*, sharing – but the traffic was too much one way, and what had she to tell in return? Nothing. Nothing comparable. She couldn't even bring herself to comment, since the hot confidences had cooled when they reached her. They were months old and, for all she knew, came from a dead man. Dead and maybe chopped into steaks? So she read them uneasily, searching for the man behind the playmate whom she knew. It was surely too late now for play? His airy irresponsibility upset her badly. Why couldn't they build proper bridges? Did he feel no concern for 'our men' when they fell off them? Or for the 'friendlies' or 'faithfuls' whose fate seemed still more precarious and whose habit of eating each other when fate struck he recorded with a shock which came close to gusto. How reconcile all this with his enthusiasm for 'our civilizing mission'?

Once – no, several times! – she dreamed that he was eating her, and woke up shaking. In the dark this seemed more memory than dream. By the time she had found matches and struck them, it had grown less compelling but still hung, like a shadow, in her mind. She had been brought up with rigid propriety, then given a playful *cours de polissonnerie*. The forbidden had become a joke. And now there were these letters. So was anything truly taboo? Even her religious practices now seemed strange, even the Eucharist, that pallid, paper-thin and 'transubstantiated' substance. What old, sly, bowdlerized lore did it really commemorate?

Shocked to find herself thinking such thoughts, Danièle began to fear that the time spent nursing her mother had spoiled her for matrimony, and that almost three years of taking decisions had quite banished her readiness to let a husband think for her. Her docile airs had misled Philibert who, sooner or later, was in for a bad surprise. Meanwhile, so was she.

For the scandal of the duel did not go away and the newspapers which continued to air the thing claimed that

Philibert had wilfully provoked his opponent. Baited and run him down as if practising a blood sport, wrote the indignant journalists. The words 'bloodthirsty' and 'barbarian' left her shaken. Moreover – she only saw this now – the *cours de polissonnerie* had left her unenlightened as to what it – what Philibert? – was all about.

Was it love that she felt for this man, she wondered? Or fear or pity? Her doubts were licensed by knowing that he might not come back. Mortality was high – his letters made this clear – in the swamps where hostile natives waited up to their necks, heads hidden behind some tuft or tree until the Belgian-led column appeared, its men holding their guns above their heads to keep them dry and offering a perfect target to spears. Small, insidious irritations could be lethal too: hookworm, mosquitoes, boils that never healed and the constant hot humidity which caused belts and boots to mould. The odds against his survival seemed greater by the day. It was even possible that she was by now a widow!

Shocked by the wily stealth of her own resignation, she shook herself into action and began, first, to say prayers for him, then, so as to reinforce the prayers' protection, to invent benign superstitions. She would *will* his safe return. By sheer attentiveness and concern, she would magic him back. One of her practices was to try visualizing his entire face precisely and all at once. This was difficult, for her memory's straining made the face shimmer like a reflection in water, so that some parts shone too brightly and others blurred or disappeared. It was as if moths had nibbled holes in it. Or leprosy! Oh dear! Oh Philibert! In flurries of pity, she moved her would-be remedial scrutiny over his poor pocked image, trying to heal each wounded section as it steadied. She was engaged in doing this, when someone knocked at her window. On the street side of the carriage, hidden from the group at the gate, a small woman wearing a hat with a grey veil was trying to attract her attention. Danièle opened the window and the woman raised the veil. Her hands were shaking. She looked about thirty.

'Madame,' she begged in a low, furtive voice, 'forgive my importuning you. I wouldn't if I weren't desperate. Will you let me into your carriage for a few minutes? Please. I need to get inside the villa to see my husband, but the doctors won't let me. He is a patient. I need to talk to him for a moment. Just a tiny moment! If he is as mad as they say he is, I shall leave. I cannot get past the servants on foot, but if I were with you ...' Gloved fingers pressed the cold window and the woman's breath was white.

She talked on, and Danièle thought, 'No!' Then: 'Why no? She is not mad. She is not an inmate here, or if she is, she is trying to get in, not out!' Then, 'Be careful!' Then, 'What can she do to me with all these people within earshot?' By now she had opened the door.

The woman stepped in quickly, closed it, then, flattening herself against the carriage upholstery, shrank as unobtrusively as she could, into the corner furthest from Danièle. She was respectably dressed, pretty, a little faded, decent, but clearly neither a lady nor a Bad Woman. Danièle felt exhilarated by her own daring and soon found her exhilaration turning to benevolence. The woman began to talk of her three children, of how it was for their sake that she had been so forward, and of how God would reward Danièle for her charity.

Danièle's benevolence flinched a little. Talk of God's rewards was apt to herald further requests, but, when none forthcame, it struck her that she was performing a corporal work of mercy and laying up divine indulgence for her own and Philibert's needs. This was a spiritual investment and insurance against possible ill fortune. Good, she thought, good, and graciously introduced herself. She was Madame d'Armaillé.

Her guest said she was Joséphine Litzelmann and that the man she aimed to see was her children's father, Monsieur Guy de Maupassant who, to be quite honest, Madame, was not precisely her husband. This revelation was made in a low and breathy tone and only half caught Danièle's attention, for something was at last happening outside, where the servants, who had been stamping about and slapping themselves to keep warm, were now gathered close to the gate. A tall young man, who had just arrived from the villa, had climbed up it and, with the porter's help, managed to disentangle Uncle Hubert, ease his foreleg back over the crest of the gate and get him first halfway down, then all the way. Moments later Danièle's uncle and his rescuer were in the carriage, taking up most of the room, smelling of mud, rubber and damp trousers, exclaiming, rubbing cold hands – Uncle Hubert's were quite blue – and describing with zest how they had managed the descent. Neither took exception to Joséphine Litzelmann's presence. If they noticed it at all, the young man, who introduced himself as Adam Gould, probably took her for a member of Uncle Hubert's party, while Uncle Hubert must think she worked here. They tapped a message to the coachman: drive on in. So in he drove them through the opened iron gates, spattering crisp, confetti-like gusts of ice flakes from under the carriage wheels and smuggling the anxious little woman into the villa. She had again lowered her veil and, as the carriage drew up to let them out, Danièle felt a cold, cotton-gloved hand clutch her own in a tight, nervous grasp.

***

Monsieur Guy's manservant saw them arrive. He was again watching from a corridor window, for Monsieur Guy would not let him into his room and seemed to feel no gratitude for the years of care François had lavished on his health – all those lovingly prepared eggnogs, purées and feather-light custards, all the concern and vigilance seemed forgotten. Well, if he must. François could put up with that. He could put up with anything if only his patience would help cure his master, who was a man in a thousand: a great, good, generous, amusing man whose needs François understood! As he had told Dr Blanche, his master's mother agreed that her son would be better off if only they could get him home.

'Not home to her,' he had spelled it out for the doctor when they spoke this morning, 'home to me. She is far too far away. In Nice. And she's not well herself. But our flat in the rue Boccador is restful. I have it spick and span now – more so than when Monsieur Guy was there, for he lived like a tornado, wet towels everywhere, stacks of papers all over the place. Now that I have it ready and welcoming, it would surely soothe his spirit to be among his own things, poor gentleman.'

The doctor shook his head. 'My poor François, he needs constant supervision. Else he might try suicide again. That wouldn't help his mother's health, now would it?'

François detected a reproach: he, for all his devotion, had not been able to keep a constant watch.

'Of course,' a warder confided later, while he and François drank their mid-morning bowls of milky coffee in the kitchen, 'suicide is the doctor's great bogy. Especially by famous patients. Those journalists out there are on the watch for just that. A good story ...'

'Good?'

'Well,' the warder removed the skin from his *café au lait* and laid it in a shrivelled puddle on his plate, 'your master wrote stories, didn't he? For money? Some, it seems, were about people he'd read about in the papers. So if he were now to be *in* one, it would be a case of the biter bitten, wouldn't you say?'

'No.'

'Why?'

François grimaced. He could not think of Monsieur Guy as a biter. He thought of dogs. He thought of a pony biting the one in front of it – *gnyam*! Full in the buttocks. Rolling back its wicked lip and snapping wasp-yellow teeth. Those were biters, not Monsieur Guy whose high spirits shed – well, used to shed – radiance on whatever he touched. Whether he was showing you how to prepare for a boat-trip, make lead bullets for pistol-practice, exercise his pretty gun dog, or restock the aviary in his Norman garden, the task became a pleasure. 'It's fun, you'll see!' was how he would introduce a new one. And, sure enough, you often found yourself enjoying it. Life brightened around him. Everyone said so. Even the tradesmen who supplied his food read his stories. Even the butcher. Why, last week when this man heard the news about poor Monsieur, he'd had to dry his eyes, while his wife marvelled, 'It's the first time I've seen him cry.' As for the stories, François himself had had a finger in several. He'd learned how to reconnoitre and ferret out facts about an interesting household and had heard Monsieur Guy tell his mother how useful he found his valet's powers of observation. Did that make François a biter too? Did it? Irritably, turning from the warder, François smeared honey on a heel of bread, dipped it in coffee and bit into it. *Gnyam*! Golden honey-eyes floated in the bowl. It was his own honey. Intending it for Monsieur Guy, he had made a special trip to the market to find the girl who brought it up from Provence. Monsieur always used to say that eating it brought back the fragrance of thyme and fennel and the high times he enjoyed whenever he moored his yacht near Cannes, and society ladies came to visit. Today though he had screamed that he couldn't eat the honey because the bees had gathered it from digitalis: foxglove, a poisoned source.

'François wants me dead,' he had screamed. 'Get him out.'

Wanted him ... Flinching, the manservant's attention swerved to the scene below his window where two women had now stepped from the carriage. One looked familiar. He tried to place her, then gave up as the memory of his master's ravings rang in his ears and distracted him. Back and forth his mind flickered, and he shook his head to empty it of hurt. For how could he hold poor Monsieur Guy's rages against him? That they were mad rages was plain from his gentleness with others, while only François got the rough side of his tongue. Maybe this was because Monsieur knew he could rely on him no matter what? In some part of his moithered mind, he surely knew that. It was possible too that he meant the opposite of what he said. He had always been a great one for reversals and practical jokes, as François should know, for *he* had often had to set them up. Nine years François had been with him. He had cooked for him, travelled with him, helped him move house a number of times, organized decorators – Monsieur's taste was opulent – nursed him with massages and cold showers and fallen in with all his whims. Some of these could be embarrassing. On one occasion, François had been required to deliver a covered basket of live frogs to a society lady and, on another, a container full of jacks-in-the-box. There had been other japes. With Monsieur Guy you had – though not everyone twigged this – to stay on the qui vive. When he flattered the titled ladies who visited his yacht, it was his valet, not they, who saw the irony behind his charm. He could be quite brusque too, and women who tried to breach his privacy got short shrift. Perhaps – it struck François as he stared out at that veiled lady whom he had better head off – in the end he himself had got too close to Monsieur Guy, one of whose fears was of meeting his double? Better think about that.

First things first though. Who were those two women? And how had they got in? No question but that *they* needed brusque treatment. François started for the stairs.

III

The to-do at the gate had been due to the director's absence. Blanche, before taking off for a taste of the salon life he so loved, had told Adam, 'Now is your chance to make amends.'

The amends were for an incident just after their staff meeting when Adam, still hot with indignation at fate, life, self, the press and the sleek Dr Meuriot, went to answer the bell at the gate and found himself confronting a reporter from *L'Écho de la semaine* – who offered him money, and whom he knocked down. Ah well. He could hardly knock himself down, could he? Or fate? Or Dr Meuriot?

He had never done such a thing before and, to his shock, relished the sensation. Till now, as he had been trained to do, he had kept his feelings in a shell. But this now seemed to have cracked, for he had to be pulled off the journalist by the porter who should have answered the bell in the first place and who, on seeing whom he was throttling, apologized. They were by now outside the gate in the rue Berton, where the man seemed to feel that anarchy should be allowed some play.

'*Désolé*, Monsieur Gould. Here. Smash the fellow's glasses.' Invitingly, he liberated Adam. 'Better still,' he advised, 'give him a swift kick in the gut! It hurts and doesn't show.'

But by then the journalist had fled.

'He,' said the porter in a satisfied voice, 'will think twice before coming back to snoop!'

This spite, so alien to the entente usually prevailing in the *maison de santé*, came from feeling besieged. So did the director's eagerness to breathe happier air.

'So you'll hold the fort here, Gould?' he had cajoled, then, sealing the bargain, flicked Adam's shoulder with a white glove which released talcum powder in airy puffs. '*Zut*! Sorry! Get them to brush that off.'

Chin-wagging in self-reproof, Blanche stepped into his carriage. Though plump, he was light on his feet and, dressed in tails and topper, was already mentally savouring the pleasures of Princess Mathilde's soirée where he was resolved, he confided with a friendliness clearly intended to make up for the spilled talc, not to let himself be pumped by Maupassant's malicious friends. Gossip, he murmured from the carriage window, was causing half our troubles. 'So: *motus*! Mum's the word!' He mimed the act of turning a key in the lock of his own mouth, then called to the porter – but did the man take this in? – that the key to this gate was from now on to be kept in his desk drawer. In his study. Understood? Only the vicomte should be let in. The doctor then sank back in his carriage and, as it clattered down the rue Berton, could be imagined drawing a happy sigh. He had delegated duties which were getting onerous for a man of seventy-two.

Adam locked the gate and put the key in the desk, but

not until the vicomte's plight grew alarming would anyone remember this arrangement. Seeing to everything in a household, as François Tassart had done for Maupassant, might be feasible when working for one man. Here the chain of command was as prone to fray as a piece of bright cord kept for playing with a kitten. The trouble was that Adam's role had expanded. Blanche was visibly aging and fading, and the other doctors were not always available. So Adam did the practical things: organized washerwomen and ordered supplies, kept accounts and was turning into a male Martha without whom all might founder. Tacitly, it was understood that he might, when need be, play doctor.

***

'More trouble, Monsieur!' The servant who had called for his help earlier was here again. With the glum relish of a man reporting trouble for which he cannot be blamed, he murmured, 'Those ladies ...'

'The ones with the vicomte?'

'That's just it. It seems that they're *not* with him – or only one is. He says he never set eyes on the other until you got him down from the gate and he found her in the carriage talking to his niece. He thought she must be a nurse here.'

'You mean that she just stepped into the carriage while it was held up?'

The man shrugged.

An intruder! And Adam had as good as escorted her in! How *could* he have been so careless? And now, said the servant,

Monsieur Maupassant's man, Tassart, was beside himself and almost in tears!

'You see, Monsieur, he blames himself.'

'For what? What happened?'

'Well it seems he asked one of the ladies who she was – confronted her like, and while he did, the other ...'

'What? Spit it out, man!'

The servant sighed. The fat was in the fire. 'She slipped into Monsieur de Maupassant's room and started carrying on. Wept! Tried to coax and cajole him. Threw herself at him! Fell or maybe was pushed off, and the upshot was that the patient began to have a fit. He gets these now, and they terrify him. The doctors say it's a false epilepsy, which is neither here nor there because *his* great fear is that if he gets agitated his brain will melt and flow away through his nose. Anyway *he* was yelling that he needed to stay calm, and *she* was wailing that he should think of her children's future – she said they were *his* children – so in the end Baron rushed in and had to shove her out the door. Bodily! He says she fought like a cat. And even while she fought, she was shouting that she loved Monsieur Guy. She was scratching at Baron's hands and calling, 'Guy, do you remember when you took me driving by moonlight? In the mountains. Do you remember what you said?'

The man began to snigger, stopped and, as though struck by something in Adam's face, said kindly, 'It's all in the day's work here, Monsieur. You have to harden your heart.'

***

The voice coming from Maupassant's room could have been

filtered through wet wool. It breathed panic and wheezed. 'Quick,' it quavered. 'Get this woman out. I'm done with women. I know what Mademoiselle Litzelmann wants, but it's not up to me to let her have it. My poor mother ...' – here the voice strangled – 'has had enough troubles. Why should she have to put up with entanglements like this at the end of her life? My lawyer has made provision for Mademoiselle Litzelmann's children. They won't starve. Is that not enough for her? Then get her out! Out! *Foutez-la dehors*! Don't come back, Joséphine.' There followed a resonant and repeated thud as though some empty vessel, possibly a tin jug, had hit the floor with such vigour that it bounced. 'Out!'

But Joséphine was already out. Even while the sick man struggled with his perplexities, she was being comforted.

Looking in through the door of a drawing room at the end of a long corridor, Adam saw the ladies sitting with their arms around each other. Which was Maupassant's visitor? The high-coloured one in the grey mantle or the willowy girl whose face reflected an elusive radiance? Come to think of it, there was a shine to them both. Tears? Wintry light shed a chill on their embrace. They were – you could see – forming an alliance. For no reason on which he could have put a finger, Adam thought of his childhood, of smells of frosty earth, straw, fungus and steaming animals, and of dawdling home through glinty northern twilight – to be seized at last with scolding tenderness in brisk, protective arms. The longer that moment was put off, the better it was.

He felt a nip of loneliness.

Perhaps he was feeling frail? Dereliction hung like a miasma in the air! It could explain the doctor's sloping off so early, the vicomte's impetuosity and the ladies' gall. Even Adam's behaviour could be due to a contagion. He was amused to recognize the source of this thought in a debate which had been rambling on in the asylum kitchens where someone had raised the fear that people dealing with the mad risked going mad themselves.

'Nonsense,' the doctors had insisted when consulted about this. 'Susceptible patients have to be kept isolated, but that's not why. Hysterics can *mimic* epileptics. There's no contagion.'

The staff, though, having often heard these same doctors offer mendacious comfort to the hopeless, were hard to convince. Anyway, what, they asked each other, about Monsieur de Maupassant? He had lately developed epileptic symptoms, hadn't he? Those didn't look like mimicry? Shuttling between worry and titillation, maids and menservants chewed over the question. Monsieur Guy's case was of more interest than most because, thanks to what Monseigneur de Belcastel called the 'forced education of the poor', several were keen readers; those who couldn't read could listen, and all enjoyed chatting about the shocking Monsieur Guy and his stories in the drowsy hour after supper over a glass of *gros rouge* or calvados.

'Just how long,' chambermaids challenged each other, 'would *you* have resisted the seducer in Monsieur Guy's novel, *Bel-Ami*? How hard would he have had to try with you?'

'How hard or how long?'

Titters touched off shy bursts of teasing. Just like drawing room folk.

Well, why not? After all, Hachette's railway-station stalls sold Monsieur Guy's books.

Oh?

Yes indeed! His vogue was wide! He had caught a mood. It was canny and in tune with the times. Reading of how the brazen *Bel-Ami* used love to leapfrog past his betters wasn't just fun. No, because the city was full of men like that who would walk across your face to get what they wanted. The book showed the dangers of hope. And most readers nowadays greeted that with a shrug: especially the hope of people bettering themselves! Before, whenever the barricades went up, expectancy had blazed – then choked. Like an unriddled stove! That had provided people with a 'forced education' all right! Maybe not the sort the monsignor meant, but it explained why the kitchen made a receptive audience when Tassart agreed to read from his master's work and defended its scepticism and taste for scandal. Tassart himself might not have chosen to reveal that taste, but, once the press did, he grasped the nettle.

The *maison de santé* was a gossip-shop, so Adam knew just which questions had been put to the valet. One was about a flayed and withered human hand which his master was said to own, but when a maid asked if he had it here, she was told to pipe down. And what about the *macchabées* – corpses – he had fished from the Marne? On his boating trips? Ten, was it? Some had been in the water so long that – but at this point the women listening would refuse to hear more.

'Stop! That's horrible!'

'I'm only telling you what he said himself!'

A footman, who had worked in a house which the writer used to visit, had heard him with his own ears describe the state to which these corpses were often reduced: a kind of swollen mush like papier mâché. The descriptions, of course, were designed to frighten ladies, to make them shriek and pretend ...

'Why "pretend"?' cut in the cook.

'Because,' smirked the footman, 'they were more titillated than upset. Some high-born ladies have appetites that might surprise you.'

'Yes, well, we'll have less of your double meanings in this kitchen, if you don't mind!'

When asked about the *macchabées*, Tassart snapped that his master was prouder of the *live* people he had managed to save. The footman, though, refused to drop the subject. He was sure he had heard that 'the Macchabées' was also the name of a group which met in a certain fashionable lady's drawing room to indulge in odd practices. 'Macabre ones!' Murmuring behind his hand, 'They say Monsieur Guy was the life and soul – or should we say the death and soul of ...'

'What? *Who* says? How do they know?'

A shrug. The footman's grin was insolent. 'They send away the servants.' Savouring his calvados, 'That in itself ...'

'What?'

'Sets minds racing.'

Hurt and indignant, Tassart spoke again of Monsieur's saving men from drowning and of how, by rights, he should have had a life-saver's medal. But the topic of contagion would not go away. A warder claimed to know that, when he had his health, Monsieur de Maupassant had attended Dr Charcot's displays of hypnosis at the Salpêtrière Hospital where the mad were put on show, and gentlemen could watch the most painful frenzies being calmed. There was even a rumour that one of the female patients – a former lady's maid – had been infected with the pox by none other than himself and that that was what had triggered her folly. This time gossip had gone too far. Tassart was upset and though the warder said that he had meant no disrespect to anyone, an all-out row was only just avoided.

'*If* my master did go there,' Tassart declared, 'it would not have been in an idle spirit, but for his research. He liked to see things for himself. Always. He was scrupulous that way.'

Aha, thought his listeners. Contagion! And felt unnerved. Later, they would exchange bracing jokes which, from kindness, they refrained from voicing in Tassart's hearing. He – 'Monsieur' Tassart to the kitchen – shone with sanified reflections of his master's raffish glory, and was treated with a pitying respect. Did it rankle that that master now refused to see him? Adam, who had taken Tassart's place today, would have liked to placate him. Guessing that he had a soft heart, he too pitied it as he might some delicate invertebrate – a sea anemone, say – which lay stranded in a drying rock pool.

Adam had, as it happened, a private reason for being wary of valets. It was clothes. Two years ago when he first left the seminary and had nothing to wear but cassocks or the cast-offs which the bursar was likely to supply, he had gone in search of a man called Thady Quill who had tended Uncle Charles in the days before this uncle went, all too literally, to the dogs and the card tables where he lost his shirt, his social standing and all need of a valet.

Thady Quill had been an apprentice jockey in Adam's father's stables, until he grew too heavy and was put instead to the trade of manservant. This was a crushing comedown for a young fellow whose sights had been set on winning the Chester Cup and other trophies. Indeed, so glum and peevish did Thady become that, as Adam heard the story later, he got on everyone's nerves, which was why, when Uncle Charles, then aged eighteen and hoping to be a painter, insisted on leaving for France, Thady was sent with him. Neither youth was to return, though for a while both wrote home. A decade later, when Adam, who was by then nearly twelve years old, found a foxed and cobwebby bundle of Thady's letters hidden in the butler's pantry, he squirrelled it off to a hideyhole of his own where he fingered his way through accounts of adventures which bemused and inflamed him. Quill's bulletins, having been intended for a fellow servant's eyes, were hard to make out, being ink-blotched, shadowy with innuendo and ablaze with the timorous amazement of a cage-born creature newly released in the wild. Thady Quill's France – Adam perceived in a stunned dazzle – was part Garden of Eden, part den of vice. As mapped by Thady – who, at the time, could not have had more than fifty words of French and whose English was half-Gaelic – it was a Kingdom of Adulthood, a predatory lottery where women were apt to be easy but poxy, brandy cost two francs a bottle and life was spirited and rash. The French he described were princely connoisseurs of the flesh, fearless, easygoing, freedom-loving and fun! Some of what he saw, Thady admitted, he had neither words nor nerve to describe and made no claim to understand. His account of it all was baffled but intrigued, tempted, yet fearful. Had people here, he marvelled, no fear of Judgement Day and getting their deserts? Had they not heard of Sodom and Gomorrah? 'Sometimes,' his letters confided, 'you'd have to wonder whether French Catholics are Christians at all!' This contradictory picture matched and expanded one with which Adam was already familiar. It was the impetuous France of Irish songs: the gallant ally which might yet help us boot out the dull, oppressive Saxon – 'Oh the French are on the say/ They'll be here without delay ...' – but also the sharp-minded nation, 'on the say' in more ways than one, which had retained membership in the Roman Catholic family while keeping its priests firmly in check. Adam, as one who longed both to be free and to belong, found that feat heartening and remembered it when, shortly after reading the letters, his own small world fell apart. It cracked open with alarming suddenness, like an eggshell around a nestling and he, the nestling vacillating on an Atlantic cliff-edge, had to think of taking flight. To where though? The first proposal was Canada. So far? Adam's shivering mind raced like windblown clouds over a cold ocean. Then quailed. No, he thought. *No*! His mother had by now been buried, and he and his father had bitterly fallen out. As his cousins were either too shocked by this scandal or too scandalous themselves to be of help, the only family left to Adam seemed to be the Church. But, though agreeing with his tutor, Father Tobin, that yes, very well, Father, maybe he'd as well go into a seminary to get himself an education, he stipulated that the seminary should be French.

By then, unknown to Adam, the Paris which Thady Quill had discovered in the wake of Uncle Charles, was quite gone. Quill's wild prediction that a storm could be brewing and the metropolis going the way of Sodom had proven sound. The Prussian invasion intervened between the writing of his dispatches and Adam's arrival in the cold corridors of his *petit seminaire*, and so had the massacres of Parisians by Parisians. Having been pent up by the Prussian siege and reduced to eating rats, they later behaved *like* rats and vented their fury on each other. How many perished? Twenty thousand? Forty? Reports varied, but agreed that the Seine had run red. Many more were transported or gaoled or fled into exile with the result that now, twenty years on, an appetite for revenge was once again biding its time. Meanwhile, Uncle Charles too had fallen on bad days and was eking out a diminished income in a cheap spa town. He had become an unlucky gambler and, even when peace and normality returned, did not recover.

Thady Quill, though, when Adam finally found him, was portly and friendly, had a French wife, spoke an eloquent, if eccentric lingua franca and was a father of three. He was prospering and kept a discreetly curtained, upstairs shop where strong smells like *essence de térébenthine* and pomander balls succeeded most of the time in drowning out less salubrious ones. His merchandise was second-hand apparel of a superior sort which gentlemen's valets and ladies' maids brought to sell when their employers fell ill, died, moved to North Africa, grew suddenly fat, came out of mourning or for some other reason, whether compelling or frivolous, wished to get rid of their wardrobe. His wife, a former lady's maid, could cut and sew, had a network of connections and had introduced him to the trade. He welcomed Adam warmly and rigged him out on tick, providing well-cut outfits with which to present himself to Dr Blanche and enable him to put his days as a seminarian firmly behind him. It was like a carnival: the speed, the choice, the faint sense of illegitimacy and impersonation. Real gentlemen would have had their tailor measure their inner calf and other specifics, which would then be carefully recorded for future use. It was unusual to buy garments which one could don forthwith or, after some shifting of hems or buttons, have delivered next day. Were Quill's customers all escapists and contrivers? Adam didn't ask.

Though pleased with his nearly-new, snuff-brown velvet jacket, striped trousers, curly-brimmed hat and fine frock-coat, he was slightly uneasy at the thought of coming face to face with their original owner – or, worse, with that owner's valet whose eye would be sharper and who, anyway, would be the man who had ripped out the label bearing the owner's and tailor's names before selling the garment on to Quill. When fashionable gentlemen came to Dr Blanche's luncheons, Adam found himself checking the width of their shoulders – his own were broad – and, since noting that Maupassant's girth must once have been close to his, felt nervous of Tassart. At any moment the manservant could exclaim: 'Ah, so *you're* the one who bought the jacket! Not too many would have the right athletic build! Bought it from Monsieur Quill then, did you?' Not that he ever would! A valet's prime qualification was a well-buttoned lip. Nervous fancies, though, were deaf to reason.

Adam knew that, in the grand scheme of things, neither clothes nor vanity mattered a jot. But then private perspectives were rarely grand. Just now, for instance, he found himself idly staring down the dim corridor to where the two ladies still sat in each other's embrace and in that of a sunset brightness flooding pinkly from a source he couldn't see, so that, like figures in religious paintings, they seemed to generate it themselves. Dreamily, he imagined sliding into it too and actually experienced waves of a mounting pleasure which dissolved his thoughts in its glow. On becoming conscious of what was happening, he found that it was his body, not his clothes, which was likely to embarrass him.

A raised voice interrupted this reverie.

As if thinking of him had conjured him up, the valet stood framed in the drawing room doorway, at the far end of the corridor, where he paused, then turned to launch some words over his shoulder. 'It is not my place to criticize, Madame, but, speaking with respect, you tricked me. *Si, si,* Madame, you deliberately kept me talking while Mademoiselle Litzelmann slipped behind my back and upset my poor master. As for the "love" she likes to talk about,' Tassart allowed himself a sneer, 'I don't think she has shown much. Love cherishes, Madame. It gives life and helps preserve it. But Mademoiselle Litzelmann has put poor Monsieur's health at risk. If he does not recover, the fault will be partly hers!'

What attachment he feels, Adam marvelled, then surprised himself by thinking 'it seems almost motherly'. Though he had lived in an all-male world in his seminary, this sort of closeness had not been possible.

Tassart now walked in Adam's direction. His lean lips were clamped in anger. He was, Adam noticed for the first time, younger than his master. As he drew level, he murmured, 'I can't think how those vampires got in! Who was in charge, Gould? You? If my master had come home with me, they would never have got near him. He would have been safe in our neighbourhood, where people are fond of him. Our tradesmen keep asking for him. They all agree that he should come home.'

Stung, Adam tried mounting a defensive attack. 'So,' he teased, 'you and your butcher and baker have been gossiping. Maybe you started the stories which reached the newspapers.'

Tassart said quietly, 'All any newsmonger could have learned from us was that my master was a straight, kind, decent man and that we are devoted to him.' He turned away, leaving Adam feeling neither straight nor decent, and just a bit embarrassed.

But already the valet was back. '*They* shouldn't be here.' Nodding towards the drawing room. 'Mademoiselle Litzelmann's name is on the list of people who shouldn't be let in. It probably tops that list. You must get her out.'

Adam did not want to expel the anxious young woman whose plight was not unlike the one in which *his* mother had found herself at the end. She too must have hoped – but he couldn't bear to dwell on that. He said, 'The other lady seems to have taken her under her wing. Madame d'Armaillé. And she *is* a guest here.'

'Maybe, but la Litzelmann ...'

'*Is* Monsieur de Maupassant the father of her children?'

'Possibly.' Tassart's face was hard. 'At all events he has provided for them. Think of it, Gould. She was just a girl in a spa, whose job was handing cups of water to the patients. What future had she? What security? She is better off now than when he met her.'

'And she wants – what?'

'Him to legitimize them. She wants respectability.' Tassart shrugged. 'His mother won't have it. Madame Laure.'

Again Adam thought of *his* mother. 'It seems hard!' he ventured.

'Gould, it is not our place to decide.'

'What has place to do with it?'

'Everything, surely. This is a nursing home. His health could suffer! I cannot think *how* you ...'

'Oh, very well! I shall ask her to leave. Come with me, will you? She might make difficulties if I went alone.'

In the drawing room Mademoiselle Litzelmann's eyelids were rosily swollen. She rubbed the back of a hand across them. Deftly, as though catching a moth, the other lady grasped and held the damp hand while hailing the two men.

'Ah,' she exclaimed, 'here is François Tassart back with my uncle's saviour! Monsieur Gould, yes?'

As if to imply that the weeping was to be ignored, she hid her companion's hand in a scarf. 'My uncle and the monsignor are conspiring,' she told Adam affably, 'so we have been excluded. I was wondering if we could impose on your hospitality. Mademoiselle Litzelmann came here on foot and is thirsty.'

'She didn't come in your carriage then?'

'Only through the gate.' Madame d'Armaillé was unembarrassed. '*Is* it possible to find her some refreshment? Barley water would do.'

Tassart, who seemed not to have heard, was staring at Adam's coat collar. 'May I,' he stepped behind him, 'see the garment in the light?' As he murmured 'It's soiled,' Mademoiselle Litzelmann retrieved her hand and blew her nose.

Soiled? Sold? Adam's body was behaving in an unaccountable way. He felt feverish.

Fingers fumbled his neck. Was the valet trying to read the label? Adam prayed not to be embarrassed in front of the beautiful Madame d'Armaillé. He was unused to being touched.

'We don't want to inconvenience you,' she claimed, but he guessed that doing so wouldn't bother her at all. His skin was hot. He wondered if the valet noticed.

'Do you want to take it off a moment? I could attend to it better.'

Adam, whose namesake had masked his nakedness with leaves, felt in need of some cover. Tassart's fossicking hands tickled and Adam spun away from them in a cloud of powder. Might his jacket have been Maupassant's?

'Talc!' Tassart was wielding a small brush. 'I always carry this. The powder sinks into the velvet pile. I *thought* I noticed this earlier. Couldn't be sure in the dark of that corridor.' Peeling back Adam's collar, he scrubbed, then, moving to the fireplace, shook his brush out over the grate. 'It can look like dandruff.'

'It's from Dr Blanche's gloves,' Adam remembered with relief. '*Il m'a blanchi*!'

Madame d'Armaillé's full-throated laugh at this weary joke was unexpected. She's young, he remembered, and felt friendlier towards her. 'Why don't we all have some port,' he suggested, 'to raise our spirits. Or Marsala?' He took decanters and glasses from a cupboard and put them on an intarsia table inlaid with festive motifs. 'We'll each drink a thimbleful, shall we? Then, though, I must ask Mademoiselle Litzelmann to leave. I have no choice. The director left precise instructions, and Monsieur Tassart may well get me into hot water over your being here at all. He is almost certainly about to say that it isn't his place to drink in the drawing room. Perhaps it isn't mine either, or Mademoiselle Litzelmann's. But, in a house like this, places shift. And many have no idea where they belong.'

To Adam's surprise, Tassart, when his turn came, accepted two glasses in quick succession and promptly drained both. They all drank, even Mademoiselle Litzelmann, who had stopped crying. Tassart looked as though he might be thinking of taking the floor.

'Biscuits?' Adam brought out a jar of *langues de chat* and handed them round. Soon there were sounds of delicate crunching and a scent of vanilla. Crumbs drifted and were brushed away.

'I have no wish,' the valet wiped his lips, 'to cause pain. But, for her own sake, Mademoiselle Litzelmann should know how hopeless her endeavours are. I understand why she keeps on with them because for a long time I too refused to accept what was happening to my poor master. There were remissions, and with each our hopes would revive. A change of air, a trip in his yacht, even a visit to a spa could brighten his mood, and when it did, how could we – he and I – help thinking he was on the mend? In the end though – this was ten months ago – I had to admit to myself that our interests were no longer the same, and that if I didn't ask him for a character reference soon I risked being unable to get employment when he was gone. Delicacy, you see, Gould, was beyond my means. Servants like me have a professional need to understand it but can rarely afford it. This is painful, and in my master's case it forced me to cause him pain too. Just now you mentioned "my place", and this reminded me that I cannot hope to find another one such as I had with him. He got me used to being treated like a man of feeling. That rarely happens to a servant. Do you mind if I take another glass of port? Thank you. Forgive me if I sound upset. I have been so for some time, you see. Not only on his account! On my own too. For nine years my life revolved around his. So did his mother's, of course, though in a quite different way. He was hers. She called him "My son the great man!" whereas I was just *his* man – a small man. But, unlike her, I was *there* all the time. Close up. Nursing and sharing. I'm a bit overcome. I'll try to be quick. I am hoping to make Mademoiselle Litzelmann see that those close to Monsieur have to give up their closeness. You'll see what I mean if you imagine my dilemma ten months ago. To ask for a reference meant letting poor Monsieur know how desperate his case was. This could damage him, but, short of destroying myself, what could I do? There was no concealing my motive. No softening pretence would have worked. Not only had he, as a writer, trained himself to see through such camouflage, but two years before, he had seen his brother, Monsieur Hervé, go mad, be committed to an asylum and die. Indeed Monsieur Guy himself had had to commit him.'

Tassart put down the glass, which was again empty. 'When I asked for the reference, he saw what was in my mind. I saw him see it. But instead of giving way to the terror I must have provoked, he took his pen, wrote out a generous *certificat* and gave it to me, and I ... well, all I had the nerve to do was sidle from the room. Just then the sane one was he, not I. Sane and gallant! I am telling you this, Mademoiselle, to let you know that I have been in your shoes. The difference is that in your case it is too late. The doctors have pronounced their verdict. No document he signed now would be legally valid. And as regards our own feelings, Mademoiselle, those of us who plan to live break faith with the dying. Allow me to walk you to the village.'

Tassart picked up the cloak which Mademoiselle Litzelmann had discarded on a chair, and put it around her.

She seemed about to make an appeal, then instead, drew herself up mutely, embraced Madame d'Armaillé, accepted her card, bowed, straightened her hat, and walked out followed by the valet. Both moved as though thwarted feelings were hampering the flow of their breath.

Madame d'Armaillé stared after them. 'I wonder,' she murmured, 'if that man is telling the truth? He seems goodhearted.' While she drank up the last of her port, Adam imagined the sweetness of it on her tongue, and his own tongue curled against his palate. 'Well,' she reflected, 'I suppose that in a place like this you must all be used to strong emotions!'

He could think of nothing to say. He and she had been left together as abruptly as two chaperones whose charges have gone to dance. For an instant he imagined waltzing with her. Not that he knew how! The only dancing he had ever done was as a child in Ireland, when he had been let join in the romping that sometimes took place on late summer afternoons, to the scrape of a fiddle, at a crossroads. Small fry like himself had rarely done more than caper back and forth, but the skilled dancers' fast footwork carried rhythms as deftly as the bow on the strings. They held their upper bodies rigid, and their motto 'Death in the eyes and the devil in the heels!' was as stern as the monastic one about keeping 'custody of the eyes'! Adam's eyes just now were in tight custody. He moved to the window.

'Will she be all right?' his companion wondered.

'If you mean will she easily get back to Paris, the answer is "yes". She can get a tram,' he told her, 'to the place de la Concorde. Or take the little train to St Lazare.' He looked out to where grimy shadows had begun to sink and thicken like tea-dregs. This side of the château faced downhill towards the quai de Passy. Outside its windows, steps, railed in by fine ironwork, divided in two elegant volutes then, when these rejoined, continued a stately descent towards a tumble of bleak, wintry lawns. Far below, the Seine gave off the opaque gleam of a great, grey eel. Bare branches scribbled on a dimming sky. To the side of the steps, two people were planting something. 'Oh,' he exclaimed, 'there's Maupassant. With Baron. They must have seen the others leave or they would not have ventured out.'

'May I see?'

Madame d'Armaillé stood behind him. Still as a birdwatcher, he sensed her shape in slight displacements of the air. The back of his neck, sensitized by the teasing of Tassart's brush, felt as if tiny antennae were embedded in each pore. He recognized a situation with which he had been trained to deal. This young, married, well-born woman was triply tabooed! In the seminary, such cases had been discussed with precision. Temptation! It was one which his clerical classmates planned to face in their future parishes as zestfully as St George had confronted his dragon. A pleasure renounced, their teachers assured them, brought more complex satisfactions than carnal enjoyment. The mind, after all ...

Heliotrope!

He inhaled. It was the scent from her dress and the name for plants which turn towards the sun! He felt the warmth of her breath. His mother had worn heliotrope.

'Which one,' she wanted to know, 'is Monsieur de Maupassant? Isn't he famous? Will he be upset if he sees us looking? Which is he?'

'The one with a beard. I'll open this window a crack. Then we'll hear what his mood is like.'

Cold air knifed in. Just yards away, the writer was too intent to notice them. Bending over a basket of whittled stakes, such as gardeners use for seedlings, he was trying to drive them into the frozen crust of a flowerbed. His voice floated hoarsely towards them.

'See, Baron, next spring, there will be a crop of small Maupassants here. Each of these sticks will grow into a Maupassant. I'm not joking! Drive in your stick and out pops your greedy, little replacement which in no time at all will be big enough to shove *you* into the earth! Soil is dangerously fertile. La Litzelmann, for instance, was fertility itself! Stick it into her once and she began to puff up. The reproduction business is nauseatingly predictable and ...'

Anxiously, Adam tried to fasten the casement but, before he could, a hand slid from behind him and pulled it open. 'Wait!' Madame d'Armaillé murmured in his ear. 'He is talking about Mademoiselle Litzelmann. We may learn something of use to the poor creature.'

She could not have understood. Just as well! But best close the window. A sheltered young woman of her sort would be appalled by what was likely to come next. 'Smelly orifices', Adam remembered with a shudder. He grasped the casement, but, when she held on, released it rather than wrestle with her. 'You may be distressed,' he warned. 'He is delirious and apt to use coarse language.'

'I am a married woman, Monsieur Gould.'

'Exactly. I am sure your husband would not want ...'

'Allow me to be the judge of that. My husband is in no way petty. He is a soldier. Fighting in the darkest wilds of Africa.'

'Well, our wilds here are dark too!' Adam was nettled by her assumption of superior – what? Knowledge? Worldliness? She couldn't be more than eighteen.

The sick man was shouting. 'Three she spawned: Maupassant,

Maupassant and Maupassant. Sounds like an undertakers' firm, doesn't it? Three guides to the evil passage! The sour and slippery way, haha! Sexual reproduction leads to death. If we never reproduced, there would be room for us all, and we could live for ever. But no! God wouldn't like that. He *enjoys* slaughter! He breeds us for it! It's why he hates us to idealize women and ...'

Adam snapped the casement to. 'You do not want to hear,' he whispered firmly.

Even now, however, the voice remained audible. 'God,' came its cry through the glass, 'cares no more for the fate of his creation than would some mindless, great fish spawning worlds in space! He has forgotten about us, Baron. You do know that, don't you?'

Baron's mumble did not reach the drawing room.

'We're nearing the end of our century! The end of our time! Doesn't that frighten you? This is 1892!'

Mumble.

Straightening up, the patient turned a bleared face towards the house. His nose ran unchecked because of his fear that if he blew it his melting brain could fall through. A related dread was that the brain contained a salt-factory worked by flies! Managed perhaps by Beelzebub? A priest, Adam thought, might claim that sending these terrors was the creator's way of calling back the lost lamb – or 'ram' as Guy had been respectfully nicknamed in deference to his well-attested sexual prowess.

Poor wet-nosed ram! Caught now in a thicket of folly! Poor wounded bull!

Wasn't it likelier though that it was the writer who had chosen to summon the creator so as to turn him into a fictional character? This let him release rage at the way his shoddily created brain was letting him down. And putting God in his story gave it magnitude.

'We're his prey,' came the shout. 'What other explanation covers the way things are? Destruction delights him. That's why he makes pregnant women puff up like frogs. Have you ever seen boys stick a straw into a frog and blow into it?'

Madame d'Armaillé backed away from the window. 'That poor woman is better off without him,' she decided. 'He's horrible.'

'But he sees his own horribleness! Most of us don't.' Adam's vehemence embarrassed him. This was the first time he had been in a tête-à-tête with a lady. How pathetic for a man aged twenty-four! Guy, he thought, is my opposite, the side of me I've suppressed. And he remembered him looking in the mirror and saying that Adam had stolen his face.

Madame d'Armaillé shrugged. It was less than a shrug, really. It was a movement so delicate that one could only admire its restraint. Adam, though, seeing it as a rejection, felt obliged to forge ahead and defend poor Guy whom he began to see as a representative of the male sex and so, ultimately, of himself. Something – the port perhaps? – had gone to his head. He pleaded: 'A disillusioned romantic!'

'Maybe. But horrible too.'

'And yet,' Adam was now in too deep to withdraw, ' I am told on all sides that he was delightful company in his time. And you've seen how Tassart worships him. They say no man is a hero to his valet, but Maupassant may be the exception. Maybe he was *too* sensitive?'

Disdain congealed Madame d'Armaillé's haughty face.

Maddeningly, this hardness made her look even more classically lovely.

Adam wished he had never begun to argue. 'His late work,' he told her meanly, 'rages against women's beauty. He came to see it as one of God's sinister tricks.'

'So he is – or was – a puritan?'

'Or a hedonist who can't bear to die.' But it now struck Adam that Guy's ranting was more likely to be a cover for guilt over failing to face up to his mother and acknowledge his children. The thought was depressing and so was Adam's fear that he had let words run away with him: an Irish habit which mentors frequently deplored.

'Billiard ball!' the sick man shouted suddenly and pointed to an upstairs window. 'Bald heads look like billiard balls! Give me a ball, Baron, and I'll score a hit!'

***

Standing at that window, in the last of the daylit clarity, the vicomte de Sauvigny ran an irritable hand over his bald head. For the last hour he had been trying to fathom Monseigneur de Belcastel who, though talkative, seemed reluctant to be fathomed. Sauvigny knew the strategy. It was one he had seen used by a fox to confuse hounds by crossing and recrossing its own trail.

'Where is this taking us?' he begged.

'We are at a crossroad,' said the reverend fox, 'and the advice from on high is that we should tread with discretion.'

The vicomte could not remember a time when advice from

'on high' – code for Rome – had been any different. 'And stick together,' he checked, 'for God and King?'

Belcastel tightened his lips. 'God should come first.'

'Of course.'

'But in practice,' the monsignor heckled, 'that only happens when it's time to pay for our allies' mistakes. The monarchists sacrifice God.'

The vicomte felt hurt. 'I ...' he burst out indignantly.

'I don't mean you!' skirmished the monsignor. 'You were a Papal Zouave and did your bit! I mean monarchist laymen here in France. Look what that connection costs the Church. It enrages Republicans who make the clergy pay. In the last twelve years,' Belcastel spread, then, one by one, folded five slim fingers, 'they tried to expel Him from the schools and hospitals of France, forced seminarians to do military service and brought in divorce. When members of the clergy protested, their pay was docked.' The hand was now a fist which the monsignor sheathed in the darkness of his joined sleeves.

Sauvigny tried to suppress a fear that the priest was turning his coat. Testingly, he asked: 'Are we still allies?' and prayed for a plain answer. None came.

If the monsignor had been a fox and gone sneaking back to his hole, the vicomte would have sent a terrier after him. Blocked up all exits but one. Then in with the dog.

'Together?' he hoped. 'Our alliance still holds? You, I am sure, are not about to join the renegades?' The vicomte laughed thinly, then, reproving himself for his distrust, managed a hearty cackle. 'You,' he challenged, 'are not that kind of man.'

Belcastel wasn't. Indeed, he could be described as a living martyr who, at the cost of his career, had taken the blame when well-born blowhards had put the Cause at risk. That, one should remember, was why he was in a madhouse. He had raced through flames to rescue compromising papers which the plotting blue bloods had left behind and, when their plot was discovered, had taken the blame. If you couldn't trust him, who could you trust? Sauvigny sighed. Maybe you could trust no churchmen now? The old alliance felt frail. There was a danger that the present pope – ironically, he had taken the bold name of Leo! – might become reconciled with the modern world.

His predecessor, Pius, had stoutly condemned 'errors' such as 'progress' and 'modern civilization' and, if alive today, would have fulminated against the godless French Republic. Pope Leo's statements were subtle, and the vicomte distrusted subtlety. Morale suffered while people wondered which way the lion planned to pounce. Up until now Leo's one telling pounce had been to order Catholic journalists to stop exasperating the French Republic. Why *should* they stop? The presage was worrying – and there had been others.

Not fifteen months ago, His Eminence, Cardinal Lavigerie, a respected and, till then, an ardent monarchist, had given in to the spirit of the age and advised Catholics to accept the Republic! Devastating though this was, worse could well follow. The renegade could be a stalking horse. Others could be creeping up behind him. It was even whispered that Pope Leo ... but the vicomte refused to pursue that line of thought. Moving closer to the window, he stared into a web of thickening dusk. Lozenges of light fell through it from casements below, and in their lambency he could make out two figures whose faces were tilted upwards as if watching him.

One shouted, 'See! Another baldy! They all look like billiard balls! Have you noticed how many there are here, Baron? This place destroys hair. Even my poor François is losing his!'

A lunatic! The other man must be his keeper. His hand hovered by the madman's elbow.

'We need billiard cues,' the lunatic shouted. 'Shall we use these?'

Abruptly, a shower of small sticks arched, flew, struck and rattled the window just inches from the vicomte's face. Luckily, none broke the glass. They were shaped like arrows and, as Sauvigny faced them, he saw himself, for a mocking moment, back in the army under fire. The old battle fever fizzed through his blood, reminding him that, instead of pussyfooting here, he could, even at his age, join up again. Go to Africa, perhaps, where the Zouaves were making themselves useful. Why not? The small confrontation with the lunatic had raised his spirits.

'Are you all right, vicomte?' the monsignor worried. 'Are the windowpanes cracked?'

'Nothing's cracked,' cried the exuberant Sauvigny. 'Only that crackpot down there.'

'Be careful. He throws billiard balls. One struck a man last week.'

'Don't worry, Monseigneur,' the vicomte insisted. 'You mustn't worry so much. You and I make an excellent team. Have you forgotten how neatly we settled Cardinal Lavigerie's hash?'

'Hush!' Belcastel's voice shook. 'Better come away from the window.'

'You surely haven't forgotten our little conspiracy? The old letter? How ...'

'Please, old friend! I implore you not to mention my part in that to anyone.' The monsignor looked as if he were on the rack.

Remorse, the vicomte wondered? Or new, contradictory orders from Rome?

***

It was now over a year since that November afternoon when, at a banquet in his episcopal palace, Cardinal Lavigerie, Archbishop of Carthage and Algiers, rose to his feet and spoke words which would scandalize the Catholic world. Forty of his guests were officers from a French naval squadron, then at anchor in Algiers harbour, and the rest were officials *en poste* in Algeria. The governor was away. So, when pudding was served, the cardinal, as senior dignitary, proposed a toast to the navy and read a speech which, by the time he had finished, so stunned his more attentive listeners that their leader, Admiral Duperré, sat down without responding. The rest of the company followed suit. There was no applause. Nobody raised a glass. Guests who had been woolgathering must have marvelled at the admiral's breach of etiquette.

Officers were traditionally royalists and unlikely to have caught the cardinal's drift at first. Having rejoiced to see men from the French civil service, judiciary and armed forces united at his table, he had expressed a wish that a similar union might soon prevail in France. Even now, the steel pricking through his rhetoric may have passed unnoticed. The Church's dearest wish, said His Eminence, was to see all good citizens united.

All! To the alert the word was an alarm signal. Some of the less fuddled nudged brother officers.

'Wake up, man! Where's the old sky pilot headed? Wants us united with everyone, does he? Is that to include the Republican rabble which murdered our relatives back in the 1790s and again twenty years ago, when – has he forgotten? – Reds shot the Archbishop of Paris in cold blood and spattered his brains on a prison wall? A chap I knew saw them. He said the bish had been a bit too much of a democrat, and the brains were pinkish.'

'Like our host's?'

'If he means what we think.'

The first accounts to reach France were confused. Listening to the cardinal was like joining a paperchase where the clues were too obscure for laymen to pick up.

'... when a people's will,' he read on in a melancholy tone, 'has been clearly asserted, when a government's form is not, as Pope Leo XIII recently proclaimed, contrary to those principles which favour the survival of civilized and Christian countries ... then it is time to bury our differences and sacrifice ... all that conscience and honour permit.'

What did that mean? That churchy rigmarole? Did it mean anything at all? Both Sauvigny and Belcastel quickly received first-hand reports. A naval cousin of Sauvigny's had actually been present at what was soon known in barracks and presbyteries throughout the hexagon as 'the Algiers toast'. The cousin must have dozed off during the speech, for all he could be persuaded to recall with any assurance was the glare from reflected sunlight – the reception was a lunchtime one – easy laughter, the gleam of buttons and epaulettes, initial disbelief.

'A row was the last thing on our minds,' said this cousin, and mentioned arranging to visit local brothels which, he had been told, offered curious and unusual pleasures. 'Jewish women, young Arab girls ...!' He had been excited at the prospect. Then someone struck a glass so that it began to sing, and there was a half-serious outcry, since if the singing wasn't stopped pronto a sailor must die. A naval superstition! After that his mind must again have wandered, for the next thing he knew they had all stood up, then inconclusively sat down again! 'I told myself, this is a rum go!' said the cousin, making a late claim to discernment.

Sauvigny ignored it. Clearly the event had been premeditated. The speech carried signals both to Republicans – conciliatory – and to the French Church: 'watch your step, brothers in Christ'. To monarchists the message was so unwelcome that some tried to dismiss it. The vicomte heard it described as 'senile', the coinage of a rogue cardinal with a grudge, at best ambiguous, at worst gibberish. If it was none of the above, then it was a slap on their collective face, not to say a brutal kick in their massed behinds. France, the eldest daughter of the Church, the land once ruled by men like Charlemagne and St Louis, was being urged by that same Church to embrace the godless Republic. But was this true? And had the cardinal acted off his own bat? Or had he been sent to test the waters? If he had, then we, Sauvigny realized, must act fast to stifle support for his policy among the French clergy. Rouse bishops. Remind them where money for their charities and pet projects came from! *Not* from the Mason-ridden state which merely paid their meagre salaries! Nor from Rome which needed money itself! No! It came from the great houses of France whose owners would expect them to condemn the Algiers toast, and whose donations, if they didn't, would dry up. Lavigerie's own ambitious good works could be starved out! Best remind him of that! And best remind others that St Peter's Pence could dry up too. If Pope Leo's head was in the clouds, he had better know that the economic ground could be cut from under his feet.

But now, fourteen months on, all this had been done, and still Rome was silent. Its newspapers were wilfully enigmatic. 'Enlighten the pope,' prayed royalist nuns. (The vicomte had his sources.) 'Enlighten him or else take him to Yourself!' It was not *quite* a murderous prayer. Pope Leo, after all, was over eighty. Still, he was surprisingly vigorous, having led a salubrious life. One had to reckon with him. So for a year now augurs had been tracking straws borne on the winds from Rome. Foremost among these was the arrival of a new nuncio who was worryingly friendly with the turbulent cardinal.

The augurs' main target, to be sure, was still Lavigerie himself. He was aged sixty-five, a priest of enterprise and vision, with a faintly elusive gaze and a range of ambitions. He had founded a missionary order, launched a crusade against slavery, built, dabbled in archeology and wine-production and shown himself politically flexible and astute. He had been a Bonapartist under Napoleon III, a legitimist in that brief moment in the early seventies when the comte de Chambord looked like taking power and now – well, what *was* he saying now?

When copies of the speech were obtained, two items attracted particular attention. One was the claim: 'I speak with the assurance that no authorized voice will contradict me.' Was Lavigerie hinting that he had papal support? Several French monarchists, both clerical and lay, crossed the Alps in person to urge Pope

Leo to disown the cardinal – and got no satisfaction. However Lavigerie – thought to be by now desperate for papal support – got none either. Spies – everyone was a spy – reported that the cardinal was sick with anxiety. From the moment when Admiral Duperré sat down without raising his glass to him, he had been confronting widespread hostility. His fear must be that the pope – if he had indeed been behind him – would now abandon him. Peter, after all, had disowned Christ.

'Admiral,' Lavigerie had begged in consternation, on that first day, as he stood alone, feeling the first shocked blast of disapproval, 'will you not respond to my toast?'

Only then did the admiral grudgingly raise his glass and say with wintry courtesy, 'I drink to His Eminence and to the clergy of Algeria.'

Then, as the guests took their leave, children from the cardinal's local orphanage struck up the 'Marseillaise'. The 'Marseillaise'! To the visitors from France it was almost inconceivable that they should have to listen to the bloodthirsty tune which had been played when priests and nobles were being carted to the guillotine!

'Can *you* understand it?' Sauvigny asked Belcastel suddenly. 'The African's enraging his guests by having the "Marseillaise" played? The rest is understandable. But that ... What possible motive could he have had?'

'It is not a revolutionary tune in North Africa,' the monsignor noted mildly. 'It is the French national anthem.'

'But the words ...'

'Nobody in North Africa knows the words.'

'Some people think,' said the vicomte, 'that too many bishops are jumped-up commoners. Men like that tend to be weather-cocks. I believe the cardinal's father was a customs officer.'

'Oh, I don't think commoners are the only weathercocks. More?'

Sauvigny let the monsignor refill his glass with Marsala. As he drank the sweet, heady stuff – it reminded him of his time with the Zouaves – he reflected that reasonableness could be a form of treachery. Monarchists didn't want reason. They wanted kings with divine right, and held hard to distinctions between 'legal' and 'legitimate' forms of government. Though legal, the Republic lacked the stamp of divine approval, and it was to ensure it never got it that they needed the vacillating, casuistic but, alas, indispensable clergy.

'You,' he reminded his host with sudden brutality, 'must be the last man alive with whom Lavigerie will want to make peace. After the way you showed him up!'

The monsignor flinched. 'As I told you, I regret doing that. It was unchristian.'

'War is war!' Sauvigny was pleased to state. 'You did the right thing for the Cause.'

What Belcastel had done was to recall that years earlier, tempted by one of those rare chances for a successful coup which arise during crises, Lavigerie had written to the comte de Chambord to tell him, in masterful detail, just how he might set one in motion and propel himself into power. His letter was of course confidential, but necessarily a few men saw it, and one of these was Belcastel. Impressed by the cardinal's lucidity and convinced that, in the hands of a more determined Pretender, the plan would have succeeded, he never forgot it, and, in his first flush of indignation over the Algiers toast, contacted the gentleman in charge of the dead Chambord's papers. Skilfully, he overcame this custodian's scruples and persuaded him to publish the explosive old letter in the *Gazette de France*, thereby discrediting the cardinal both with his new Republican allies and his Church.

'It exposed him doubly,' Sauvigny gloated. 'A brilliant stroke!' He laughed.

As Belcastel shuddered, the burned side of his face flashed in then out of sight, like a palmed card. The reverberations had been scurrilous. 'It was uncharitable!'

Sauvigny made a rude noise.

'I told myself that he in my place would have done the same. Publishing the letter, you see, was a sort of coup.'

' A Republican-style manoeuvre.'

'I was going to say the opposite. Men like us gamble on a coup because it invites a miracle and gives God a chance to intervene. Rationalists have no such excuse.'

Sauvigny wondered if his leg was being pulled.

'Now though,' the monsignor mused, 'the cardinal's claim is that Chambord committed political suicide by refusing to make concessions. That, I'm told, is why Lavigerie now wants to cut the Church free of your party. You, runs his argument, would drag us down with you, but no one has the right to commit suicide.'

'And are *you* jumping ship too, Monseigneur?'

'No! But remember that, though your ship is the monarchy, mine is the Church. And before you say that we are venal and stay with you because we need your money, remember *why* we do. We need to fund independent schools because of the Republic's *lois scolaires* for which ...'

'... you blame us. When we enrage the Republicans and they strike back, you get caught in the middle. Let's admit that we are in your debt! Money can settle that. So pour me more Marsala and I shall propose my own toast. The Auteuil toast! Are we in Auteuil here?'

'Passy, but we're smack on the border!'

'Border people! How fitting.' Sauvigny raised his glass. 'I drink to the French monarchist clergy. And,' teasingly, 'to the temporal goods we plan to provide for them.'

***

'Well,' François Tassart turned his back on the departing carriage. 'They've gone!'

Adam locked the gate, and the two walked quickly back to the house. It had started to freeze.

'Good riddance!' Tassart stamped cold feet. 'That countess wanted me to tell her how to get my master to recognize the Litzelmann children. She cornered me. Did you hear her mention paternity suits?' As he smiled, his teeth slid over his lower lip as though cancelling the smile. 'My master used to say of young women like her that they're brought up in convents, then never learn how to live in the world. Mind, I should not have let my feelings run away with me earlier. Perhaps that encouraged her? Speaking with respect, she's a child herself. Pretty, though. My master would have had an eye for her in his day.'

Adam swung the key-ring on his finger. 'And would it have been right,' he queried, 'if *he* let his feelings run away with him?' They had reached the hall where their ways divided.

'It's not ...'

'... your place to say! But?'

Hearing themselves laugh at the same moment, both men paused, then laughed at their laughter.

'I have no place now!'

'I have never quite known mine.'

'Because you're a foreigner?'

'Perhaps.'

That wasn't why, though. Adam never had known it. Place in his Ireland had been a slippery notion; in the seminary it had been provisional, and here – ah well, in Dr Blanche's establishment, the only one worrying about such things might be Tassart. Adam was amused by the manservant's attempts to hold on to notions of hierarchy while enjoying its occasional collapse. Tassart's stock phrase – the one which had made them laugh – was 'It is not my place to say, *but* ...' There were a great many 'buts', for the valet's position with Maupassant must have been like that of a dumb-waiter: that small domestic hoist which glides between kitchen and dining room, servant's sphere and master's, and belongs in both. As though acknowledging this, Tassart, when remembering those days, always spoke of 'our' flat. Even his readings from Guy's stories staked a claim. Perhaps he planned to write himself? Adam had seen pencillings on his cuffs. Notes? For a memoir? Maupassant had written about servants. Could he have guessed that one might turn the tables? What, after all, could be more just than such an appropriation of the reflective, upper world which servants enabled and often saw from closer than the upper folk guessed? One of the male nurses here had worked in a house where concealed corridors, running parallel to the visible ones, allowed chamberpots and the like to be discreetly spirited away. Bandages, blood, clysters ... Unseen, behind panelling, tiptoeing servants bore off evidence as alertly as mice or spies or – come to think of it – writers. So why should Tassart not change trades? According to Baron, he had told the kitchen that, though he had always refused to wear livery, he felt a bond with fellow-servants and was indignant when they were misrepresented in books.

'He'd have us believe,' had been Baron's half-incredulous comment, 'that he and his master talked about this. Well, maybe they did. I'd have said though that custards and shoe-polish were more in a manservant's line.'

Reminded, Adam now asked Tassart about these conversations, and was amused by the valet's indignation.

'I hate the picture,' he told Adam, 'that my master's friend, Monsieur Zola, draws of domestics in his books. Perhaps you've read *Pot-Bouille*? It is painfully misleading, a contemptuous, mean-spirited cartoon. Gentlemen think we use bad and incorrect language but, in twenty-five years' service, I never once heard a maid use the sort of filthy words which Monsieur Zola puts in the mouths of maids and cooks. And people reading his books believe that that's the way we talk! "It's not right, Monsieur," I told my master. The real lives of girls in service are worth writing about, but not, as Monsieur Zola thinks, because they might hide lovers behind the kitchen door so as to smuggle them up to their attic. Few do that. They don't dare. Besides, unlike the ladies who visited my master, they're too decent. No, what's interesting about those poor girls is how careful they have to be and what a lot they have to put up with just to earn their thirty francs a month – most of which has often to be sent home to their needy families. But the worst thing is that they have to bottle up their feelings and can never let off steam. In most households servants are expected to have no character at all. Men like my master are rare. He respects character even in a servant.'

'Talking of letting off steam, did you hear about his throwing sticks at the vicomte?'

'At his "billiard-ball head"? I heard. Yes. His mind is on heads, poor Monsieur! That's because he is worried about his own. He keeps saying, "I'm going at the top!" It's heartbreaking. He thinks I stole his brain. Why would I – even if I could?'

Again Tassart looked ready to weep. And, though Adam tried to comfort him, he wondered too whether Maupassant's instinct wasn't sound. It looked as though, in a way, the valet was indeed hoping to steal his master's brain.

IV

Reflections float; air is buoyant, and the eye ambushed by surprises. Those specks by the perron now are not snow but snowdrops, for winter is on the wane. But change can be disturbing. Some inmates grow restless, and there are scuffles in the *cour des agités*. Maupassant's mood veers between ravings and remissions attended by attacks of keen anxiety.

'My mind is mush. Gone soft! I *have to die* before I lose it.' These words sound as cold as if he had been keeping them on ice.

'You seem all right now.'

'Oh, it stages the odd reappearance.' His chill words pop like spat pips. 'I *think* it sidled onstage today, and am pitifully glad. I couldn't bear to end up like your terminal patients. They're animated ... bags.' He frowns, then speaks in a rush: 'What matter, you may think, since I wouldn't know? What matters is that my mother would.' He nods. 'She'd get reports. Not from poor François, mind! *He*'d spare her, but gossip wouldn't. Its source is our very own Dr Grout, who is courting poor Flaubert's niece, Caroline de Commanville. You've met her! At lunch, remember? Well, Caroline's an indiscreet old friend whom my mother will pump for details. I know she will because *I* trained her to. For years she used to collect anecdotes for me to write up. "Get details," I'd insist. "Details are what makes a story live!" So she developed a nose for them and will get them about me – then be devastated!'

Guy looks steadily at Adam. 'She calls me her great man! Such a man – don't you think? – ought to kill himself while he's still lucid. Will you help me do it, Gould? When the time comes? I wouldn't ask if I hadn't made such a poor fist of it last time.' He runs the tip of a finger along the scar in his neck where the sliver of broken glass must have slipped. Missing the artery, it left a pink, satiny crease studded with nodes no bigger than lettuce seeds or the beads in a baby's necklace. 'No use asking the doctors.' He lifts an eyebrow. 'Their oath, you see! The hypocritical, Hippocratic one!'

His smile pleads. Guy the seducer.

He means it, thinks Adam, then wonders: is there a 'he' there now? Dr Blanche's notes on this case describe: 'Acute disorder of the intellectual faculties characterized by melancholy ravings ...'

'Gould?'

'We're hoping to get you better.'

'What if you can't?'

Adam can't bring himself to say. After Guy's last attempt his neck wound gaped like a split pomegranate.

'Yes? No?' The straying mind is back, focused by need.

'Do you,' Guy presses, 'mean "maybe"?' His hair has fallen out in handfuls, and he hates letting the barber trim his beard. Naturally, he cannot be allowed to trim it himself. 'I know I don't sound the way I used to.' His once robust frame is a ruin. 'Unfortunately, I can see how things are.' He waits. '*Well?*'

Adam shakes then stops shaking his head. 'Maybe,' he says, then: 'Let's wait a little. The topic sharpens your mind wonderfully. Maybe you will cure yourself?'

Afterwards he can't be sure whether he made a promise and whether, if so, it is binding. Now that he has decided – this was quite recent – against going back to the seminary, by what rules will he live? He wonders if Guy recognizes him as a rudderless man.

***

More damage by *Dynamitards*!! Anarchists attempt to destroy the barracks in the rue de Rivoli where the Garde Républicaine is quartered. No lives lost.

Adam is now the house press censor. Each morning, before patients receive their newspapers, he checks them for references to Guy, pen poised to ink them out. Happily, a series of outrages has diverted public attention and Guy is forgotten. This is a relief. Adam, when inking out his name, always felt a small, superstitious shiver.

Anarchist-Trial Judge's residence bombed. Further attacks feared.

Republicans are now thought to regret alienating so many Catholics. When trouble explodes on your left, you look the other way for friends. But the Right is skittish. Its organ,

L'Autorité, has been printing a heated correspondence about a proposal by the bishops that their flocks should agree to respect the government. Readers – who may not be readers at all, but the editor in disguise – reject the notion. Insults like 'morally defrocked' scorch through letters from 'An anxious Catholic from Saint-Malo', 'A troubled father', 'A loyal subscriber' and many more. Most claim to be laymen, fear change, and are outraged to find it coming from their Church. 'Any priest who supports the proposed compromise must,' says 'A betrayed and bewildered member of the faithful', be 'either mad, vicious, a gull, a joker, a double-dealer or a liar.'

Adam asks Blanche whether this fury could affect patients? 'Should we stop their newspapers altogether?'

'If we did,' says Blanche, 'how could we ever get them ready to return to the great madhouse outside? You too, Gould, may have trouble adapting to it! How come you're so unlike your madcap uncle? He told me your papa was a bit of a wild man too.'

'Maybe that's why I'm cautious. I'm fearful of damaging people.'

'Did you ever?'

'Yes.'

'Well, I won't probe.'

***

Days go by. The thaw expands. Sap rises. Moisture glints.

' ... two ... three.'

In one of the exercise yards to the side of the old château a voice counts. It rattles with brusque precision through the kitchen window to where Adam and the cook are sitting at a deal table planning the week's menu. Repeated scrubbings have so stripped the grain of the deal that its fibres feel to their fingertips like string. Adam thinks of Guy's softened brain.

'Calf's head,' licking her pencil, the cook writes greasily, 'for Wednesday. Monsieur le Directeur is partial to it. We'll need several. *Salsifis* would go well with them and plain boiled potatoes. I'll make a sauce. For pudding ...'

'One ...'

'Poor gentleman!' She shakes her head. 'He's fighting duels. In his fancy of course. Been at it since breakfast! A lot of them do that. Pull the trigger. Bang! I suppose it's a relief. Is it something he read in the paper that got him agitated?'

Adam admits that they haven't worked out how to keep the papers from Maupassant.

'A shame!'

'Yes.'

'Not that I took to those things of his that Monsieur Tassart read to us. My little kitchen maids are so young. I had to send them away. Can't have their minds corrupted before their bodies. I could do sweetbreads for Thursday, if you like, or pigeon pies, then turbot on Friday after a clear soup. No, I don't like stories about low life. Keeping that at arm's length is hard enough for decent people. So why read about it? Plain folk have to mind their step. As I said to Monsieur Tassart, one slip can topple you. Fast! No need at all to read about what's below! Never look down, is what I say. Looking up to your betters can teach you things. Oh, you may laugh if you like.'

Working in an asylum has made the cook contentious.

'Bang!' shouts Guy.

'That's right,' shouts Adam boisterously. 'Bang!'

Reading Guy's stories has expanded his view of the world. They disconnect doom from licentiousness. Maybe this is what worries the cook who, on second glance, is younger than she chooses to seem, possibly still in her twenties, with tender, blanched flesh. Trussed into a tight topknot, her hair pulls at her facial skin. Perhaps she thinks of prettiness as a lure? Something for which she could be blamed? Perhaps she craves the guard-rails with which Guy's tales do away. The fallen women in his brothels are more cosy than randy and as easy to chat with as – well, herself.

'Life's a tightrope,' she says now, while writing '*compote de pommes* or *crème caramel*?'

Reading this upside down, Adam asks greedily, 'Why not both?'

She smiles.

'One ...' Guy's footsteps pound monotonously back and forth. 'Two ...'

Listening for fear in these shouts, Adam hears only rage and wonders whether this was always Guy's trouble. 'Cook, do you think fear keeps the world in order? Are you a timid person?'

She, thinking he's flirting with her, snaps her notebook closed and stands up. 'I'm not a rash one anyway.'

Dismissed, Adam leaves the kitchen, still wondering whether Guy's rage began when he lived like the poor clerks in his early stories. Confined in their rabbit-hutch lives, their only safe outlets would have been visits to sanitized brothels supervised by the Paris police. Might Guy still be sane if he had stuck to those? The doctors are unsure how much the pox contracted in his youth weakened his constitution.

'Am I a prig?' Adam worries. Priggishness is the mark of the 'spoiled' priest or seminarian who, as they say here, flings his cassock in the nettles. A stinging image!

In the courtyard the shadow duellist is still fighting. The male nurse with him is Baron who, though mild-tempered, has wide-spanned, capable hands, able, if need be, to overpower a violent patient.

'I could take over,' Adam offers. 'I'll take him in.'

Baron grins doubtfully under his ticklish, barley bouquet of a moustache.

'There's coffee in the kitchen. And cook needs cheering up.'

Baron leaves. Guy keeps counting.

'Bang!' says Adam. 'Bravo. You've decimated your enemies. But the weapon that really flattens those swine is your pen. As they know! Even their attacks are a tribute. I see,' nodding at an old newspaper in Guy's pocket, 'that you read the one in *L'Écho de Paris.*' Why, he wonders, was the paper not taken from him?

'One ... two ...'

'Guy, you mustn't keep rereading that. Here, give me your copy. Just listen to the envy: "The author of *Notre Cœur* used ether to quicken the ink in which his brain dissolved ..."'

'... three.'

'Why not challenge the shit? Prove him wrong? Write something, and we'll send it to the papers with today's date on it, just to confound them, what do you say? Hm? Here, give me that gun.'

Guy has no gun but lets himself be taken through a pantomime in which he hands one to Adam who breaks it open, swivels the drum, removes imaginary bullets, then puts gun and bullets into different pockets of an equally imaginary bag which he slings over his shoulder.

'If your eyes are too bad for writing, you can dictate.' Adam takes his arm. 'If we're to get you better, you've got to help. Making those bastards look silly will do you more good than any medicine. Are you listening, Guy?'

As they walk into the house, Adam slips the copy of *L'Écho de Paris* inside his shirt.

Back in his room, the patient flops on his bed. The pupils of his eyes strain in two directions. Strabismus is part of his condition. Strabismus and doubleness.

Sitting by the convex window-grating – it stops patients getting near the glass – Adam leafs through a file of newspaper cuttings. 'Look what I've got here, Guy, your occasional pieces. My favourite is about boating at Argenteuil. Watching the dawn. Remember? It describes frogs perching on water-lily leaves to cool their bellies, while a kingfisher slips through tall grass. It is a lovely piece of writing, and – do I imagine this? – thrums with sexual excitement when the grasses part for that sleek, flashing bird. You must have pleasured a thousand hankerers – sad dreamers like *you'd* been when you were stuck in an office living for your next chance to get out on the river. But what's odd is that the piece then grows glum. Why, Guy? Here's some paper. Can you write? Can you tell us why you followed your account of radiant, moonlit water with the complaint – these are your words: 'this symbol of everlasting illusion was born for me on the foul water which sweeps the filth of Paris down to the sea.' Am I misreading you? Maybe it's not a complaint? Maybe you were *glad* of the filth-borne radiance? Maybe you were reflecting that we were all born in shit? As priests say: *inter faeces nascimur* so – *Guy*! Calm down! Don't stab yourself! Here! Let me have the pen. That's right! Easy now. Lie back and we'll forget about writing. Just be glad that the radiance you described still thrills people! You can still turn pessimism on its head.'

Silence. Guy breathes hard. His eyes fail to focus. Is he reflecting that, whatever the fate of his books, he himself is ending where he began! In the shit! *Merde*, thinks Adam. Why did I mention it?

'Guy?'

More silence.

Adam moves closer. '*Guy?*'

The patient doesn't answer. His mouth sags, and saliva threads shine on his chin. His beard sprouts sideways like a ruff. Aged forty-two, he looks like a half-mummified and obsolete life-form.

***

Elsewhere in the *maison de santé* the post had been distributed.

Monseigneur de Belcastel received a parcel and slit it open with a gold paper-knife which, according to asylum rules, he should not have had in his possession. Naturally, those rules were sometimes bent a little – indeed, in his case, they were bent a lot for, after all, he wasn't mad. However, from politeness, he usually kept the knife concealed.

The parcel contained no letter, just a copy of *Le Petit Journal*, dated 17 February. In it was – but this was so unheard-of that he had trouble taking it in – an interview with the pope. In the popular press! The condescension was troubling, and the monsignor's first impulse was disbelief. His next thought was that the newsprint must be counterfeit, a squib put out by some inky anarchist – or unhappy monarchist? – eager to imply that papal pronouncements were now much like those of the popular press. 'A penny encyclical'! He could just hear Sauvigny's drawl. *'Une encyclique à un sou*! Today's Church, *mon cher monseigneur*, is ...'

What? Time-serving? A heresy-shop? He blotted Sauvigny out.

For of course the thing must be a sham. But reading on, he saw that it was not. He knew the tone: roundabout but firm. The Petrine Rock had found a voice and, astoundingly, it was that of a reporter called Ernest Judet in *Le Petit Journal*.

Rome -- here came the real shock – had pulled the rug from under monarchist feet!

After so long! It must be a good fifteen months since the Algiers toast. And *all that time* the pope had kept disquietingly quiet! Were we to think that mists, only now lifted from his eyes, had blinded him to his temporal responsibilities? How could we when the main trust of Lavigerie's – presumably ventriloquized? – speech had been that an authority which failed to hold things together lost legitimacy?

Restlessly, the monsignor smoothed the newspaper back in its folds then laid his paper-knife flat and spun it like the spoke of a golden wheel. Round and round it spun. A molten dazzle. The implications of Lavigerie's thinking – which, it now transpired, was actually Pope Leo's – could lead far.

For how legitimate by its gauge were kings-with-divine-right, or popes or divinities themselves, if they did not procure peace and goodwill? Whether or not God existed, faith in Him should surely be able to do that.

Unnerved, Belcastel's thought turned back in search of God, faith and safety. For God was glue, and doubt led to thinking for yourself, which could restart the cycle of revolution, retaliation and rage. But the pope, in the copy of *Le Petit Journal* once more unfurling on the monsignor's desk, had told his interviewer, 'I want France to be happy.'

'Happy!' Belcastel spoke the word aloud and tried to think no further.

Not thinking, though, left a void and into this surged contradictory sensations. The first was shame over what he had done to Cardinal Lavigerie who had, now at long last, been vindicated. His Eminence had, after all – this interview proved it – been the pope's stalking horse and scapegoat. He had been his apostle too, his John the Baptist, whose voice, valiantly crying its message to hundreds of ill-disposed French presbyteries, had prepared the way for Leo XIII's public volte-face. For fifteen months the Vatican had left the sixty-seven-year-old Lavigerie to swing in the wind, a lone target for every kind of offensive abuse including – this had been reliably reported by the presbytery servants' bush telegraph – anonymous letters smeared with excrement, sniping innuendos in the Catholic press and frontal attacks by former friends, among whom Belcastel had in all honesty to number himself. *His* strike had possibly been the most hurtful.

Mortification reached the capillaries in his face. Feeling it burn, he guessed that his unblemished cheek must be as red as the scarred one.

His paper-knife, having slowed and regained knifishness, had best be put away. Opening a desk drawer, he thrust it out of sight. As he did, his hand touched the box of monarchist mementoes which had accumulated during his stay in the *maison de santé*. Most had been gifts: offerings to the living martyr which the more excitable party-supporters held him to be. The blue leather missal, for instance, with the gilt fleur-de-lys had been sent by the duchesse d'Uzès. He could hardly send it back.

Returning to the paper, he found His Holiness taking the view that, since France badly needed a stable government, its citizens must accept the legality of the status quo. 'Everyone,' conceded the pontiff, 'is entitled to his private preference, but, in practical terms, the only existing government is the one that France has chosen. A republic is as legitimate a form of government as any other ...' An encyclical dealing with this matter at more length would, said *Le Petit Journal*, be published by the French Catholic press in four days' time.

The monsignor refolded his paper and sat staring into space.

***

Guy's remission was holding. Tassart was allowed to sit with him again, and tremulous foretastes of spring had been carried indoors in the form of potted narcissi. Sometimes, when the windows of the main part of the old house were open, shouts floated from the annexe where the writer was lodged.

'*Mère!*'

Tassart wrote bulletins to his master's mother, assuring her that the women she had blacklisted were being refused access to her son. She herself couldn't come, he told anyone who asked. She was too ill. Too delicate. Too old.

'Too selfish!' murmured the nurses, who were used to patients' relatives.

'*Mère de ... merde, mère de Dieu.*'

Seeing his valet with a pen bewildered the writer. He accused Tassart of writing to God accusing *him* of having buggered a goat and a hen.

'To whom I *am* writing,' the valet told him, 'is your mother. Madame Laure. And I haven't stolen your ideas either!'

'They were too salty. So was my wit!'

'If you shout, I shall have to close the window.'

'We are all pillars of salt. You too, François! You should stop writing. Never look backwards! Never turn round!'

There was still no mention of him in the press, which had found other fish to fry. Cardinal Lavigerie had been right to warn of dangers threatening the country. The Panama Canal scandal was dragging through the courts; ruined investors suspected the government of corruption, and the labour movement was gathering strength.

'People outside this place are all madder than we!'

'You could be right.'

'But there are more thieves in here. They stole my brain and my hair! They'll be back. Do you hear them?'

Shrieks rose from the exercise yard where the more dangerous cases were allowed to take the air.

By contrast a cannon, which had lain in the asylum lawn

since the Prussian invasion, twenty-two years before, had settled into the ground, acquired a tilt and a patina and looked as peaceful as the cows chewing the cud further down the hill. Paris seemed unimaginably distant when you stood here where dense groves gave an impression of great space, paths disappeared among them and tall trees hid the perimeter wall. Only the Eiffel Tower, rising above the highest branches, spoiled the pastoral effect. It was now three years since its official inauguration.

In Dr Blanche's drawing room a mild sloth prevailed, a readiness to sink into a deep divan and sigh. On a rug, a cat, flat as spilled gruel, meticulously stretched each limb. The doctor himself, plumply dignified in his skull cap, puffed at a pipe and delegated more and more practical decisions to Adam. His attention sometimes faltered now, succumbing to a haziness not unlike the morning mists which in this season masked views from the windows and swaddled the villa in threads of sieved sunlight. In a studio in the grounds his son, Jacques-Emile, led his own life, painting portraits and entertaining English friends.

***

Another damp day. Fractured sunlight blazed, and sparrows, apparently mimicking pockmarks on the shine of a wet wall, could turn out to be real bullet holes surviving from the last time Paris tore itself apart. Cardinal Lavigerie's warning about fresh slaughter and outrages should be borne in mind. The monsignor decided to make peace with His Eminence even if he had to abase himself.

***

Dearest Guy,

It was horrible to have to leave the other day without having a chance to explain why I came or to tell you how sweetly and often the three little ones ask about you. Lucien who, as you know, is now nine, is naturally anxious about his Papa's disappearance from his life. I tell him you are in a hospital too far away for us to visit and that he will now have to be the father of our small family. This usually cheers him for a bit, though of course he still worries and misses your visits. His small sisters talk fondly of you too. They are all affectionate children and I had fancied that seeing them might have done you good. In fact it was to propose this that I came. I do see, though, that, as things are, bringing them would be unwise.

I am hurt that you thought my visit self-serving, since I never asked for more than the security with which you generously provided us. The dream of a marriage – have you forgotten that it was once your dream too? – has long faded. Perhaps if we had been alone the other day, we might have taken a kind and even affectionate leave of each other. As it is, this letter will have to do. François Tassart, who was in a friendly mood, told me that you have good and bad moments. My poor, sweet darling, I do so wish I had seen you in a good one. Please save this letter to reread when the next of those comes and remember that both I and your children cherish memories of you at your best – which was dazzling! I feel like one of those mortals who had a quick fling with some god, then found the rest of the world forever dull. To be sure, I have my little demi-gods to prove that I didn't dream it all. I do feel flayed though. I have to tell you that! Scarred and damaged. But I wouldn't wish the past undone.

With all my love,
Joséphine

***

'So why won't he see me?'

The vicomte had arrived unannounced. After all, he may have reasoned, Monseigneur de Belcastel could not go anywhere. And perhaps his aim had been to catch him unprepared? Doing what, Adam wondered? Entertaining Freemasons? Belcastel had said to say he was ill.

'How ill?' The vicomte, who was leaving town, claimed he needed urgently to see the monsignor before he did so. 'What's the matter with him? He was fit as a fiddle last time I came.'

Adam improvised. 'He gets migraine headaches,' he decided. 'Quite severe. Has to lie in the dark for a day or so.' The one who had had migraine headaches was Adam's mother. He had borrowed a detail from a lost life.

'*In the dark*?' The vicomte seemed to find this perverse. 'Has he seen the *Petit Journal*?'

'I've no idea.'

The vicomte had a copy. 'Well, give him this,' he instructed. 'Can I trust you? You're the ex-seminarist, aren't you? No doubt you studied things priests don't need to know instead of those they do? I'm not blaming you! That's how it is now. Young clergy, I'm told, study the -isms: Kantism, Cartesianism and so forth. Well, we know what they produce – disloyalty! A few swift kicks in the backside would do some of our Reverend friends more good than any -ism. I am not talking of anyone we know, you understand, but of certain puffed-up personages who need bringing down to earth with a reminder of who butters their bread. The Count of Paris – this is what you're to tell Monseigneur de Belcastel – has warned in private letters that if Catholics do badly in next year's elections, persecution will start again. *Then* the clergy will see that they've backed the wrong horse! Can you remember that?'

Adam said he could.

'There's something else.' The vicomte worried. 'It's confidential. All right? Our agents have learned that, last winter, telegrams signed by a certain cardinal's valet reached Rome warning confederates there to prevent French royalists being granted an audience. The confederates had a code. The nuncio was referred to as "a salesman", the Church as "the business" and the pope as Petronillo.' The vicomte grimaced. 'Their metaphors betray them. Indeed, who is to say that they are metaphors at all?' Running a hand over his bald head, he asked, 'Are you taking this in? Do you even know who I'm talking about?'

'Yes. You are talking of mad or vicious gulls, jokers, double-dealers and liars among the French clergy.'

Sauvigny stared, then nodded. 'That is exactly who I mean.'

***

Dear Mademoiselle Litzelmann,
I am writing on Monsieur de Maupassant's behalf to say that,
although he cannot write letters any more, yours was read
to him during one of his remissions and moved him greatly.
He asked me to tell you that, although it is too late for him to
make any formal decisions about anything – his condition is
volatile and, as you saw, we have to be careful not to get him
agitated – he understands your distress, reproaches himself for
failing to appreciate the generosity of your impulse in visiting
and begs you to believe that, in moments when he is most fully
himself, he remembers you and your precious Lucien, Lucienne
and Marthe-Marguerite with warm affection. He wants you

to know that what he feels for you all is unique in his life. He enjoyed domestic calm and closeness with nobody else. Not even in his own childhood. He trusts you to bring up the children better than he could have done. He too feels flayed and scarred, and perhaps the fact that you both suffer means that you have come closer to him than anyone else.

He asks me to assure you of his affection and esteem.

Signed (on his behalf): Adam Gould

***

In the monsignor's apartment, discomfort writhed, and new urgencies rasped visitors' nerves. After the vicomte's departure for Belgium, military-looking men of a certain age started to arrive by the carriage-load, closeted themselves with Belcastel and could be heard wrangling in lowered voices. When they left, he was ironic and prone to paradox, which, with him, was a sign of unease. He had rings under his eyes and was not quite his old affable self, although he still insisted on offering his guests Marsala and slightly stale cakes which stuck in their throats. Adam heard them coughing and was called more than once to bring jugs of drinking water. The monsignor did not lay out his monarchist regalia for these visits, and, after the second one, remarked that though a small dose of madness could generate energy and courage – consider the saints – it could not safely be given free rein.

'That's particularly true in politics and religion,' he told Adam. 'I hope I'm not shocking you. I am too worn out to curb my tongue. I have just spent two hours with some virtuous, but dangerously mad friends.'

'Trying to curb them?' Adam ventured.

'Well, we have more than enough of that sort of thing right here, wouldn't you say? Listen to that.'

'*Mer-de, de, de* ...' It was Maupassant's hoarse, tense voice. '*Dieu de merde! Merde de Dieu!*'

***

To the Provincial of the White Fathers

My dear Father de Latour,
Presuming on the bonds between our families, I write to beg your intercession with Cardinal Lavigerie. Knowing his magnanimity, I am praying that he may see his way to forgiving the injury I did him. Your advocacy could tip the balance.

I have only just learned for whom he was speaking when I emulated his militancy and, having a weapon to hand, used it against him. Need I say that I am devastated and anxious to make any amends which, if I may quote his words, 'honour and conscience permit'. As a young priest, I admired him intensely. Later this admiration led me to use his methods rather than to respect his person. Now that his calvary is over, mine has begun.

Can you, as a successful crusader – even Arab slavers acknowledge the White Fathers' success – imagine my mental agony? I struck a blow against our own side! To say that the lines were camouflaged only aggravates my anguish. For why did God not enlighten me? Remorse corrodes, and a man in my plight can think the unthinkable. You see how I need His Eminence's forbearance. Will you speak for me? Might you come here and let me explain myself? I cannot come to you – though this may change. Once the civil authorities are satisfied that we have indeed broken with the monarchists, charges against me could be dropped. Dare I ask if you might help with those too? I know the government values your order's contribution to France's civilizing and scientific mission. How could it fail to, since your missionaries so often go ahead of the fighting men? You once wrote to me from some wild outpost near Lake Tanganyika where a small group of you were – I quote from memory – 'devoured by insects, living on stale hippopotamus meat and upholding the honour of the flag, while awaiting the day when France can take possession of these lands.' A half joke? A true hope? It shows why, as the great Republican, Gambetta, told His Eminence ten years ago: 'anticlericalism is not for export'. Today it is even less so. Thanks to men like yourself, France has so far outstripped all other missionary countries that – I read this in one of your pamphlets –75 per cent of those in the field are French. Bravo, mon Père! *Can you use a scrap of your credit on my behalf so that I may leave here, serve the Church again and atone for my mistakes?*

You have a right to know my (pained) opinion of the royalists, which is that we should distance ourselves from a party which, for all its conspiracies, has proven incapable of winning. Making it a point of honour to bury oneself in the folds of its vanquished flag is an indulgence which we owe it to the Church to forgo.

Please accept the expression of my respectful devotion,

Belcastel

***

A pale sun slides its arc across a swampy sky, and Adam has again been asked to talk to Guy, who could benefit from stimulus.

'Never mind,' say the doctors, 'if you get no answer. Just keep trying.'

'Do you remember my telling you,' he asks the patient, 'that I couldn't bear to talk about my mother?'

Guy's red, flaking eyelids quiver and pleat.

'That,' Adam decides, 'was because at one time I'd talked about her too much. I kept telling about her suicide in confession in the hope that the priests would say she couldn't have done it. She was pregnant when she died, and I needed to think that no Catholic woman would risk condemning two souls to hell, hers and her unborn child's.'

'*My* mother,' Guy squinnies from a single eye, 'suffers from goitre. The light makes her scream. Once it drove her to try and strangle herself with her hair and they had to cut it off. She mustn't see me like this.'

'We won't let her come.' Adam wonders if he should stop humouring Guy.

'Tell me more about yours. Do you think she did kill herself?'

Adam pictures and tries to shrink his old pain. He sees it first as a brown cloud, then as blood soaking the front of his mother's riding habit when she fell at a fence she should not have tried to jump.

Remembered voices mumble.

'... while the balance of her mind ...'

'Shush!'

Another wonders, 'Did she not see the wire?'

'Saw it too late, maybe. Maybe it jumped up after a horse ahead of her dislodged a stone!'

'That rogue of a farmer shouldn't have had wire there at all!'

Rags of memory gleam like blanks in a negative print. Or a stack of prints. Under that dark wetness must be whiteness, and under that more blood. And deep within, though he never saw it, the foetus. A male, he heard later. A brother.

How, some priests queried, could *he* have seen anything at all? Aged twelve? Wasn't all this imaginary? Honestly now! And he, having encouraged their incredulity, wanted to agree but knew that she must have been taken from where she fell and that he must have followed. He would have been on his pony and she perhaps in a cart. Unless they rigged up some sort of stretcher. This bit is blank, so he can only guess. Taken, anyway, to a cabin where her clothes were cut open with a tailor's scissors. Even now he can summon that sound of steel labouring through layered wool. Failing to cut, then cutting. After that, memories of confessionals and cabin get entangled because someone was praying in both. Reciting the *Memorare*, begging for a miracle. The next thing he remembers is her coffin.

'I used to gabble the *Confiteor*,' he tells Guy, 'at top speed. Remember how it goes? "I confess to Almighty God, to Blessed Mary Ever Virgin, to Blessed Michael the Archangel, to ..." And so on, empanelling half of heaven. Busy priests like you skip the names, but I never would because I needed those authorities to reinforce the confessor's opinion when he shot my story full of holes. I craved disbelief. It consoled me – but the odd thing,' Adam confesses, 'is that their disbelief in my story undermined my belief in the Christian one. So I ruined my own stratagem. My doubt spread like rain over a watercolour painting until ...'

His listener has fallen asleep. So Adam rings for one of the nurses to come and make up the fire and put him to bed properly, which is their task, not his. He walks into the garden and breathes in smells of sap and lichen, wet earth and mulch. The air is mild, for they are between seasons. Half daydreaming, he blots out what is in front of him and guesses that his mother used to do that too. A gambler, like Uncle Charles, she must have played with fate and taken the tricky fence while hoping to get safely over it. Praying as she did, perhaps? Saying the *Memorare*.

***

My dear Monseigneur,
Love, they say, is blind, but friendship rests on knowledge. So I,
who know your staunch heart, am confident that our friendship
will survive the present crisis. I plan to cement it, moreover, by
bringing you a first instalment of the money with which you feel
our Party should compensate the Church's losses.

I wonder what you make of Pope Leo's journalistic ventures.
Rumour whispers that he wants us to enter the Republic so as to
change it back to a monarchy – but would Republicans let us?
He is badly advised and too politic. Also: saying one thing urbi
et orbi *and quite another in our private ear does not inspire*
confidence.

You should know that there is talk of freezing the money
collected for his succour – St Peter's Pence – and lodging it in a
bank for the use of his successor. The funds I shall be bringing you
are from quite another source. They are for royalist clergy, so any
attempt to send them to Rome would be a breach of trust.

Bombs explode in the streets and scandals in parliament.
Anarchy's motto is 'Neither God nor Master!' And here we
have its fruits!

Don't worry, old friend, I am not trying to persuade you!
I trust you.

You may wonder why I am writing rather than visiting.
It's because I am in Belgium where some old comrades have
gathered: ex-Zouaves. They have been in Africa helping to fight
Arab slavers and scout out commercial opportunities in the ivory
and rubber trades. I shall tell you more when we meet. What
about Monday?

Yours, etc., Sauvigny

***

Monseigneur,
Indeed yes, we must get your talents back to work. His Eminence

is only too eager to forget the past and will be glad to have you with us. He, as you surmised, has been suffering the torments of Job, for not only did he lose friends, he has material anxieties too. Donations to his charities and to our order – which he of course founded – have dried up. It is not at all sure when they will start to flow again.

In that connection, it will be better if you sever yours with Sauvigny. Our missionaries have picked up unsavoury rumours about the Congo Free State, where King Leopold's troops allegedly force natives to provide him with great quantities of ivory. This would explain why Antwerp is now the greatest ivory market in the world. Do ex-Zouaves and the rest of his bullies take a percentage? If so, that particular royal connection may be more dishonourable than any Republican one.

I have some ideas for your future and am eager to visit and plan your rehabilitation. Would Monday be a good day?

Latour

***

Monseigneur,
I take the liberty of begging you to help me resolve a moral dilemma which confronts me. Though we have not met often, we are, as you know, distantly related and can trust each other.

It is hard to say more in a letter. My situation is delicate and I must therefore ask you not to mention this appeal to my uncle. He will not be back from Belgium until the middle of next week, so I could visit you on Monday without embarrassment. May I? Please let me know whether the date suits and, if it does not, whether you might consent to a visit at some other time.

Your devoted and obedient relative,
Danièle d'Armaillé

***

Paris police discover a manufactory of bombs in a coach house in the St Denis quarter. Sixteen persons arrested.

***

'Glass of wine?' Belcastel sounded as if he himself might have had more than a glass. 'Join me,' he invited. 'I am practising for my return to the world. Perhaps you would like to come with me? Be my secretary if my future post,' he made a grimace, 'is of an elevation to require one? I am endeavouring to keep overweening fantasies in check. Sit down and tell me about yourself. Do you like claret?'

Adam sipped. 'I am learning to.'

'Well,' Belcastel admitted, 'I may have to do the opposite, since who knows where I shall in fact be sent? I should not be raising our hopes.' He wondered if he had become ambitious. Well, if ambition helped one do good, why not? Picking up the hem of his cassock, he ran a fingernail along its frayed edge, then scratched at a wriggle of tidemarks left by walks in the wet grounds while reading his breviary. There was a darn there too. Never mind! He might soon have new cassocks and they might be edged with purple piping now that he was to join the side which God seemed to have chosen. 'God?' he said aloud and marvelled at the word's new shiftiness. Belief hadn't faded. How could it? 'God' was a word – like 'and' – with which one could not dispense. But aspects of its meaning had flaked off. Belief, like images in run-down chapels, was now vulnerable to bad restoring practices. All the more reason for a disciplined obedience to Rome, he decided.

'In unity lies strength,' he told the refreshingly simple young

Irishman who, though visibly taken aback by the suddenness of this remark, raised his glass in assent.

The monsignor's room struck Adam as looking unusually shabby. On closer inspection, he saw that two curved swords which had hung on its walls had been removed, leaving bright silhouettes of themselves on the faded wallpaper. Most of this was pink, but the commemorative curves were a grinning crimson. What other changes had been made? Ah, the photographs of royal pretenders had gone, too.

The monsignor followed Adam's gaze. 'As you see, worldly glory has once again come a cropper. Always a painful business. By the way, lest I forget, I shall want you to send telegrams to several addresses. The message for all is the same: "Monday impossible. Letter follows, Belcastel". More claret?'

***

Another dynamite outrage in Paris leads the police to arrest fifty persons.

Bribery alleged in Panama case.

***

It was the day of Madame d'Armaillé's visit. Seeing her was a way of doing her uncle a favour and so dissipating some of Belcastel's moral discomfort over his impending betrayal of that same uncle.

The discomfort was undeserved, for he was following his conscience. As always. What was new was having to do so alone and to rely on his inner lights. Like a Protestant! How arrogant one must become, it struck him, if one had to do this all the time. He, at least, was now conforming to the Roman line. It was a pity that *that* had not been made clear sooner – but then the pope too, poor man, had found it hard to embrace change. He had had to reconcile loyalty to his predecessors' infallible judgement with – but best not become embroiled in such thoughts when a guest was due to arrive. Happily, her little feminine troubles were unlikely to be taxing. Belcastel found himself looking forward benevolently to supplying her with guidance.

***

The niece wore grey, had a hat with a thick veil and was in every way appropriately turned out. Unfortunately, Tassart's account of his master's last mistress, the prodigiously lustful '*dame en gris*', had so echoed through the *maison de santé* that what that sober colour now evoked for its staff was lubricity. Watching the footman's face as the guest was shown in, the monsignor judged that she might as well have had the words 'priest's whore' emblazoned on her forehead.

'I would offer you tea,' he told her when they were alone, 'but, since you asked for discretion, I arranged for Adam Gould, who normally gets it, to take some hours off. I don't trust that footman' – whipping open the door to make sure that the fellow had quite gone – 'whom I suspect of thinking ill of clerics, but am not allowed into the kitchens myself. So sorry, no tea.'

They sat on either side of his fire and a filigree fireguard, which protected them from sparks. It was shaped like a peacock's tail and may have reminded her of the grille in a confessional, for she said, 'Monseigneur, though I have a confession to make it is not about a sin which has taken place but one which may be prevented. What I need is worldly advice as to how to do that.'

Wincing at the word 'worldly', he hoped she hadn't heard he was precisely that.

'It has,' Madame d'Armaillé said carefully, 'to do with my uncle, who – this is not easy to say – is aroused by me, though for now he hasn't let himself know this.' She seemed unable to go on.

Belcastel was unsure what to do next. A smile would be out of order. A glum face might silence her. Standing up, he presented her with his back and, with his head in a cupboard, called out, 'I'm listening, but I have some wine here. Perhaps a little drink would make things easier?' Affably, he emerged with a decanter and poured her a small glass of Sauterne.

She held, then put it down. 'Thank you.' Still tense. 'This isn't imaginary.'

'No.'

'Though nothing has happened. Yet.' She stared at her yellow wine. 'Only that my aunt – she's a nun – went back to her convent. She was staying with us for the past year, and now my uncle claims that I don't need a chaperone, though I disagree. You see his caresses are ... ambiguous. A goodnight kiss can become something else. One can't finger the moment. It's ...'

She must be waiting for a word of help. He chose not to supply it.

'I don't want to hurt him.' Another pause. 'Nor to *name* things, because that summons them, doesn't it? But if I don't, what can I say?'

'To him?'

'Yes.'

This time the pause was a long one. Qualmish, thought Belcastel and wondered if the aunt was to blame. Qualms throve in convents. Desire disguised as repulsion? All this could be a fantasy. Perhaps the thought showed on his face, for his guest's expression changed.

'The truth is,' she took up in a rush, 'that when Uncle Hubert cuddles me, I *like* it. I'm tempted. I don't want anything to happen, but if I stay in the house with him, it will.'

Feminine vapourings, thought the monsignor. They get bored and fanciful. He was about to tell her to pray when it struck him – growing fanciful himself? – that she might be the White Fathers' pawn, sent to turn him more fully against his old ally, her uncle. But for that to happen she would have to be not merely corrupt but treacherous. So might she not simply be telling the truth? He asked: 'You're sure *he's* susceptible?'

'Quite sure. And there I am dangled, you might say, before him. At all hours. Just now he doesn't see the danger because he's upset – unbalanced by something else. He's going through some trouble, a sort of despair. He has fits of fury when he reads the newspaper.'

The monsignor grew interested. 'Which one?' He leaned towards her. Dear God, he thought, don't make poor Sauvigny suffer. He is a good man driven beyond his strength. 'Was it *Le Petit Journal*?' Belcastel's mind was clouded with fears he'd like to shirk. He asked the niece, 'Can you describe these fits?'

'Well, he shouts a lot. I don't know which newspaper. Once he burned a picture in the drawing room grate, and the smell of singed varnish hung about for days. It was a picture of St Madeleine-Sophie Barat.'

'The nun?' So perhaps the vicomte's troubles were not the monsignor's fault after all? But no, he got his fits over the newspaper! Nuns were contingent! 'Does your aunt,' Belcastel asked anyway, 'belong to St Madeleine-Sophie's order?'

'Yes, but I should have told you that he seems ill. He's been taking too much opium. I've seen him, when he thought no one was watching, hold his stomach. He seemed to be in pain.'

It was now Belcastel's turn to suffer qualms. If all this *is* my fault, he begged his diminished God, spare him and punish me. 'Did you ask him if he was in pain?' he asked.

'Yes, and he said "yes", but *then* he grabbed my arm and threw back his head and said he needed comfort, and I thought something appalling was going to happen. Happily nothing did – well, not to me.'

'To him then?'

'He ...' Madame d'Armaillé foundered, blushed, then whispered that, because of her husband's teaching, she knew only the coarsest terms for what she wished to say.

'He had an emission?'

She nodded. 'If it happens again ...' Her difficulty recurred.

'You fear violence?'

'No, no! I fear I might lead him on. So I shouldn't stay in his house exposing us both to temptation. On the other hand, where can I go? Both my brothers have been posted to North Africa.'

Belcastel quite saw why Sauvigny disliked the nuns who had fostered his niece's self-important virtue. Though he too was to blame. Why, for instance, did he not use a brothel like everyone else? Stop dangling around his niece? But the reason was obvious. Sauvigny, an excitable man deficient in common sense, had modelled himself on monumental figures like the royal crusader St Louis, and could not now settle for second-best. No brothels for him. Sadly though, those he served *were* second-best: a politic pope, a false friend – Belcastel could see no way to become less false – and a political party which had about as much hope of taking power as the chorus line in an Offenbach opera. Poor vicomte! What a torment to him his pretty niece must be! She was his kin, so he could trust and honour her, but this put an intolerable strain on his trust in himself. No doubt, too, she reminded him of the Roman girls he could have married when he, aged twenty and hailed as a hero, was defending their city against Garibaldi? She looked, come to think of it, like a Fra Filippo Lippi Madonna. Her neck was as pale as a snowdrop, and the sight of her, slipping away from him around corners and the bends of stairways, must be like the incarnation of his life's elusive hopes. Sighing, Belcastel told himself that this was the wrong sort of thinking for a confessor.

She acknowledged his sigh by arguing with it. 'If I stay, I'll end up as Uncle Hubert's concubine, and he will come to hate me. He already hates what I make him feel. I can tell by the way he uses idiotic pet names like "bunny rabbit" and "little squirrel". He's trying to pretend I'm someone else. I've been having nightmares.'

'What help do you think I can give you?'

'He trusts you. You could maybe ...' She paused hopefully.

'Talk to him? Impossible!' He saw her shock. 'I'm sorry.

Trust between us now is, well ... under strain. Have you another plan?'

Again she blushed. 'It's to work,' she told him. 'Women in our family never did anything like that, of course, but I nursed my mother. I could train to be a mental nurse. Here. In this house. I was hoping you could perhaps put in a word for me with the director? Might they let me live in? I know female nurses do.'

Before he could answer, she added, 'In the long run the experience could be useful.' She explained about her husband being in Africa and how, having had no letters for a while, she had sought out returned missionaries at the White Fathers' Paris house to ask for news.

'You visited the White Fathers?'

'Yes. And if Philibert comes back in the state I found some of them, I'll *need* to have had training. Many are as mad as hares.'

'Was there news?'

'No. I was almost glad.' She clasped her hands. 'Don't be shocked, Monseigneur. If I could *do* something for him I would. Truly. If he lost a limb or caught some tropical disease, I would go and nurse him. But I can't stay idly at home wondering about a man who may be dead. Until recently I kept making superstitious bargains with God. Then I saw that they were affecting my mind. That can't be good, can it? What if poor Philibert survived, came home and found a mad wife?'

Belcastel, as if emptying his head of his own bargains, shook it and agreed that it couldn't be good.

'At the missionaries' house,' she told him, 'I heard that cannibals attacked a mission near the Upper Ubangi river and ate six priests. Philibert could have been there. I think I remember his mentioning the Ubangi. Those cannibals, the missionaries said, are of a refined ferocity. They break their captives' legs and leave them, still alive, in running water. The next day the skin comes off like the peel of a fruit. I have had to put away my rosary beads. Shall I tell you why? It's because now the crucifix reminds me of how the two thieves' legs were broken.'

'That story comforted people for nineteen hundred years.'

'But stories go bad. I imagine that this house is full of people who fell into their stories the way you might fall into a well.'

Belcastel, before he knew it, found that he had promised to ask Dr Blanche to consider taking her on as a trainee. Why had he, he wondered, then saw that it was because he envied her nerve and candour. He himself lacked both, being so caught up in compromise that, having hit the cardinal when he was down, he was going to have to do the same to the vicomte. What she had said about stories going bad seemed to apply. This amazed him. Out of the mouths of babes!

By the time she left, escorted out by the same grave footman whose face was now deferent to the point of irony, Belcastel was feeling such gloom that when Adam Gould came in he asked him for morphine.

***

Dear Monseigneur de Belcastel,
Contrary to recommendations in my last letter, His Eminence asks you to postpone severing your ties with the party you served so well. Its members are now as mad as wasps and likely to do something intemperate. Having a friend who is privy to their

*plans and able to restrain them may be useful. So, for now, not
a hint about your change of heart.*

More when we meet,
Latour

What a reproachful phrase, mused Belcastel: change of heart!
Why had this never struck him before?

***

Ouf! Danièle was glad to have got that over. Indeed, so relieved
was she that, on collecting her maid, Félicité, who had been
gossiping in the asylum kitchens, she suggested a turn in the
park when they got home. Her cocker spaniel, Lulu, would
love it. All three could do with some fresh air.

'We'll give him a run in the Luxembourg Gardens.'

Félicité, who had an eye for the students who might be
idling there, was all for this. She was a neat little person,
with a plump, kissable mouth, and could be nobody's idea
of a chaperone. The outing, however, had to be put off, for,
when they got home, Uncle Hubert was there before them.
He had returned unexpectedly soon from his trip to Belgium
and wanted Danièle's company. His work for the Cause was
looking up, he told her with a pleased grimace, though he must
not, for now, say more.

Where had *she* been, he wondered, and was mildly surprised
when she said she had been to confession to Monseigneur de
Belcastel – which was true in a way.

'What's wrong with our local *curé*?'

Her fib had the merit of not reflecting too badly on the
poor man. She said his breath smelled of onions.

***

Floral smells slid through the slats of blinds along with Guy's blasphemies.

'Shut the window,' Belcastel instructed. 'I keep wondering why that poor devil isn't an atheist. He would be more at ease. But no, he's like an escapee from some old tale called *The Sinner's Conversion*.'

'Where debauchery is a way of refusing mediocrity?'

'That's it! The old sermon-writers had a soft spot for extreme conduct.' Belcastel sighed. Changing the subject, he asked Adam why he had left the seminary. 'Were you unhappy there?'

On the contrary, said Adam. He had been as snug as a seed in a seed plot, which, after all, was what a seminary was. 'It was only when the time was approaching for the seedlings to be transplanted that I began to panic. I had been uprooted before, and it is easier to go than wait to be pushed ...'

When he paused, Belcastel apologized for upsetting him.

'Oh,' Adam claimed, 'it's easier to talk about it now.' Turning from the window's stippled damp, he told the monsignor, 'My father threw me out when I was twelve. Me and my mother. He had never married her, you see, and – it was a shock to us to discover this – was now planning to marry someone else. For money. He had lost most of his, and it looked as if his estate would have to be sold up, just as several neighbouring ones had been. I, of course, understood none of this, but others must have seen the blow coming. Things had been bad since the famine thirty years before, when *his* father lacked the ruthless-ness needed to evict the starving, clear the land and turn from wheat to pasture. Landlords who did that prospered. Those who didn't – didn't. I suppose,' Adam heard himself say, 'my papa felt it was now time for heartlessness.'

His voice cracked.

'Is he still alive?'

'I don't know. I sent back his letters for a while. Then they stopped coming.' Abruptly he admitted, 'That's untrue. I know he's alive.'

'I imagine that if he had lost the estate, you and your mother might have been no better off.'

Though this view had not occurred to Adam, he was prepared to consider it. 'He did cry,' he remembered, 'when my mother died. Crocodile tears? Maybe not? Anyway,' he hurried on, 'thanks to my tutor who had studied there himself, the seminary took me in. Le Séminaire d'Issy. I spent ten years there and couldn't bear to wait to be put out again when I was twenty-four. So – I left. Two years ago.'

'But you wouldn't have been put out. You would have become a priest.'

'Ah, but the seminary was like a regiment. I belonged there as I never could in a parish where I'm told there are now such feuds ... Also, I hated having to get a dispensation to be a priest because of my ...'

'Illegitimacy?'

Adam looked away.

'You are right about feuds.' The monsignor spoke from the shadow of his deep leather chair. 'Nowadays one has to choose one's side and can find oneself *having* to betray people. Someone said to me just yesterday that we can fall into our own stories. That may have happened to your father. You don't have to be over-reaching. Just unlucky. Talking to inmates here is instructive. Most seem sane except for the odd one who thinks he's Napoleon. But then, as the joke goes, Napoleon too thought he was Napoleon, and how sane was he? It's all to do with winning. As long as he did win, he was admired.' Belcastel sighed. 'You said your uncle gambles. Well, all France does that now.'

Adam felt it was his turn to change the subject. 'What,' he asked, 'about Guy? You said just now that he would be happier as an atheist.'

'Only because ideals torment realists. People like him try to embrace and control reality. And he did for a while. Then when he no longer could he must have longed for a God to help him, but couldn't believe in one – and was ashamed, I'd imagine, at even wanting to. So he's enraged and torments us with his shouts. I suspect he began by wondering what might be *hors-là* beyond ordinary reality. Then – you see this happen in stories like *Le Horla* – his inventions began to take control of him.' Turning his burnt cheek towards Adam, Belcastel confided, 'When he stares at my scars, I am sure I remind him of his Horla. He could do something ...'

'... violent?'

'Oh easily.'

'*Mère de ... de merde ...*'

The window had come unlatched. Adam closed it.

'Do you correspond with any of your family?'

'Never.'

'Your mother died? Before you left?'

'Yes.'

'Perhaps you should try to forgive your father. That's just a suggestion.'

But Adam wanted to drop the subject.

***

For the Goulds, property and religion were psychically entwined. This was because they had been Catholic landowners at a time in the past when the English Crown had aimed to make their kind obsolete, and tales of the stratagems by which the threat was foiled were still part of their heritage. These hinged on the plight of the single 'renegade' son, who, in each generation, had had to pretend to convert to Protestantism and risk his soul so as to keep the patrimony intact. Though the renegades counted on heaven's allowing them to repent of their apostasy in time to earn a deathbed absolution, a stigma could not but attach to them. For how could relatives be sure that, one day, a false renegade might not keep the estate for himself and cheat his family? Or die unshriven and go to hell? God too, being part of the equation, came to be seen as untrustworthy. So though the Goulds pulled through with their property intact, a propensity for double-dealing remained bred in the bone. Or so neighbours claimed.

Adam's father, Garret, was considered a typical throwback. His guile and optimism were viewed as incorrigible, and stood him in good stead when he was running his racing stables or riding one of his own horses in a reckless steeplechase. Brave as a stallion and tricky as an eel, he would jump any obstacle for a wager, including the spiked iron gate at his own front entrance. He had a disarming smile and relished risk. Women forgave him his deceptions, but men were leery of doing business with him and accused him of trying to ride two – if not three – horses at once if he thought he could. This was a reference to his ten years spent as a member of Westminster Parliament where, having simultaneously courted the landlord and tenant vote, he ended by losing both. It was even said – Adam, when at the crawling stage, heard things from listening-posts under benches and tables – that Gary Gould had not only spoken up for Irish tenants in the House of Commons, but was a member of a secret sworn brotherhood, a Fenian, and had tried to keep in with the nocturnal ribbonmen who favoured direct action and whose aim was to terrify landlords like himself into lowering their rents. Yet how could he lower his? He couldn't. He needed money. His roof leaked and was for ever threatening to fall in. Jokes were made about its loose slates and those in his own head, and some of his son's earliest memories were of listening to water falling into the pots marshalled in the library and drawing room to catch drips whose sounds varied with the recipient's fullness and capacity. Rolled up to one side would be Persian rugs bought in London when Gary was flush. Profits from the stables had soared when – a fluke – a horse, foaled by a mare taken from between the shafts of the Gould carriage, won the Chester Cup in England then went on to win more purses. For some years after this, money eased Gary's choices; his oratory won him favour at the hustings and the rugs with their fanciful designs turned his front drawing room into a bower.

This was when he fell in love with his sixteen-year-old cousin Ellen, whom he swore to marry as soon as he could get a dispensation to do so.

Or maybe Gary never did quite swear to this? Wary of that old adversary, the law, he would, Adam guessed with hindsight, have shied from committing promises to words, let alone paper. He imagined his young father's courtship as teasingly tempestuous. Combining cousinly tenderness with some playful bullying, he must have broken down the unpractised girl's defences before she knew it.

Adam had adored him. He remembered lively returns from London when his father produced gifts, tossed him in the air, then soothed Ellen with hugs. He had an eager grin, a quiff of curls high as a cock's comb, and played his role of father with élan.

Love of horses drew the cousins close. The great glossy creatures thundering under them must have magnified their sense of their own possibilities. Poor Ellen! How could she guess how narrow were the limits of her and even Gary's power? It had taken Belcastel to point them out to Adam! His memories were evolving.

Ellen sank her interests in her cousin's. She kept his accounts, tried to bring order into their forests of wild figures and took on the thankless task of trying to make the racing stables pay for his political career. Running things at home when he was in London, she campaigned with him when he came back.

'We've got to keep in with the priests,' he kept telling her. 'They'll deliver the Catholic vote. Then we can cock a snook at the old landlords.'

'But Gary, you *are* a landlord,' argued Ellen Gould, whose surname was conveniently the same as his. 'You have twelve thousand acres. Supporting five thousand souls!'

'Mostly bogland, Miss Gould!' Teasingly. 'And supporting neither them nor me in any degree of decency.'

'Miss', slurred to 'Missus' in blandishing mouths, lent itself to jokes about 'missing the ring' when Ellen's back was turned. By the time he was six, Adam was catching hints of malice. These puzzled him. 'Little pitchers ...' murmured gossips.

'Wouldn't you think she'd send him home to her brothers? Plenty of his kind there!'

'Afraid maybe? Some don't make old bones.'

'Shush!'

'They don't like my mother,' he marvelled, 'why don't they?'

Looking back, he saw that the realities around him had been as shifty as clouds and that early on he had grown used to knowing alternately more and less than he thought. Insinuations spread like ragweed, and it must have become increasingly difficult for Gary to keep in with priests who were scandalized to find that the pretty, nubile Ellen Gould was living, ostensibly as a housekeeper, in his house, and twice as scandalized that she should have produced a son whom, as if foreseeing his and her fall from Eden, she chose to call Adam.

It was a ramshackle Eden, but Adam had loved it. As he grew, though, so did the scandal, though some people affected to believe that he was his mother's nephew.

***

On being turned away for a second time from Belcastel's door, Sauvigny grew haughty.

'Who did you say is with him?' he harried. 'A priest? What kind of priest?' In his boyhood members of the lower clergy had been sent to eat in the kitchen, and no gentleman would have been kept waiting on their account. 'How long will he be?'

The Irishman went to inquire.

'Say,' Sauvigny could not help calling after him, 'that I brought what I promised. It's here.' Slapping his leather bag, he opened the glass doors to the terrace and shot outside. The rebuff irked him, for he had hoped for plaudits, as why shouldn't he? He had gone to Belgium on what had looked like a wild goose chase and, to his own amazement, brought back gold.

For years, his family's handling of money had been so queasily inept that they had grown wary of dealing with it at all. He himself had once had a chance to marry a great fortune, then, on finding that there was a scandal attached to it, was glad he hadn't. He had had a lucky escape, and the memory had almost prevented his undertaking last week's mission to Brussels. Once there, however, he had had a stroke of luck. Falling in with some old comrades who were fresh back from the Congo, he asked if they could advise him how to raise funds and found that they could do better. They had funds themselves – bounties from the Belgian king for their success in fighting Arab slavers – and were ready to donate large sums. Truly? To the poor boxes of the French royalist clergy? But of course, *cher* Sauvigny, what better cause? They, it turned out, had been looking for just such a deserving one to endow with a fraction of their windfall fortune and purge the rest of some unspecified taint. 'Let's not go into *that*,' they murmured to his relief. Soldiers' tales! Having known men who thought you could see their crimes imprinted in their eyes or, contrariwise, that a dead man's stare reflects his killer's face, he had no urge to probe such vivid guilts. Some, who had fought to save the last pope's lands, then fought again in America, were on their third and, they hinted, grimmest war. He wouldn't give much for their stability. God knew how much they drank. He guessed them to have minds like magic lanterns for, having left home as hardly more than schoolboys, they had the sketchiest image of normality, and he learned with surprise that he, who had thought himself one of them, stood, in their eyes, for France, sobriety and virtue.

'The donation will be a baptism for the money!' Captain Joubert had gravely confided, adding that he hoped to make considerably more on his return to a small, personal fief, deep in the bush, which he had carved out for himself and where he had an African family. Didn't the missionaries object, Sauvigny asked, and was told that, in an inferno like the Congo, priests learned to be flexible. After all, the ex-Zouaves were protecting *them*, and worse was going on than bigamy or miscegenation. 'Cardinal Lavigerie likes to say,' Joubert told him, 'that we are raising the poor, benighted blacks to our level. If he saw what I've seen, he'd know that benighted darkness comes as much from us as from them. Can you imagine a Belgian throwing an infant against a rock so that its head burst like an egg? To force the parents to surrender loot? It's true! A white man from Antwerp! Probably called himself a Christian! I witnessed that. And, before you ask, I couldn't stop him. Take the money and remember us in your prayers.' There was a hard set to Joubert's mouth and a wavery depth to his glance, and when asked why he was going back to that place, he shrugged.

In Antwerp, the shrug implied, they worshipped the golden calf. But the gold was imported. By the likes of us, said Joubert. Under two species. 'We still communicate these days, under two species. These are no longer bread and wine but rubber and ivory!'

So here was Sauvigny back in the rain-rinsed grounds of

Dr Blanche's establishment, with as yet unbaptized wealth in his bag, feeling nervous and impatient. Unable to quite clear his mind of the yarns he'd heard in Brussels. Loitering and vexed. Ready, because of this, to condemn the flexibility of priests. Pope Leo's betrayal of the French monarchy had enraged the Vatican's old French defenders – many of whom had fought for the last pope-king as a way of fighting for their own would-be king. Joubert, noting that Zouaves were often described as mercenaries, had sourly observed that the Church was more mercenary than they. 'This is for the spiritual mercenaries,' he had quipped when hefting Sauvigny's bag of gold. '*We* fought for *them* for nothing.' Joubert, older than Sauvigny and now in his fifties, had been with the French *Guides*, who had been forerunners of the Zouaves. 'We provided our own uniforms and horses and were expected to have an income of 4,000 to 5,000 francs of our own to spend. But the Church forgets what we did for it. Here, take the money. It may jog some memories.'

Later, Sauvigny met and duly thanked other contributors to the sum in the leather bag, then joined them for an impromptu banquet. Toasts were drunk and speeches made, whose promise not to spoil the occasion by speaking too much of the Congo was more eloquent than speech. Seeing in their eyes something of the trusting bewilderment that sometimes gleams in the eyes of old dogs, Sauvigny guessed at the terrifying moral vacancy which these old warriors must have found in themselves. The impression sharpened when he heard them argue for restraint, discipline and a rigid chain of command. And it was with the pride of distilled pessimism that he and they stood up to drink the ambiguous toast: '*Vive le roi.*' They were the *Franco-*

Belges, and what was known of their respective monarchs was disheartening. The French one lingered in a country house in England because he was not allowed into France, while the Belgian Leopold was whispered to be a rapacious despoiler of the native peoples of Central Africa. Yet the ex-Zouaves, including Joubert, stood, squared their shoulders and drank the toast without a tremor. They were, it struck Sauvigny, drinking to imaginary, ideal leaders who represented the best of themselves. To the silver thread of loyalty which could unite and empower them. He felt moved and sad and soft and foolish as he, too, said the words. And ready, if he only knew whom to attack, to forge a fierce persona out of the opposite qualities and kill all round him.

V

'Where?' A cry rose from the shrubberies.

A second voice soothed. 'We'll ask the gardener to find it.'

'What? No! I have it.'

'Calm yourself now.'

There was some rustling and mumbling. Sauvigny ignored them.

Stepping back from the house, he stared up at the monsignor's window and, framed in it, was shocked to recognize the tall silhouette – there couldn't be another so tall – of the Reverend Father de Latour. Pale as limestone in his missionary's robe, Latour was one of Lavigerie's White Fathers! What business could *he* have with Belcastel? Should Sauvigny hail them? Before he could decide, he heard someone cry, 'Don't', then something hit his head and lights flashed inside it. The flash coincided with the thought that any conspiring going on must be on our behalf. A clever man, the monsignor! Best not upset his stratagems. Staggering, Sauvigny told himself,

'I mustn't fall', then did. Again lights razored past his vision, then waves of darkness rose.

'Bull's eye!' came the madman's shout. '*J'ai fait mouche*! He has my brains in his bag.' As the darkness lightened, Sauvigny saw the lunatic make a rush towards him, then, to his relief, a *gardien* caught and hustled him away.

By now several people were in the garden. One was a doctor. 'How,' he asked the madman's keeper, 'did he come to have a billiard ball?'

'He plays billiards, sir, quite well. We think it helps him keep calm.'

'Another time frisk him when he leaves the billiard room.'

'Thief! Thief!'

Pain blossomed thickly in Sauvigny's head, and something trickled down his temple, as officious minions tried to seize his bag. He fought them off. 'I brought it *in*,' he argued. 'I'm a donor, not a thief.'

Luckily the Irishman now reappeared. 'Monsieur le Vicomte, what happened? The monsignor said to say ...'

'That he's busy with Father de Latour. Yes? Never mind. Never mind. I'll wait.'

'Well, let's have one of the doctors look at you. I'll get some brandy.'

***

Latour, still at the monsignor's window, had been watching the scene in the garden and now turned back to Belcastel. 'So he brought you money,' he guessed. 'A large sum? Is that the message you just received? From the Irishman?'

'How can I tell you?' Belcastel tried not to show petulance. 'It was in confidence. Do you want to dishonour me totally? I suppose you must, since you let him see you!'

Latour shrugged. 'Honour is starting to seem a quaint notion. If he did bring money, what do you plan to do?'

'Refuse it.'

'If you do, he will know you have changed sides. *Then* you will be unable to atone for the wrong you did the cardinal.' Latour's smile must have tightened during his years in the tropics. His lips were as thin as cat-gut. 'Hypocrisy – a humble virtue – can be used to a good end.'

'You want me to pretend I am still working for the royalists?'

'Why not? Drawing wild elements into a facsimile plot could stop them engaging in a real one. That strikes me as useful. Meanwhile, you can keep us informed of their plans. This is a delicate moment, as you may imagine. Republicans don't trust us.'

'You?'

'Me, you, us. But the pope wants us to win their trust. Your friend out there,' nodding towards the garden, 'and *his* friends are likely to spoil our hopes of so doing by some ill-conceived coup. You might help prevent it. Surely this is worth one or two lies? In the interests of peace.'

'I'm to be a safety valve? A *soupape de sécurité*?'

Latour smiled his dry smile. 'A sub-pope and papal pawn? Why not? What do you suppose they expect you to do with the money?'

'I haven't said there was any.'

'But if there were?'

'I would use it for some safe and worthy cause. For our schools, perhaps.'

'Safe?' Amusement wavered across Latour's face. 'Schools, Monseigneur, are minefields. Have you followed the Catechism Scandal? Then you'll know that the reason the government stripped five bishops of their salaries is because catechisms in their dioceses teach that it is a Catholic's duty to vote against *it*, and understandably, our Republican masters are displeased. Some of our bishops are firebrands. And laymen egg them on. Between ourselves, I can tell you that neither the nuncio nor the minister wants trouble, but to men like ...' Another nod towards the garden.

'Poor Sauvigny?'

'Trouble is the breath of life to men like him.'

'Well, if he brings me money,' said Belcastel, 'note I say "if", I shall take and give it to some harmless recipient: a fallen woman perhaps?'

'I shall applaud.'

***

The blow seemed to have affected the inside of Sauvigny's head even more than the outside, though this had begun to sport a bump which might soon reach the size of a gull's egg. He was lying in a lunatic's cell.

He felt feverish. The ache made him whimper. His skull felt porous, and he pictured meaty memories being shaken through its passages as ruthlessly as, on the feast of St Januarius, a vial of that saint's dried blood is shaken in an attempt to liquify it. The fall seemed to have sprained a rib! How dangerous peace-time could be! He laughed. The laugh hurt and more memories were shaken up ...

The vicomte rarely pictured his person, for he had not been brought up to consider his looks. Men like us, his father and his father confessor had told him gravely when he was a small boy, need neither looks nor learning. Others may use such folderols to help them inch up the social ladder and become prime ministers or the like. Not we! We do not 'become'. We are. Honour (said the father) and religion (said the priest) must be at the forefront of your mind. So Sauvigny, who was disinclined to study anyway, joined the pontifical army at the age of seventeen and found himself being fêted in Roman drawing rooms where his looks, to his surprise, turned out, after all, to be quite pleasing, and helped a lot with the ladies. What helped even more was that, taking his father's comments to mean he was ugly, he had learned not to notice looks much. He danced with plain women, lacked vanity, gave himself no airs and was held by the beauty-worshipping Romans to be little short of a saint. Some mothers thought of him for their daughters, but when they learned that his father's high-mindedness had reduced the family to penury, they backed off. Married women, eager for a gallant dalliance, were more persistent and, by the time he was twenty, the young vicomte had had a number of happy experiences. The ease with which these happened, together with his enjoyment of soldiering, and keyed-up friendships with two young men who were killed at the battle of Mentana within months of his meeting them, all bred a reluctance to become attached to worldly or even otherworldly hopes. He fought in the skirmishes which bandits and Garibaldini conducted on the frontiers of the diminishing papal state, danced in princely palaces back in the city, hunted in the Campagna, made love to yet another married lady, failed to notice that this one was dangerously in love with him and waved away friends' warnings about trouble impending from that quarter. 'Careful, Hubert!' murmured the friends. 'Hot blood, you know! Southerners aren't like us! They can be a bit extreme in their behaviour. A bit operatic!' He hardly listened. The end of an epoch was impending too, so how could he give thought to the end of a love affair?

Sure enough, four years after he got there, the papal state and the pope's role as a temporal monarch came to an end when the Italian army broke through the city wall and the pope, whose small force had no hope of winning, forbade it to put up more than a token resistance. This, to Sauvigny, felt like the end of the honour and religion he was there to defend, and the sight of the white flag fluttering from the cupola of St Peter's sickened him. He slept that night with his fellow Zouaves under Bernini's colonnade, and, next day, stood with them for the last time to cheer the pope as king. Then, still numb and only half alert to what was happening, he went to say goodbye to his mistress and found, to his alarm, that she had packed her bags. Shutters were being drawn and dust covers laid over furniture. She knew that the Zouaves had just been disbanded and that he was now free to travel wherever he chose. So, she informed him, was she. Switzerland, Canada ... The old world had just died. The new, modern one was their oyster. Reopening a shutter, she let in light, handed him a glass of champagne and proposed a toast to honesty.

'We can go wherever you like, my darling,' she cajoled, hold-ing out the glass which, as she had demonstrated on more intimate occasions, fitted perfectly over each of her exquisitely shaped breasts.

He mumbled, sipped and wondered what to do. She was rich, and he had learned that rich mistresses could be masterful. Even now, he was only half taking in what she was saying. His senses felt as though dust covers had been laid on them too.

'I'm coming with you.' Her husband, she reminded him, had died some months before. Then, when he started to commiserate, 'Wait! Do you know how he died? No? Of poison. Yes. You heard me. Poison. I fed it to him. Slowly. Just as you slowly poisoned me.'

He had no idea what she meant. He was still only twenty-one, and in the morning light she seemed ancient to him. Black did not suit her. He had been seeing less of her and would have broken off sooner if he hadn't known that he would be leaving anyway. He saw now that their passion had been one-sided. Rome had been bad for him. He had come here to devote himself to the pope's cause and instead had grown worldly. He was not the shy, generous boy who had been ready to die when he first came. He was vain and carnal, and aware that his mistress's sallow skin had the unpleasant texture of a dried-out field-mushroom. He disliked himself for thinking this. Appearances and surfaces were now all he ever saw. He tried and failed to remember how the priest's words went on Ash Wednesday when rubbing ash into people's foreheads. *Quia pulvus sumus*, was it? Dust and dustcovers, he thought, is all any of us are. Noticing that she was wearing too much white powder, he had an impulse to laugh. Possibly lack of breakfast had made him lightheaded.

She was still talking.

'You poisoned me with love,' she accused. 'Love dosed with indifference is a kind of torture. It's what I got from you.'

'*That's* the poison I fed you?' He remembered his friends' warnings about Southerners and was disgusted. Her mind, he thought, is the ugliest thing about her and, as dislike of himself turned to dislike of her, absolved himself of blame.

'You drove me into a fever of need. I couldn't sleep or rest. You poisoned my dreams. That's why I did what I did to poor, unsuspecting Massimo. I poisoned his body because you had poisoned my soul.'

He did not ask whether the two poisons were equally fanciful, but was informed that they were not. She had, she claimed, truly, physically and with her own hands administered arsenic to her husband over a long period in small, patient, imperceptible and continuous doses. This was a local art, often talked about, probably less often practised, but one which she, she swore, had used. Sauvigny affected to think – indeed did think – that her story was a trick or a metaphor, but was assured that it was not. He told her that, whatever the truth, he could not take her with him, whereupon she said that her pharmacist suspected her, and that she had to leave. The wretch claimed to have kept records of the amounts of arsenic supplied to her household. Her sister-in-law too had been snooping about, questioning the servants. And her nephew.

'If I go, they will let things die down. I can buy them off. I may have to let them have this palazzo, even though it came from my family.'

He told her that there was no place for her in his life. She wept and said he must be in love with someone else. He denied this. She clung to him; he managed to remove her, but even then felt unfree. He was caught in a quicksand of nausea.

'I'm sorry, *cara*, I am planning to become a missionary priest. I had it in mind to do that anyway and what you just told me has helped me decide. I would rather deal with pagans than with the corrupt. Everything which happened in this city in the last weeks appals me.'

She looked at him coldly. 'That,' she said with a contemptuous grimace, 'is a base improvisation.'

'Like your own?'

'No.'

She said no more then, but sat slumped and silent in an upright, seventeenth-century chair which did not accommodate slumping. For perhaps a minute, he was tempted to wonder whether what she had said could, after all, be true. But no, she was more likely to be engaging in a kind of charade. All Rome was doing this. People's feelings were so suffocating and unprecedented that they needed to devise ways to release them. Days ago the seventy-eight-year-old pope had climbed the Scala Santa on his knees; last night the Zouaves had slept under the Bernini colonnade; Sauvigny himself had just devised a fantasy to trump what he took to be another fantasy. His felt half true, for he did feel appalled and thought he *might* well renounce the world which would now be run by makeshift measures and shabby contrivance. The old moulds had broken. In the long run disarray would surely spread everywhere, and already here nobody knew how to behave. New roles would have to be learned, and meanwhile Romans were hiding indoors. This had been strikingly obvious yesterday and this morning on his way here. The invading Italians had been neither reviled nor welcomed and the usually demonstrative Roman crowd was as much at a loss as a theatre company which has lost its props. No doubt, Sauvigny thought sourly, they were wishing they could put on the masks behind which they so enjoyed hiding in carnival time, when men and women did things which they undoubtedly denied later even to themselves. Not that he was any better! He was in a self-lacerating mood, and memories of his own lucky and light-hearted adventures sickened him. News that the white flag raised over St Peter's was a domestic bed sheet supplied at the last minute by the family of some minor Vatican employee seemed emblematic. He imagined imperfectly washed stains sunk deep in its weave. He imagined smells.

Play-actress, he thought, as his mistress again began to sob, then, overcome by shame at his eagerness to get away from her, began, almost involuntarily, to play-act himself. He asked: 'Is there a foreign flag on your roof? I forgot to look. Prussian? English? So many of the palaces have them. The pope was making sour jokes about it. At the moment of his Gethsemane, palaces belonging to Rome's greatest Catholic families are flying foreign flags and claiming protection from foreign embassies to ensure that they will not be looted by the invaders. Am I your foreign protector or have you others? France, as you must know, has just been defeated by Prussia, so I suggest you look to a stronger power.'

She said she didn't know what he meant. He – revelling in the chance to move – jumped up, opened a casement, ran out onto a balcony, looked up and saw an Austrian flag on the front of her palace. He laughed. She slapped his face. He left. Some time later he heard that a police inquiry – conducted by the Italian police who now ran Rome – was under way and that she had been charged with murder. Only then did the full horror of his self-deception register. And his shame, for of course she must have loved him.

But what, now, could he do about that?

He did not become a priest, but neither did he marry or take another mistress. His half-measure matched the – possibly venal? – decision eventually reached by the Italian authorities that there was insufficient evidence to bring the suspected murderess to trial. Arsenic proved to be native to the soil of the graveyard where her husband was buried; the pharmacist had withdrawn his testimony, and this reduced the evidence against her to hearsay and speculation.

**

At tea-time on the day after her visit to Monseigneur de Belcastel, Danièle's uncle surprised her in her dressing-gown. She and Félicité had been caught in a downpour earlier when walking with Lulu, whose fault it was that the two young women got drenched. The previously docile little cocker had revealed a reckless streak and would neither come to heel, nor – greatly mortifying them both – stop trying to mount and, failing that, sniff the *cul* of an unsuitably large mongrel bitch. In the end the bumptious Lulu, while defending his untenable position from rivals, all but lost one of his pretty, silken ears.

'It's not his fault. It's nature. She's on heat,' Félicité whispered while resourcefully ogling a sturdy young bystander who obligingly, and bravely, broke up the fight, then, as it was starting to rain, and they couldn't find a cab, carried the loser home in his arms. The footman was dispatched forthwith to take Lulu to have his ear sewn up, while Félicité led the rescuer into the kitchen, to have *eau de vie* dabbed on his bites and scrapes and receive a glass of the same cure-all to keep up his strength. Danièle was upstairs towelling her hair when she heard the front door open and, glancing over the bannisters, saw Uncle Hubert move unsteadily in, looking, for all the world, as though he too had been brawling. His head was bandaged.

'Uncle, what's happened?' Seen from above, the bandage was alarming. Running down to embrace him, she recognized the young man – Mr Gould, wasn't it? – from the *maison de santé* walking in behind and cried, 'What have you done to him?'

'Madame, he had a small accident and I was asked to bring him home.'

'Not his fault, not his fault!' intervened a genial Uncle Hubert. 'A billiard ball went astray. Monsieur Gould is a Good Samaritan.' Her uncle's breath smelled richly of brandy and his hug disarranged the flimsy dressing-gown in which she would not have chosen to be seen by either man.

'The doctors have seen to him, Madame. Doctors Grout and Blanche. There's no need to worry.'

'A billiard ball?'

'It hardly grazed me. Calm down, little rabbit!'

Their guest's smile at the endearment made her fear that what she had told Monseigneur de Belcastel had already become the subject of gossip. Provokingly, Uncle Hubert repeated 'twitchy as a rabbit!' and stroked her hair. Though of course the monsignor must have respected her confidences. As a gentleman. Besides, it had been a sort of confession. But the young man was still smiling. Perhaps he too had been drinking brandy? Didn't rabbits have an unfortunate reputation?

'Your uncle,' he told her, 'is not badly hurt. You may safely try out your nursing skills.'

Mention of those told her that they *had* been talking about her! What else had been said? When Uncle Hubert went to look for some book he wanted to show Monsieur Gould, she had to stop herself asking. Instead, mounting her high horse – a nervous habit which she *knew* she should break – she couldn't help giving her uncle's medical history with a silly loftiness. Ninny, she told herself. Be quiet!

But Adam, who was used to terms like 'the tabernacle of honour', saw no foolishness in her using it of the battle in which her uncle had got an early wound. He was, besides, feeling charmed by the domestic untidiness into which he had intruded. He had not known the like since leaving Ireland. It struck him as intriguingly unpredictable and, in that, quite unlike the institutions – seminary, *maison de santé* – in which he had spent the last dozen years. There was a sameness to those, a reliability and a lack of mystery about arrangements which made him relish the feeling here of improvisation and – was it tolerance or forgetfulness which juxtaposed a gaudy religious chromo with a delicate watercolour and jammed a matchbox under the unsteady leg of a fine ormolu table? The seaweedy scent of his hostess's hair was pleasingly intimate. The hall was a jumble of hats, shawls and walking sticks, and the room into which she now led him was a forest of furniture through whose cosy murk there pulsed, like carp in pond-water, the vehement colours of several hectoring, historical paintings. These were so large that she, in her silk dressing-gown, could have just stepped from one of their frames. Of whom did she remind him? Lucretia? Susanna? Leda, perhaps? Cheeks flushed, hair rough from the towel, you could see in her any of the victim-heroines of antiquity, and it was reassuring to see that she, who had been so stiff when they met before, now seemed a little at a loss. Echoes from his school readers came to mind: 'sweet disorder' and 'the tangles of Neæra's hair'. He couldn't voice them though. They were too delicately indelicate – and anyway not his! He had had no live experience of women. Humiliated at having a mind papered with other men's dreams, he turned away his head.

Taking this for disapproval – the monsignor *must* have been indiscreet – she felt the need to explain that her tender devotion to her uncle was in part due to her hope that someone in faraway Africa would be as kind if her husband should ever find himself in need of a corporal work of mercy. Oh *zut,* she thought as soon as she'd said this. How priggish! And into her head shot the child's word 'pi'. It summed up her vexation. She had been pi!

Again little Lulu was to blame. Danièle had been unsettled by Félicité's confidences during their walk home through the rain. While the wounded Lulu's rescuer clumped behind, carrying him in his coat, mistress and maid had kept softly bumping umbrellas as Félicité leaned close to describe the erotomania of her last employer, a rich foreign widow now back in her own country. She, Félicité murmured, had said that, just as the cure for hunger was to eat, so the cure for uterine need was ... Danièle shushed her: a purely formal move since Félicité could not be shushed for long and in next to no time was again shocking them both by accounts of the widow's views. The link, of course, was with the incident just now in the park. Males *knew*, Félicité asserted. They sensed female readiness and could not help but respond. Willy nilly! Nature took charge. There was no choice involved. Widows … At this point Danièle, feeling a cold drip from her umbrella on the back of her neck, turned, saw that the fellow carrying Lulu had his ear cocked, told Félicité to hold her tongue, then marched testily ahead of her.

Félicité's former employer's notions amounted to a subversion of everything that Danièle had ever been taught. Poor, darling Philibert's improprieties, being conjugal and blessed by the Church, could never be as shocking as this. His were technical. The widow's tackled the soul. If there was *no choice*, my goodness, it meant that we were all as free as little Lulu, and the only considerations which need restrain us were the equivalent of the good canine sense which might have prevented the near loss of his pretty, silken ear.

Danièle was so dazed by the principle that she did not at once apply it to her own case.

Later, though, while towelling her wet hair, a little before the arrival of Uncle Hubert and Monsieur Gould, she had the alarming thought that if widows gave off such blasts of uterine power, then she too might be emitting signals. This would explain poor Uncle Hubert's unhappy fumblings and made it her duty to either (1) move away, (2) become repellently nunlike or (3) – though this choice could not be seriously entertained – eliminate her ardours by satisfying them.

***

Sauvigny's wound throbbed, and he could see cobwebs on the

ceiling. He was lying on his study floor where he had collapsed while hunkering down to take a book from a floor-level shelf. Best stay here for now. Mustn't worry Danièle by presenting himself like this. He had let himself get deplorably unfit and, while crouching, his blood flow seemed to have got cut off at the knees. The room was rotating. That was the brandy! He and young Gould had sat drinking it after the doctor finished with his wound. They had been waiting for Belcastel to liberate himself from his guest, and in the course of their chat it had turned out that Gould had had a black-sheep cousin who died at Spoleto, fighting for the pontifical army.

'The Italians called us *all* black sheep,' Sauvigny reproved. 'You don't want to go repeating their slanders.' But Gould said his cousin had been the genuine article: dyed-in-the-wool black. All his cousins were like that, and two had died jumping high walls for wagers. They had shared the use of a mean-looking nag which could outjump any thoroughbred. 'It was more cat than horse and, for a while, earned them a tidy income. Nobody bet against it twice, but they tended to bet heavily the first time.' Gould laughed and Sauvigny had to tell him he disapproved of men who laughed at their kin. Plenty of wild fellows, he told Gould instructively, had signed with St Patrick's Battalion, and some had died and died well. General de la Moricière, who, in an earlier war, had moulded a tribe of wild North Africans – the first Zouaves – into crack troops, would have done the same with the Irish if time had not run out on the Eternal City! Time *and* rifles! 'Rome expects miracles', the general used to joke, 'but can't supply them – or indeed much else.' Three ha' pence a day was what the rank and file were paid when they could have had a shilling from the British army. *And* they'd had to fight with muskets.

Sauvigny remembered clearly now that it was a search for a memoir about all this which had led to his dizzy fit. So here he was! On the floor! He had rung twice for the footman, but the wretch must be asleep. Even reaching for the bell-pull made his head swim. He had felt worse in the asylum. It had taken his last grain of willpower to put the bag of gold into Belcastel's hands as soon as Latour was off the scene, and he had had no strength left to ask about *him*. Just as well, maybe. Let Belcastel stew in his shame if he *had* been conniving. Meanwhile, where was that footman? And Félicité? What was that little piece up to?

Very gingerly, Sauvigny got to his feet and, being too dizzy to bend and put on his shoes, padded down the stone steps to the kitchen in his stocking vamps and opened its door to find Félicité in the arms of a rough-looking thug on whom he had not set eyes before. 'In the arms' was putting it delicately, for her bodice was undone and a black-nailed hand was burrowing between breasts where Sauvigny had sometimes imagined sliding his own. Imagined only! He had never permitted himself an impropriety with Danièle's maid.

Danièle! Oh dear!

She must be in the drawing room just now, unchaperoned, dressed in her *peignoir* and alone with the young man whom Sauvigny himself had brought to the house! He trusted his niece. But trust must not be tried too hard. Besides, one thing led to another, as what was happening in front of him made abundantly clear. The two had their eyes shut as the boy's other hand reached under Félicité's thick skirt and began clumsily raising it. Up her thigh he inched his handful of bunched cloth, peeling and rolling so that the watcher could see stretches of goosepimpled skin. Up, up ... Surely they must have heard the door? Taut with insult, Sauvigny caught the thug's shoulder – ecstasy seemed to have made him deaf – spun him round, propelled him towards the outer basement door, flung it open, then kicked the fellow out. Pity he hadn't shoes on to kick harder! Turning to Félicité, he raised his other hand, saw her flinch, then flinched himself, as pain shot up his wrist. Guessing that he must have injured it earlier when he fell, he watched the hand change course of its own volition, take flight and land, like a homing animal, in her warm, tabooed and beckoning cleft. He withdrew it, turned away, then back, saw her smile and left the kitchen. He would not, she was clearly thinking, turn her out now. Nursing the hurt hand, he went back to his study where he managed, with some difficulty, to put on his shoes.

Minutes later, erupting into the drawing room, he found the two young people there sitting yards apart and in total propriety, his niece having at some point draped herself in an ample cashmere shawl. Seeing their surprise at this sudden entrance, he felt his face redden and, to justify both redness and suddenness, told them of his embarrassment when, as he was ready to leave Passy, Dr Blanche had asked if he thought that Madame d'Armaillé was serious about wanting to do a *stage* at the *maison de santé*. Sauvigny, having had no idea what the doctor was talking about, must have cut a poor figure.

'You might have told me,' he reproached Danièle.

She said – he didn't hear what, for it was dawning on him that, like himself, she might have thoughts which she preferred people not to know. Well, she was a married woman, after all, and not the maidenly Mystic Rose he sometimes liked to imagine. Just now, with the wet tendrils of her hair tangling around her, she looked in no need of the protective *noms de guerre* from the Blessed Virgin's arsenal which he had mentally staked around her. ('Hope of the ship-wrecked! Tower of ivory!') His blood was pumping hotly, and the hand warmed by Félicité's cleft was tingling. Maybe it would be as well to let Danièle go on that training course. Félicité, since she was clearly useless as a chaperone, could be otherwise employed.

***

On his return by tram to the *maison de santé*, Adam told the director that the vicomte was unlikely to make trouble with regard to his accident. He then went upstairs to make the same report to the monsignor whose mind, however, was full of his own concerns. These touched only obliquely on Sauvigny's accident. What was bothering Belcastel was that the clergy were no longer quite trusted by laymen, that Sauvigny didn't quite trust *him* and would be wise not to trust him at all.

'The sad thing is that he stood in the garden looking up at my window where he saw Father de Latour, yet refused to draw the obvious conclusions.'

Adam said nothing. And Belcastel continued to muse about the vicomte's motives in entrusting money to him after he had seen him with an enemy. It was, he decided, a challenge. 'A challenge to me to be as honourable and simple as he wishes the world to be.' Belcastel's laugh seemed to Adam to mix self-dislike with indignation. It was hard to be sure, for the monsignor's mood was mercurial. Moments later he said that, in the world in which we now lived, scruples and delicacy were unaffordable.

The day's events had keyed him up. Teasingly, he noted that, though he would like Adam's frendship for himself to be unreserved, his friendship for Adam meant that he must advise against this. 'For both our sakes,' he said, 'if, as I hope, we go into the world together, you may as well learn by my mistakes. Cultivate suspicion. Allow for paradox!'

He talked then of his experiences with the cardinal and Father de Latour. 'You read the piece in *Le Petit Journal*? Yes? So you see why I feel that treachery is rarely the simple turning of a coat. Loyalty, in difficult times, can be a savage option. Blinkered! Harsh! When troubles ease, it is only fair to remember this when judging people's past conduct. Do you follow me?'

'I think so. You're thinking of my father.'

Belcastel nodded. Ireland, he observed, was a bit off the map. Would he be wrong in supposing that options there were more clear-cut than here? Harsher therefore? Priests must be simple souls.

Adam, remembering conversations with Thady Quill, said it was a quicksand and the home of paradox.

'My tutor was a priest,' he told the monsignor, 'Father Tobin. He may have sympathized with my father's contradictions. Anyway, he didn't – perhaps couldn't – force him to commit himself. He colluded in the fantasy that my papa was only waiting for a dispensation to come from Rome to marry my mother.'

Belcastel sighed. 'For twelve years? Was anyone really taken in? Well, you *were* living in the backwoods.'

'I think people were used to closing an eye.'

'I see. Well, Rome, they may have told themselves, was far away, and canon lawyers likely to be – what? Over-conscientious? Corrupt? Many reasons could be thought up. Meanwhile, I would guess that Father – what's his name? – was giving your father a chance to put things right. Hypocrisy can often be a form of charity. When it is, I am all in favour of it.'

'I suppose *she* should have guessed?'

'That he was paying court to another woman?' A veteran of the confessional, Belcastel dismissed the idea. 'It wasn't in her interest to guess. Anyway, how can you let yourself believe that the person you love is a liar? Human love is a poor mirror of the divine, but we keep pursuing that life-redeeming image.'

'Seen in a glass darkly?'

'It's the best explanation I know for irrational hope. Which reminds me,' said the monsignor with a change of tone, 'that I need you to take a letter to Latour. By hand. The post is sometimes pilfered and interfered with. Not by Republicans either, I may say. No, the bribes paid to have telegrams copied and letters opened and read are paid by those we think of as friends.'

***

There was a press of people trying to get into the church of St Sulpice, where Cardinal Lavigerie was expected to show his controversial face. To be sure, his purpose today was to raise funds, so he was unlikely to say anything piquant. Besides, he had been vindicated, hadn't he? Perhaps he was a saint? Or – oddly, a Republican minister was said to have said this

– a Richelieu? A man who in another era could have run the realm! Saintly or scandalous, it would be interesting to see him. He was a big man, big in every way, and could have posed for a portrait of the fat St Thomas Aquinas. The Divine Doctor!

Apologetic jostling melted any shyness people might have felt, and Adam was not surprised to see a lady smile at him. Then he recognized her.

'Madame d'Armaillé!'

'Monsieur Gould! This is Monsieur Gould, my cousin, Gisèle Coutelier! And you know Mademoiselle Litzelmann.'

Held back by the bottleneck at the church doors, the young women were caught in a crush which swayed like a turning tide. Inside, white-robed missionaries pushed and nudged. There were excited nuns here too in starched coifs, and ladies whose feathered hats recalled the equatorial lands where missionaries worked. Pinned to an easel were freehand maps of some of these territories and a picture of a black madonna. Tables piled with tracts were manned by seminarists, and black children were handing out small, gaudy, religious pictures tailored to fit between the pages of a missal. Some were three-dimensional with silk embroidery, done perhaps by nuns.

A priest whose skin was as crumpled as a much-used paper bag accepted several, fanned them like playing cards and thanked the black child in some African tongue. The boy looked puzzled, and the priest shrugged as he caught Adam's eye. 'Wrong language! There are so many!' He laughed then, abruptly, sighting a priest he knew, whirled, pushed towards him, greeted him with an elated bear hug, and cried, 'Twelve years since Ujiji. Twelve! Ah, *mon père*, there aren't many of us from those days left!'

The other man kept nodding his head and saying, 'Not many. No! We were the pioneers!' Wiping their eyes, the two passed a single, grubby handkerchief back and forth. Above their heads the choir sang exultantly, then paused for a sermon.

'Let's sit!' Discreetly vigorous, Madame d'Armaillé pushed into a small space on a pew, forcing those already there to move along. 'Come,' she told Adam. 'There's plenty of room.' Her cousin and Mademoiselle Litzelmann had disappeared in the crowd. 'Gisèle,' she explained, 'went to subscribe for us both to a mission magazine.' At the high altar, surrounded by more black boys in lace surplices, a stout prelate with a hoarse rolling voice began explaining why the missions needed funds.

'That's His Eminence,' whispered Madame d'Armaillé. Then, *sotto voce*, during a listing of those who had already made donations: 'Do you know what Mademoiselle Litzelmann told me? She got an answer to a letter she wrote to Maupassant! Isn't that good news? Do you think he's softening towards her?'

'No,' Adam told her. 'He never read it. We were afraid to upset him. It was I who wrote the answer to her letter. And signed it too. Didn't she tell you?'

Madame d'Armaillé sighed. 'No, but, come to think of it, I more or less wrote *her* letter. I dictated it.'

'So you and I have been corresponding with each other!'

A muffled laugh united them. When a nun looked reproving, they hid it behind their hands.

Lavigerie, whose great white beard was shaped like the letter W, cried out, 'The slavers kill ten natives for every one they catch. And then they kill the weak ones and the children if we don't buy them off them. Yes, dearly beloved, I said "kill". He paused before adding in a matter-of-fact voice, 'That's where your money goes. These,' he waved at the small black altar boys, 'will be tomorrow's Christians.'

A smear of colour from stained-glass fell across the pew, reddening tears in Madame d'Armaillé's eye, and Adam, shocked to find he was still smiling, blushed.

'Oh,' he heard her murmur, 'I left my purse with Gisèle!'

'There are places today,' shouted the cardinal, 'where you can buy several women for a goat, and a child for a packet of salt.'

Someone shook a collection plate in front of Adam, who put down more than he could afford, enough maybe for half a goat, then saw that his motive was vanity and a desire to impress Madame d'Armaillé. Never mind! Amounts, not motives were what mattered. Perhaps he should empty his pockets? But he needed what he had left to bring him to his next pay day. Oh God! Were children being eaten because he needed to ride the omnibus? He owed Thady Quill too for some shirts. Well, Thady would wait. It was all right to bilk one's tailor, and, anyway, Thady was not so much his tailor as an impossible mix of mentor, vassal and possible future employer who, sooner or later, would get his money's worth.

'In the wilder parts,' the cardinal was telling the congregation, 'humans, not cowrie shells, are the preferred currency for making small purchases. I leave you to guess the ultimate fate of those we fail to buy.'

'I can't listen to this.' Madame d'Armaillé stood up, grasped her skirts and stepped with nimble energy past the knees and feet of those in her way. 'Excuse me. Sorry, but I might be sick. It's nausea, morning sickness, you've got to let me pass.'

'*Is* it really?' Adam had followed her nervously.

'Of course not,' she whispered. 'How could I have morning sickness? I haven't seen my husband in a year. He's with the Force Publique in one of those awful places. I'm here to ask if anyone has heard anything about its officers. Some of these missionaries might have.'

'*I'm* here to deliver a letter to one of them, Father de Latour. Maybe he can tell you something.'

But Father de Latour, when found in the sacristy, had no news. A bony, pale-eyed, sandy-haired man, he seemed to be run off his feet. Pocketing the letter Adam had brought from Monseigneur de Belcastel, he explained that he would have to wait until later to read it and that, as he was kept busy nowadays running the White Fathers' House here in Paris, he no longer travelled to Africa. However, on seeing Madame d'Armaillé's distress, he remembered that there *were* priests here who had recently returned from Boma at the mouth of the River Congo. They might have heard something.

'I'll send for them,' he told her and dispatched several black children through the crowd to seek them out. 'Meanwhile, Madame, you had better sit down. You don't look at all well.'

The first man to appear was one of those who had earlier been weeping into a shared handkerchief. Father de Latour left him and two younger priests to sit in the sacristy with Adam and Madame d'Armaillé who had grown pale and kept pressing a handkerchief to her lips. The weepy priest, Father Augier, did all the talking, and it was soon clear that his gabbling was nervous and his nerves shot to bits. Shaking and shrugging, he said that when he left Boma there had been no news for months of the men in the Force Publique, and that they might well have come to grief, since the average Belgian – most FP officers were Belgian – lacked the stamina to make long treks. Back home they had been softened by the introduction of the tramway, so how could they survive in Africa? Piqued, Madame d'Armaillé protested that her husband *had* stamina, which prompted one of Augier's companions to murmur audibly in his ear that he should not distress her. But Augier had the bit between his teeth. 'Europeans,' he rattled on, 'die there like flies. They succumb to disease, drink, women and' – here the companion gave him a visible kick – 'manic rage! The *furor africanus*!'

The other priest now tried to intervene, but Augier, talking him down, raised his voice to list further risks, including the use of native soldiers. He was talking, *bien entendu*, of the rank and file. 'The FP, sadly, has no choice. It relies on volunteers and impressment. Wives tag along, and so do attendants and dependants who of course pillage and ...'

'I don't think, *mon père*, that Madame wants to hear ...'

'... orgies of cannibalism after every battle. The moral degradation is contagious.'

Madame d'Armaillé looked about to faint.

'Some witnesses say the Belgians are now worse than the natives. You hear of women's hands being chopped off ...'

Adam stood up.

'... to get the gold bangles.'

'Stop! Silence!' Adam used a dog-trainer's voice which was surprisingly effective. 'You'd better get him away,' he whispered to the other two, thinking that they and he might have been dealing with one of Dr Blanche's patients. And perhaps the thought showed in his manner, for they did as he said. One furtively touched his forehead.

'Our poor friend,' he murmured, 'has had appalling experiences.'

'I understand!' Adam turned back to tell Madame d'Armaillé, 'I'll see if I can find a cab and take you home.' However, he was unsure about leaving her even briefly and felt relieved when Father de Latour reappeared to offer a loan of a carriage and promise to reassure Madame's cousin and friend if they should happen to come looking for her.

At the church door, Adam and Madame d'Armaillé caught a last glimpse of Father Augier. He was dictating names to a seminarist who was writing them on a blackboard: 'The Reverend Father Xavier Le Blanc,' intoned Augier, who was too absorbed to notice them. 'The Reverend Father Jacques Georgel, Father Louis Lebrice ...' After each priest's name, instead of a prayer for eternal light to shine on him, came the words: 'killed and eaten, killed and eaten, killed and eaten'. Each time he said them, Father Augier's lower teeth shot forward and bit the air. They were neat, yellowed teeth and reminded Adam of the ivory hair combs which had been appearing more frequently in shop windows since the interior of Africa had opened up. '*Tués et mangés!*' the priest repeated, and his lips closed like a noose around the 'u' of '*tués*'.

Perhaps the seminarist saw Adam's surprise, for he turned from the blackboard to ask, 'Should I write "martyred" as well, Father?'

Augier's head jerked upwards, 'Yes. By all means do. They were all doubly martyred! Just going to that place is a martyrdom. Going there is a martyrdom and coming back is a miracle. Have you any red chalk?'

'Red, father?'

'Yes, *fili mi*, the liturgical colour for martyrs.'

Madame d'Armaillé's face was still frozen, and Adam couldn't tell whether she had heard. He felt relieved when they came out into the winter daylight. In its shine, her forehead had the clarity of mother of pearl.

***

After they had settled in the carriage and told the coachman where to go, her expression remained congealed, and he didn't know whether to be as reticent as she. On impulse, he decided to break the silence. 'Madame ...'

She managed a twist of a smile. 'Oh, I think you can call me Danièle. Formality, after what we've just heard ...' She waved it away.

'Very well, and my name, as you know, is Adam.'

'Adam!' A spurt of nervous laughter ran out of power. 'What a pity I have no apple to tempt you! Yet here we are in a carriage which must be the modern equivalent of sitting under the tree of knowledge.'

'I don't understand.'

'It's just that carriage-rides are seen as great occasions of sin, are they not, since the one in *Madame Bovary* by poor Maupassant's friend? I imagine poor Mademoiselle Litzelmann – oh dear, why do I keep saying "poor"?' She shivered, and he saw that the effort to make conversation was too much for her.

To soothe her, he said, 'That priest wasn't reliable.'

'The Congo is a terrible place.'

'But there are miracles.'

She said drearily. 'I don't think *he* believes in them, do you? His faith is full of holes.' She fell silent for moments, then said thoughtfully, 'So is mine. After all, my husband may have become morally degraded, as le Père Augier would say, or his body may have been divided among the Bantu.'

He was unsure what to say to this and, though raw with sympathy, feared to make her anguish worse. He would have liked to put an arm around her, but didn't dare. He felt his hands open, then close. Being invited to call her Danièle was not, he guessed, an encouragement to make advances. On the contrary, it granted him a brotherly status, which in itself was a sort of taboo.

'If someone ate his flesh ...'

Seeing his shock, she stopped, then, after perhaps a minute, added, 'It's all quite mad, isn't it? Grotesque!' Her tone was cooler now, and before he could speak, she said, 'Wait, let me get my thought clear. You were in a seminary, yes? Someone said so. Then tell me: if we're all to rise glorious and immortal on the last day, *bodily*, as we learned in the catechism, but someone has eaten Philibert's flesh, who gets it on the last day? Do the Bantu have to cough it up?'

'Madame ...'

'Danièle!'

'Danièle! Stop. You're hurting yourself.'

'Well,' she said steadily, 'if I had been tied up with a rope and wriggled out of it I would chafe my flesh, but then I'd be free. My mind is in a tangle, so I *have* to hurt myself.'

He thought: she's telling herself that if she imagines the worst, it needn't happen! To let her know he had guessed, he said: 'You prefer magic to miracles? I remember when I did.'

'When you were a child?'

'Yes.'

'When I was one I didn't think about either,' she told him. 'Until three years ago I was in boarding school where everything was quite sensible and predictable and things were controlled. Then they decided I knew enough and sent me home. But being an adult is not how I thought it would be. Nothing is predictable at all.' Her laughter lasted a little too long.

Hysteria? He wondered whether morphine might have helped. If they had been in the *maison de santé*, he could have asked one of the doctors. 'I'm sorry,' he said humbly, 'that you're unhappy! I wish I could do something.' This sounded pathetically weak. 'Oh,' he raged, 'that sounds weak! And evasive!'

'Is it?'

'Maybe. But you must see that I daren't take any initiative with you. And what can I do about your husband? If there *were* something I could do, I would. Yet it sounds like bombast to say so.'

'Why are you timid?' She turned to look fully at him, and her face now was flecked with red patches which contrasted with the polleny whiteness of her neck. Wondering if she was angry reminded him of Maupassant. He thought: if she is, the anger is a distraction. It's to keep her from going to pieces.

'Are you asking me,' it occurred to him, 'to help distract you? Tell me how?'

'You *are* timid, aren't you? Is it because you were too long in a seminary? Did they breed your instincts out of you?'

Controlling his own anger, he said, 'So tell me what to do.' He thought her pitiful, beautiful and infuriating.

'Instincts, Adam! Summon them. Wake them up.'

'I don't have to. They're as rampant as the Bantu's but ...'

'What?'

'You came here to find out about your husband ...'

'Don't think about him. *I've* thought too hard about him. So now I want to paint over his image in my memory as painters paint over images when they change their minds. Is that called *pentimento*? Or is it the other way round? Is that when you scrape away one to find another underneath?'

Pentimento? Contrition? For what? Was she taunting him again about his time in the seminary? Wondering whether he had 'made himself a eunuch for the love of God'? Shouldn't he stop being touchy about such things? After all, the *pentimento* was hers. Her unhappiness was so palpable that he imagined he could take hold of it. He imagined grasping its head as he would a shot pigeon's and wringing its iridescent neck.

'Which is it?' she insisted. 'A painting over or a scraping away?'

'I don't know.' How should he know how painters used the word? Anger, like flame, had now definitely passed from her to him. Unsure whether he was being enticed or warned off, he felt his lips tighten and resolved not to speak again. What right had she to mock him? Her pain? Well, did she think she had a monopoly of that? As he fumed, Carmen's challenge to Don José danced into memory. '*Et si tu m'aimes, prends garde à toi.*' Last year, Thady Quill, on finding himself with a spare ticket, had taken Adam to hear the opera, and those words had stayed in his head. Alluring! Dangerous! Surely Madame d'Armaillé – Danièle – could be neither? But the carriage-wheels took up the beat: *Et si tu m'aimes, tralà lalà! Et si ...*

It had stopped. Opening the window, he leaned out and saw

that they were stuck in traffic. A crowd had gathered on the street ahead. People were running. Someone screamed, and he thought: an anarchist bomb! Two had been thrown in the Paris streets last week. His sight blurred and he thought of the red chalk Father Augier had wanted. The singer playing Carmen had worn a rippling red dress. An ominous cascade of a dress. What if the horses were to panic? Rear? Bolt? I could die, he thought, right here, in the next minute, and never have kissed a woman. Turning back from the window, he closed it and asked: 'Are you teasing me? Taunting?' He drew breath, then risked: 'Encouraging?' A shudder passed through him.

She smiled.

'Why would you pick me?'

'Because rules can seem pointless, don't you think? They're part of a game which we only choose to play. *And* you're a handsome fellow! *Un joli garçon* – and, better still, you don't know it! Take my hand. Do you feel feverish?'

'Yes.'

'Pull down the window blinds. Take me in your arms.'

He did, felt unfamiliar sensations, and forgot his pride. Her smile lingered, and he saw that the thought of bombs hadn't entered her head. Good! Protectively, he pressed himself around her, and the force of their connection made him think of magnets hurtling. Or meteorites! His surge of feeling amazed him as did an absurd sense of empowerment. Like courting animals which showily swell and expand, he felt as if he had grown proof against bombs. His soul had magnified itself. His boundaries seemed to melt. It was as if he and this woman had no skin and their bloodstreams had run together. Salmon, a fisherman back in Mayo had told him once, turn crimson and bloat when they are about to spawn and soon afterwards die. A myth?

She nuzzled his neck. 'Not angry any more? Open your mouth and close your eyes.'

His nerves shuddered. He thought: it's the bomb! It's fear. Or maybe fear, releasing some volcanic smoulder in himself, had found sensations in his body which had never come alive till now. He felt a tingle in the arches of his feet. Baptism by fire, he thought, I'm a new man.

When they paused she touched her forehead to his and said, 'Good, isn't it? Here, put your hand here. That's right! Move over a bit and let me ... That's it! Do you know what this is called? No? Or this? Ah, Adam my sweet, I can see I'm going to have to give you a quick little *cours de polissonnerie.*'

In his excitement he hadn't noticed that the carriage had set off again, and that whatever had been holding them up no longer did. There was no bomb. No thunderbolt! Hooves and wheels whirring through frills of mud had found a new, triumphant jingle. It whispered, fizzed and caressed the air. *Gaudeamus*, he thought and the hooves took up that rhythm too.

She challenged: 'Say something saucy!'

'We're not going to die!' he told her. And wondered why she was laughing.

After dropping her off at home, he heard nothing from her for weeks.

***

May brought a plump softness to the air; fibres relaxed and Dr Blanche wore a protective fez in all weathers and began to show his age. His attention was apt to falter, as though blurred by the morning haze which often muted the garden's gaudiness and bound it in threads of sieved sunlight. By noon, heat had usually burned it off and was shrivelling this year's first foam of blossoms. Already pinks had turned brown, and chestnut candles speckled the ground.

As windows stayed open longer, Maupassant's shouts grew harder to ignore. He had had no remissions for a while; his personal habits had grown repulsive, and the other day Dr Blanche had shocked the staff by murmuring, 'He's turning into an animal. *Il s'animalise.*' This, applied to the prince of lovers, a man from the doctor's own social circle and that of the late emperor's cousin, the princesse Mathilde, brought mortality disagreeably close. Worse, it put paid to the buoyant trust in progress which doctors and the tired century itself had once enjoyed.

Adam, coming from where he did, had never enjoyed this, nor had Belcastel who, when told of the incident, wondered whether Blanche himself was growing brutal. Of Guy he said, 'He's trapped in a story no crueller than those he wrote. You've read them, I suppose? They cut us down to size.' Delicately, Belcastel touched a finger to his scarred cheek. A joke? 'Sadly,' he told Adam, 'he knows his France. It is the one that Pope Leo wants us to accept, and Sauvigny can't. When I read Monsieur de Maupassant's views of it I don't want to accept it either. What, I ask you, have the great stories which console humanity in common? A recognition, I say, of our divided nature. Of our aspirations as well as our failures. In *his* stories, though, what triumphs is a clever meanness.' As if breath were failing him, Belcastel sighed and shook himself, while a change of feeling seeped across his face. 'Well ...', he grunted, 'maybe that *is* what we must cope with? Now? In the Third Republic! Maybe we are *more* necessary to our flocks than ever?'

***

At first Adam was so full of his adventure with Danièle that when she failed to contact him he felt no impatience and even relished the chance to relive their carriage-ride in solitary daydreams. Daringly expanded, the memory grew radiant. After a while, though, he began to worry at it and pull it apart until, like a sundered onion, it sprayed bitterness. And hurt. For where was she? He couldn't go to her, could he? No. Nor write? Nor hang about near her door? Doing any of those things could compromise her, upset her uncle and provoke a humiliating rejection. He daren't even send her one of those Parisian telegrams which the monsignor now received quite often. A *petit bleu*! She, though, could have sent one to him. Why didn't she? Tenderly, he imagined himself opening it. She was to have started working here. What had happened? The monsignor didn't know, and the director, taking to his bed with influenza, had left Adam overworked and with nobody to tell him what was happening. Did she want to avoid him? Or did she not even think of him? Was he foolish to have hoped she might?

Supposing he were to send her flowers? Anonymously. Would *that* be indiscreet?

Probably.

White flowers or red?

What a torment hope was! That and lack of information!

No wonder religion made so much of both. Doubt. Clouds of unknowing. All those prayers had been a camouflage. While thinking he was learning to renounce the world and the flesh, he had, he saw, been preparing to embrace both – if they would have him. Would they? Would she? Shame confused him. Had he been used? Treated – his thought punished itself – as a temporary convenience like one of those menials who, if gossip was to be trusted, serviced their mistresses in all ways: sweaty stable-boys who were transformed by folktale into frogs which, if kissed – and no doubt washed – grew princely? Translation: the mistress might marry and raise them up so that they got her property and with it leisure to evolve the souls they lacked. Dr Blanche's clinical aside about Guy –'*il s'animalise!*' – must have touched off the thought, but it went back, too, to Adam's childhood and the shock that ended it. Old susceptibilities throbbed like a wound beneath a scar.

Was he – had he become – a frog?

In his early experience of hierarchy there had been the base and the proud and little in between: stable boys on the bottom rung, landowners on top. (The middle was empty but for the odd priest or rural usurer.) Rarely – scandalously – extremes might mate. The frog could leap, the high-perched spinster lose footing. Disparagement was hard to conceal. That was how it had been in County Mayo, and why Guy's fictions intrigued Adam. They showed how much more slyly the French jostled up and down their ladder, and he read them as reports from real places: beds, ports, railway coaches, streets, boats, private rooms in restaurants, newspaper-offices and barracks, watering-places, dance-halls, rooming houses, drawing rooms and, of course, brothels. There was even an account of a lunatic asylum in North Africa.

Adam had rarely put foot in any of these, but Guy had sized them up zestily, and what he had had to say was a corrective to daydreams.

Reading him supplied Adam with the smell of jaded distaste as figured by shucked oyster-shells in stuffy rooms, careless lies, hastily cast-off breeches, champagne left uncorked to go flat in its bottle and the cold pleasures of revenge. More cheeringly, it conveyed a sense of urban savvy, and of contrivances unimaginable in Mayo. Bourgeois resourcefulness despised by Guy – in this, oddly at one with the squeamish Monseigneur de Belcastel – seemed wonderful to Adam who shrank, anyway, from harsh judgements. They or the fear of them had, in his opinion, killed his mother. So he made none and hoped to avoid incurring any either. To be alert was to forestall, as his mother clearly had not done. Love was a dangerous business. Even friendship – surely an apprenticeship for love? – was something Adam had hardly known. Who were his friends? Guy? The monsignor? Thady Quill? At a distance, Father Tobin? He, over the years, had sent the occasional letter from Ireland with news which was by now more outlandish to Adam than Guy's fictions. Dutifully, Adam had replied, sometimes sending along a cutting from a Paris newspaper to assuage Tobin's provincial greed for news. But he had not got close to another human being since he was twelve. He lacked instinct. Not only had he no carnal knowledge of others, he had little of himself. Was he, as Danièle had said, a pretty fellow? Assessing the glances women shot at him in the streets of Auteuil and Passy, he guessed he was. He had milky skin, blue veins, dark eyelashes and a supple figure, so perhaps he could count on his looks. But inexperience left him vulnerable. 'I might as well,' he saw, 'have been raised as a wolfboy.' Reminded of Tassart, he told himself, 'It's not that I don't know my place. I don't *have* one.'

Suddenly light-hearted, the good side of this struck him: 'I can be what I like. I can soar. First though, I must learn the *earthy* things.' As that word took on colour in his mind, he caught the erotic drift of Guy's account of pigeons pecking seeds from dung. Guy's thinking had been, in some ways, like that of a medieval monk. And now, the poor wretch, imagining he had diamonds in his belly, was afraid to shit. And – there were those yells again! – in pain.

'I should help him,' Adam reproached himself, 'to put an end to his agony.'

Oddly, he felt no religious scruples about the idea, but feared that putting it into practice could be terrible. Besides, if there were to be pain – for Guy – in the process, what would be the point? It would be easier for everyone if the unfortunate simply died in his sleep. How much morphine would be needed?

Meanwhile the conjunction of shit and diamonds returned him to more personal uncertainties. He wondered whether women – decent ones – acknowledged having thoughts about such things? Remembering his own fiercely fastidious adolescence, he guessed that they hid them from themselves and managed to ignore how animal we all were. How then could a man ever fully open himself to a woman without fear of horrifying her? Mentally? Physically?

Danièle had not seemed shy.

Remembering Guy's love of water and hydrotherapy, his

mind turned to hygiene and he wondered if he had smelled on the day of the kiss. Might she have a taste for abasement? Women weren't often – were they? – as forward as she had been with him. He thought of consulting Thady Quill about this, but knew the brave Thady would fail to see the dilemma. Adam could just imagine Quill's cheerily quoting – as he often did quote – Little Bo Peep: 'Lave her alóane/ And she'll come hóam/ And carry her tail, haha, behind her!' Thady would be a useless guide to feminine caprice.

It would be better to consult a woman, but the only one with whom Adam was on easy terms was the cook. A lady was what he needed, but few sane ones, apart from Dr Blanche's wife and Guy's childhood playmate Caroline de Commanville, lodged here or visited at all regularly. Even Madame de Commanville now came rarely, for she had moved to Antibes.

When, therefore, on a sunshot late May morning, he came on these two chatting on the terrace, he seized his chance.

'What,' he asked, 'would you ladies say was the secret of Maupassant's charm for women? I have been reading *Bel-Ami* whose hero's amorous success is both amazing and persuasive. The author must have known something like it.'

The ladies agreed that, by all accounts, Guy had.

They were seated on garden chairs, flicking through newspapers, while waiting for lunch. Sunlight, filtering through the elder lady's sunshade, threw rippling reflections on the pages. 'Attentiveness,' she decided thoughtfully, 'was a great part of his appeal. He shared his fun with women. That is rarer than you might think. And what men might call cheek. He seized his opportunities.' The old lady smiled with the tolerance of a spectator at a play.

'Yes,' said the other lady surprisingly, 'he made us laugh.' Madame de Commanville, whose bearing was ramrod stiff, had endured an unhappy marriage – her husband's business failures had ruined her uncle – and didn't laugh easily, which could be why she liked remembering occasions when she had. 'He was a lively talker,' she recalled. 'Though one often found that he had been trying out things he meant to write up. He loved organizing parties and was vain even when he was small. He liked people to say he had a Roman emperor's profile! But I agree about seizing opportunities. The parties, of course, created them.'

Dr Grout, who now joined their group, began to tease her about her enjoyment of such worldliness, and for a while Maupassant was forgotten.

'*Some* of the events he got up,' said Madame Blanche, who must have been pondering the topic, 'were said to be quite depraved. The few society women who attended enjoyed condoning this. I believe Princess Mathilde had to be dissuaded from putting on a mask and going to a private cabaret in which he and other male writers appeared dressed as naked women. They wore skin-coloured *maillots* with obscene embellishments which – well, I leave you to imagine! Seeing what should not be seen can be piquant.'

Adam saw that the thought amused her, even though she herself was impeccably proper and went regularly to mass.

Madame de Commanville noted that her uncle, Gustave Flaubert, had been almost as outrageous as Guy, and that the two were so devoted that when her uncle died Guy laid out his body with his own hands. 'Poor Uncle had put on a great deal of weight, so of course Guy had help. But he did most of the job himself. Wrestled his flesh into his clothes. Combed his hair and fluffed up his moustache! He had a good heart. Poor Guy! To think he used to be so athletic! I remember someone sneering that he didn't look like a gentleman at all because he lifted weights and had muscles like a coal-heaver. And look at him now. When I saw him I had to hide my tears.' And possibly to hide more tears, she launched into a distracting little anecdote about Guy's encounter at the age of sixteen with an English poet called Swinburne. Something to do with an ape. The story started nobly with Guy's rescuing the Englishman from drowning, then grew increasingly disturbing as the poet bestowed a flayed human hand on his rescuer and invited him to a lunch which involved near-cannibalism and other odd practices. Just what happened could not, it seemed, be rendered intelligible without violating decency.

Somehow, talk now turned to Monseigneur de Belcastel who, in his day, said Madame de Commanville, had also appealed to ladies. Oh indeed, she insisted. There was a story about that too. Had none of them heard it? Glancing up at the asylum windows, she lowered her voice. 'I shan't tell unless you all beg me to. Why should I let you revel in what you hear, then have the luxury of disapproving. Do you beg?'

They begged and were told how, on the night of the famous château fire, Monseigneur de Belcastel had been in a married lady's bedroom. Since he could not be seen emerging from it, without damaging both her reputation and his own, he let her leave ahead of him, then lingered behind until the coast was clear before doing so himself.

'By then the wooden panelling was breaking up and, as he crossed the hall, a burning piece hit him on the face, which is how he got his scar. It is said that, when the conspiracy was discovered, he took the entire blame for it so as to atone for his sin!'

Adam, who guessed that Belcastel was now sacrificing his old allies to a new atonement, wondered how the monsignor could ever pay his serial moral debts. But perhaps this latest story wasn't true.

**

Another week went by with no sign from Danièle, and Adam, encouraged by what had been said about the appeal of the forbidden, thought of pursuing her. How though? Her uncle was clearly possessive. The way he had burst into the room where Adam and she were sitting had been alarming. Besides, remembering her anxieties about her husband shamed him. Then he heard that the uncle had gone back to Brussels, taking her with him.

'Sauvigny,' Belcastel revealed, 'hopes to raise more money with which to buy my loyalty. It seems King Leopold's circle is awash with African profits, but he will have to stay there a while if he is to find out how to get any. No doubt he felt he couldn't leave his niece alone, but didn't want her to come here either.'

Adam winced, decided wincing was presumptuous and turned the conversation to his patron's affairs.

Belcastel hoped to leave the asylum soon. He and le Père de Latour had been promised help by friendly government ministers, and Adam had been sent with several coded messages to the telegraph office. Because missionaries' work abroad helped the country's prestige, Latour had access to circles otherwise closed to the clergy, and a project was afoot to found and edit a newspaper which would promote the *ralliement*, as the truce with the Republic was now called. This task was daunting since the old Catholic press had taught its readers to view Republican Catholics the way a fox views the hunt. But Belcastel had agreed to take it on once his civic status had been straightened out.

'There will be a position for you,' he assured Adam, 'if you want it. You're surely not planning to stay here? Dr Blanche can hardly remain active for much longer. Dr Meuriot will soon be in charge and has already made it clear that he will run this place on more orthodox lines. So you won't fit in, and Madame d'Armaillé won't either. Ladies complicate life in institutions – except, to be sure, when the institution is run for and by them like the notorious Belgian one which houses the deranged Empress Charlotte of Mexico whose keepers collaborate with her illusion that her asylum *is* Mexico. Madame d'Armaillé might be more at home there than here. Refusal to acknowledge reality is part of her heritage. After all, her uncle refers to the Count of Paris as Philip VII of France. I know what you're thinking. So used I. Well,' Belcastel laughed with rueful malice, 'times change, as they say, and we with them. If we're sane.'

By the way, he added, Madame's reasons for going to Brussels were to make inquiries about the men in the Force Publique. 'It seems that there's been news about her husband. Contradictory, but worth pursuing.'

Adam's hopes now took a new turn. What if the husband were dead? Fool, he berated himself. If he were, she would look for an advantageous match! Marry again for birth, rank and money! She wouldn't think of you!

***

Some time later another chat between the two men was slowed by a rain shower during their morning walk. Though the air was thundery, neither had an umbrella, and, as they loitered under a tree, Belcastel said he was sorry if he had lately seemed self-absorbed. 'I keep fretting,' he explained, 'about this move I have agreed to make. Sometimes I think of that deranged lady I mentioned who reigns over an imaginary empire, and it seems to me that the Church is full of men who are mad in precisely the same way as she.' Pausing, he clenched his mouth so that the skin on his jaw whitened. 'The trouble is,' he took up, 'that I was used to our old, honest madness, and, in spite of myself, despise the sane trimmers with whom I shall have to work. Latour was telling me about the unfortunate natives in the Congo who are caught between Arab slavers and rapacious Belgians. As he described it, there is a sort of Christlike grandeur in their sorrow. He says they sing, over and over, in their own language: "Let us die! We want to die!" One can't help reflecting that none of *our* friends think like that! So, why feel bad about deserting them?'

Adam watched the unscarred cheek flush darkly.

'Mind,' Belcastel rallied, 'I would not be waffling like this if I did *not* feel bad. It's a stark choice when His Holiness does a 180-degree turn. Yet I, I tell myself, have some leeway, unlike the natives of the Congo. Our world is myriad. I can learn to trim. I can even teach you to help me, Gould.'

Adam made a supportive grunt.

'Yes, well!' The monsignor, after – presumably – turning for
moments on the spit of his conscience, admitted being in two
minds about the paper he was to edit. But then, as Latour had
pointed out, a man of two minds was just the man for the job.
'Knowing how opponents think helps. Besides, if I get abuse
from my readers, along with shit-smeared letters, why – dixit
Latour – I'll be working off guilt for having caused similar
abuse to be hurled at His Eminence. Clemency is not much in
evidence these days among the senior clergy. They're too busy
walking their tightrope towards the secular world! Ours is an
unpromising time.' Belcastel waved at a heavy raincloud. Fat
drops were starting to fall.

He and Adam were now heading for shelter by making
zigzag dashes between protective clumps of trees. The lawns
had been mown the day before, and the hem of the monsignor's
cassock was crosshatched with grass cuttings. Walking – a new
habit with them – had drawn them close, for both favoured a
lively pace and Belcastel talked volubly as they strode.

Though Adam was the vicomte's replacement as Belcastel's
confidant, there could be no confidences going the other way.
He could not confess his interest in Madame d'Armaillé,
although he enjoyed bringing up her name. Even the shape
of its syllables in his mouth gave him pleasure and, as with a
prayer, the sounds seemed to make a connection with her. It
had been a surprise when this shivered along his nerves the first
time her name was spoken – not, as it happened, by him but by
Belcastel who, shortly after her visit to *him*, asked Adam if he
thought she would be a useful element in the *maison de santé*.
Was she, he had wondered, quite stable? A flurry of feelings

had promptly assaulted Adam – suspicion that he was being tested, contempt for his own caution, eagerness ... In the end he said 'yes'.

Then she didn't come.

***

As it turned out, far from being suspicious, Belcastel was disarmingly trusting. Last week he had asked Adam to open a bank account into which to put Sauvigny's money. No, not in the name 'Belcastel'. This wasn't feasible while its bearer was officially a lunatic. But, once the charges against him were dropped, he could be declared sane. The men he had been shielding were now out of the law's reach in London and so could be safely named; the climate was conciliatory and the cardinal's influence would help. But such things were slow, and the money could not stay here.

'Might be snaffled! By magistrates, as some sort of fine! Why let that happen?' It wouldn't do either to involve Father de Latour who would want it for the new pro-*ralliement* newspaper. That would be too unfair to Sauvigny.

To explain his clash of scruples, the monsignor sketched the history of his moral shift. Fourteen years ago, he revealed, when the last pope died, Sauvigny and he had revived a long defunct secret society, les Chevaliers pour la France et pour la Foi or CFF. Ensuring that France and Faith were equally well served was not easy but, as in a three-legged race, it was vital to keep in step. That was what the original CFF had been for. Adam hadn't heard of it, had he? No! Secrecy had been its strength. Other networks – pious masonries really – sworn to revive the old order, had been more visible. The CFF kept to the shadows. If one of Belcastel's granduncles had not been a member, he would never have known of it.

'It was pious and ruthless and was dissolved in 1826. Did you know that the confessor of Louis XVIII's mistress used to prepare her for sessions with her royal lover? Drilled her in politics!' Belcastel smiled. 'We may presume she needed no other coaching. *Our* target was Rome. We hoped to softsoap the new pope's advisors and so secure support for our monarchy. The activities of our wilder elements – blackmail and bribery – were never part of our plan. We tried to win a hearing by making donations to the papal coffers.'

'That didn't work?'

'No. So some of us began to feel that God wasn't with us. Don't look surprised. You may prefer not to say "God". Say "the spirit of the times". You see we couldn't control our wild men.'

'And this new money?'

'Was to be used here in France to win churchmen's sympathy – starting with mine. Sadly, it came too late. Now I have other loyalties – which can be uncomfortably demanding. My new masters want me to trample on the old. But I shan't do it.' Belcastel straightened his shoulders. Why, he challenged, should his change of allegiance not be effected in an honourable way? Why should only rogues change their minds?

This was the nub of his torment: fear of becoming a rogue. Warily, he and Adam circled the dilemma: giving the vicomte's money to his opponents would be unfair to him; returning it to him would be unfair to them.

'Put it in *your* name,' Belcastel finally told Adam.

'Adam Gould?' Laughing.

'Yes.' Belcastel was grave.

'But I could make off with it and cheat you. Or people could think I had.'

'Ah, yes.' The monsignor nodded. 'In today's France people could think anything. I,' he made a point of insisting, 'trust you.'

But Adam insisted that they must sign a contract before a notary whom he would fetch here for the purpose. It struck him, as they agreed to this, that he and Belcastel had more in common than either had supposed. Their inner lives were vivid. Scruples and doubt were filters between them and action. I must *do* something, Adam resolved, and I must do it soon. If I don't, the dreamy, mad contagion which the kitchen staff fears will stupefy me.

As they stepped up their pace to avoid the coming rain, the monsignor's comments came in short, asthmatic gusts. 'When Madame ... d'Armaillé comes here,' he panted, 'you must not ... tell her any of this.'

'About the money? The newspaper?'

'About either.'

'Very well. But *is* she coming?'

'I believe so. Any day now. Didn't the director tell you? Ah, of course, he's been ill.'

The mist was condensing in fat drops. There was a flash of lightning followed by thunder.

'Best get out from under the trees.'

'We'll be drenched!'

'No,' Adam remembered, 'I know a place where we can shelter.'

He led the way through the kitchen garden to a loft above some disused stables which he had come upon last year when following a hen which was laying out. He had found her eggs in a nest of old hay and guessed from the musty fragrance that this had once been a storage place for apples. He now hid there when he wanted to be alone and, over some months, had rigged up a hammock, brought in a supply of candles and stacked books on the airy, porous shelves which must have been designed like that so as to keep the apples dry. Sometimes, while lazing in the hammock, he wondered about the hen whose place he had taken, for once he cleared away her eggs – there was a surprising number of them – she stopped coming back. A loner, was she? Or a hen with a yen to be let hatch out chicks? But she hadn't done that and the eggs, when smashed, had proven as rotten as a madman's dreams. Sometimes, when he came here, Adam studied a manual of stenography, but mostly he just mooned, telling himself that he was making plans. Thady Quill had offered to take him into his business, and Adam had not yet said no. He shied from the notion, though. An old-clothes man!

'There's money to be made,' Thady had urged. 'And what else counts these days? Look at this government! Every second minister is for sale. Have you followed the Panama Canal shenanigans at all?'

Thady didn't remark on Adam's lack of expectations from his father. The offer made the point.

'Are you going to go back to the sem then?'

'I don't think so.' Moodily.

Remembering this much chewed-over exchange, Adam felt suspended between personae. Belcastel had now as good as offered him a position. But it was contingent on the monsignor's hopes of having himself rehabilitated – and how serious were those?

VI

Rain drummed; drips from a leaking roof stirred memories, and an old rhyme blew through Adam's head.

> A red rosy apple,
> A lemon or a tart?
> Tell me the name
> Of my sweetheart.

While the storm lasted, the monsignor stayed cocooned in the hammock and read his breviary. Gusts rattled the tiles and Adam lay on a storage table redolent of long-gone apples: a cidery reminder of childhood and Hallowe'en, that day of days which had licensed rowdy behaviour.

Drowsily, his train of thought shunted back to those old festivities and the man who planned them. Wanting companions for his pupil, Father Tobin used to invite locals in for 'a spot of rough and tumble' – which could turn rougher than foreseen. One game required players, with hands behind them, to seize apples from a tub of water. Good training perhaps for hobbled lives? Other apples hung on strings, and Adam's memories now bobbed as elusively. In one his father's mouth nuzzled under a skirt, steadied a low-hung apple against a leg and bit – what? Mama's shriek was startling, but Papa denied he had bitten her. Of course not, silly! It was the *apple* he had bitten! His laugh froze when Father Tobin banged down his glass of mulled wine and walked from the house. This was unusual for Tobin, a tolerant man, educated in France, who was said to have been banished to this bog because of 'dangerous thinking'.

'Ah yes, poor Tobin!'

Last year Thady Quill had confirmed the old rumour while measuring Adam for a tailor-made overcoat. 'Didja know that at one time there they were grooming him for a position in Rome? That was *before* he published his pamphlet saying usury was a sin. How are the shoulders? Tight? I could ease the cloth. What the Reverend T. didn't know was that the Vatican had been borrowing from the banks. Strictly speaking – as I heard it – Tobin was right, so his superiors couldn't deny him. He'd boxed them in, God love him! And how could they forgive that?' Quill laughed with the relish of an agile man who had himself escaped his box. 'He was too strict for Rome!'

In Adam's memory, the priest had not been at all strict. But neither, good lord, could he condone Adam's papa biting Mama's leg in public! Maybe his papa had been drunk? Maybe remorse for what he feared he must soon do to her made him unstable? By then his debts must have been mounting.

With hindsight Adam marvelled at his own failure to guess any of this. The signs were there to be read! The most brazen turned on another Hallowe'en feature: rings or rather the one his father stole from the festive barmbrack. This was tampering with luck, and Adam had been shocked to see his papa pick shamelessly through fruit-flecked slices, find the ring nestling among currants and sultanas, then slide it from its greaseproof wrapping and onto Mama's finger.

Ping!

She dropped it in his plate. The time for mollifying her with baker's rings was past. How old was Adam then? Five? To this day his mother's taut, white face was vivid in his mind, and so was the shine on the ring which his father began to polish on his coat. Doing that gave him a pretext for keeping his head bent, while the glint in his eyes was a little too bright.

A sourer row started with a pudding called 'apple snow'. While savouring it one lunchtime, Father Tobin may have felt the need to fill one of those silences now frequent between the Goulds by recalling that the Latin word for apple meant evil too. He addressed his remark to Adam and later swore that innuendo was the last thing in his mind. He had, for goodness sake, been praising the pudding when he made his mild joke about good apples: *bona mala*. *Malum* was a vocabulary item in Adam's primer.

'We,' Tobin told the parents, 'have started on the dative. Show them, Adam. Give us the Latin for "The sailor gives the girl an apple".'

Perhaps Adam was slow? Anyway his papa got in first.

'Ha!' Gary Gould must have had too much claret. 'The poxy sailor gives the girl – what? What sort of *malum* is he likely to give her? Eh?' Half rising from his chair, he seized the bowl of pudding and threw it on the floor where it cracked so that its foamy contents spurted through the cracks. Gary sat down. 'Let's have no more of your hints, Tobin,' he said quietly. 'I'm the evil one here, am I not? I'm the snake. Say it. Speak your mind like a man. Or did they emasculate you totally the last time you did that?' Gary beat the table with his spoon.

It was upsetting to see a man use a child's gesture to defy that other intrusive 'father', the priest. Nervously, Adam began repeating Latin verbs in his head. *Amo, amas* ... Like the sheet which he pulled over his eyes at night to keep off ghosts, this stopped him hearing what was going on. By then he must have been older. Eight? Six? Impossible to work that out now. He had no event by which to date things, nor any fellow pupils against whom to measure his age. Father Tobin's efforts to recruit companions for him failed. Nobody else studied with the priest, over whom a small cloud malevolently buzzed, the way flies did over cowpats, and midges over the sweat that foamed on Adam's pony's coat when he rode the animal in warm weather.

'Here,' his mother handed him a bracken frond when they rode out later that day in an attempt to clear their heads and forget the unpleasantness. 'It's for the flies. Wave it. Chase them away.'

***

The rain had thinned. Smells of rinsed greenery seeped in through a half-open door.

'There's something I'd better tell you.' The monsignor closed his breviary. 'Maupassant's man, François Tassart, came to see me. Surprised? So was I. It seems he is at the end of his tether. His master won't see him now at all. He says you have taken his place.'

'But I've hardly seen Guy lately.'

'Well,' Belcastel pried a spoke of hay from the stuff of his sleeve, 'Tassart says he has proof that you promised his master to help him do away with himself. I imagine he meant me to warn you.' Belcastel fiddled with the clasps of his breviary.

'I see!' Standing up, Adam moved to the edge of the loft floor. It extended only halfway across the width of the storey below, before ending like a shelf. Squinting down at the door, he reported, 'I think the rain is slackening.'

'The director wouldn't like talk of suicide.'

'No.' Adam raised a hand to steady himself against a rafter. There was no barrier to stop anyone falling off.

'He was out when Tassart was here. Luckily.'

Adam asked: 'Was this yesterday?' He guessed it must have been because he had seen Tassart shortly after Guy's lost 'manuscript' turned up. A maid, finding the dog-eared sheaf behind a cupboard in the billiard room, had recognized the foolscap on which the writer had spent his first days here scribbling, and brought it to Adam. Inky bladders, dark with afterthoughts, crammed its margins. One said: 'I am flickering out like a lamp without oil.' The smudged paper had been worn furry.

Finding Tassart posted outside Guy's door, Adam pressed the sheaf into his hands.

The valet stared at its scribbles, read the words 'I'm flickering out', and said, 'If this is a signal, he's past meaning it. Leave him alone.'

'I don't understand.'

Tassart drew a strip of pasteboard the size of a bookmark from his pocket and held it up. 'He called me "Adam" just now.' Shrugging, 'He mixes people up. Poor Monsieur! He knows that the doctors are doctors, but not which one is which. Ditto for the rest of us. "Don't tell François," he told me when asking me – whom he took for you – for some "help" which you seem to have promised. It's not hard to guess what sort of help. "François," he said, "stopped me last time and he'd do it again." Well, I would. Read this.'

It was the strip of pasteboard. Stacked on it, one word above the other, like print on a sauce-bottle label, was the statement, 'I refuse to survive myself.'

Tassart plucked it back from Adam's fingers. 'That's *two years old* and was written in a black moment. He had a lot of those, poor Monsieur Guy! I sometimes thought that it was to keep his demons off as much as anything that he liked to have women around. Not that he wasn't hot for them in between times. He cheered up after he'd written that, so when I found it I hid it. Maybe he'll cheer up again. If he's allowed to! But suicide tempts him.' Tassart nodded. 'He was fond of saying that he had "burst into literary life like a meteor and would go out like lightning". Those were his words. Always the same ones! Working himself up! I used to worry when I'd hear him say them and had no way – or only small ways – of taking his mind off killing himself. He's right to think I'd stop him if I could. But how can I if he won't see me?'

'Maybe he will if you give him this.' Adam handed over the wadded-up papers.

So Tassart took them into Guy's room from which, Belcastel now reported, he was soon ejected. 'It seems his master is suffering from that hallucination he gets – auto-what?'

'*Autoscopie?*'

'Yes. When he saw the valet holding the manuscript, he took him for a vision of himself and began shrieking that this self was looking at him with contempt. Tassart had to leave. He kept the papers which, he says, record your promise to his master.' Belcastel swung his feet out of the hammock, heaved his weight onto them and stretched his limbs. 'It strikes me that the sooner you and I leave here the better.'

'Are you telling me *not* to help Guy die?'

'Do you need to be told?' The priest's tone was sharp. 'I imagine that what poor Guy hoped not to survive was his dignity, but now he has. So any promise you may have made ...'

'I'm not sure I made one.'

'There you are then. Anyway, how could a promise bind you now? Who would keep you to it? Not Guy! Nor God. God is against suicide. The taking and giving of life is His prerogative.'

Adam said nothing.

The monsignor buttoned on his oilskin coat. 'I'm in no position to give advice. I suppose my new project could be described as helping the monarchist party to commit suicide. Sorry. Too flippant. A human being's death is a great deal more serious. Though, barring a miracle ... Ah, I *said* I wouldn't preach. We'd best get back. Father de Latour is coming for lunch. We mustn't show long faces or he'll think he's picked the wrong man to run his new paper.'

Wet surfaces glinted as the two picked their way past muddied lettuces, around the house and in by a side door.

'The director was looking for you,' Adam was told while they hung up their coats. 'He needs you to speak English to someone.'

The monsignor turned to look at the front garden. 'Isn't that Madame d'Armaillé down there? She must have come with Latour.'

***

Danièle had been shown to the room which would be hers by a nurse who told her where to put her things, promised to help her settle in properly later, then excused herself and raced off. There was a crisis with which she had to help. Danièle did not grasp its nature. Meanwhile she, the awed nurse told her as she left, was to take lunch in the director's dining room in less than half an hour.

'With *Monsieur le Directeur*. And his guests. You'll hear the gong.'

Nurses, it seemed, ate somewhere else. So what was Danièle? Realizing only now that her status could give trouble, she thought of the troubles others had suffered because of theirs. Among them was the princesse de Lamballe, who had once owned this house and whose elegant head had ended on a pike. Ninety-nine years ago! A martyr, thought Danièle, and fingered a red silk thread which she was wearing around her neck. In the past, women in families like hers had worn threads like this in memory of guillotined ancestors. Her own mother sometimes had, and today Danièle was wearing hers in memory of her mother. She had come upon it while packing her things after the scene with Uncle Hubert, and, on impulse, put it on: a gesture of family piety and remorse.

Poor, darling Uncle Hubert! She had not meant to mortify or hurt him. Indeed, no sooner had she made a stand by declaring her determination to come back to Paris to work in this *maison de santé* – sorry, uncle, but her mind was made up! – than she was tempted to stay with him in Brussels. She itched to throw pliant arms around him and kiss and make peace.

She did not, though. It would have undone whatever good she had achieved by being firm. Instead, she claimed to have an irresistible vocation to be a nurse and pointed out that he, anyway, might quite soon be travelling through Africa on behalf of the Belgian king. There was serious talk of this. He might make all their fortunes – his, hers and Philibert's, about whom he would, besides, be able to keep constantly informed! As the king's representative, Uncle Hubert's position would be both safer and more exalted than those of the officers in the Force Publique.

'If I stayed here I'd be holding you back,' she had argued. 'Don't you see that my plan is really quite practical? You'd worry if I were alone.'

His answer was to look her gravely in the eye and say that he would joyfully give up any position, however lucrative, if she needed him. Delicately, starting at the back of her neck, he ran the tip of a slim finger around her throat, and smiled.

For moments neither said anything.

She went to her room.

Alone in her slightly down-at-heel, damask-hung bedroom – in Brussels she and he stayed with Belgian cousins – she was obliged to lie down. A fit – what else could it be called? – swept through her, and her pulses leaped. She shivered all over, and her teeth chattered. She thought of the catch in fishermen's baskets: silver scales glistening, flame-shaped bodies thrashing, just as hers was doing now. She wasn't alarmed, although she had never heard of the like happening to anyone before. She guessed, though, that the nerves which she had controlled so sternly while Uncle Hubert made his appeal were seeking a release. It wasn't painful. If anything, it was a relief to let her baffled body be and to feel no responsibility for its leaps and twitches. In the days when people believed in demons she might have thought herself possessed.

Oddly, much of what Uncle Hubert had said about himself could be applied to what was happening to her. He had spoken of the brimming up of natural needs and of how such brimmings sometimes found outlets which, though unorthodox, were fulfilling. In among his obscure and obscurely reproachful appeals – instinctively, she kept throwing them off course – came reminders of his affection for herself and her dead mother, of his loyalty, family feeling, pride of caste, fidelity, integrity, solidarity and general good intentions. Holy, holy, holy, she thought sarcastically, then grew ashamed of her sarcasm, and began to pity Uncle Hubert whose excitable state must be due – he had hinted – to recent betrayals by former friends and allies. He had had news too, he now confided, of a lady whom he had known long ago in Rome and who had recently died. He felt, Danièle learned, that he had been unkind to the deceased and had wasted both their chances of happiness. Lack of generosity could ruin lives. One saw such things too late.

'I was too rigid,' he lamented, 'intolerant, cruel and young!'

Young?

The words hung in the air.

Did he mean them to apply to her? Don't ask, she told herself, then saw, with a throb of secret hilarity, that what she had better be was just that: rigid, intolerant and, yes, maybe cruel! Her hilarity worried her. Might it be hysteria?

'I'm going back to Paris,' she decided. 'I'll travel with Father de Latour who is leaving in some days. I know you don't like his opinions, but he'll be a safe companion.'

Uncle Hubert gave in. Potent loyalties kept him in Brussels where Zouave veterans, gathering like starlings, were blackening each other's skies with chatter about the misadventures, schemes, deaths, and in one or two cases, amazing good fortune of former friends and comrades. As most of them these days were mercenaries of a sort, their life spans were apt to be short. This drew survivors close, which was why Uncle Hubert might well, thanks to their networks and connections, have landed a splendid appointment. If he had, it was a piece of sheer, unearned luck. For he had not – his niece guessed – come here to intrigue, but rather to join in the bittersweet hobnobbing which he and his fellows had not enjoyed for twenty-two years. Where and on what pretext could they have met? Papal Rome no longer existed. Republican Paris was uncongenial. Besides, the years had scattered them. Some had signed up to fight in the Americas, some in Africa. One or two had married landed widows and settled down. But working with a Catholic king to fight Arab slavers and possibly make their own fortunes in the process – *there* was an exhilarating goal. Like old hunting dogs sniffing a gamey breeze, they had found a new lease of life.

Danièle needn't worry. Uncle Hubert was in his element.

So here she now was, almost carefree, in the wet, glittery garden of the *maison de santé*, fingering her commemorative neck thread and feeling contrite about having slipped too quickly from her uncle's embrace at the Brussels railway station.

She had dreaded some sort of display. But he, to his credit, had managed to appear unruffled. Both, she hoped, would in time be glad of the oblivion to which the small episode could be consigned, like an unusable trousseau to a cupboard. What Uncle Hubert wanted of her could not be right.

His ferment, though, had affected her. If he, aged forty-two, was admitting to having once wasted his chances, what about her? Women could hardly wait to be forty-two to find their element. Arguments against Danièle's seeking hers could be summed up by the name Philibert. But concern about him was mixed with impatience. A recent letter from her elder brother showed that he felt the same way. Gérard did not plan to marry until he was in a position to settle down. To do so would not, he explained, be fair to his fiancée. Perhaps, thought his sister, he had forgotten to whom he was writing.

We wait too long in our family, it struck her. We think we're wild, but we're as thrifty as petty shopkeepers – only what we save up are our lives. Again she fingered the vivid thread on her neck. Saving up your life was like saving bread: it could grow stale before you enjoyed it.

Bright drops hung from the wrought-iron railings by the garden steps. The gate on the other side of the house – also wrought-iron – on which Uncle Hubert had got stuck was, according to Father de Latour, an example of the purest eighteenth-century craftsmanship. Chatting on the train journey here, the priest had talked about the *maison de santé* where he had lately taken to visiting Monseigneur de Belcastel, about its past, its architecture and what he had been told about Maupassant's attacks of *autoscopie*. Odd, wasn't it, he marvelled, that seeing *himself* should cause a man so much horror? Did self-sightings materialize the act of examining one's conscience?

It struck Danièle that this busy chit-chat must be designed to throw her off some scent. Which one? Hadn't Uncle Hubert mentioned rumours of trouble in the Congo? A blink of fear passed through her.

'Please, Father, has there been news?'

Latour told her that the last batch of letters had been so delayed by events that their news was quite out of date when they arrived. Word was, though, that a fresh consignment had reached the White Fathers' mother house in Paris where they would be kept until the information in them could be pooled.

Delayed by what events? What had happened?

Latour promised to go straight to the mother house on reaching Paris. If there were letters there from the Upper Congo, where the Force Publique was now thought to be, he would bring them to luncheon at the *maison de santé*. Whoever was bound for home was entrusted with letters. But she mustn't be too hopeful. Often, he warned, those from outlying stations had to wait so long for such a courier that when they reached their destination, the sender was dead. Communications with the Independent State of the Congo had grown harder since King Leopold started discouraging French missionaries.

'He got the pope to agree that if enough Belgian priests could be found, we should hand over to them. Leopold fears French influence and may even be wary of Cardinal Lavigerie's anti-slavery campaign. I seem to remember,' the priest said slyly, 'that your uncle's family is part-Belgian?'

Danièle was disconcerted. Uncle Hubert called Latour *le Père Tartuffe*.

***

Her skirt brushed and broke off the rain-soaked heads of some delicately pleated red poppies. Gathering up the least damaged, she tried to recall what Uncle Hubert had said about the king's having collaborated with Arab traders until Cardinal Lavigerie's influence made this difficult. It was confusing. How *could* the king collaborate with slave-traders while promising to stop that trade? Well, it seemed he no longer could, but that changing allies had left some of his officers perilously exposed. Two who had been residing at the headquarters of one of the Arab leaders had – what? Nobody knew. It was while trying to reassure her about this that Uncle Hubert first became emotional.

The cousin with whom they had been staying in Brussels thought the talk of bringing civilization to Africans had one aim only: to boost the sales of Congo Loan premium bonds. What was more, the Congo didn't even belong to Belgium! It was the king's. A private fief. Run for profit. The cousin was critical.

'Some,' he mocked, 'see it as "a testing ground for gallantry", *et patatati et patata*. Such phrases fly around. "Free from the canker of money" is another. Recruiting-officer's patter. You may think me cynical, Hubert, but, if you will forgive my saying so, a little cynicism would do *you* no harm!' The cousin had flashed a mollifying smile at Uncle Hubert, then taken a moment to fill his pipe. 'We all admire your *élan* and courage,' he said, without looking at him, and struck a match. 'You're one of the ornaments of our family, and we'd hate you to be disappointed by our revered monarch. It could happen! Things go in threes, don't they say?' The pipe was now alight and the cousin looked steadily at Uncle Hubert. 'All your life you wanted a king to serve. First you fought for one who was too spiritual to hold on to his temporal kingdom. Next you championed an heir to the French throne who was too noble to compromise. You must sometimes have yearned for a leader with a bit of greed. Well, beware of having your wishes granted. It's true,' the cousin added quietly, 'that if you do go to the Congo you'll have a chance to prove your mettle, collect ivory and rubber, organize river transport, manage slaves ...'

'Slaves!' Danièle protested at the slander.

The cousin turned to her innocently. 'Don't Philibert's letters mention them? They're what this little war is about. Nothing's known for sure, but the rumour is that our lot simply take them over and use them in new ways. Commerce. Railway building. Who do you think supplies the labour? Best not to even imagine the methods used! A small force has to be ruthless, and there are no more than 120 European officers in the Force Publique. If the Arabs weren't totally disunited ...'

Uncle Hubert's restraining grip on her wrist reminded Danièle that they were staying with this cousin's family. Gently does it, Danièle! Mustn't take umbrage! Whatever one felt about their king, Belgians were ... well, Belgian! A little too straightforward, perhaps! But well-meaning! Best, she had interpreted the grip to mean, to let their truculent relative feel he had carried the day.

There was the gong! She climbed the curving stone perron

leading towards the house, paused as a light flashed, and saw a woman who had a thin red gash across her throat as though her head had been severed, then reattached. There were scarlet flowers in her hands. As Danièle opened her mouth to cry out, the woman did too – it was her own image in the swinging pane of a French window.

Her fright broke the ice and provoked little cries of sympathy and amusement, all of which made the luncheon party unusually animated. Adam, who arrived late, had to have it described to him, so that it became an anecdote which could be embellished with remarks about how pale Madame d'Armaillé had been, and how her shock had shocked *them* who were as surprised by her cry and her red neck-thread as she had been by its reflection. The incident drew them close. They had it in common, bickered, laughed, made knowing reference to the ghost of the guillotined princesse de Lamballe and were soon as much at ease with each other as people who have been travelling together or shared the excitement of a game.

Adam and Danièle waited for the rest to drift off, then stood looking at each other.

'So you're to work with us after all!' Flatly. Waiting.

Perhaps he had looked forward too much to seeing her? She was less intimidating than in his memory; there were shadows under her eyes and she had dressed almost like a nun. Might she be in mourning? Surely he would have heard if the crusading husband were dead? Of course he would! Besides, if she were a widow, she would not be here. No, indeed, she would then be free to seek friendships with men of her own station, and *his* moment would not recur. So: 'I hope,' he said quite sincerely, 'that you have had reassuring news of your husband.'

She said she had not, but that Father de Latour had brought reports about the situation in the Upper Congo. 'As you see, he is already here.' She nodded towards the other side of the drawing room where the priest was talking to Madame Blanche. His birdlike profile moved observantly, keeping the company in view. 'He is to show them to me after lunch.'

'And you are seriously going to learn to be a mental nurse?'

'Why not? It is a useful skill.'

'Indeed.' He thought: how curious it was that she should have come to this asylum, then: how curious that anyone should. This was a parenthesis of a place, a limbo. The reflection saddened him. Only in a limbo could he and she come close. With sly temerity, and at a rarely acknowledged depth of himself, he believed the opposite of this, but hedged his hopes for fear of a massive disappointment. His dwindling religion had left him with a residual habit of using small mental tricks and rituals to keep his feelings in control. Judiciously dosed dips into a layer of hidden optimism buoyed him up like a drug.

The reason he was late was that a German doctor had been examining Maupassant. He had not much French, so Adam had been sent to beg him in English to temper his Teutonic thoroughness and join the company at table.

He had found Dr F. in Guy's apartment, making excitable entries in a notebook. He showed these to Adam. 'Is the French correct?' he wanted to know.

Adam read: 'thick, short nose; low forehead; brutally sensual mouth; brow prominent as in a Cro-Magnon skull. Erotic dementia an early symptom of mental decline.'

'I need to discuss this with some of the students at the Hospital of the Salpêtrière.'

'Me-eh-eh ...'

The murmur trickled into inaudibility. Guy, slumped in an armchair in a kind of torpor, must have been sedated. Baron was holding his hand.

'His are the typical characteristics of a sensualist,' said the doctor, whose own characteristics were a small, goatish beard, pale eyes and a skull so flat at the back that it looked vertically scalped. Europe, he confided, France to the fore, was sinking into degeneracy, and writers like Maupassant had led the way. A man 'predisposed towards a cellular deficiency triggered by debauchery', the patient was now in the throes of leucoencephalitis. 'Read his work,' challenged the doctor. 'Read what he wrote about *smells*. He could write whole paragraphs on a topic which is at best trivial and at worst obscene. Yet he lavished talent on this least noble of the senses and his skill testifies against him. His revelling in morbid sensations points to cerebral exhaustion.'

Guy's eyelids flickered. Could he see? Or hear? Adam hoped not. He wished, perversely, that Guy would give one of his fierce cries of revolt.

Dr F. adjusted his lorgnette, stared at the comatose patient and shook his head. 'This,' he said disdainfully, 'is a man whom the French public idolized! You're not French, are you? No. No French blood? Well, you may depend upon it, his disease progressed from the nerves to the white substance of the brain. The decay is a moral one and emblematic of our time. Sensations squeeze out the healthy feelings which keep families and countries together.'

'The gong has sounded for lunch,' Adam told him. 'The doctors will be eager to discuss all this with you.'

But Doctor F. said he could hardly tell Frenchmen that his plan was to write an account of French degeneracy. 'Sensual excess,' he kept murmuring in English, as Adam herded him down stairs and corridors to the dining room, 'and drug abuse played their part. Misogyny too! Yes, young man, libertines are misogynists!'

Merde, thought Adam, remembering how much poor Guy had hated Prussians. He should not have been exposed to this.

At table, the guests flicked open their napkins and started sniffing the aromas being released from silver covers with a gusto likely to confirm Dr F.'s opinion of French sensual excess.

After the meal Danièle and le Père de Latour disappeared upstairs with Monseigneur de Belcastel. A little later, passing the monsignor's door, Adam thought he heard sobbing, but was unable to pause as he was still with Dr F. who had asked to be shown the bathroom where some patients, including Maupassant, were given therapeutic showers and baths.

***

'There can be no invasion of privacy here,' Latour told Danièle. 'Letters from the priests of our order are addressed to our whole community and have no secrets. However, I have folded these in such a way as to cover sections which can be of no interest to you. I shall attempt no censorship, but, for your own sake, you should remember that news from the Congo is rarely reliable, and that if you read something disturbing in one letter, it may well be contradicted by another. The monsignor and I are going for a walk, so that you may read in peace.'

Danièle sat at the monsignor's desk, drew the folded sheets of paper towards her, closed her eyes, fished one out and read,

> *... Brussels was not, by all accounts, ready for a break with the Arabs, so peace was preserved and only broke down when the Force Publique forced the Bantu vassal of an Arab leader to defect and join it. The ensuing troubles led to two European officers who were resident in the Arab town of Kasongo (population 30,000) being turned overnight into hostages. The fear is that they may now have perished.*

Here a fold in the page interrupted the narrative and, on opening it out, Danièle found that the writer had turned his thoughts to heaven. He and his fellow priests were recruiting the hundred or so freed and baptized slaves who lived with them to help pray for a satisfactory outcome to all this. The next letter she picked confined itself to a description of a mission village.

Dipping into the papers was like a game of divination. A frightening one! Might Philibert be one of the two officers at Kasongo? No. When a letter yielded up the – now dead – men's names, his wasn't one of them. And it was with shamed relief that she learned of how their hands had been cut off and sent to the Arab leader of that town. At about the same time, it turned out, the Force Publique, ignoring 'impossible' orders from Brussels to restore peace, had massacred three thousand men.

'*The Christians were implacably bloodthirsty and the battle terrifying*,' declared a missionary whose handwriting might have shrunk from terror, so tiny were his words. Perhaps the taut neatness of his lettering was an attempt to keep order in the one, small area where he felt confidently in control?

One of our priests – Father Aubert – who went to comfort the dying, found that the losses were almost entirely on the other side. Our Bantu allies, whose defection from the Arabs had caused all the trouble, were looting and worse. When he saw a group cooking a human leg, he begged an officer from the Force Publique to interfere, but was told that we must pretend not to see since we were in no position to object. We hadn't the power, and anyway, everyone knew that it was to get meat that they had agreed to fight. Besides, these practices were, the wretch – a Belgian – added, hygienic, and left the battlefield clean. And indeed, Father Aubert could not but notice that as fast as the Arabs and their vassals were killed, the Bantu ate them up.

The European officers are cockahoop at their victory, and it must be said that it was clearly their eagerness for the spoils of battle rather than any distaste for the slave trade which finally led to the break with the Arab slavers. Brussels didn't want this, but God surely did, and, though His Belgian agents are far from being in any way admirable – indeed many of our Bantu converts are more pious – the outcome is to be welcomed.

As Danièle riffled through a bundle of crisply folded letters, phrases flashed out at her. Some meant little. Two or three made her tremble: 'further battles may ...'; 'skulls hung up like hats'; 'commission to be made on the ivory one buys'; 'captured Arab towns with orchards, gardens, fine furniture, silks and amenities such as the officers had not seen for years ...'; 'Thousand and One Nights ...'; 'one officer, Philibert d'Armaillé ...'

On sliding that letter from its bundle, she learned that a party of French officers had brought gifts to a mission station along with news of friends known to its priests. Among those mentioned – she smoothed the paper and drew breath before reading – was, yes, *her* Philibert, who had been left in charge of a captured Arab town where, though there had been considerable danger for a while, there was none for now, and 'the brave Philibert, when last seen, was living like a pasha, eating like a milord and enjoying the favours of several pretty Arab women ...' The case-hardened priest hardly bothered to deplore this tasting of the Mohammedan warriors' paradise. Neither could Danièle. Poor, hot-headed Philibert deserved a few houris. At least, thank heaven, he was alive! And apparently intact! Indeed, hale and hearty! He had, said the report, fought gallantly and could, along with quite a number of his fellow officers, expect to be decorated. Money, moreover ...

She put away the letter.

The sobs which Adam had heard through the door had almost immediately turned to laughter, signalling – oh, relief, then deliverance from the need for relief. Pain. Anger, and a slow recognition of its absurdity. She felt released! Almost light-hearted. 'Pretty Arab women' indeed! Well, that was Philibert! That was how he was! It was as well to know it, and useless to take it to heart! 'Oh dear!' she thought, '*O mon Dieu*!' And this time the blubbering and chuckling merged.

A little later, overcome by a great wave of fatigue, she folded her arms on the monsignor's desk, let her head sink on them and fell into a remedial sleep. When Adam, who had finally finished with Dr F., knocked at the door, she sat up and managed to ask calmly: 'Is there somewhere in this madhouse where we too can be mad?'

'You and I?'

'If you'd like that?'

Wordlessly, he drew her after him out of the door and upstairs to another floor. He had, he explained, access to all the keys.

***

An hour later they had hardly spoken more than thirty or so words, but their fever had peaked, been assuaged, then peaked again. The air around them felt used up, and their skin was slick with sweat. A clock struck five.

Adam broke from their embrace. 'We'd better go down.'

'Yes.' She turned. 'Can you help with this?' It was the thin neckband whose fastening had become entangled in wispy curls at the nape of her neck. Though his fingers were at first all thumbs, he got it free, then took this for a promising omen. Perhaps he could free her from other attachments too. He was still keyed up.

'Do you feel as if we'd passed into another dimension?'

'Yes.'

'Can we live in it for a while?'

'I don't know.'

They were in a room reserved for inmates, where thick, convex bars bellied back from the window to prevent suicide attempts. Looking out, they could see nothing of the foreground, only a pale-gold horizon frayed by the tops of distant trees.

She said, 'Our horizon is in a cage!'

'We mustn't think like that.'

Drawing her to him, he examined her face. It was calm.

Already the bed on which they had been lying had been smoothed in case a maid should come in after they left. They had also, while exchanging few words, straightened each other's clothes and hair – the room had no mirror – and agreed that she should leave first. If she ran into someone who wondered what she was doing on this floor, she could claim to have got lost on this her first day. But, as she was unlocking the door, he pulled her back in.

'You said we should be mad,' Adam reproached. 'I don't want you to feel that. What I feel is that I am saner than I've ever been. I feel whole for the first time in years.'

'In how many years?' Teasing. 'With whom were you whole before?'

'My mother when I was quite small. Am I ridiculous? Is what I feel now an illusion? Don't tease me.'

'I won't.'

'This has to be serious. If not, let us stop now. I couldn't bear for you to disappear again. It's too painful. Do you know that it has been the best part of three months since we met?'

'Do you want a promise?'

'Do you *keep* promises?'

'Ah you don't trust me! You're thinking, "She's an adulteress; by being here she's breaking a promise"! Well it's not quite like that. Philibert ...'

'I don't want to know about him.'

'But you must! How else can I explain how much of me is free? You say you feel whole. Well, I don't and ...'

'What?'

'How can I tell? You have to let me feel my way away from him and towards you.'

'But you might go back to him?'

'If he needed me I'd have no choice. Wait. Think.' Putting two fingers on his mouth. 'Suppose he were in need. Ill, wounded ...'

'Mad? I remember. That's why you're taking up mental nursing?'

'Now you're being cruel.'

'I'm sorry. Maybe we shouldn't talk. Words are dangerous. You see I am feeling a bit mad – yes, I know I said we shouldn't say that, but I was thinking of the sort of madness which afflicts people here. *My* madness – jealousy – is allowed for by the law. Do you know that if I killed you and pleaded mine was a *crime passionnel*, I might escape the guillotine?' Playfully, he plucked the red thread from her fingers and held it across his throat. 'After the way you tormented me!' He whipped it away. 'Whereas people like, say, Guy ...'

'Maybe their feelings are real too? You asked whether I kept promises. Well, tell me: if you had made a promise to one of *them*, would you keep it?'

'You mean to ... Guy?'

'Yes. Would you?'

'I can't answer.'

'Don't look so upset!'

'There's a reason. I'll explain about it another time. Why did you ask about Guy?'

'Because not all promises remain binding. I was thinking of mine to Philibert who – no, let me speak – has not kept his to me. That is a kind of release. Isn't it? Or maybe it isn't? Perhaps I'm deluding myself.'

'Do you expect him to consider any of this when he comes back?'

'I'm not thinking of what *he* will consider.'

'Can we put off thinking about it?'

'Yes.'

He checked the corridor. 'Quick! The coast is clear.'

She left, and some minutes later he went up to the attics then, by a roundabout route, down to the kitchens to talk to the cook. Elation made his knees rise as though he were levitating or were a soldier going smartly through his paces: up, up they came as he sped along corridors. Up almost to his chest! This time he must not let happiness disappear as had happened when he was a child and taken by surprise. Sternly he warned himself – the sternness was ballast for fly-away hopes – to ensure that each of the two of them always knew what the other was thinking. Could this be done?

He thought: I haven't told her I love her. The word frightened him. To love was to risk being hurt and hurting others. Then he remembered that it was she, worrying about her husband, who had reminded him of that. Sensible girl!

While telling the cook about two extra guests who would be coming for the evening meal, he marvelled to hear himself talk with cogent sobriety about sorrel soup and plum compote and whether to spit-roast a few extra plover. At a side table two menservants were cleaning silver and discussing the Panama scandal. One quoted the newspapers, and the words 'man of straw' tripped Adam's attention. Is that what I am, he worried, a man of no substance who can offer her no future? Never mind! *Tant pis*! My straw is dry! I'll burn well! Maybe I'll set the Seine on fire? I must remind the monsignor of his offer to find me a position.

He felt tipsy, though he had drunk nothing.

Crossing the hall, he passed François Tassart who turned away and refused to acknowledge his greeting. Adam wondered whether to stop and mollify him, then reflected that this could take a while and that he had fallen behind with his day's tasks. The couple who were to dine here were old friends of Guy's who would want to greet him if this was at all possible. Best go and find out from Dr Blanche if the patient was in any condition to be seen.

However, when he reached the doctor's drawing room the visitors were already there, drinking lemonade and exchanging reminiscences. The wife, whose parents had rented a seaside villa one summer in Étretat, Normandy, where Guy's mother then lived, had sparkling memories of him as a golden lad. He was employed in Paris at the time and only came for visits, but she had caught glimpses of him, wearing stripy *maillots* and straw hats, pulling jauntily on his oars, then, as his boat shot forward, flourishing them in bright dripping arcs. Harnessed rainbows! Leaping prisms! She had been ten years old and dazzled.

'He'd have been this young man's age.' The husband, nodding at Adam, was possibly feeling his mortality and touching the keys in his trouser pocket – iron for luck! – while his wife's mental snap-shots of Guy ricocheted along the surface of their minds: muscular and proud, a lost image.

Another she produced was of Guy putting or pretending to put a small frog down the front of a lady's dress – a favourite trick.

'Then he tried to persuade me that he had found it in my

pinafore pocket.' She shuddered comically as her listeners imagined the creature's frantic pulsing and the fragility of its skin. Guy himself, as Blanche and Adam knew, was now frequently as frantic as that frog.

'Memories!' the young wife sighed. 'Is it sadder to have or to lose them, as he must have done? Will he know us, do you think?'

Blanche could not say.

Talk turned to Guy's racy novels which her mother had forbidden her to read because, being sold in railway stations, they were disparaged as '*littérature de gare*'.

In Adam's mind, the word *gare* – which also meant 'beware' – began to flash and redden. He was remembering Carmen's cry: 'If you love me, beware!' But he had had earlier warnings about love.

***

When he was twelve his papa, who was spending more and more time in London, seemed hardly to come home at all. Oh, reasons were given: the worst harvest in living memory, tenants' demands for rent reductions, agitators' threats, rumours of violence and attempts by Papa and his friends in Westminster to bring in new, mollifying legislation. These things would be settled there, not here. If at all. Adam's tutor and his mother shrugged. We must all be patient, Adam! Just as soon as he could, Papa would be back home and would expect him to have made progress with his studies. His Cicero and, yes, algebra too ... No, we're *not* just saying this! Of course he'd be back as soon as he could and *of course* he loved Adam. He loved us all and was working for our futures. That was why he stayed away. It was a paradox. Did Adam know what a paradox was? It was a seemingly self-contradictory truth! Seemingly only! Well then!

Father Tobin traced Papa's journey to Westminster on a map. His pointer slid across the prawn-pink cluster of the British Isles, showing Dragon England, with pronged coastline, chasing the flayed, scampering, bear-cub shape of Ireland. The pointer then skipped to the violet hexagon of France: a Catholic country. Well, less Catholic than it had been, but congenial. It had rules we could understand.

'It's Catholicism with a small "c"!' said Father Tobin, who seemed to see this as an advanced and on the whole noble state of mind in which you absorbed the best of your opponents' ideals. It was *not* like Protestantism. No, nor like anything in these mist-sodden islands. It was a way of thinking which kept you on your toes! You could so easily be seen as a heretic.

'A paradox?'

'That's it!' said the priest happily, then grew glum as he remembered that, in his youth, he had not kept on his toes and *had* been seen as a heretic. He taught Adam to speak and sing in French, which Adam did boisterously for he was seething with eager, impatient energy and missed his father who had taught him to jump double ditches and unreliable dry-stone walls which fell apart behind him. His mother didn't like his doing this by himself, but he did it anyway, for he was afraid of growing soft, living as he did now among priests' and women's petticoats. Sometimes there was barbed wire hidden in the walls which sprang up when one of the stones fell. Maybe the agitators were to blame? If a second horseman arrived just as the wire rose, it could trip his mount and bring it down. Adam had seen this happen and had seen horses' and riders' limbs broken. The horses had had to be put down, which was sad, but, in this part of the country, if you neither rode nor raced, you grew dull.

***

Guy had been sedated. Why did they think he didn't know? Syringes, drinks, tablets, food and, for all he knew, flowers, carried secret drugs into his body and had peculiar effects. Just now he couldn't talk. His tongue had swollen and seemed paralysed. It filled his mouth and gagged him. He could think though, and judge what the spectators in this one-man zoo were thinking. Here were two old friends – friends? – pretending to be distressed for him. Maybe they were distressed? Probably they were! But, woven through their distress, was a steely thread of relief that Fate, for now, had picked off someone other than themselves. He saw it in the glitter of their eyes. He remembered feeling it himself when his brother, Hervé, went mad and was locked up and screamed, just as Guy, who had had no choice but to do this, was leaving him in the madhouse: 'You're the madman of our family, Guy. *You*, not me!' Terrifying! Guy had fled in shame, pity and fright. The pity was for Hervé. The shame and fright were for himself. Later, in Morocco, where he had gone shortly afterwards on his yacht, a madman in an asylum he had visited – why *had* he? – yelled that everyone was mad, including the sultan.

Just as well his tongue was the way it was, or who knew what he might have yelled! He felt as though someone had stuck a penis into his mouth. Just as well to be gagged! If he shouted, he might shout for his mother. '*Mère*!' was the word he must stop himself yelling or, if he failed to stop himself, must at once disguise. If he did not, some well-meaning busybody might think he wanted her to visit him.

Just as well to be gagged!

After the doctor took away his visitors – 'Goodbye, Guy,' they cried with false good cheer, 'we'll come again!' – Gould came in with a new nurse called Danièle Something-or-other who said, 'Good evening, Monsieur Guy, can we get you anything?' Nurses were of more interest than visitors. At least they'd be here tomorrow, which visitors would not, and this one was worth looking at. She had the flesh of a Flemish Venus. Curdy. Firm. Probably salty with sweat. He imagined the taste of it on his tongue, his poor paralysed tongue! Curls like licks of flame nibbled her neckline and a flush reddened her fingertips. Ears like small shells. He had known so many girls like that – so many that in memory they all fused, then scattered like a shoal of silver sprats or like the earth which would soon be flung on his coffin. Like himself when he rotted inside it. Everything now reminded him of death. Not that he minded. On the contrary. What was that line of verse about sleep and death being kindly sisters? With luck one might lead him to the other. He mustn't be buried in a lead coffin. No. He wanted to reunite as fast as possible with Mother Earth.

Mère – deddde!

***

When Danièle left the room, Guy seemed to wake up. Lying

quite flat and staring at the ceiling, he murmured fretfully, 'Gould!'

'I'm here. Are you uncomfortable?'

'Uncomfortable? I'm in the Circle of the Envious, watching your dallying.'

'Mine?'

'Dillydallying with the Flemish filly! The one who said she'd just come from Brussels. Do you know what Dante did to the Envious?'

'Sewed up their eyelids.'

'I knew you'd know.' There was a pause, then: 'Gould. I want to ask you something urgent. Wait. You're not going?'

'I must. Dinner will be starting any minute, and I have still to talk to the coachman. Sorry. We'll talk tomorrow.'

'You're dodging me, aren't you?'

'Only for now. Sorry, Guy, I'll send up Baron.'

'Gould! Adam ...'

'Here's Baron now. He'll get whatever you need.'

***

News came that Adam's father was coming at last. With a house party. Oh? Yes, so the place had to be got ready and, as there might not be space for everyone, Adam and his mother were to move out and into the gate lodge. Several of the rooms in the main house were too damp to be used. Those leaks in the roof had grown worse. Besides, the guests would bring their own servants. And a cook was to come from Dublin.

'So we'll be moving out. Just while they're here.'

'Who are they?' Adam wondered. 'The guests. Do we know them?'

It turned out that they did. A year ago the same group had stayed in a castle some thirty or so miles from here, and the two households had met at a point-to-point race in which Adam's father was riding. Some days later they had met again for a picnic. There was a girl called Kate who was five years older than Adam. English.

And now he remembered. She had been surprisingly bold, perhaps because, though not quite adult, she wasn't a child either and could shuttle between selves. Her hair wasn't up yet, nor her skirts down, but she told him that she was obliged to be ladylike and begged him to lay a bet for her without her mother knowing. Nobody would object to a *boy* talking to a bookie.

'You are a brick!' she commended while slipping him money and a piece of paper with the horse's name. 'But you mustn't tell anyone it's for me.'

'I'll happily oblige,' he told her, looking at the paper, 'but maybe you should have another think.' For her bet was on a horse which he, knowing the local form, told her had positively no chance. 'I could give you a better tip.'

'Really?'

'Honour bright!'

She took his advice and, when she won, wanted him to keep some of the winnings. A tip?

'I accepted yours!'

He was offended. So she laughed and dared him to help her take a bottle of wine from one of the hampers that her party had brought along.

'To celebrate! We'll need a corkscrew too, and glasses. I'll hide the wine while you go back for those. Don't let yourself be caught.'

He managed this and they drank it secretly behind a haystack well out of sight of both their mothers. Kate had learned to like wine in France where, she told him, even nuns drank. She had been in school there for two years. So she and Adam had France in common and he, emboldened by drinking, sang her *sotto voce* one of Father Tobin's French songs. Why had she gone there, he asked. To France?

'Oh, my mamma says a plain girl like myself needs every accomplishment. She sent me to Austria too. The other girls in the school, though, had a more likely explanation. *They* said that all our mothers wanted to be rid of us so that they could pretend to be years younger than they were. Having big, hulking daughters around would cramp their style.' She swung her long braid over her shoulder. 'It's also why my mamma won't let me put this up.'

'I don't think you're plain.' This wasn't quite true. He hadn't thought it until she said it, but now saw that there was something of the cottage loaf about her knob of a nose, wide, puffy cheeks and small, currant eyes. Plain! But lively! It made her easier to talk to. Less of an adult, somehow. 'Even if you were,' he comforted her, 'you could develop into a swan.'

'It's nice of you to say so, but I'm resigned, and it won't matter. I'm rich enough to get a husband.'

***

'If proof were needed,' said Belcastel, 'that, in a time of change and in the absence of a tightly organized religious institution, men slip into folly, we'd find it in the example of poor Sauvigny who, according to Latour's latest telegram, has got wind of our plans. It seems that he's making wild threats and telling everyone in Brussels that he regrets letting his niece come to live in this coven of traitors. Luckily, he's to sail for Africa shortly. His appointment has been confirmed.'

'In what way are we traitors?' Adam hoped his face didn't betray him.

The two were again strolling in the grounds where the storm had left the grass flattened and slightly mangy after a previous dry spell.

'I'm the traitor,' Belcastel told him. 'Why include yourself? Unless ...' He paused. 'I hope you haven't – have you – fallen in love with his niece? Surely you haven't had time? Traitor though I be, I'd rather the vicomte didn't see me as something worse. All this bears out my belief in the need for order. He's unhinged now and may well charge over here like a rogue elephant before leaving for the Dark Continent. Father de Latour, who makes it his business to know everything, knew that there was some bee in the Sauvigny bonnet, but didn't guess that there might be two! Mind you, Latour sends good news as well. We can soon leave this place. He has found premises for our newspaper, which is to be called – provisionally – *The Rallying Cry*. Be careful, meanwhile, what you say to Sauvigny's niece. I shan't preach morality to you, Adam, but I do preach prudence. For my sake as well as your own. Above all, don't mention the money her uncle brought.'

They walked for a while in silence, then Belcastel said, 'Forgive my asking but, sooner or later, everything here reaches one's ears and it has reached mine that you've heard from Ireland.

I've been wondering whether you would like to make a quick visit there? I could advance you the money. You can take it from the account held in your name.'

Adam thanked him, but said no. It was true, he conceded, that he had had a letter telling him that his father was ill of a wasting disease and had expressed a desire to see him. The letter was from his father's doctor. It would be the Christian thing, the doctor had written, to let bygones be bygones and visit the sick man. There was an implication that it would be in Adam's interest to come, and this – plus the fact that his father did not himself write – made him recoil. He could imagine the gathering of his father's barren wife's clan and the sort of looks they would give him: falsely welcoming, anxious and – in the case of his old tutor, Father, now Bishop, Tobin – timidly congratulatory. No!

Why, he had wondered, did the doctor write? Was there some hidden motive or – surprising him, the language he had heard murmured in kitchens and pantries as a child erupted in his memory with the needed phrase – *uisce fá thalamh*, underground water? Meaning an intrigue? Whoa, Adam! Halt there! Suspicion dries the soul.

'Thank you, but no,' he told the monsignor. 'I feel more filial affection for you than I have felt for a long time for my blood father.'

Though this was true, his mind drifted away from the monsignor's gratified reply. For the spurned summons had upset him and was almost certainly why he kept dreaming and day-dreaming of his sad, disabling past.

***

'Do you want to lay another bet? On my father's horse?'

'Will it win?'

'It's young, so we're not sure. You'd be betting on *him* really. He can ride anything. He usually wins.'

'All right then. Put it on for me. Wait though. Have one of these.' She produced peppermints. 'So they won't smell the drink from you. I'm afraid I've been leading you into bad ways. Can you walk straight? I hope you won't start falling about and embarrassing me?'

'You drank most of the bottle,' he told her. 'Besides, I'm used to drinking altar wine.'

'Is it awful?'

'No, Father Tobin buys his own. I think he knows I help myself and feels it's educational for me to drink good stuff.'

'He sounds all right.'

'He is.'

Kate was all right too. When she asked him how old he was, he lied. When they said goodbye, they agreed that they might meet again next year – meaning now.

***

'Why do we have to stay in the lodge? Are we to take our meals up at the house? Some of our meals?'

'That's what I was going to tell you,' his mother answers. 'The plans have changed. You are to stay with your cousins instead. Beyond in the valley. Your papa's is to be a working holiday, you see, and the London guests are political allies. English ones. He wants them to meet his friends here and work out how best to deal with the land agitation. It will be confidential.' She says all this as if she had learned it by rote. She even closes her eyes. 'He won't,' she finishes quickly, 'want to be distracted during the discussions.'

'Will those be going on even at lunch and dinner? Every day?'

'Yes. While his guests are here. The work is pressing.'

'But are their wives not coming? Will there be no children? I could help with them.' He is thinking about croquet games and race meetings, but doesn't ask about Kate.

'I don't know.'

'You must know, Mama, if they're going to need all that space. Are *you* going to be staying here? Where will you have your meals?'

His mother turns away. She has begun to cry.

It is impossible to ask about this. Too painful. His pain for her – the knowledge is dawning in him – lurks in a tender, speechless part of himself which has intuited everything. Maybe it is what people call the heart? He distrusts it. If he were smaller, he would put his arms around her and console them both. As it is, fear of inflaming her hurt confuses him. He tiptoes away.

Later, though, she tells him that his father plans to ride over to the cousins' place and spend a day with him just as soon as he can. Maybe early next week. He wants to have a long chat with him, man to man. About what? She claims not to know and, again, looks dangerously close to tears.

'She's ill,' her maid warns Adam quietly. 'She's not herself. Don't upset her.'

'Ill how?'

'Women's troubles. She'll live. She's just feeling a bit low, so don't keep questioning her.'

But who *can* he question? Or upset? Nobody. Father Tobin has, quite unprecedentedly, gone to visit *his* mother, and his parish duties have been taken over by a substitute priest.

***

As an amateur and a lady, Danièle's status at the *maison de santé* meant that she made her own rules. She thought briefly of refusing the privileges granted her by Dr Blanche, then saw that she needed them if she and Adam were to have any time together. So, her room was in a different wing from the dormitories where the other nurses lived; her hours were short; she ate with Adam and the doctors and didn't wear a uniform.

'Which means that Dr Meuriot won't take me seriously, I shall never earn a nurse's diploma, and he'll be rid of me the minute Blanche retires. See what I'm sacrificing!'

This was both a joke and not a joke, because the future was a taboo topic.

Rumours of further battles in the Upper Congo made any hopes that Adam and she might have of prolonging their love affair seem murderous. The usual promises were impossible. They could say 'I love you', but not 'I shall be with you next year'. Being hedged into the present made their sense of it fragile and avid. They had to be furtive. They walked together in the grounds, but not too often. They made their separate, circuitous ways to hiding places – the apple loft, empty apartments, her room, his – then came back separately. This took time. They had not been out of the asylum grounds since her arrival. Gossip could so easily trickle back to Brussels. Shame heightened their need.

'I hate skulking. I wish we could be together openly. Even for a bit. Nowhere's safe though. Certainly not Passy village, let alone Paris. Watering towns are the worst. Spas. Watching for illicit couples is their prime sport.'

'We could visit Ireland. Hire horses and gallop on a beach. Some are quite empty except for seals and gulls! If you've got the stamina you could swim in the very cold, very buoyant Atlantic.'

'Could we pretend to be married?'

'Maybe we could rent something. Play house. I haven't lived in a private house since I was twelve.'

Sometimes they studied the papers, less now from interest in Guy, who was no longer news, than to see whether the world's excitements might affect their own, and whether impropriety, being widespread, had become acceptable. They hated having to hide what felt like a state of steamy grace. Infringing a rule might have turned them into anarchists, if they hadn't known the risks of thinking one's own eye wiser than the world's.

Falling foul of that gaze held menace.

'We'd best be careful of Tassart. He was lurking outside Guy's room when you were telling me about how he begged you to kill him before he got any worse. When I came out of the room Tassart gave me a murderous look.'

***

So Adam's clothes are piled into a box and put into the dog-cart, and he and they are dropped off at his mother's relatives, who live in a remote, highland farmhouse by a black, reedy lake which, until now, he has only visited on fishing expeditions or to bring medicine when someone was ill. The household consists of his grandmother, who in her old age has reverted to speaking exclusively in Gaelic and to whom he is therefore not required to speak, his cousins and their exhausted-looking Ma and Da. The da – his Uncle Patch – is his mother's older brother but looks old enough to be her father, and the whole family has kippered skin and mottled shins from sitting too close to the turf fire.

The cousins are wiry and numerous. He forgets how numerous. Eleven? More? Two died. Some are girls. There is always a damp toddler and often a new baby. All have hair the colour of wet hay and none use handkerchiefs. Their eyelashes are transparent; their pale, blue-veined arms are dappled with freckles and dirt, and, as they wear each other's hand-me-downs, it is easy to mistake one for another and give offence. Adam rarely sees and hardly knows them. Or rather he sees them regularly, but only in certain situations. They come to the house at Christmas to receive presents and at Hallowe'en to play the apple-games on which they impose their sly, clannish truculence. He greets them – sometimes warily and from afar – at races and fairs. He has on occasion caught lice from them. But till now he has never stayed in their farmhouse which is cramped, under-furnished and, somehow, accusing. Trying not to show that he feels this, he has often stood by the door in their dim kitchen or sat perched on an edge of its settle, smiling and answering questions about his parents' health while willing himself to ignore the sour smells of mildewed thatch and dung. He has tried to think that the farm's remoteness explains the uneasiness he feels in his cousins' company; while fearing that this has less to do with miles than with pity and his discomfort at feeling it. He has squeamishly tried not to feel discomfited by their having neither running water nor a privy nor by the smells of pigswill in their clothes. The lines on their palms are etched with emphasis, as though fate's soiled network held them tighter than it does him. Well, it does, doesn't it? Once, as if in defiance of this, three of them forced him to watch them torture a cat, and though he has had nightmares about the incident for years – the cat's tail was slowly and inefficiently hacked off with a blunt shearing knife – he has never felt able to tell anyone about it. There is plenty of brutality around his father's stables too, but it is random and inexpressive compared to the cousins' act, which seemed malevolently aimed at proving something to him. Proving what? Their strength? The opposite? He can't work it out. Sometimes, in his nightmare, one of them is the cat, and he holds the shearing knife. All this is disturbing. Now, sleeping head to toe in the same bed with three of them, he is confronted by another conundrum.

'You,' says the one called Bat – short for Bartholomew – 'don't belong in the big house. You belong here.'

A test? How can he answer? Adam tries teasing, 'Are you claiming me? Should I be flattered?'

But Bat is grave and not quite friendly. 'I'm tellin' you how things are. You don't belong there. Ask yer da if you don't believe us. You're not one of them. You're one of us. You're a Gould, but you're *our* kind of Gould!'

Fully aware now of malice – a familiar miasma – Adam, as a way of ignoring it, begins boisterously tickling a small, giggling cousin into near-hysteria, and, by dint of horseplay, hides his unease. He is afraid to answer, much less argue, lest there be some furtive and horrid truth to what Bat just said. He doesn't believe there is. Not really, but – well, why did his mother cry? Why is he here? How many kinds of Gould are there? Don't ask, he tells himself. Never look weak! This is animal instinct. He trusts it. And laughs cheerily aloud.

'Your ma used to sleep in this bed.'

'Not always alone neither!'

Meaning what? Again, don't ask. At best the answer would be, 'Nothing! But *you* thought it did! *You've* got a dirty mind!'

Has he?

To stop this baiting, Adam jumps onto Bat's chest, puts a bolster over his face and holds it there until a bigger cousin joins in and – what *is* this one's name? Owen? Dinny? – subdues Adam by painfully twisting his arms.

'That'll teach ya manners!' pants Owen-or-Dinny, 'since they didn't do it in the big house! Teach ya not to come the nob with us!'

Has he 'come the nob'? When? How? His arms hurt. He wonders if his wrist is sprained.

'Betcha don't even remember my name,' says Owen-or-Dinny. 'Ya don't, do ya? No more than if I was one of the dogs. Think yer Lord Muck, dontcha? Last time we met, ya said "Hullo Cathal." My brother, Cathal, went to live in Cork two years ago. Well, what *is* my name then?'

Adam doesn't risk a guess.

Later, after blowing out their candle, the cousins tell grisly ghost stories and, later still, when he has to go outside to relieve himself, someone hidden behind a windy holly bush makes would-be blood-chilling noises, and throws drops of what Adam hopes is water on his head. Well, if *that's* their worst, he decides, let them do it! He, after all, may be the most challenging novelty to reach this bit of bog since the botched French invasion of nearly a hundred years ago. His bogmen cousins are touchy about being bogmen, and may, he guesses, feel obliged to show that they're neither impressed nor awed by his big-house ways. All right, he decides, *all right*, he'll allow for their need to take him down a peg. They find it hilarious that he wears pyjamas so, to avoid providing them with further amusement, he makes sure that they don't see his slippers. They're a smart pair in soft leather, which his father sent from London, but he wraps them round a stone and slides them into the lake.

Over the next two days, things go more smoothly, and his cousins seem to be observing a truce. Even so, when a groom delivers his pony along with a note from his mother, he is glad to get away on his own. So out he rides across the bog, canters about a bit, jumps a few fences and is wondering where to head next when he sees someone else practising jumps. At once the dull landscape acquires focus and he starts to watch. But his hovering must have unsettled the rider, whom he sees now is a woman, for her horse refuses a jump, stopping dead so suddenly that she looks like landing in it head first. While she's righting herself – luckily, she grasped the mane – Adam rides towards her and recognizes Kate. She is wearing a smart riding habit and hails him cheerfully, calling out that he needn't worry, a miss is as good as a mile. Then she asks where he has been and why he wasn't at dinner last evening.

He can't think of a lie. His mind freezes. Telling the truth would entail the mortifying admission that he may be the wrong sort of Gould and have to live from now on with smelly, ill-disposed cousins, so he bats back the query. What about her? What is she doing so far from the big house? Alone? As he hears his own questions, they worry him. Could she have heard gossip? And what if one of the cousins – say Owen-or-Dinny, whose actual name he still doesn't know – were to pop like a leprechaun from behind a turf-stack and insist on inviting her to the farm for an insanitary cup of buttermilk? This is just what the cousins would love to do with a '*céad míle fáilte*', in the name of Irish hospitality, from malign curiosity, the joy of embarrassing Adam and in the hope – *Oh God*! – of a tip. And she'd go! Of course she would! From politeness and – why not? – a touch of malign curiosity. And might even distribute small change.

At this point – 'coming the nob' inside his own head – he panics and becomes briefly convinced that he sees a composite cousin approach. This cousin is wearing a length of thick, hairy string around his waist to keep up his ridiculously low-forked, adaptable, hand-me-down clown's pants and has a sack over his shoulders in lieu of a jacket. Not that Adam should care! Imaginary or not, the cousin is his blood relative, and Adam should not be snobbish about smells or lice or hairy string or even badly washed cups of buttermilk. '*Pauvreté n'est pas vice*,' is what Father Tobin always says: 'It's no sin to be poor.' Maybe not, but, as even Adam knows, poverty can bring shame and meanness, exasperation and a hardening of the heart. The reason Father T. coyly makes the claim in French is because he knows it too. (Like a demon sprinkled with holy water, the visionary cousin has now evaporated.)

Meanwhile, listening with half an ear, Adam has heard Kate explain that she is practising for her next riding lesson. She hopes to go out with the hunt, possibly even in the next day or so, but is wary of the double fences they have around here. 'We didn't ride much in my French school. I nearly came a cropper just now,' she admits. 'You saw me. What did I do wrong?'

'Lean forward as you approach the bank,' he tells her, 'then lean back when your mount changes feet on top of it. Watch.' And off he wheels, jumps a combined bank and ditch and, while he does so, makes a quick survey of the reassuringly empty bog. No cousins in sight! Not even a distant turf-cutter. Not a soul. He feels a guilty relief.

'You've put your hair up,' he notes, smiling, as he trots back. He can see, though, that it doesn't suit her. Too severe.

Laughing at herself, she says she's a young lady now. Seventeen! No more tippling behind haystacks! 'I've put childish things behind me.' This, it turns out, includes school. 'I'm on the marriage market. My mama can't keep me abroad for ever and, as motherly concern is definitely not her forte, we've agreed that she should arrange to marry me off as soon as we can find someone nice whom we both like. If I were clever or were a boy I might do something more challenging, but as I'm not ...' Kate shrugs. 'Maybe, if she fails, I'll end up as a missionary nun? It's the only career I can think of which combines adventure with propriety. Meanwhile I am trying to jump fences.'

'Do you want to try a few more?'

'Why not?'

So he gives her a lesson, after which, tired but pleased with themselves, they dismount, let the horses graze, spread out his mackintosh and sit on it eating sandwiches which she foresight-edly brought with her. No wine this time, but above their heads the sun gilds a flicker of damp birch leaves which remind them both of coins. This prompts him, when they see a rainbow, to tell her about the crock of gold which is said to be buried at the end of it. 'My family,' he jokes, 'could do with one of those. My papa is always saying so.'

Pulling off her riding hat which leaves a pink indentation on her forehead, Kate leans back on her elbows, arches, gazes at the breeze-blown birch leaves and says, luxuriating like a happy cat, 'Remember I told you I had money? Maybe *I'm* your crock of gold.'

'Why mine?'

'Your family's, then.'

'Sorry, I'm being thick.'

'Guess who else has been teaching me to jump fences. Your papa.'

'My ...?' Adam's impulse is to sort this claim under the same heading as crocks of gold and spectral cousins-in-clown's-trousers. Delusions! What else? How could a busy man who has not yet found time to ride a dozen miles to talk to his own son be teaching someone else's daughter to jump fences?

***

To Monsieur le Vicomte Hubert de Sauvigny

Monsieur le Vicomte,
He who writes this note has been trained to know his place and would not divulge private information if the need were less urgent.

Your niece has fallen into dangerous company at Dr Blanche's asylum where an Irish adventurer is taking unscrupulous advantage of her affections. Worse: he is just as unscrupulous in his treatment of the unfortunate inmates of that place and has been heard plotting to give a lethal dose of poison to the most distinguished of them, the writer Monsieur Guy de Maupassant. If there is a scandal, your niece risks being touched by it unless someone rescues her first.

A well-wisher

VII

It was twilight.

'I've had an odd telegram.' Danièle's shiver was restless. 'Uncle Hubert may be coming to say goodbye.'

'In what way is that odd?' Adam had been savouring the moment, telling himself, 'We're together now,' then trying to make the 'now' last. It was a game children might play. 'Because he's in Brussels, and his ship sails from Antwerp.' She shivered again. 'Coming here is the wrong direction for him.'

Leafy reflections shone. In their radiance her limbs looked ready to escape human embraces. Her shiver had flicked the thought into his mind.

She said, 'We don't want Philibert hurt!'

'Philibert?' He took moments to understand. Then: 'Are you afraid that if your uncle comes he will guess about us, then report to your husband? In Africa?'

She was watching his face. 'You think I'm fanciful?'

They laughed, aware that without fancy, they could hardly

have talked at all. So many topics were embargoed, among them his dream that one day she might get a divorce or – here it was his turn to shiver guiltily – be widowed. The sorest was their lack of funds. Backing from it, they returned, with relief, to their transgression. Desire was so obsessive that the stealth of their arrangements could seem the healthiest thing about them. At least, while deceiving other people, you gave them your attention. Surely that was better than spending your waking hours in a clammy smoke of lust?

'If you do go to Ireland, could I join you there?' A pause. 'Discreetly.'

'I don't know.' His mind slid between cunning and impulse. Both their minds were tossed coins turning in the air: heads, tails, heads ...

Solemn as bookies, they reckoned up their hopes. Her readiness to run off to the pastoral wilds of Ireland reminded him of how those wilds had failed love in his parents' case.

He had had another letter from there, this time from His Grace John Joseph, who wrote,

> I make this appeal on your father's behalf. Have you got it in you to forgive him? In person? He'd die happier if you came. His marriage was not a good one and, though I can't expect you to pity him, I do ask you to help him die in peace – especially as that might bring you peace too. You cannot be totally at ease over what you did.

Adam's father, Tobin reminded him, had not in the end married the young English heiress – '*you'll* remember why' – but an older, less well-dowered neighbour who had proven barren.

The estate, Tobin warned, was again encumbered and run down.

Mention of the heiress – Kate – brought back aspects of the story which Adam had managed to forget. Discomfort pricked. What had the dying man been saying?

The possibility that his father might think himself a victim was startling. But then, being a victim excused a lot, and the old man had a lot to excuse. Emerging from some sour cellar of memory rose a Gaelic jeer often flung at a loser: a *mí-ádh*. Gaels, being connoisseurs of loss, were quick to deride misfortune's stratagems, self-pity for one. Had Adam and his father, each in his own mind, played the *mí-ádh*?

Tobin seemed to take no position on the matter. Clearly, the years had taught him to sit on the fence.

Danièle, when shown his letter, took a cheerful view. Of course Adam must go to Ireland! For his father's sake – but also for *them*!

'Adam, how can you hesitate? One doesn't pass up possible legacies. I'll bet that the estate isn't all that run down. What might you get?'

This, though he tried to think of it as candour, shocked him. Remembering talk of how King Leopold aimed to milk the Congo before handing it over to Belgium, he reflected that the wellborn were not brought up to be mealy-mouthed.

So where, he wondered, did we small folk get our prayerful dreaminess? Where but from an education tailored to suit the interests of the propertied! If we were to manage their affairs without bilking them, we needed scruples – and humility. Amused, but also a little sour, he recalled Sauvigny's opinion that the lower clergy should be sent to eat in the kitchen. That for all his eccentric airs, Sauvigny was self-servingly shrewd, was an insight which Adam owed to his reading of poor Guy's lucid and indignant tales.

So, if scrupulousness went with low birth, might not Adam, as his father's son, have a streak of the opposite? Indeed, if he wished to prove himself a true chip off the old block, might filial piety consist in being callous? A thought to keep to oneself!

'Could we live,' Danièle was back in the embrace of fancy, 'on your father's estate?'

'On it, but not off it,' he told her, practising plain speaking. 'The land is poor; the income, here or in London, wouldn't be much. On the spot, though, you could have a great life.'

'There's no reward here or in heaven,' she told him forth-rightly, 'for failing to claim your inheritance.'

'What about *noblesse oblige*?'

'The *noblesse*,' she said tartly, 'might, like my poor Philibert, feel obliged to kill if insulted but never to give up money. They need to have it so as to serve their ideals.'

'What drew him to the Congo? Adventure?'

'I told you. He killed someone in a duel and was advised to make himself scarce.'

A duel! Lord! Should Adam learn to shoot? He asked: 'But why there especially?'

'Romance. King Leopold's speeches. Philibert has a bit by heart about how "the universe lies before us, steam and electricity have abolished distance; all the unclaimed lands on the surface of the globe are ours for the taking." That thrills him – or did.'

'But isn't it an invitation to steal other people's land? We Irish are touchy about that. It was done to us.'

'It's not the same, though, is it? Africans don't *use* land any more than animals living in a forest develop or claim it. So how can we say it's theirs?'

'Is that *his* argument?'

'Yes.'

Cherishing his contempt for her dashing, bone-headed husband, Adam said no more.

But, while handing out blame, he couldn't absolve himself. What about his promise to Guy? Might some noble callousness make that easier to keep?

***

Racing in the wind, a cloud passes overhead, the sun's dazzle returns, and perspiration shines on Kate's forehead. She rubs it with the back of her hand. 'You don't believe me, do you?' She gleams as if suppressing a laugh. 'About your papa giving me lessons.' Then, after an artful pause: 'What if he were courting me? How would you feel about that? Seriously, would you like me as a stepmother? I'd promise not to be a wicked one.'

'As a ...' Telling himself to stop parroting her words, he says with dignity, 'I don't think you should be making jokes about things like that.'

'I'm not. I wouldn't. Look, I know he's twice my age, but you see I've always wanted to marry someone older. I want to be *cherished*.' She is grave and seems – foolishly? – to swell with hope. 'I never have been, you see. Cherished! And I know I'm not beautiful, so a younger man would never ...'

'Stop! You mustn't talk like this. Not to me. Not about my father.'

'Nor,' he could have added, 'about yourself.' He feels as if he has opened a privy door at the wrong moment. Has she no instinct for self-protection? She seems not to have. How, he wonders, can anyone like that survive? Could living with French nuns have turned her into a misfit? Maybe she was sent to them *because* of being a misfit?

Or maybe English people, being cocks of their walk, don't need – or think they don't need – caution? Maybe she fits among them? Not here. He likes her, though. Her forthrightness excites him. Nobody he has met till now ever exposed their private selves like this.

'But Adam, I don't want to do things behind your back! I want things to be above board if I'm to join your family.'

'How could you join it? Is that what you were after last year? Why you came looking for me?'

She is shocked. 'What do you mean? Last year we were children. We were closer in age to each other than to anyone else in our party. That's why you helped me place a bet. Don't you remember? I didn't even know your papa then. But some months ago in London, he approached my mama with a view to ...'

Adam covers his ears.

'No? All right. I'll let *him* tell you. All I need to know is whether you would object.'

'You're cracked!'

'Look, I'm sorry. You're right. I shouldn't have spoken.'

But of course he can't leave it there. 'You,' he guesses suddenly, 'must be the one who upset my mother and ...' He trails off, unwilling to fit the bad jigsaw bits together: his father's absences, the cousins' sniggering. She couldn't have caused all that. Could she? Might she? His world has begun to wobble.

But now – another surprise! – it is she who seems shaken. She stares at him. 'Your mother? She's dead surely? Isn't your papa a widower?'

'My mother is not dead. My mother is Ellen Gould. You've met her.'

Her hand flies to her mouth. 'Ellen Gould? The housekeeper?'

'She is not a housekeeper. She's my mother.'

'She is? But then what can your father have been thinking of? I don't see how both my mama and I could have misunderstood him.'

'No?' Adam is shaken.

'Not really. No.' Her voice trembles.

Noting the tremble, Adam takes heart. 'Perhaps,' he argues defiantly, 'he was joking and you didn't realize. People here joke a lot! And flirt. It doesn't mean anything. It's a game. You'll have heard of Irish charm? Blarney? We call it *plámás*. It's a sort of practical joke to lead people up the garden path! We like things to be double-edged and to get people eating out of our hands while, inwardly, we're laughing.'

With laborious patience he lays out a view of things that calms his fright and aims to baffle off unwelcome news. And as he elaborates his argument he starts to believe it. Clearly, he decides with satisfaction, it is she who has got the wrong end of the stick. Famously, the gullible English often do. Sobersides! Simple Simons! He watches her ponder. She is brave, he thinks, in spite of himself, as she turns away then, abruptly resolute, back. Plucky! His papa must have thought of her as a child and teased her the way you do a pert little Miss. Maybe he'd been a bit thick-skinned? Teasing – Adam has seen this happen – can go too far.

'Adam!' Her face is on fire. 'I must – I have to ask you: are they married? Your father and mother? Is she his wife?'

Is she his ...? Is his mother *married*? 'Of course she is!' But even as he speaks, doubt ruffles his certitudes. He gets to his feet. 'I think we should stop talking about this.' He feels an answering flush blaze up his own cheeks. 'I have to go. Maybe we'll see each other at the hunt.' This is not meant to be taken seriously. He hopes never to see her again. And waits for her to remove herself from his mackintosh.

But she stays sitting on it. 'I'm sorry.' She shakes her head. 'I didn't mean to upset you.' And watches him with the same – he guesses it to be the same – offensive pity with which he watches his cousins. Seeing her come to a conclusion, he half reaches it himself: for what if his mother were *not* his father's wife? That would explain everything! All the jigsaw spats and hints and innuendos! What are the odds? Fifty-fifty?

No, it's worse! In a reluctant bit of his brain, he has sometimes, hazily, half guessed this without accepting it, yet braced himself for the day he might have to. An eldest son's first duty – this dogma, having been obliquely conveyed, feels hard to refute – is to preserve and hold onto his estate. A natural law? And *is* Adam such a son? Or not? His father *is* and so may feel obliged to marry money, even if this entails taking a wide-eyed, helpless, puffy-faced, sixteen-year-old heiress into his bed and betraying his true family.

'I didn't,' Kate pleads, 'plan any of this when I came to look for you today. All I wanted was to get things straight. You see

I didn't just chance by. I knew you'd be riding here. One of the grooms gave me directions. I guessed things were being arranged behind your back and thought I should find out how you would feel if – but it may not matter now.'

'If what?'

'I think it doesn't matter.'

'Goodbye then.' He has to get away.

Later, reviewing her image in his mind's eye, he will notice that she was crying. Later still, it will strike him that she was the first person he ever met who had the nerve to go straight for the truth – and that he thought her mad.

Now, though, they get back on their mounts and head in different directions. To his surprise, his cousins' farmhouse feels like a haven.

***

Sauvigny did not give much credit to the unsigned letter from the lunatic asylum.

Yet he could not dismiss it, for it revealed malevolence, and he hated to think of his niece being surrounded by that. Wondering whether to warn her, he considered posting it on to her, then rejected the notion. He thought next of sending it to the Irishman, but decided that people working in asylums were unlikely to need cautioning. They must be used to malevolence and lies! To whose malevolence did the letter testify? To the lunatic writer's? To those of whichever near-lunatic had smuggled it out? In doubt as to whether he could have conjured the thing from his own raging imagination, he forced himself to reread it to make sure that he had not. That done, he folded it into his waistcoat pocket where a probing fingernail could, at any moment, check its small, arid, monitory crackle.

It was a season of rumours and alarms.

His cousin had advised him against going to the Congo, and Sauvigny had listened closely to his dissuasions then refuted them in his head. The worse the place was, the plainer it became that he must go there to confront the demons which had been playing grandmother's steps with him since he was seventeen. They were drawing closer. But if evil in the Upper Congo was as impudently visible as was claimed, he could find solace by going there to do what he had been trained to do: fight.

His readiness to do this was connected with a very particular demon! 'Call it by its name, Hubert,' he admonished himself. 'Your ruling passion is a carnal one for Danièle. Once distance has helped control it, you must set about finding the hare-brained Philibert, and make him see that it is his duty to come home. No sane man leaves a pretty young wife alone for the better part of two years.'

Sauvigny did not want to leave her alone either. But he distrusted his inclinations. The demons! In his mind they were an army of ant-sized parasites whose uniform he sometimes imagined as red like the Garibaldini's shirts and sometimes black like the coats of Republican deputies. Laying siege to the seat of his emotions, they might yet adopt it as their *grand quartier général*. They would run his mind.

When he stared at a flame, then closed his eyes, the colours he saw were theirs. Flight was the way to defeat them. He *must* go to the Congo.

A more immediate reason for going was an all-too-plausible rumour about Belcastel.

The ex-Zouaves had now migrated back to their far-flung lairs and niches. Before dispersing, they had pooled their news. Many had female relatives who were senior members of religious Orders or were married to leading members of opposing parties and nations. Several knew secrets or shreds of secrets and, as a result, patchwork accounts of Father de Latour's activities had reached Sauvigny. Some of these were made up of echoes bounced back from distant missions and embassies; others came from Republican clubs in Paris and clerical coteries in Rome. Belcastel's name kept cropping up. Converging, the scraps pointed to an unequivocal conclusion. Monseigneur de Belcastel had joined the opposition.

Though Sauvigny would once have blamed his friend bitterly, he didn't now. For the charges the monsignor might make were hard to refute. Far from ensuring good order, French monarchism had subverted it, and the twitching agonies of its last adherents called for a *coup de grâce*. One read of oriental widows choosing to be burned on their husbands' pyres and of vassals killing themselves so as to join dead overlords. Christian loyalty was less extreme. Living on after the disappearance of our lovers and leaders we clearly had no choice but to adapt. And the line between doing that and turning one's coat was hard to draw. Inside Sauvigny's head, something had begun to turn.

News of his former mistress's death had rattled him.

If kings with divine right had so manifestly failed, might not the Kingdom which theirs prefigured be failing too? The notion was both satisfyingly sour – the priests' day of reckoning would avenge their betrayal of the Zouaves – and frightening since, if there were no absolutes, how did one live? With what right, for instance, had Sauvigny, who had killed for love of the pope, spurned the woman in Rome who had killed for love of him? And why, come to that, should he not try to seduce Danièle? They were fond of each other and he guessed that, if ardently pressed, she was unlikely to spurn him.

Unless the lunatic letter was telling the truth?

But there was no space in his mind for such a likelihood.

He had been having intoxicating dreams. He found he could entice them by thinking of her before he fell asleep. Her image blended with that of the Roman woman to whom he had been cruelly harsh. In the dreams he tried, remorsefully, to comfort *her* and once or twice found, with shocked pleasure, that he was embracing his naked niece.

He had thought, while drifting into sleep, of how her skin glowed like the inside of an oyster shell; of the shadow pool in each cheek; of the blue veins in the crook of each arm and of parts of her body which he had never seen. The veins were the colour of wind flowers. She was as delicate as that.

Several times he had woken up in states of vivid excitement. Had he brought them on? Connived or merely consented to them? How culpable was he? He wouldn't consult a priest since in his mind the clergy were to blame for the whole phenomenon. Once the armouring of certainty thawed, their rules were worthless.

Mostly he deplored this licentiousness and regretted the days when he had liked and respected himself. Now he didn't.

The thing to do was leave. Cut all ties. Do what good one could elsewhere. But first he meant to make peace with his old associate. There was a danger that Latour – a gossip and intriguer – might report some explosive comments which

Sauvigny had made to his face on learning of his and Belcastel's latest project. Sauvigny now regretted these, since, if they were repeated to Belcastel – whose conscience was a good deal tenderer than Latour's – he would be painfully flayed by remorse. Poor, delicate-minded old B! 'I must reassure him,' Sauvigny decided, 'grant him my absolution, set his mind at rest. And I'll take the opportunity, while I'm at the *maison de santé*, to say a few wise words to Danièle.' Maybe, he thought in a flush of optimism, he might persuade her to leave France for Belgium, a less frivolous and happier country whose Catholics had known how to keep the population on their side and hold on to power. If she was so eager to be a nurse in a madhouse, why not go to the one set up to humour the troubled brain of its only inmate, the deposed Empress Charlotte of Mexico? Surely there must be a dearth of attendants capable of pretending the place was a royal court? There Danièle would be with her own kind, and King Leopold, as Charlotte's brother, could arrange the thing in a trice. Such a move would be honourable and edifying. After all, many well-born saints had in the past chosen to nurse lepers. Madness could well be the new leprosy. Danièle might have received a higher call.

Sauvigny planned to make this point forcefully when he saw his niece.

Meanwhile, he had to argue no less forcefully with the doubts that crept into his mind each time he thought of the lunatic's letter in his waistcoat pocket.

Shortly before he boarded the train for Paris, a friend showed him a more cheerful and very different sort of letter. This one was from a prelate who had travelled to Rome to find out how those who mattered there felt about the pope's policies towards France.

> *Many cardinals,* claimed this prelate, *think as we do and are horrified. Their outspokenness is surprising. There is a boldness in the air just now which is both very Italian and typical of the end of a regime. Leo XIII is healthy but bloodless. One thinks of a lamp running out of oil ... The real disaster is 'the African' (Cardinal L.). Some Romans claim he has hypnotized the pope. What would people say, after all, if the next pope were to force Catholics to become royalists? Anyway, good lord, what business is it of any pope's to dictate our politics?*

As Sauvigny sat in the train, these questions thumped through his head. One shake of the kaleidoscope could change everything: the death of an old man. Pope Leo was eighty-two. Maybe, after all, Sauvigny should open his heart to Belcastel who, in many ways, must be in the same boat as himself? The tide, he could remind him, might be about to turn.

***

The bog must have eyes, ears and feelers, not to mention mouths, for the cousins already knew about Adam's meeting Kate! How? Through whom? A talking sheep? Adam was almost certain that nobody had seen them together. Never mind! Never mind how people knew things. The point was that he needed to know them too.

'Yer ma wouldn't like ya hobnobbing with her!'

'Why?'

'Don't pretend, Adam. You must know yer da means to marry her. He's set on doing it, and yer ma's desperate. She's got herself pregnant a second time so as to try to force his hand. Get the priests on her side. The English girl's a Catholic, you see, so they might be able to stop the marriage. Father Tobin's been trying to do that, but it'll take more than him. He's not in with the powers that be.'

'So they're not married? My parents.'

'Ellen and yer da? Jesus, Adam, are ye that green? Hey, listen to this, lads: Adam here didn't know he was born on the wrong side of the blanket.'

'Ah, will yiz shut yer gobs and leave the poor bugger alone!'

Amazingly, the cousins were sorry for him. Unmanned by this, Adam had to bite his tongue to keep from crying, and, just as he heard them say that blood was thicker than water, tasted his own.

'Don't take it so hard.' Owen-or-Dinny punched him lightly in the chest. Now that Adam had been taken down, not one but several pegs, they were rallying to him who was, they reminded him, 'one of ourselves'.

God forbid, he raged haughtily. But need overrode pride and, listening to their jabber with a new attentiveness, he began to get some things clear. One was that Owen-or-Dinny had not two names, but three. He was Owen-Dinny-Dan, meaning Owen son of Dinny, son of Dan, because what was the use of calling yourself Owen Gould if half the neighbourhood had the very same name?

'Sure we all come wan way or another from the wrong side of the blanket,' said Owen, making no bones about this. And went on to explain that '*that* had been goin' on a long time.'

'What?'

Goulds from the big house sleeping with girls – 'and not

only girls!'– from the tenements. Bastards being defiantly recognized (by fathers), foisted (by mothers) on unsuspecting spouses or (by both) stealthily farmed out. Comings and goings. Inbreeding. Face-saving. False entries made in parish records so that nobody knew who was kin to whom. Brothers, affirmed Owen, had been known to marry their half-sisters, because those who knew what was happening lacked the nerve to tell the priests.

'You couldn't tell a priest a thing like that! So people made their own arrangements.'

'That's why there was likely no real impediment to yer da marrying yer ma. She may be his cousin twice over in the flesh but if she's not one on paper, the story of waiting for a dispensation could be all my eye. How – or why – would anyone explain the like of that to a canon lawyer beyond in Rome?'

'Bat, you have it wrong. It *was* on paper. Ellen said so.'

'The word was made flesh!'

' It's what held them up.'

'Did she, personally, check the parish records?'

'Listen ...'

'No, you listen!'

Two cousins started to pummel each other and were separated with some violence by Owen-Dinny-Dan who wanted to get things straight.

'If the gee-gees had still been making money, he'd a married her like a shot. He was mad for her at the start. First cousin or not!'

'Ellen was a lovely girl.'

'Still is.'

'Ah, but the iron has to be hit while it's hot! She's afraid he'll want to emigrate her to Canada now. A clean break.'

'Maybe he will.'

'I'm not so sure. That English girl is terrible plain. What if he picked a plain girl to make it easier to get Ellen to stay and accept some new arrangement?'

'What sort of arrangement?'

'Who knows? Foxy as he is, he'll want to have his cake and eat it too. Two cakes if he's let.'

'Get away! Two on the one plate!'

'Well, there's Father Tobin gone to visit his mother. He never did that before. I wonder does he have a mother at all?'

'There's more going on than meets the eye.'

'And some are hoping others will turn a blind one!'

'Ellen won't!'

'Not yet!'

'Maybe never.'

'No. Ellen's proud. The Lord between us and all harm, but she could easily do something dangerous!'

'Listen, Adam,' said a thoughtful Owen-Dinny-Dan, 'yer ma's already half out of her mind. When she hears that you and that English filly have been conniving she'll be convinced that yer da plans to keep you here after emigrating her – which could be true. I wouldn't put it past him to have sent the girl here today so as to encourage the pair of you to get friendly. Anyway, true or not, the danger is that Ellen will think it is. Just now she'll be imagining the worst. Didn't the girl say she asked one of the grooms how to find you? So by now the stables know, and that means the kitchen does, and how long can it be before yer ma hears it? So you'd best have a word with her at the hunt tomorrow. Soothe her down! Tell her you love her. Promise whatever she wants. Don't worry. She'll be there all right. Timmy who brought yer pony over said she would. She gave orders to get her mare ready.'

***

At an alarmingly early hour Dr Blanche came to the monsignor's room and woke him to a dawn slashed by gleams as half-hearted as the shine on a scuttleful of coal.

'Forgive the intrusion.' Closing the door, Blanche struck a match and lit a candle.

Odd, thought Belcastel, not to have lit it before coming down the dark corridor. 'Something's the matter, isn't it?' He was anxiously alert.

The doctor's tone was brisk. 'I had to see you before Adam did. It's to do with Maupassant. Adam offered him poison.'

'Ah!' The monsignor who, though warned by Tassart, had failed to prevent this, felt more guilt than surprise.

'Things could be worse,' Blanche admitted. 'The poison was spilled, though no thanks to Adam. However, there is likely to be gossip, so I am advising him to leave for Ireland, and hope you will support me. Later, he can either come back here or join you elsewhere, but for now he should be off the scene. My fear is that he may resist us. Hang around, draw reporters on himself. Lurk in some *louche* hotel.'

'Because of ...?'

'Her.' The doctor's shrug – it was more like a spasm – expressed weariness tempered by resolve.

Ah, thought Belcastel again, and burned as though the

indiscretion had been wholly his. They've guessed it, he saw! Got the scent and run it to ground! Love. Eros! The smell of musk. He – having sniffed it before they did – should have acted. Becoming eunuchs for the love of God was meant to make it easy for clerics to regulate other people's conduct. His trouble was that carnal folly interested him about as much as tiddliwinks. But what if it were one's duty to focus one's mind on tiddliwinks? He told the doctor, 'I am sorry I encouraged you to employ Madame d'Armaillé.'

Blanche did not pretend to misunderstand. 'We have both been careless.'

The monsignor wondered whether his own guilt was misplaced. Maybe he should feel it instead over his failure to spring to the defence of his young protégé whose actions, after all, had clearly been motivated by a misguided charity. He suspected Adam of having lost his religious faith, which meant that he was adrift without rules. So, being sorry for poor, mad Guy, he had tried to succour him. He, Guy and Madame d'Armaillé needed some sober person's help and protection. They needed a good Samaritan, but, dear lord, thought Belcastel, *that* role had never been easy. The priest who shirked it in the parable might have had other obligations – and so did he whose first duty was neither to lunatics nor lovers but to his superiors who had a right to expect him to steer clear of scandal. After all, the last time he stuck his neck out he ended up in here. Belonging, as he did, to a spiritual army, he could not risk being cashiered a second time.

Nonetheless he put in a plea for leniency. 'Adam', he argued, 'will be leaving with me soon. Couldn't he stay here till then? We could both keep an eye on him.'

But Blanche too had an institution to consider. 'I'm afraid he must leave now, before the press comes nosing round. The thing could too easily be misrepresented.' What had actually happened, he explained, was that the patient had again begged to be helped to die, whereupon Adam, who was in a susceptible state – 'One forgets how young he is!' – brought him an overdose of opium. No sooner had he done so, however, than the lunatic started to rave that Adam was his other self and must drink the poison. He then thrust it so fiercely at Adam's mouth that the mug cut his lip. In the scuffle a table fell, and a brass vase went bouncing. This, said Blanche, was a piece of luck, for he, who had been patrolling the corridors, as he sometimes did when suffering from insomnia, heard it and rushed in. On tasting the spilled dregs, he guessed what had happened and made Adam confirm his guess. Baron, who arrived close on his heels, must have guessed too.

'Will he talk?'

The doctor's face lengthened as flesh sank, like molten wax, to collect along his jaw. 'If we keep our nerve, that needn't matter. My colleagues, though displeased, will hold their tongues.' In the grey light, the stubble on his cheeks was the colour of ash. 'A scandal,' he pointed out, 'would do none of us any good, so I told Adam that I want him gone before others hear what happened. He has agreed and is now with Madame d'Armaillé. I had to let them have a moment together. I imagine you'll want a word with him too?'

Neurologist and priest exchanged nods. Both were used to soothing vehement frets.

'He is a good young man,' the doctor acknowledged. 'I

believe you offered him a position? So, once this blows over
...' His hands levitated hopefully.

'I shall still want his collaboration.'

'And for now? Perhaps you could advocate prudence?'

'I shall write him a letter,' decided the monsignor. 'In the
state he is likely to be in, he wouldn't get the hang of anything
not laid down in black and white.'

Blanche left, and Belcastel, still in his dressing-gown, sat at
his desk, laid blank sheets of paper on the blotter and stared
at the mean mouth of the irreversible inkwell. It struck him
that his own passions were as good as atrophied. For a man
about to return to the world in the hope of wielding influence
in it, this was a handicap. His whole training was a handicap.
It had led him to avoid the kind of feelings he now needed to
address – sudden, giddy ones of a sort that could unforesee-
ably affect conduct. He had had no truck with those. The story
peddled by his enemies was false. On the night of the château
fire, he had not been in a lady's bedroom. On the contrary, he
had been in her husband's adjacent one, ensuring that papers
which could compromise their group were put back in their
box. Tact was second nature to him. He disliked sensational-
ism and feared that, like a huntsman who has no feel for his
quarry, he might, when he began to run a newspaper, be unable
to catch his readers' interest, much less persuade them to do
an emotional about-turn. A pity, perhaps, that the burn on his
cheek had not been incurred during some gallant frolic? But
just as well if rumour led the impressionable to take him for a
bird of their own feather.

The thought returned him to Adam, who was so good with
the mad and whose impulsive sympathies he had hoped to

enlist. How long, he wondered, would the boy be in Ireland? His leaving was badly timed.

Adam, to be sure, claimed that, far from being impulsive, his method with the mad was as coolly controlled as the bird calls by which he sometimes entertained the monsignor during their walks. Imitating these was a skill, he had explained, a trick learned in boyhood. 'You intrigue them, so they think you're one of their sort and come close enough to be caught. We'll do the same thing with our readers.'

'Do you,' Belcastel had asked suspiciously, 'do it with me?'

Adam hadn't hesitated: 'Oh, I do it with everyone. You see, I haven't really lived much for a man my age and I have no trade. So I try out personae. Maybe journalism will suit me and I'll settle. My father was a great man for politics and wrangling.'

'*We* are to avoid both.'

Their prospective paper would be pledged to promote unity and have no party affiliations. This was Father de Latour's plan. Yet established Catholic journals had already taken umbrage at the news that a new one was even deemed necessary. A circular to the bishops of France aimed at raising funds had been promptly leaked. Episcopal palaces were sieves. Vanities had been hurt. Latour's decision not to employ men compromised by old polemics had raised hackles. Preaching unity to *them* would not be easy. And, as more than one bishop had already warned, moderation did not attract readers.

Glumly, the monsignor's eyes slid to a stack of papers whose warring words he had underlined in blue ink for Republicans and purple for monarchists. *La Gazette de France*, *L'Observateur français*, *La Croix*, *L'Univers*, *Le Monde* and *Le Gaulois* bled like beetroot salad and pumped out bloated phrases such as

'Both our Christian conscience and our honour as journalists oblige us to say' or 'We would rather break our pens than fail in our duty to tell ...' And what they said and told was always very sour.

He had been taken aback by their delirium. Hatred of the Republic to which *he* must persuade readers to rally was bred in the bone. Heartened by its troubles – anarchist bombs and so forth – conservatives argued that, since it was on the brink of collapse, rallying to it would be folly. Anyway, they hinted, the present pope must surely die soon. All we need do was sit tight and wait for one or both of these events to save us. *L'Autorité*'s latest blast, occasioned by the Panama scandal, described the French state as a 'foul, swollen carcass' which 'had left its stink on the banks of the current which was now carrying it off'. Readers with a taste for such abuse would need to be frightened, even threatened and, only when thoroughly softened up, gently cajoled into considering their opponents' arguments.

Belcastel was planning a feature to be called – provisionally – *Bogies and Bugbears*, aimed at softening rigid views on topics such as divine right. This, he would boldly tell readers, was no more nor less than the mark of divine approval attaching to *any* legitimate authority.

Could minds be changed, or were hearts more responsive? When doctrine failed, could these guide our sympathies? The monsignor was tempted to hope so, for his own shrivelled feelings had proven unexpectedly susceptible to the contagion of another man's fervour. Adam had actually led him to admire writings by Maupassant, which he had expected to loathe. If this could happen to him, might not readers, who must surely be tiring of the old papers' diet of spleen, be weaned from it?

France, as Pope Leo hoped, might be the happier.

***

The meet was closer to his cousins' place than to his father's, so Adam was able to get there early, then stay out of his father's sight. He couldn't bear to confront him and, anyway, needed to see his mother first. However, there was no sign of her, so he hung back when the hunt moved off and soon found himself with a group of stragglers who had backed away from an intimidating jump and were looking for a gap. Seeing Kate among them, he opened a gate for her, waited for her to ride through and tried to avoid conversation. She caught him, though, as he was securing the hasp.

'Adam, I want you to know I'm not your enemy. I'm telling you this because it looks as though things may work out after all between me and your father. I spoke to him last night, and ...'

'Kate, I don't want to hear what he said. I can imagine it, anyway.'

'Can you? He swears that what you denied yesterday is true.'

What had he denied? He couldn't remember having been sure enough to deny anything. He said, 'I don't want to talk. Enjoy your ride.'

As he turned to ride off, he heard her voice behind him. 'Adam, just remember: I want us to be friends.' At the same moment he found himself within a yard of his mother who had clearly heard too and looked stunned. He saw her hand tighten on her reins.

'Mama, wait. Please. I've something to tell you.'

She had gone white and her lips were clamped firmly shut.

'Mama!'

Perhaps she couldn't trust herself to unclamp them, for she didn't answer his greeting, much less ask why he was here. Instead, she took off at a gallop, jumped two fences and disappeared over the brow of a hill in the wake of the main body of riders. Guessing that she would join his father, he decided not to follow.

It was the last time he saw her alive.

***

Belcastel dipped his pen and wrote very fast:

Fili mi,
I am not writing as a priest, but as a friend, so shall stick to things temporal. You will surely know that it is affection which leads me to warn that you are on the verge of scuppering our plans and your future.

Since you must be in distress, I am putting a few thoughts down as clearly as I can. There is unlikely to be time to convey them to you any other way. The first is this: don't brood or blame yourself too much!

What has happened with poor Monsieur de Maupassant is regrettable but, after all, no harm was done since he is no worse off than before and a scandal can be avoided if you will only take the director's advice and leave at once for Ireland. You will recall that I have always urged you to make peace with your father. Well, now there is a further reason for going. You are kind-hearted with others. Why not with him?

Your place on The Rallying Cry *will be waiting for you. So start thinking up clever ideas for it. Working together, we will each have a chance to make up for earlier errors – mine were more culpable than yours! – and to redeem ourselves by doing good. There will be time later to discuss all this. I only want for now to remind you that you have a worthwhile future.*

Allow me, meanwhile, to say that your impulse in trying to help the unfortunate Maupassant shows a generous nature and a lack of cool thought. You felt you had made a promise and had to keep it. Since you must by now see the rashness of this, I shan't dwell on it. Instead I beg of you to make no promises at all for the next few months. Do not bind yourself or anyone else. That is all I ask. Is it too much?

Dipping his pen back into his inkwell, Belcastel delicately shook off superfluous drops, held it poised, decided against mentioning Madame d'Armaillé, then signed off with a blessing and a flourish.

Having sealed his letter, he quickly wrote another, then rang his bell and summoned two servants to witness his signature. This done, he inquired whether one of them would accompany him downstairs, since it was against the house rules that he go alone, and he didn't want at this late stage of his residence to upset the doctors. Where, by the way, was Monsieur Gould?

He had been seen, said the servants, walking in the *potager*. 'Maybe half an hour ago? With Madame d'Armaillé.' Neither knew where they were now.

'Probably he came in,' one guessed helpfully, 'when it started to rain.'

Rain! Belcastel had failed to notice it, but there it was, slyly licking his windowpanes. What had brought the word 'sly' to mind? Remembering the apple loft with its airborne hammock gave him his answer and, mindful of his duty to prevent further improprieties, he practically raced his 'escort' down the stairs. Midway, they were met by news that the vicomte de Sauvigny had arrived unexpectedly and begged a few moments of the monsignor's time. He was between two trains. Had to turn around and leave in under an hour. He'd asked to talk to his niece too.

'The gentleman's in the morning room,' said the maid who brought the message, 'waiting'.

He wasn't, though.

'Well, he was a minute ago! I left him right here, chatting with Monsieur Tassart.'

'Tassart was here? Are you sure?'

'Oh yes, Monseigneur. He was talking about having noticed Madame d'Armaillé's neckband hanging in the apple loft. It's where he stores his master's tricycle, which is to go into an auction with the poor gentleman's other things. That's what he came for, but now he seems to have done a disappearing act too. I expect he went to the kitchens for coffee.' She looked out of the window. 'Why, there's the vicomte now! In the *potager*! And look! He's out in the rain without an umbrella!'

Belcastel looked and saw Sauvigny striding in the direction of the apple loft. Fat bars of sunshot rain enclosed him! An omen? The monsignor felt a constriction in his chest. Here was a warning that his friend could end up *behind* bars for some intemperate act! The monsignor did not, of course, believe in omens, but recognized this one as a nudge from his conscience, a reminder that, because he had again failed in his custodial duties, the vicomte could be about to discover his niece and Adam *in flagrante delicto*. Belcastel felt his brain heat and his forehead sweat. It sweated so profusely that drops slid into his eyes and stung them. Abruptly, to the maidservant's amazement, he too shot out of the side door and into the rain without either hat or umbrella and, worse still, in his dressing-gown.

By now the vicomte was out of sight.

Slithering in the mud – he was wearing slippers without heels and kept stepping on the sagging hem of his dressing-gown – Belcastel pondered the odds and prayed he was being fanciful. *Were* Adam and Madame d'Armaillé in the loft? Oh dear, it did seem likely. Making love? Likely too. Remembering her confidences about her uncle, he grew increasingly alarmed. How absurd – and dangerous – human behaviour could be! 'Please God,' he begged, while quickening his pace, 'if You avert this danger, I shall never ask You for another thing. Nor mix Your interests up with the pope's which are, I admit, lax, secular and full of compromise! So are the cardinal's. Yes! We have all grown lax. The comte de Chambord was right. The only Catholic king worth having would be an absolute one! His was a noble failure whereas, win or lose, the *ralliement* is likely to be squalid! He was absurd – but absurdity is what defeats the vainglory of the so-called Enlightenment which was just another of Lucifer's meretricious mirages. I renounce it! *Credo quia absurdum est*! Grant me this intention and You can ask me for anything at all! Just make Adam and Danièle not be in the loft!'

Its door when he reached it was open. Inside was Stygian! Black as fur! Blinking into the dark, Belcastel was dazzled by the after-glare of the sunny rain outside, and again felt sweat sting and blind his eyes. He caught a faint smell of fish.

'Vicomte!' he called. 'Sauvigny!' Then, raising his voice: 'Hubert!'

***

Sauvigny heard the shouts but paid no heed.

The news that Danièle's crimson neckband had been seen hanging from a beam in a tricycle or apple shed was the shake to the kaleidoscope which can change everything. His mind had instantly rearranged itself, and its components now spelled out a new message: the demons were not in *him*! They were in the others. There was an impertinent mockery to the neckband's being there which could only mean that she, as women did – just think of the whorish wretch with whom he had dallied in Rome! – had forsaken her old loyalties for some new alliance.

As he sighed, his chest swelled and the paper in his waistcoat pocket crackled. The madness in this madhouse had reached his niece! What else could he think when just now he had walked into the outbuilding and seen, exactly as Tassart had said he would, the glimmering neckband – thinner than his little finger – hanging from a peg on a rafter? It was like an obscene symbol! Deeply offended, he had made straight for the iron ladder, which he would need to climb in order to remove what in his mind was a sacred heirloom and in his niece's, he must now suppose, no more than a love trophy. While looking up at it, he knocked his shin against something – the place was littered with impedimenta – stumbled and, groping for support, caught hold of a dangling rope, jerked it without meaning to, then heard something bang somewhere above his head and found himself in darkness. Guessing that he had accidentally closed the shutter of a skylight, he pulled the rope again, then jiggled it hopefully, only to find it come away in his hand. The thing had broken. A minute or so later he heard Belcastel's shout.

'Sauvigny!! Hubert! Don't go up! It's dangerous in the dark and, anyway, there's nobody there!'

A lie, concluded Sauvigny and, as he had now managed to locate a rung of the iron ladder, quickly began to climb. He was getting used to the dark, could guide himself by the light coming from the open doorway behind him and hoped, besides, to be able to reach the skylight shutter and open it once he was on the platform above. So he ignored the mendacious plead-ing below. Clearly Belcastel had been pimping for his young protégé or anyway closing his eyes to his fornication and now feared that light – literally! – would be thrown on what was going on. Well, one way or another, that was going to happen – though, of course it mustn't! Sauvigny's niece's honour must be protected! *Honour*? Ha! Pulled up short by the sound of his own sour and unintended laugh, Sauvigny found that he had torn the crumpled letter from his waistcoat pocket behind which he had just felt, or imagined he felt a pain in his heart. Clapping his hand to the stricken place, he dropped the paper. Never mind, he thought, then with a tremor of fear: 'Am I fit enough to be going to the Congo?' But maybe the pain was in some unimportant muscle? Hearing a clash of metal below followed by gasps of distress, he guessed that the monsignor had bumped into one of the pieces of domestic machinery that had been visible before the shutter closed. Sauvigny was startled to find himself almost relishing the sounds. Anger, like a rough drink quaffed at one go, left him exhilarated and giddy. It was as if his mind were being shaken again: shaken and shaken so that he could not get his bearings. He felt a thrill of satisfaction at the prospect of catching out the lovers – and at the same time a desolate horror at the pain he knew he would feel once rage had worn off. 'Honour!' he found himself repeating silently. 'Horror!' What did the words mean? The shock to his mind had drained everything of meaning.

Feeling someone seize his foot, he wondered if he was between two dangers: the monsignor below and, possibly, the Irishman above. Was he up there? Silently waiting? Armed perhaps with some sort of club? Surely he wouldn't strike Sauvigny in Danièle's presence? But maybe she wasn't with him?

The door behind banged shut and the dark became total. He couldn't move his foot.

'Let go!' he shouted at Belcastel, but the fool wouldn't and kept exhorting him to come down.

'Please,' he kept maundering. 'Let's talk sensibly! Surely we should be able to do that?' And other blandishments.

Sauvigny wriggled his foot.

'There's nobody up there.'

'Then let go.'

But the grasping hands were now climbing up Sauvigny's leg. Next they clutched his coat, pulling him off balance so that his other foot slipped. He regained purchase on the rung, but, instinctively, as he did so, lurched out with the knee the other man had released and felt a crack of yielding bone which must, he guessed, be his opponent's face. Possibly he had broken his nose? There was a cry followed, as the hands released their grip, by sounds of a fall then a dull collision with something below. Then nothing. The next cry came from the vicomte's own throat.

'For God's sake,' he called. 'Is anyone up there? The monsignor may be injured. Can you let in light?'

Nothing.

Groping his way cautiously – he had glimpsed an unstable-looking scythe earlier – past a wobbling tangle of tools, he climbed down then reached the door. Once propped open, it let in enough light to reveal that the monsignor's head had fallen against the edge of a garden roller and was bleeding. Blood, pouring down his face, hid the gash of his old scar and soaked the quilted silk of his dressing-gown. A large tricycle had rolled almost on top of him. By the time Sauvigny had pulled him clear and found a place to lay him flat, his pulse had stopped. The vicomte, who, in his fighting days, had seen many dead men, was confronting another.

***

It was less than an hour later.

Adam and Sauvigny sat in silence as the hackney cab left the *maison de santé*. Each was amazed to find himself in the other's company, but neither had had a say in the matter. Slanting rain streaked the windows as though repeatedly crossing something out. Both their minds were choked by the knowledge that their silence, though an admission of shame, was impossible to break. Dr Meuriot, limply assisted by a defeated, waxen-faced Blanche, had settled them firmly into the cabriolet, then waved it off.

'To the railway station,' Meuriot told the cabman. 'These gentlemen have trains to catch.' He spoke with authority and in the mild tones of a man who knows he will be obeyed. Having commandeered the vicomte's cab, he had asked the coachman to take both men to the Gare du Nord. Clearly, he couldn't wait to be rid of them and free to start spreading healing lies and Hippocratic balm.

'It is in both your interests,' he had explained.

So here, to their exquisite mortification, they sat avoiding each other's eyes. Neither could think.

'Here still,' was all Adam's frozen mind could manage: 'Here still!'

He wasn't sure what he meant by this nor what he ought to do. Surely it could not be his place to speak first? To do so might even be dangerous. Anyway what was there to say? 'Would you have preferred,' he would have liked to ask the vicomte, 'that the accident had happened to me?' He couldn't ask that. No. But what *could* he ask? What possible words – what bridge? – could be found between the awful thing that had happened and their joint flight in a hackney cab? In normal circumstances the proper words would be: 'Poor Belcastel! He was a good man. May he rest in peace!' And so forth. *Lux perpetua luceat ei*! Amen. But if circumstances had been normal, Belcastel would be alive. Poor, affable Belcastel! He *had* been a good man! And if there was to be an eternal light, it would surely shine for and on him. Adam wished he could scream. Was it my fault, he wondered. How *much* my fault? Then his mind froze again. Maybe it was as well to let it freeze? He had begged to be let stay for the funeral, but the doctors wouldn't hear of it, and neither would Danièle. Danièle ... Slowly, like invisible ink yielding up secrets, the confused words which had just now flashed through his head yielded a melancholy meaning. 'Here still' meant that he was still near – fairly near – her but might not be again! Dr Meuriot wouldn't have him back, and even if it did come into being, the newspaper would close its doors to him. Would she? If he came back? Things had moved so fast at the end that the promises they had exchanged earlier this morning might no longer count.

At the last minute, when the vicomte and those taking leave of him had already gone out to the carriage, Meuriot had drawn Adam into a small cloakroom smelling of oilskins and galoshes. 'The police,' he warned quietly, 'may not think that the monsignor's death was accidental. If they open an inquiry, they will want to talk to you.'

'Me?'

'Oh, I know you were with the director when it happened.' Meuriot's tone consigned Blanche to the category of the unreliable, too vague or possibly complicit to supply an alibi. 'But this was found near the body. Read it.' Adam read and learned that he had been accused of corrupting Danièle and planning to murder Guy. The unsigned letter was addressed to the vicomte. 'Naturally,' murmured the doctor, 'I shall destroy it, but whoever wrote it may write again. And any rumours that get about will make for appalling publicity. Remember the trouble we had with the press over the unfortunate Maupassant? Well, this could be ten times worse.'

Who could have written such a letter? Adam couldn't remember antagonizing anyone – except perhaps the vicomte. But the vicomte could hardly have written a letter to himself. He must have read it, though, and this made sitting in this carriage with him excruciatingly uncomfortable. Did he believe the accusations? Why did he not say something? Adam's fists were so tightly clenched that his nails were piercing his palms.

On leaving the rue Berton, the cab clattered along the quai

de Passy, and with every hoofbeat, the gagging silence grew more unnatural. Anxiety sharpened Adam's faculties, and, as worries began to prick and stab, like ice fragments, through the cold mud of his mind, he saw that, even at the cost of disregarding etiquette and possibly his own physical safety, he, the junior man, was going to have to speak first. He *must* find out what Sauvigny had made of the letter and what advice he was likely to give Danièle.

They were now crossing the river whose pallor glimmered like the track of an enormous snail. Ahead lay the short drive across Paris to the Gare du Nord where they would begin their separate journeys to Ireland and the Congo. There wasn't much time.

Adam reviewed his recollection of what had been said on Dr Meuriot's return to the library with Sauvigny in tow. The two had by then been back and forth to the loft from which two *gardiens* had meanwhile removed Belcastel's body.

Dr Blanche had left these arrangements to his colleague. He was propped up by cushions, on the library divan, recuperating from the shock of learning that the status quo which he had managed to restore after Adam's scrape was now threatened by something worse. How much worse, he asked. What exactly had happened? He addressed his questions to the vicomte, but it was Dr Meuriot who replied.

'An accident,' he interjected curtly, when Sauvigny tried to describe the new mishap. When he tried again, Meuriot cut him short. 'Vicomte, with respect, I beg you to hear me out before you speak. We are, after all, discussing my patient.'

As if poor Monseigneur de Belcastel – by then lying under

a sheet in the morning room – were alive and suffering from some faintly disreputable malaise!

Sauvigny, perhaps from military instinct, let Meuriot pull rank, and Dr Blanche did not protest. He had spent his last energies on Adam, with whom, not long before, he had been *en tête à tête*, when Meuriot walked in, accused them of sweeping something under the carpet, and demanded to know what it was. There had been nothing for it then but to give him a sanitized account of the fracas with Guy in which the opium was not an overdose but an appropriate quantity which had been prescribed by Blanche. Meuriot accepted these mitigating points, but Adam saw that the real significance of the exchange was that Blanche felt obliged to provide them. Meuriot had taken over.

It was no surprise then, that, when news came of the monsignor's accident, Blanche could not cope. He closed his eyes, and his face crumpled. Quite suddenly he had to lie down.

By contrast Meuriot, when he returned, looked forceful. He presented a persuasive version of events. Belcastel had been responsible for accidentally closing the shutter; he had stepped on his own dressing-gown as he climbed the ladder – there was a tear to prove it – had lost his footing and had fallen against the garden roller. He had been alone. Two questions remained to be settled: why had he gone there at all and how had the vicomte come to find him?

Meuriot's jowls shook impressively as his large, authoritative head, amplified by a vigorous growth of grey side-whiskers, slewed about. 'You,' he eyed the vicomte, 'were no doubt looking for him? The maidservant, who says he followed you outside, must have got things wrong. She is a young featherhead and quite undependable. *You* followed *him, n'est-ce pas?*'

'I ...'

'And found him dead. In the dark? You had come here, I am told, "between two trains", precisely to see him? So you were in a hurry and when you saw him making for the loft, you followed him. It is perfectly logical. Nobody is to blame. It was, as I said, an unhappy accident – especially so as the poor, dear man was cured and due to leave us in a day or so.'

Blanche, Adam and Sauvigny were silent. Each may have been waiting to see if one of the others would speak. Then the moment for speaking passed.

Meuriot nodded. 'The other question remains. Why did the monsignor go to the loft in the first place? Mmm? Someone must have an idea.' Waiting, he sighed irritably. This time silence wouldn't do.

To his own surprise, Adam heard himself say, 'He sometimes went there to read his breviary. He liked to lie in the hammock. It was a place to be alone.' This was almost true. The monsignor had, after all, gone there once.

'In the rain? In his dressing-gown?'

'Perhaps he had left the breviary there and was anxious about it? It was a gift from the comte de Chambord and very precious to him.' This was an outright improvisation.

Again Meuriot nodded. He looked relieved.

Adam had spoken from habit. Fixing things was what he had done as Dr Blanche's factotum and right-hand man. The question remained though: what had really happened? Better perhaps not to know. Monseigneur de Belcastel would not have liked a scandal.

A milk dray was holding up the hackney cab. Looking out, Adam saw that they were nearing the station. They could be there in five minutes. The silence felt like metal, like stone. He *must* break through it. 'Well,' he managed to say, 'between us we averted a scandal! It was the least we could do for poor Monseigneur de Belcastel.'

The vicomte sighed.

Dazed, Adam decided. Not angry: dazed. Hoping to rouse him gently, he sighed too. It was the pitch of the voice, he had found with inmates, which mattered most. 'Don't worry,' he cajoled soothingly, then, more soothingly still: 'I know that it's hard. I myself sometimes worry that I bring bad luck to people I care for. It's like a fate.'

This, it struck him, might not be a wise thing to say if he wanted the vicomte to consent to his friendship with his niece. Not that the vicomte was listening. His hand moved. It had pulled something from an inner pocket. It was Danièle's crimson neckband. Sauvigny dangled it on his forefinger.

'Oh dear,' thought Adam. '*Zut!*'

'I took it,' the vicomte told him, 'when I went back in. From the nail on the rafter. I couldn't leave it there.'

'You know how it got there,' Adam was inspired to lie. 'Madame d'Armaillé gave it to the monsignor after he persuaded her to trust His Holiness. As a token of her trust.'

Sauvigny screwed up his eyes and held the red circle so that it caught the sunlight that was now breaking through the rain.

'I thought you'd like to know,' said Adam. 'You see, he and she were in the garden one day when the rain came on, so they took shelter in the loft. He had been telling her about the pope's hope that all Frenchmen could be at peace. So, as the neckband was a memory of the guillotine ...'

'A memory of our relatives' martyrdom.'

'And an incitement to revenge ...'

'Did he say that?'

'He said that making a cult of the wrongs done to us bred pugnacity and self-righteousness. His mind was full of the topic. You see, he was preparing to write some articles ...'

'... for his newspaper?' The vicomte nodded knowingly. 'I heard about that.'

'Well, it seems he was persuasive. So Madame d'Armaillé took off her neckband and ...'

'Ah,' said the vicomte, 'I see! I see! You have set my mind at rest. I knew I shouldn't pay the least attention to that base, disgusting letter.'

Adam pretended not to hear this. Instead, he went on talking about the dead man and, quite soon, both he and the vicomte were obliged to take out their handkerchiefs and flick away tears.

'It *was* an accident,' Sauvigny said abruptly. 'Not planned. Not controlled. An accident. And of course it happened in the dark.'

'Yes.'

'We always thought we should control everything. It was why we wanted the king – and indeed the king pope, *il papa re*. But, well, there you are, everything ended in a muddle, and now we have a new, treacherous pope, so it's just as well that he's *not* a king, but is penned up like a lion in a zoo in his little toy leonine city, ha. That's its name, did you know? And he's

Leo! I shouldn't laugh. It's a shame that poor Belcastel died violently. He was a man of peace.'

'Yes.'

'Well, I'm glad anyway that I learned the truth.'

'Yes.'

'I wish,' said the now garrulous vicomte, 'you weren't leaving. Poor Danièle will need a friend.'

Neither man believed that he had been lied to, and each knew that his own lies had been benevolent. When they parted at the station, they embraced.

VIII

While watching the vicomte's train steam from the station, Adam realized that he was free to miss his own. This thought so compelled him that, by the time the engine smoke dispersed, he had found the *consigne*, dropped off his bag and headed for the post office where he composed a telegram urging Danièle to send a reply care of Thady Quill.

Remembering Dr Meuriot's warnings against lingering in France upset him briefly and he spoiled two telegraph forms. But seeing his message set out on official paper put him in good heart.

Some things were not yet out of his hands!

He would stay at Quill's. She could meet him there or, if the place was distasteful to her, in a tearoom. Perhaps in the Bois? She could wear a hat with a veil thick as a bee-keeper's, and who would know her? He imagined her muslin frock – green and pink – flowering under it. They could go where they liked, even boating on the river as Guy used to do – though it was now too cold for that.

Was his idea reckless?

By striking down Belcastel, death had made lesser risks look puny. Poor troubled Belcastel! Wincing, Adam crumpled the form, nibbled a hangnail and stared, for an unseeing moment, at a blotting-pad where traces of past urgencies cringed in mirror-image. Then he picked up the scratchy, post-office pen, rewrote his message – practice was improving it – and sent it off. If he and Danièle were to have a future, they must meet. Talk. Make plans! There was no need to leave today. There would be later trains. There would be trains next week!

He had some cash: his salary and a small amount belonging to the dead monsignor who would not have begrudged its use. It would do for now. He set off on foot for Thady Quill's.

His step was buoyant and the air fresh. Street vendors were selling hot buckwheat pancakes and roasted chestnuts, and on a poster a red-gowned woman danced. Capering in parody, a bearded beggar raised imaginary petticoats, and for seconds was a woman too. Laughing, a real woman threw coins into his cap. Paris had never seemed so pleasingly protean! Adam, as he told Thady, whom he found mouldering drearily in his shop, felt as though he had emerged from a cocoon. It was maddening to have to leave, but he kept quiet about why he must. Thady – a gossip! – had best be given an edited account of his plight.

'Arrah go on!' was Thady's puzzled response to this shifty rigmarole, followed by: 'Breaking outa your cocoon is what you shoulda done years ago!'

Thady's mood was fractious. His wife had scolded him in front of two of their employees, so to punish her he felt obliged to punish himself by refusing the lunch she had prepared as a peace-offering. No self-respecting husband could afford to be won over by a dish, however tasty, of *blanquette de veau*! Thady was proud of his wife who was shrewd, personable and worked hard. But in any partnership showing weakness was unwise. The upshot was that Adam too had to forgo the *blanquette de veau* and eat with Thady in a greasy *gargote* smelling of reboiled soup. The bench they sat on was bolted to the floor, so they had to stand up when other clients needed to squeeze past. There was a dead fly in the water-jug and the cloth had gravy stains.

When they were finally settled in front of a litre of *gros bleu* and wedges of greyish bread, Adam asked what had started the conjugal tiff.

'Nothing. Next to nothing! But that,' said the didactic Thady, 'means everything, as you'd know yourself if you'd ever lived with anyone. Ah, but sure you're the nestling that fell from the nest too soon to learn about families. Any news of your old man?'

'He's dying.'

'Ah God, Adam, I'm sorry to hear that.'

Adam burst into tears. It was a nervous reaction. Mechanical. He had felt nothing until he saw Thady's sympathy. Now he felt deceitful.

'Ah Jesus! And he's only how old? Fifty-five, is it now? Did you say he had a wasting disease? Ah God love him!'

The good side of Thady's gossipiness was the interest he took in other people. 'So that's why you're off to Ireland! I was wondering. Well, you're doing the right thing! You'll be a comfort to him now, and knowing that will be a comfort to you later. You're like all the Irish! Good-hearted! All soul! Warm!'

Adam didn't argue. He guessed that the ulterior aim of

this praise was to set up a contrast between high-hearted Irish dash and the narrow views of Thady's French wife. In the war museum of Thady's mind, Adam – like one of the tailor's dummies in Thady's shop – was no doubt at this moment wearing a heroic and slightly battleworn uniform. Madame Thady, if represented in this same imagined space, would be wearing blinkers.

'She's a valiant woman,' Thady acknowledged. 'But unforgiving.' He ordered two glasses of *marc* and, after downing one, was moved to claim that we Irish, due to our long acquaintance with grief, had achieved a spiritual development rarely found in others. As our bodies suffered, so our souls had thrived. Ergo, he argued, while absent-mindedly sipping Adam's *marc*, we were less attached to property than the money-grubbing French, and wouldn't kick up a huge fuss when someone made a small mistake and maybe lost a little family money. Despondently, he emptied the glass and stared at the wall.

Adam didn't ask what mistake Thady had made, but was led by some injured muttering to connect it with a consignment of carefully mended dress uniforms which had not been rendered proof against moths. Had the oversight been Thady's? The topic, clearly, was best left unprobed.

'Look at you,' Thady enthused sadly, 'rushing to forgive your old man who, there's no denying it, made a right balls of his and your affairs. The French say you can't please the goat and the cabbage, but *he* did neither. If we say *you* were the goat – no disrespect intended – and his estate was the cabbage-patch, well ...' Thady's quick-snipping tailor's fingers mimed havoc. The goat had not been let near the cabbages. Yet where were they? His fingers sank limply, abandoning their mime.

'You mean there's nothing left?' Adam had had hints in letters from Ireland that he might be his father's heir. Heir to what, though? Debts? A thankless duty to come and maybe – oh God! – take responsibility for the widow? 'How bad is it? Have you heard?'

Thady either hadn't heard or wouldn't say. But what, he challenged, sticking to his theme, did money matter when in the long run we'd all be dead? Charity, not blame, was the mortar that kept things together. A man like Adam's father needed it more than most. 'He'll blame himself,' said Thady. 'He'll be haunted at the end! But you'll be there to comfort him and redeem the past!'

Fortified by another – then another – *marc*, he gloated grandly over Irish high-mindedness and so praised Adam's good heart that Adam, who had not drunk at all, was fired by this vociferous approval.

It struck him, though, that Thady, being used to promoting moth-eaten goods, might be a poor judge of affection, and he began to pity his father, who perhaps deserved better than Adam had it in him to provide. He would have *liked* to love his defeated old progenitor but, remembering his trouble with Guy, feared unmanageable pity, and to cool things, reminded Thady that to err was human and to forgive divine.

'I'm not a god yet.'

Thady grew worried. 'You don't hate him!'

'My father? No, no!'

'And will help him die in peace?'

'I will. Of course! If what he wants is a ceremonial absolution, he shall have it! "*Absolvo te*, Papa! Die in peace."'

Adam tried to say all this lightly. In his mind he hedged

his promise between quotation marks and, like a man holding a bucket of burning pitch, did his best to keep its brimming heat at arm's length. Touched, though, by Thady's sentiment, he secretly melted.

After all, he saw he could do for his unhappy papa what nobody had been able to do for Belcastel. One should seize such opportunities.

And yet ...

Maybe he did hate him? Hatred was a horrid affliction. But could you have love without it? It was easy for Thady to talk about 'redeeming the past'. That, in Adam's mind, revolved around his mother.

***

After her accident, he had been so numbed by the rush of events that what he remembered later was fitful and overlaid by hearsay. One exception was his memory of how, at dinner that evening in Dr Keogh's house, his vision had become distorted. It had not been like – or did not feel like – going blind.

'You'd best stay with my family tonight,' the doctor had insisted after twice seeing Adam turn his back on his father and refuse to speak to him. Adam had then rushed from the cabin and, a few discreet minutes later, Keogh came out after him and led him a little way off to make sure that they were not overheard. He was their family doctor, a robust, big-bummed, generously built, hunting man who had been out with the field that morning and was still in his riding boots. He had sons of his own. 'I'll drop you off at my place,' he decided, 'then come back here and explain to your pa where you are. It will be better to do that when you're out of the way. Give you both a chance to simmer down. Wait a minute now, while I go back in and attend to a few things. I'll meet you by my carriage.'

The doctor returned to the cabin where women were starting to lay out Adam's mother's body.

Earlier Adam had heard one of them ask, 'Are they not taking her home?'

'Careful, Bríd!' another whispered. 'Little pitchers! But no! Mr G. said no. *He* wants the corpse to stay here!'

'Are you quite …?'

'Amn't I telling you?'

After that the voices sank and Adam heard no more. But when his father returned and tried to talk to him, he turned away. His father had been shuttling back and forth between the cabin and outside where a few carriages were drawn up. There wasn't room for any more people in the cabin. And perhaps some were afraid to intrude. The English guests might be, in any case. Some of the servants from home had been fetched, then Adam's father had ridden off to get a priest and again to make who knew what arrangements.

Adam didn't want to know. 'Bundling her into the ground', he thought furiously. 'Keeping her out of the house even now!' He felt something stony inside him and revelled in his anger, sensing that, once it passed, what followed would be unbearable. He had trouble catching his breath.

He prayed, 'Let her not be dead.' But had little hope, since God, though not bound by time, was unlikely to reverse things for those who were. Then: 'Let her not have done it to herself.'

That prayer, since nobody knew whether she had or not, felt

more hopeful, so he kept repeating it until the words meant nothing. They formed a kind of rope, though. 'Not, not, not ...' he repeated and felt the words change to 'knot, knot' as though he were threatened by a hurricane and the rope held him. He was still murmuring them when Dr Keogh appeared with his whiskey flask and persuaded him to swallow some to steady his nerves.

'Ready then? Shall we go?'

'Yes.'

The doctor drove at a smart trot to his own house by pony and trap. Dinner, when they got there, was already being served and a place was quickly set for Adam.

'I'll be back,' the doctor told his family, 'before you finish your fish.' And left Adam to explain. But Adam was past explaining anything.

The fish was pink salmon served with a green cucumber sauce on blue-rimmed plates. But when Adam looked at his portion what he saw was a swirl without contours or consistency: a blur. He was dry-eyed, so this was odd. He kept staring, but what he saw didn't change. The colours coiled and merged like pigments on a wet palette. Looking up, he half expected the room too to have dissolved. But no. There it all still was: chairs which were still load-bearing and still chairs, the doctor's live wife ladling out sauce to family members who remained solidly intact, with their blood neatly packed inside their skin. They ate quietly, and spoke in lowered tones from respect for Adam's loss. Only what was on his own plate swam smearily like the design on a spinning top. By an act of will, he focused on the smear until he had made it separate into its components, then, as these again began to mingle, forced them apart once more. He was reminded of stained-glass reflections and of vomit. Trying to focus stopped him dwelling on what had taken place when the doctor came out of the cabin for the second time and led the way to his carriage.

Then, too, Adam had been dazed and half-blind and had kept wanting to go back in to have a close look at his dead mother. Because of lagging behind the rest of the hunt, he had heard the news early, had been among the first to reach the cabin and had seen what now haunted him: her half-bare body when they used the tailor's scissors to cut open her riding-habit. He thought he had seen the scissors pierce her flesh.

'Adam, they didn't,' Dr Keogh had assured him. 'I promise you that you imagined that.'

Adam knew that this must be true.

He had been taken outside as soon as someone noticed him looking, and when he was let come back his mother was covered by a sheet. They had put a handkerchief over her face, but he took it off and touched her hand and her grey forehead. Her eyes were closed. That time too he heard whispers. 'Four months,' he heard. 'Four months gone. Mr Gould was over from London four months ago.' Then there was shushing followed by a shocked silence. Unless that came later? The unpleasant incident did, anyway. It must have. It happened outside by the carriages.

When the doctor came out for the second time, carrying his bag, he produced a pocket flask, unscrewed the silver cup from the top, filled it with whiskey and offered it to Adam, saying that it would steady him. Adam, who was unused to the stuff, took a mouthful, which burned his throat and made him cough.

He was still coughing when someone stepped down from a carriage drawn up next to the doctor's. It was Kate. Her mother, still inside, held the door open and seemed to be hissing at her to get back in. But Kate ran forward. She was no longer wearing riding clothes, so more time than Adam guessed must have gone by since he saw her last. Hours? A whole day? He saw luggage strapped to the roof. The girl looked younger than he remembered. He thought: she is as helpless as I am. He wondered whether it had been to talk – perhaps argue? – with her mother that his father had been going back and forth. Bargaining?

'Adam, I am deeply sorry. Truly! We all are. It was a terrible, unpredictable thing! They say the rider ahead of her displaced a stone which was holding down some barbed wire, and that it leaped up just as her horse jumped. We are deeply, deeply sorry.'

'Sorry? How sorry can you be?' he heard himself spit the words at her. 'You thought she – my mother – was dead before, didn't you? Well now she is. You should be happy! Your prayers have been answered. I hope this fits your plans.'

Her crumpled face reproached him, but her tone was steady. 'Mama and I,' she told him, 'are leaving for England. We shall take the train this evening. The house is free of us. We shan't be coming back. Tell your father he can bring her body home. Tell him we shall write. Goodbye, Adam.'

Later, he would wonder if she had produced the story of the wire – it was one sometimes told to visitors as a warning – so as to prevent him thinking that his mother had taken unnecessary or deliberate risks. She was clever, he thought, quick-witted and would have made a good friend. He wished he had not insulted her – and would have liked to embrace her. But that was impossible. He couldn't embrace anyone lest he break down.

***

At dinner in Thady's house, the *blanquette de veau* finally made its appearance and was as succulent as Thady had hoped. While he worked his way through two helpings, Madame Thady – her formal title was, of course, Madame Quill – plied Adam with friendly questions. As she did, she turned her body as fully towards him as if they had been dancing.

The manoeuvre was almost certainly designed to allow Thady – who liked to slurp his food as though from a nosebag – to do so behind her back. Adam knew from Thady himself that she deplored his table manners. This evening though, he was clearly to have *carte blanche* to savour her meat as he chose. Adam saw the concession as proof that the tiff had been a mere conjugal readjustment.

Thady's '*tendre moitié*' – it was odd to hear him talk French – had a neat, no-nonsense *chic*. Her grey eyes were clever, her eyebrows finely arched, her dress well cut – which, since she was a dressmaker and an ex-lady's maid, should be no surprise. Her upswept hair rose from a strong neck in an elegant curve. Socially she must have been several cuts above Thady, but perhaps did not know this, since Ireland would be as strange to her as the Congo was to the White Fathers. Adam remembered one of *them* talking approvingly of an ex-Zouave officer who had settled down with a Bantu wife and 'raised her to his level'. Not that Thady would see himself as being like a Bantu! Or if he did, he would – no doubt like the Bantu themselves – feel cheerfully confident of his worth.

Come to think of it, Thady had been prized in Adam's father's racing stables for his hands which could gentle even the most skittish horse or mare. He had his own kind of subtlety which *la tendre moitié* must have divined. Adam, who had spent his childhood observing a doomed domestic union, was cheered to see a promising one. He smiled at Madame Quill.

'So why,' she quizzed, 'are you leaving us?'

Behind her, Thady's bony head dived like a cormorant for his plate. He made munching sounds.

She ignored them. 'How long,' she asked Adam, 'will you be in Ireland?'

With measured candour, he told some of his story and of how, after being obliged – ordered! – to leave the *maison de santé*, he had sent a telegram to a friend, asking that an answer should be sent here. Madame Quill agreed to deal with this and expressed sympathy over the monsignor's accident, which she described as 'a piece of appallingly bad luck'. This view, by turning the death into a fluke, shrank Adam's responsibility.

Thady's feeding sounds stopped. Running bread over his plate, he marvelled, 'Jaysus, Adam, you're a dark horse!' He had lapsed into Hibernian English, and his and Adam's attempts to translate this for Madame Thady were hopeless.

In what way, she inquired patiently, if Adam was to be a horse, was this horse *'ténébreux'*? Was the expression droll?

The men had to admit that any drollery there might be was elusive, having to do with parody and exile. Indeed, now that they thought of it, drollery itself was 'a dark horse', something which somehow brought the distant close and made the here and now feel strange. Did she twig? *Non*? They laughed, and she looked mildly riled.

Wait, though! Was there not, she remembered, a brand-new song, '*Twiggez-vous*?' Sung by Marie Lloyd? '*Nous twiggons*,' she sang, and the men applauded: '*Elle pige*!'

Thady in French was only half his Irish self – and this helped Adam to shed his caginess.

'You eat,' Madame Quill had encouraged her husband when they first sat down, 'and let me talk to Monsieur Gould.' Which was why, freed from the mockery with which an English-speaking Thady would have greeted Adam's revelations, Adam had felt able to make them.

Wondering if she guessed at the slyly defensive, volatile element in which her husband's mind moved, he considered warning her – then saw there was no need. Thady's agility of mood, like his ex-jockey's bandiness, had survived its usefulness. Both were adaptations to circumstances which would not recur.

Adam, by contrast, should sharpen his defences before heading back to their tribal and waspish province. For now though, the bed-time tenderness which he felt rise like steam between his hosts made him envious and he wondered wistfully whether, before he left, Danièle and he might manage to be together for a few bonding, private, frolicsome days. His telegram had begged her to turn her mind to this.

***

Next morning, when he rose at an impatiently early hour, there his answer was: a telegram.

YOUR MESSAGE JUST FORWARDED STOP MEETING IMPOS-
SIBLE STOP AM WITH DR AND MADAME BLANCHE IN
NORMANDY STOP BEST WISHES D'ARMAILLE

Gone from Paris then! Was the formality discretion? 'D'Armaillé'!
All those stops, then 'best wishes'. Of course it was! It must be!
He himself had warned her of how telegraph employees had
been known to copy messages that passed through their hands.
Some of Cardinal Lavigerie's prudently encoded telegrams to
Rome had been intercepted by monarchists.

***

'I'll be in the post office later. Shall I send a telegram for you
to someone in Ireland? To say when you'll arrive?'

Madame Quill and Adam were dunking stale bread in
their *café au lait*, which did not taste of coffee at all but of
toasted barley. He welcomed the revelation of how the married
lived: fine food for company in the evening, then, when one
penetrated behind the scenes, thrift.

'That would be kind.'

He gave her the address of his father's doctor.

***

Panama Affair: Trial Starts in Paris. Senators and Deputies
Indicted.

The saloon of the Irish mail-boat was almost deserted. Adam,
too restless to stay in his berth, gripped a rail and flicked
through newspapers bought in Holyhead. He had already
checked the foreign news and found nothing about Belcastel.

Looking up, he locked glances with the only other man in the bar.

'Nasty night!' The man seemed eager for company. 'Whiskey?' he suggested. 'Settles the stomach. Can I get you one?' His soft tongue changed 'get' to 'guess'. That, Adam remembered now, was how people 'at home' talked. Engaging dubiously with consonants, their breath hovered as though hesitancy were a form of politeness. 'Yes?'

'Thanks, but I'm not sure enough of my sea legs.'

The fuzzy-looking man – he had a pepper of stubble on cheeks and chin – raised an eyebrow at the headline in Adam's paper. 'Still risky, eh, to be a French politician? How long is it – a century? – since they were sending each other in tumbrels to the guillotine! Now I'm told they go in carriages to the courtroom!'

An old joke. The floor lurched, and the other man's drink drenched Adam's chest. Amidst apologetic moppings, names were exchanged.

'Gould?' The drinker was a Blake. His tone now was businesslike. 'You,' he scrutinized Adam, 'must be one of the Goulds from ...?'

A lie shot from Adam's mouth. It was as if he were dodging himself. 'I have no relatives here,' he blurted, aware that what he *was* dodging was a despotic tribal gaze that turned you into what it chose. He had seen Thady mesmerize fellow-Irishmen with this in Paris and seen them do it to him.

Cannibal-like, the tribal eye reduced you to matter for absorbing or spitting out. Adam had been spat out before. Maybe – as must have happened to his young father – it was worse to be swallowed?

'I,' he improvised, 'come from Canada.'

It could have been true. His tribe had planned to 'emigrate' him there.

Blake's scrutiny sharpened. Seeking a resemblance? Adam did not think he would find it. He couldn't believe he looked like Gary Gould who, he had come to think, must always have been coltish and immature. It was the kindest view: an irresponsible, aging child! Even his father's blithe monicker suggested this. It was a buck's name. A rosy-faced sportsman's name, it hinted at 'score' and 'galore' and hopes of more and more unearned luck!

Which, by all accounts, had run out.

Again the boat heaved.

'Are you all right?' asked his companion. Then, hopefully: 'Staying in Kingstown this evening?'

'No.' Adam said something vague about a train. Not vague enough, though, for Blake guessed that it must be the one for the west.

'God help us, the Wild Irish West!' He listed its troubles: a recurrence of potato blight and the Congested Districts Board's efforts to get landlords to sell. 'Land purchase,' he sneered. 'Helping tenants to buy. They call it "giving them a stake in the land". The crowd beyond in Westminster aim to kill Home Rule with kindness! But sure once you give land to pooreens, what do you think will happen? It'll be let go to thistles and ragweed.' Blake ordered another whiskey. 'You won't join me?'

Adam shook his head.

'Sure? The worst is behind us. The barman says they've sighted the Bailey light. You can be glad, anyway, that you're not one of those Goulds I was thinking of. They're a rackety lot.' Blake sipped irritably. 'I should know. My first cousin married one, and,' he lowered his voice, 'it looks as though I may end up with her on my hands! Between yourself and myself, it's why I'm here. I've been summoned to give support. But it'll be a poor lookout if I have to take her home. My wife can't stand her.' Sobered, he stared glumly at his glass. 'The cousin's a difficult woman. Bitter. She had no children,' he confided, 'so there's a strong chance that her husband, who's at his last gasp, may have made a will leaving their place – which is badly encumbered anyway – to a by-child he had years before he married her by some ...'

'Stop! Don't say it!'

Blake stared.

Adam's face was burning. 'Sorry! I had to stop you! I *am* one of those Goulds. I'm the by-child.' A 'pooreen', he thought, a bringer of thistles! Practically a thistle himself! Had his father thought so? But now what Blake had said about *him* began to register. 'Is he,' Adam asked, 'Gary Gould – it *is* him you meant, isn't it? – is he really at his last gasp? Close to dying?'

'You ... Oh Lord ... Listen now, Mr Gould, I'm truly sorry if ... I meant no offence. You mustn't take it to heart.'

'Is he?'

The other man gabbled on, as upset at having given offence as Adam could ever be at taking it.

Not that Adam had! He shook his head. 'My fault! I shouldn't have misled you. Will you have a drink with me?'

'I will. Of course. A large Irish, please.'

'Two,' Adam told the barman, 'neat,' and when the liquid blazed in his throat felt a quiver of relief. The tribe, after all, was divided within itself. Not compact at all.

'Now you must have one with me? Another large one?'

'Thanks.'

'*Sláinte.*'

By the time they had drained their glasses, the gangways were in place. They joined the passengers crowding down them, and, on leaving the jetty, Adam felt the land of his fathers underfoot.

The 'auld sod', he thought, and in his ear the words had Thady's self-mocking lilt. Feeling an abrupt and painful onset of cramp in his foot, he flexed it hard, raised the toe until his calf hurt, lowered the heel and got rid of the sensation. Maybe it had never been there?

***

Waking, hours later, somewhere in the flatlands of middle Ireland, he looked out of the train window at a mare with her tail up racing through mist. It brought to mind the stories of fairy horses – 'pookas' – which his mother used to tell. Wild as fate, these challenged travellers to climb on their backs, then carried them off to a timeless land. Had the thought come to mind as a cypher for something? Love? Mourning? Encumbered legacies? He closed, then opened his eyes and this time saw a sheep so deep in sedge that it looked like sedge itself. Grazing nearby, a pony had a coat as rough as grass. Next to it Adam's father lay on his back and stared at the sky. He didn't blink when the pony – somehow Adam was now on *its* back – raised a hoof and held it poised over his face. There were no reins. In a panic, Adam seized the creature's mane, jerked it to one side and kicked its opposite flank. This had no effect. As the hoof descended, there was a splintering of bone. His fingernails, when he opened his eyes, had pierced the skin of his palms.

He wondered if his father had just died. Or whether the dream had mixed the dead Monseigneur de Belcastel with an image of the young Gary Gould.

For of course it had been a dream, a guilt-and-worry dream, touched off by what Blake had told him. Remembering his promise to forgive his father, he felt relief at the prospect. Perhaps, after all, the tribe's embrace need not shrivel a man's sense of himself? Perhaps it could expand it?

Thinking of Blake made him wonder whether there hadn't been something odd about him, even a little mendacious. Was it possible that the estate was *not* encumbered? He imagined Blake seated in a Kingstown hotel, eating hot buttered scones and jam, while wondering how effectively he had frightened off the by-child.

Gazing vaguely out at the mesmeric bog, Adam saw his mother. She was mounted on a chestnut stallion.

This was not a dream. His eyes were open. She was there. As she galloped along beside the train, he saw her from quite close then, more completely, from further off. It was she! And not a day older! Neatly dressed in her familiar riding habit, she wheeled away and began jumping fences. Her hair, as always, was in a bun and her riding hat pulled low on her forehead.

Adam, who had paid little attention when psycho-physical phenomena were discussed at the *maison de santé*, now wondered if he was about to witness a re-enactment of the old disaster – the one he had not seen but had endlessly imagined? Thinking, half credulously, of the belief that bad events could leave their mark like a photograph on a place, he began to brace himself for the accident and felt an access of mounting battle fever. Surely it must soon happen, then be over. Now? No, *now*! But not at all. Easily and efficiently, the *amazone* – the whimsical French word domesticated her – cleared her fences. Then her hair came loose. She paused, pulled off her hat, twisted a new bun in place, secured it with a few salvaged hairpins and jammed the hat back on. Her nose must have started to run, for she wiped it lavishly with the back of her hand. Surely no ghost would do that? After a while, the train left her behind and, although he continued staring out at the boggy flatlands, he had no more visions.

How odd that he had had none while in Passy and two now! Maybe, after all, dealing with the mad kept one sane? And making too much of the past might do the opposite? Turning his mind to the here and now, he hoped his father's doctor had got Madame Thady's telegram and would meet the train.

***

'It is Adam, isn't it?'

The doctor, a chatty, quick-moving young man of about Adam's own age, smelled of tweed and cloves. His rust-coloured hair jutted in crinkly sprigs from under his hat and tickled Adam's ear when they embraced.

Almost at once, as if dissatisfied by the slackness of Adam's hug, he pushed him away, held him at arm's length and looked him reproachfully in the eye. 'Adam, I'm Conor Keogh! *Con*! You haven't forgotten me surely? We poached a salmon together one time that was nearly as big as – well, nearly half as big as one of us. We were about eleven years old and it was a huge bugger! Or so we told everyone, though there's no way of knowing now. We sold it to the parson's wife. She cheated us of course.'

Adam stared.

'We raced ponies!' Keogh could not believe he had been wiped from his old confederate's mind. 'Snared rabbits. Nearly burned down a barn.' A bonding life of petty crime seemed to lie behind them.

Then Adam remembered: 'But of course! Con the Bad Influence! Father T. used to say you got me into bad ways. I suppose it was because you were a Protestant.'

'Not at all,' Keogh told him. 'He told my mother that with your heritage you had to be kept on a tight rein. It was all right for me to be a bit wild, but not you!'

'What a foxy old cleric!'

They laughed and hugged again.

'Hop in,' Keogh invited, as they reached his horse and trap. 'Put your bag there. We'll go straight to your father's just in case he might be in good form and recognize you. Don't be disappointed if he doesn't. He's in a coma a lot of the time. In and out. Sometimes he raves and thinks he's a boy again and back in school. Bad memories there it seems! One of my nieces is sitting with him.'

'Tell me,' seizing his chance to get a word in, as Keogh clicked his tongue and the horse took off, Adam asked, 'is there a woman living somewhere around here who looks just the way my mother used to? Her exact image?'

'Dozens!' Keogh told him. 'There's a local face. Well, there are several. But there's one rather beautiful one. That's the face your mother had. Why do you ask?'

'I think I saw her from the train.'

The trap jolted them past squat cabins fuzzed with mist: a wizened world. These looked as though they had half emerged from the soil but, like wormcasts, were attached to it still. Men standing in the low-lintelled doorways had something earthy about them too. Like serfs *adscripti glebae*! Adam shuddered. Here was a surviving bit of the old regime whose lost sweetness – '*la douceur de la vie*'! – haunted Sauvigny and his friends. Would they find this sweet?

'Your Mama's double?'

Adam described what he had seen from the train. 'It could have been her ghost!'

'It could have been Cait,' Keogh guessed. 'Your stepmother banished her. She won't have her in the sickroom, so she – Cait – went riding. That's why my nieces are relaying each other by the bedside. I wanted *her* there. I've been training her, so she's a better nurse than either of them, but no point having rows.'

'Is ... Cait a cousin?'

'Yes.' Keogh added, 'I daren't leave your stepmother alone with your father – I mean alone without someone I trust. Many's the dead man's signature was witnessed by a legatee's friends, and his will could be changed in two flicks of a lamb's tail. Not, mind, that I know for sure what's in the present one, though I did try to use my influence in your favour.'

'Isn't that improper?'

'Like poaching salmon?'

'I suppose.'

'Recognize this?' As Keogh turned in a long, unadorned drive, they faced a distant granite box of a house that could have been built to imprison murderers. Bleak, bare, barracks-like and domineering – was this Adam's childhood home? His memory had softened it.

'So you think they ... her side of the family ...?'

'... could – would – concoct a will to suit themselves? Yes.'

'Even if he's in a coma?'

'Oh, they're great ones for mobilizing corpses – not that your papa is a corpse yet, but ...'

While Keogh talked about the law's intricacies, Adam looked around at cows and a muddy lake. Dry stone walls ran hither and yon, made, he remembered, more to clear the stony land than for any positive purpose. Ragged thorn trees leaned away from what must be the prevailing wind. A gate sagged. The land, he heard Keogh urge, needed attention.

'And I need help with the co-operative creamery we're planning. We need you, Adam. We are about to set up a cottage hospital too. It'd be great to have a landlord here pulling his weight, which he hasn't been up to doing this long while, and Mrs Gould never would.'

Adam wondered who hadn't been pulling his weight? Ah: his father. Mrs Gould of course was his father's wife and the cousin of the man on the mail-boat. Keeping track of all this was like learning positions in cricket: short slip, silly mid-on ... All he remembered about this stepmother was that when he was small, she had been one of the Miss Blakes and reputed to have a face like a pike – the fish not the weapon. Some of the second meaning clung though: pugnacity, stealth. Pikes were the weapons favoured by moonlighters.

In a late gleam from the wintry sun, the house's windows

turned a fluid white. One thought of a pack of dogs with pearly cataracts.

'This young woman,' he persisted, 'looked exactly ...'

'Well, Cait wears your mama's old riding clothes. She inherited them, so of course she wears them. For her the price of a new riding habit ... But never mind that now. Here we are. Listen.' Keogh spoke fast and furtively. 'If you're asked where you're staying, it's with me. Yes? That'll save embarrassment all round. You wouldn't want to stay here.'

Jumping down from the trap, he produced a key, opened a side door and led Adam through familiar-unfamiliar spaces to a room with an enormous bed. Everything here was some shade of grey: the light, the sheets, the shine from the medicine bottles and even a bunch of papery, half-dry hydrangeas. In the middle of all this a supine figure lay breathing noisily through a hole in the middle of its face. The hole was mouse-sized, centripetal and black. The lips had been sucked inwards. No teeth, Adam realized. There was a sandy stubble on the cheeks. Nothing about the dying man looked like his memory of his father. As he watched, an unexpectedly live strip of grey-pink flesh slid from his father's mouth, lolled a while, then withdrew. His tongue? Adam's own tongue froze. How was he to talk to this unmanned near-corpse? Forcing himself, he picked up one of the hands, but it felt as limp as a package of liver.

'Papa,' he tried, 'I'm Adam.' Then stopped. His prepared speech about reconciliation had lost meaning, and other conventional words that came to mind seemed uncaring and bumptious. Indeed, his own grossly healthy presence felt like an affront, and he feared that saying goodbye might frighten this relic of a man. 'Goodbye' had a callous ring. He couldn't say it. Instead he repeated, 'I'm Adam,' and, when he tried to let go of the dead-liver hand, felt ashamed.

A freckled girl wearing an apron had meanwhile risen from a chair and been presented as Keogh's niece. She struck a match, lit the wick of an oil lamp and in its flare proved to have her uncle's colouring in a fresher, red-cheeked version. Its vividness drew Conor Keogh's boyhood self from the dusk of Adam's mind so that he could hardly believe he had ever forgotten him. There he was in memory: as bright and speckled as a robin's egg. Today's Keogh took on some of that recovered gleam. His father who, of course, had also been the local doctor, was the very one with whom Adam had stayed for some days after his mother died. Conor, one year older than himself, must now be twenty-six.

'No change,' the girl was saying, 'except that we got a little food into him.'

Keogh mouthed: 'Mrs Gould?'

'Upstairs,' the girl whispered. 'He was awake before. Raging at her. He's full of rage. She had to leave.'

Keogh nodded. 'Mr Gould,' he addressed his patient, 'your son has come to see you. Adam.'

At first there was no response. Then: 'Adam,' came a voice from the bed, 'ruined my life. Did it from malice. He frightened away the girl I meant to marry, and when I wrote asking him to write and beg her to come back, he never answered. It might have made a difference if he had.' In the reptilian face, two slits of eyes, grey as wet slate, had half opened. 'She was a sweet girl.'

'Now, now,' Keogh put his head close to the dying man's

ear, 'we've been through all that. That story can be told two ways. It all depends where you start it.'

'He ruined Kate's life too. Kate was the girl. Did you know that she became a nun?'

'In Belgium. Yes. But her letters say she's happy now. She found what she needed. And he's your only son. Have you forgotten that you agreed to forgive him?'

'Who?'

'Adam.'

'Adam?' The grey face crumpled in disgust. Then it widened in a grin. 'Adam and Eve and Pinch Me,' said the mouth in a singsong, petulant voice, 'went down to the river to bathe. Adam and Eve were drowned. So which of them was saved? Answer. Answer!'

'Pinch Me,' said Keogh. 'That's an old trick.'

'Aha, it *is* old. It's an old schoolboy trick. Schoolboys are vicious beasts. I was a beautiful child. That's how I know. The beautiful are prey!' Again the mad old mouth took up the schoolyard riddle: 'Adam and Eve and Pinch Me ...'

Adam expected the hand he was holding to try to pinch him. But it did not. Perhaps the life force no longer reached it? The mouth though was still alive.

'I shall pinch you,' it threatened.

'Do,' Keogh challenged. 'Let's see your strength. Pinch me and say you forgive him.'

But the pleated lids, grey as cockleshells, had closed over the dim, angry eyes. A sound of intent, greedy breathing filled the room.

Adam, deprived of the excitement which had been sustaining him, felt that he might faint. He had not, it occurred to him, eaten all day. And back on the boat he had had two double whiskeys.

***

On their way out of the house – no point waiting any more for now was Keogh's opinion – they were held up by a small group arguing at the front door. A manservant with his hand on the knob was keeping it half closed to prevent someone coming in.

'Now Miss Cait,' he was saying, 'you know I'd not stop you if it was up to me, but I have my orders.'

A second man stood behind him, clearly ready to lend assistance. Adam was reminded of the *maison de santé*. From outside came a woman's voice. 'Brady, all I want is to come in for a tiny minute.'

'He's out of it, Miss. He won't know you.'

'Well, but you can let me see him. Just a quick look. I'll be gone before – ah, Dr Keogh. You'll let me in, won't you?'

There, in the now open doorway stood the *amazone*. Cait. Though still in her riding habit, she was hatless and agitated: exactly as Adam's mother had been the last time he saw her. 'Psycho-physical?' he wondered, unsure whether he had dreamed up the resemblance. Just now he distrusted his perceptions – but couldn't let himself fail this woman. He pushed forward, bowed, claimed cousinship and begged her to return with him to the sickroom to view his father. Without knowing it, he had perhaps been thinking of paintings by Greuze with titles like 'The Deathbed', and 'A Late Reconciliation', for he found that, with old-time gallantry, he had offered her his arm. She took it without a word.

Keogh told the manservant, 'Brady, this is Mr Gary's son. He's back from France.'

Brady threw up his hands. 'I hope you'll explain then, doctor, if there are ructions.'

'Right you are, Brady. I'll take the blame.'

So back they trailed to the sickroom where, although the patient was now comatose, the *amazone* seemed satisfied. Perhaps it had been a mere matter of pride with her to defy Mrs Gould?

As the three returned to the hall, Mrs Gould – who else could it be? – came down the stairs. She was small, wispily pewter-haired and clearly on edge. She paused meaningfully on the bottom step, stood her ground and let them come to her. Yet she looked, Adam saw with relief, in no way formidable – just a little long-nosed and probably unhappy. Her mouth was quivering, and if they had been in the *maison de santé*, he would have suggested she sit down. Here, that could seem intrusive, since an intruder, if not indeed a marauder, was clearly what she felt him to be. Her eyes fastened on the crook of his arm through which the *amazone*'s was still defiantly wound.

He couldn't think what to do about this.

Keogh introduced him.

'Well, Mr Gould,' his stepmother sighed wearily, 'I suppose you are all set to take over.'

He shook his head and would have condoled, but feared that condoling could be construed as an insult. 'I'm sorry,' he said, leaving the cause of his sorrow vague.

'Ah, but to say that,' she said, 'can mean "I shall do as I

like, but mustn't be blamed." It is – *was* – one of your father's tricks.'

'I don't think you have had time to know that we play the same tricks.'

Mrs Gould glanced again at the linked arms. This time Adam tried to disentangle his, but gave up when his companion tightened her grip. He hoped Mrs Gould hadn't seen this, but rather thought she had. 'Miss Lydon,' she observed, 'has wasted no time getting in with the new master. New masters and mistresses do sniff each other out fast, don't they?' Her slightly prominent front teeth gnashed the words, as though she would have liked to bite.

Unsure why he was being scolded, Adam's instinct was to smooth things over. How could he judge the rights and wrongs of quarrels raging here? Besides, if his father's will was worrying his stepmother, then he, as the intended beneficiary of Keogh's conspiring, might seem to blame. But he was reluctant to snub his new-old friend by a parade of scruple – especially as Keogh could be telling the truth when he claimed to be preventing, rather than mounting, a conspiracy.

'All I meant,' he told Mrs Gould firmly, 'is that I never intended to barge in. But, as you weren't here, and we feared that there mightn't be much time, we ...'

'So you are already "we"?'

'I don't understand.'

'No?'

This was a quicksand. Bowing, he turned away. Best let Keogh take over. He, after all, was the sick man's doctor and here as such.

Cait Lydon now slipped out of the front door. By the time

Adam had collected his coat and hat and gone after her, she had vanished. Staring about, he saw that the landscape had improved. Low, bleached light softened its lines and, where shafts of this caught the damp, broke into prisms. He had forgotten how totally – and fleetingly – such effects could transform this dour country. The thought revived memories of chill, shadowy air and of how eager this had often made him to get indoors to fires and light and any company at all, even that of animals. To be alone here was peculiarly mournful. A spasm of pity reached him for the prone figure he had left lying between life and death. Poor Papa! How unfortunate that they had failed to make any connection, and that Keogh held out little hope of their making one now! Might it have been different if Adam had come earlier? Perhaps he should come back soon and try to make peace with the difficult Mrs Gould? She was clearly in a bad way and it would be a kindness to his papa to soothe her anxieties.

***

He had already written twice to Danièle when an envelope with a French stamp arrived. It was from Dr Blanche, who was still in Normandy, and explained that Adam would find enclosed herewith the letters which he had sent to Madame d'Armaillé. They had happily just missed her.

Happily? Why happily? Adam had trouble with Blanche's handwriting, which had begun to blur. He seemed to have something in his eye.

> She left here almost immediately after our arrival, in response to news that her husband is on his way to Belgium, where an

*aunt has put a house at their disposal. He has been wounded,
but we don't know how badly. His letter was vague, and one
must deduce that he plans to break things to her gradually. This
strikes me as a mistake.*

*The house where they are to live needs renovating, so she
left at once to see to this – and also with the idea of making
a quick, clean break. This, my dear Adam, is why I have not
forwarded your letters.*

*Before leaving, she asked me to tell you that she begs you to
refrain from corresponding with her behind her husband's back.
It is now her duty to try to rebuild their marriage, so she wants
neither to hurt his feelings nor to add to other hurts with which
he may have to contend. Clearly, your duty is to keep away. I
am sorry to be the bearer of such news.*

The rest of the letter was about recent public events,
pessimism, the new broom in Passy, news of Adam's uncle
who was suddenly quite ill and being cared for by nuns, and
of Maupassant, who no longer recognized anyone. Blanche,
now that his own prospects were poor, had begun to see
shadows everywhere.

This [he added] *is of course poor Guy's native stretch of coast,
so we keep being reminded of him. How sensitive he was to the
way things were going.*

Adam tried not to brood on how they might or might not
go.

It was a time of waiting. The sundial in Keogh's garden rarely
received enough sun to tell the time. Adam's comatose papa's
stamina defied medical expectancy, and a rumour got about
that a bookie was taking bets – not for the first time – on the
former gentleman-jockey's staying power.

Adam, who had settled in with Keogh, took his advice and put off calling on Mrs Gould 'until things were resolved'.

'You mean his death?'

'Death and property, Adam. No point being mealy-mouthed.'

No, since nobody else was, there was indeed no point. Local people peeped at him from beneath shawls and hat brims.

A Mrs Ross, who said she had known him as a boy, called by to ask after his father and find out whether Adam planned to hunt. Not now, perhaps, but later on? She was a vigorous lady with a florid face who spoke wistfully about the splendid refreshments which, when the Goulds' racing stable was doing well, used to be brought to the meet and served on their fine but sturdy hunt table.

'Not recently though,' she admitted. 'Thin times, I'm afraid. I was wondering if you would lend us that table while you're in mourning. You'll not be needing it. By the way, best have an inventory made of the furniture just as soon as you get the chance. Things disappear at a time like this. That hunt table did not belong to your stepmother. Remember that. A lone man is easily preyed upon. I suppose,' she admitted, as she rose to leave, 'all this is a little premature.'

He agreed that it was.

'Well, *adiós*.' Self-mockingly. In the last century, her family had made their money by settling some of its members in Spain to export wines.

Twice Adam glimpsed Blake – the man from the mail-boat – in the village 'main' street, a straggle of snail-grey houses. They hailed each other, with jovial caution, and promised to get together quite soon for a chat. That, Adam supposed, would be after 'things' had resolved themselves. For now, the word from Keogh, who was in daily attendance at the sickbed, was, 'Your old man's dying hard. Living on his will. All spirit when spirit is no use to him.'

Bishop John Joseph – 'JJ' – Tobin came, administered the last rites, dined with Keogh and Adam, drank to the dying man's safe passage to the right place and spent the night. He relayed gossip and inquired fondly about France. Death, having no lasting dominion, need not spoil a convivial evening. Sitting up into the small hours, the three stared into the turf smoulder, riddled away powdery ash when it choked the flame, drank port and brandy and corrected each other's reminiscences. Adam's mother's death was duly lamented. An accident, of course. He, the bishop assured, said mass regularly for her soul, God rest it. As for Gary Gould, he was no longer making sense. Indeed, most of what he said now was the opposite of what he meant.

'Ludicrous,' was Tobin's response to reports of the old man's paternal curse. 'You had nothing to do with the heiress leaving. How could you have? You were only twelve! No, the match was doomed once *her* mama heard the news about your neighbour, Captain Boycott. Till then she had never looked long enough from her carriage window to note the difference between Connaught and Kent. House parties in both were no doubt alike, so imagine her shock when she learned what the Land Leaguers could do to a genteel household! Invasion by the mob! Servants refusing to serve! What worse upsets to the social order could be devised? The captain, his good lady and one or two hangers-on had to do their own milking! And *everything* else! It seems that the thought of emptying her own slops upsets a wellborn Englishwoman as nothing else can, and that Kate's mama would have faced the French Revolution with more sangfroid! Spilled blood can be commemorated, spilled urine never. And the Orangemen who came to defend the Boycotts were said to be a case of the cure being worse than the disease. That sort of rumour could make a regiment of match-making mamas turn tail. You weren't to blame, Adam. She needed delicate handling and who was to do it? Your papa was too taken up with politics to pay attention to his courting. And who's to say he wasn't half-hearted about it anyway?'

'What happened to Kate?'

'Kate,' said his Grace, 'took against the secular world. A blessing, perhaps? In the long run. But let's talk about now. Tell me about France – not the tin-pot republic! Tell me how His Holiness's policies are being received by the French people. Did you read where he said that they have a keen mind? "Keen and generous, *vif et généreux*?" I think that's true. Especially now that French Catholics are grown wiser and milder! They're burying the old malice, aren't they? Burying their hatchets while we sharpen ours!'

Adam chose not to disillusion him.

***

'The silver lining,' said Blake, 'is that my cousin plans to go and live with her sister. The cloud is that the annuity you have to pay her may beggar your estate. Will I top that up?'

Adam handed him his glass.

'Maybe,' Blake mused, 'you should give her a few sticks of furniture in exchange for withholding her annuity for a year or so? Until you can afford the cash? I wouldn't think she'd want to arrive at her sister's with one arm as long as the other. She'd want to be seen to be bearing gifts. Making a contribution to the household.'

'I'll have to take advice,' Adam told him.

'Do that,' said Blake.

Adam looked around him. They were in what was now his house, although he had not yet seen it properly. From discretion, he was still staying with Keogh.

Things had resolved themselves. His father had died, slipping away quietly for all his tenacity, and the will brought few surprises. It assigned an income for life to Mrs Gould and the residue of the estate to Adam. The funeral had unfolded with the efficiency of a gymnastics display.

'Don't worry about a thing,' well-wishers had told Adam. 'We're great at funerals here. We're practised.'

This proved true and his own role slotted in smoothly, as he helped shoulder the coffin to the hearse, then followed it on the two-mile walk to the church. During this, the mood lightened as if, well before seeing the coffin stowed in its vault, the mourners' image of what was inside had dissolved in a blur of souls gathering for flight on some baroque ceiling. Prayers were in the plural. 'Eternal rest grant them, O Lord.' Gary Gould had shed his singular self.

At the reception, Adam mistook relatives for their fathers. Mrs Gould, too, was being condoled with, so, as he stood with her, they must have looked like mother and son. Faces merged, and he was soon emotionally tipsy.

Somewhere someone was singing one of those old airs whose appeal is almost embarrassingly direct. Curious, he shouldered his way down a corridor to where a niece of Keogh's sat at a grand piano accompanying Cait – then on to where he could listen in privacy. His mother had sung that song. In what spirit, he wondered? He hoped there had been irony.

'No, the heart that has truly loved never forgets,' Cait sang, 'But as truly lives on to the close.

'As the sunflower turns on her god when he sets 'The same look which she turned when he rose.'

There was an interruption, a raised voice and a brisk clack as though someone had forcefully closed the piano lid. Then no more singing.

He got the explanation for this some hours later from Cait herself, who came home with Keogh to share a cold supper and have her feathers smoothed. She was still upset.

Mrs Gould, she reported, had burst into the music-room, mortified her in front of everyone and said it was disrespectful to sing love songs at a funeral. Which nobody believed. No, the true reason for this scene was that Cait reminded the widow of Adam's mother, of whose memory she had always been jealous.

'I felt,' Cait sobbed, 'like a kicked dog!'

Adam soothed her, praised her singing, and wondered privately whether his presence could have caused the acrimony. Rousing his stepmother's fears of being left in poverty, his return after such a long absence could look like revenge from the grave and even a small-scale episode in the land-war. Cait, meanwhile, was saying that, though she had not learned to play the piano, she had always wanted to. Both men assured her that it was not too late. Then Keogh turned the talk to good works. He wanted Adam to help him stimulate cottage industries which, in this soggy pocket of the bog, had hardly started to exist. He meant to install looms for the weaving of homespun.

'The gentry here,' he told them, 'are bone idle and the Home Rulers want the economy to stagnate so that they can keep blaming the English.' Keogh was a dynamo converting hope into plans.

Adam was stirred. Triggered by the love song, the thought of Danièle had been tormenting him all day. No: it wasn't a thought! Memory's irruption was tactile. It was the spill of her breasts; it was the down on her neck puckering his tongue as though he had licked the husk of a green almond. Even the tangy smell of chrysanthemums – church and house had been full of it – had reminded him of the tousled softness of her pubic mound and of his telling her that the Gaelic word for soft was the Russian word for God: *bog*. 'Maybe,' he had argued when she laughed at the useless information, 'God's goodness for some tribe which moved west came to mean softness. Mildness! *La douceur*! That's not utterly useless, is it? Not if it jogs your mind and makes you wonder about things.'

'So,' she had asked, 'are the Irish soft?'

Well, were they? Mrs Gould? Blake? His father-the-centaur? Keogh? The bishop? Adam's mother? Thady Quill? No, but sometimes – in songs for instance – they mimicked softness. You admire what you want but perhaps cannot afford, so he had wanted softness to be his and her element, like the swansdown cloak in the fairy tale which made wearers invisible and enabled them to fly. Enticing her into its shelter, he told her, 'In Gaelic they say "Be soft with the world and it will be soft with you."' A half-truth? Perhaps, but half-truths let one off – gave one escape routes, safety valves and ways of having things both ways. He needed these now that Danièle had retreated into a way of thinking which ruled that concern for the returning Philibert rendered her taboo. Even in his mind she had become that, since he could neither let himself think 'I hope he dies, so that we may marry,' nor 'I hope he recovers, so that I may persuade her to go on deceiving him.' His rational self knew that he should not think of her at all.

To keep from doing so, he flirted playfully with Cait and made promises about the piano, which were soon to get him into trouble.

***

As soon as the will had been read, he decided that he ought to reassure his father's widow. Her behaviour to Cait betrayed unhappiness, and it was clear that her married life could not have been made easier by knowing that her predecessor had been a beauty, while she had a reputation for being 'difficult'. Her cousin didn't want her. Where could she go now? The least Adam could do – like it or not – was offer to let her stay in what had been her home. Accordingly, he set off to call on her.

He went on foot and, on his way up the drive, rehearsed ways of soothing and – why not? – charming her. He had been good at this with the patients at Passy. Perhaps he should have brought flowers? But the best ones in this boggy outpost grew in her – now his – garden. So: no. Perhaps he would tell her a joke? He imagined kissing – or better, holding her hand comfortingly in both of his. Impossible to plan. He must trust his instinct.

However, when he reached the house she was out.

This was how he came to have his long-postponed drink with Blake, who told him that she was soon to leave for her sister's place.

'So you won't have to worry about her,' said Blake, adding that this was a blessing since what Adam *had* better worry about was the house. He would see why in two ticks if he let Blake take him on a tour of it. 'What about now?'

But Adam didn't relish the possibility of being caught by Mrs Gould gloating – as she would construe it – over possessions which had been hers. He knew what it was like to be expelled. Sipping his drink, he tasted blood on his lip. The glass was chipped. And the Venetian chandelier above them had lost beads. His eye swooped about, noting further signs of wear and tear. The poorer the objects he took from her – such as crazed dishes or ones with rivets – the more humiliating for them both. He imagined darned, intimate things that might even date back to his mother's time. For moments he would have liked to see the whole place burned – or to board the next train and go back to France for good.

'Well, take my word for it,' said the increasingly unbuttoned Blake, 'this house needs serious injections of cash if it isn't to collapse altogether. And raising them won't be easy. Insurers are reluctant to lend to Irish landowners.'

It was then that he proffered the suggestion that his cousin should be allowed to take some furniture.

***

'No,' was Conor Keogh's reaction. 'Neither lend nor lease as much as a pincushion. Let the Blakes take a parcel out of the door and you'll never know what was in it. Nor will you see it again.'

It was some days since Adam's chat with Blake, and news had come that a waggon, pulled by two farm horses, had trundled up the Goulds' drive. At this moment the grand piano, on which Adam had promised Cait should learn to play, had had its legs removed and was being covered with blankets prior to being carted who knew where.

'You *said* I should have lessons on it,' Cait reproached. 'Did you even know it was your mother's?'

'Possession is nine points of the law,' warned Mrs Ross, the lady who had her eye on the hunt table. She and Cait had arrived some minutes apart, having been alerted by well-wishers too shy to bring the news themselves. Nobody likes to be seen to tell tales.

'Did you say,' Adam was asked, 'that they could take the piano?'

He said he had not and asked what else was likely to be taken.

'Jimsy Flynn says they're after moving twenty dining room chairs into the hall.'

'You'd best get up there,' Keogh advised. 'Take the trap. Don't embarrass the Blakes but make sure they unload the waggon. Wait till you see it done.'

Adam did this. Colluding in a show of good humour saved everyone's face. He was offered tea, and when it grew clear that he would not leave until he got what he wanted, the furniture was unloaded and restored to its place in the house.

'I'm sorry,' he told Mrs Gould afterwards, 'that your cousin and I made such a muddle. If there are pieces you especially want, then you must have them. I'm afraid, though, that I can offer neither the piano nor the hunt table.'

She nodded, then, moving to the piano, which had been freed from its wrappings, sat and began to play. It was something wistful and maestoso which, however, ended bravely and con brio and had, he suspected, been picked to show off her talent. For, though he himself was only moderately musical, he could tell that she had talent and knew it. Glad that she had something vital of her own, he praised it with such persuasiveness that she accepted his invitation to come here to play whenever she chose.

When he went out to where he had left the trap, Cait was sitting in the front seat. It was now almost dark, and he did not see her until he got close, but she had seen him through the window sitting in the lamplight with Mrs Gould, listening and applauding and turning the pages of her score.

'Well, you're a double dealer!'

She was, he could only suppose, jealous, so to calm her, when they had left the Gould house behind, he stopped the trap and took her in his arms.

Some days later, he moved into the big house and on his first afternoon she and he hid from the servants and made passionate but cautiously inconclusive love. She seemed adept at this.

IX

Mayo, Ireland, December 1892

Dear Dr Blanche,
Forgive my not reminding you sooner of the bank account which
Monseigneur de Belcastel instructed me to open in my name
but with his money.

I enclose particulars so that that money may now be made
available to his heirs.

Please commend me to Madame Blanche and allow me to
hope that the sea air in Dieppe has restored both your spirits.

With esteem and affection,
Adam Gould

***

For AG to wish him a happy and a holy Christmas:
Rennes, December 1892

Dear Adam,
Though I once hoped that you would become my brother in
Christ, I now pray that you may find fulfilment outside our

ministry, which is a bed of thorns. The sharpest are the fault of Catholic politicians who – this has been a shock – despise priests, require us to deliver the vote, but care nothing for our advice. Meanwhile their activities make it difficult to get our flocks to vote for them.

Think hard before joining us and pray for me as I do for you,

Your old classmate,
Jean Barat

***

Paris, 10 March 1893

My dear Adam,
I am back in Passy. The bank, on learning of the deception practised on it, informed the police, who have been interrogating me and would like to interrogate you. I have tried to discover what will happen next, and believe the answer may be: nothing. In this election year a 'Belcastel case' would profit no one, since the government (weakened by bombs and bribes) needs Catholic support. Police zeal is being discouraged.

Nonetheless, you and I could be charged with professional misconduct – especially as a will has turned up whereby the monsignor left the money in the account to you. The question arises: was he of sound mind? If it is decided that he was, you may inherit and I be in trouble, since why was a sane man under my care at all? If he was not, you risk being accused of abusing your position.

So our interests diverge. You had better come for a visit. We need to talk.

With warm regards,
Emile Blanche

***

So the doctor was back in Passy – and might have news of Danièle. Curbing his hopes and anxieties, Adam packed his bags, paid a promised visit to Bishop Tobin, then started the slow trek back across a chilly Ireland, England and northern France to the *maison de santé* where his first encounter was with a monitory letter.

***

Mayo, 18 March 1893

My dear Adam,
Do not be alarmed to receive this letter.

You need to know something which I meant to tell you at the station then funked. Did you wonder why I raced your train down the platform? I had been planning to speak just as it left, but saw, as it picked up speed, that I would have had to shout out news which should only be whispered.

Unfortunately, even now, there is no way to be tactful.

The matter, as you will have guessed, is delicate, and I am afraid that learning it is bound to upset you, but there is no help for that, since you ought to know what other people think they know. This is that Cait, from when she was not quite sixteen, was reputed to be your father's woman. The story is that he hoped to have a child by her and, if he had succeeded, would have cut you out. People said – forgive my telling you this – that he wanted a legitimate heir. You mustn't hold it against either of them. After all, Adam, you never wrote. The thing is that you should settle something on her. From discretion he chose not to do so in his will. But she is tainted in the minds of possible suitors, and it will take a dowry to efface the taint. He would have wanted you to arrange that.

I know cash is short, but our hospital, when up and running, may provide a solution. Cait might find a salaried position there as good as a dowry.

Hurry back and help me deal with priests who don't like the 'Protestant doctor' butting in on their territory. Did you know that they warn their flock against me, and that the flock, when sick, slinks in here after dark?

You and I must stick together.

Affectionately,
Con

Adam pictured his friend raging at the indelicacy of their situation and steaming with philanthropy. This, though due to his being a generous Protestant in a place where Protestants were privileged, could seem meddlesome – as, to be sure, was this letter.

Cait?

How to link her with what he had seen on his father's deathbed? How could she have got close – how close? – to the mouth Adam had seen simmer like bubbling gruel as it made a last, desperate gulp for life? Gary Gould had died as he lived: reaching for more than his due. With angry pity Adam imagined her lying next to the *macchabée*.

Had she really done that though? Almost certainly. Gould Senior would have grabbed her, just as the Cretan Minotaur had grabbed adolescents. That tale had all the air of a truth that could not be plainly told. For surely it must have been old, frightened men who gave the Greeks the idea for it in the first place? Needy patriarchs, caught in time's labyrinth and gulping for the breath of youth!

Had she offered herself from pity?

Adam tried to expel her from his mind. Emigrate her, he thought wryly, and crumpled the letter, which had reached France before he did, due to his having broken his journey to visit Bishop Tobin.

It had been waiting for him at the *maison de santé* when he got out of the *fiacre* and learned that Dr Blanche, though out, would soon be back and looked forward to seeing Adam at dinner.

He left his bag with the porter, a new man who didn't know him.

'And here is a letter for Monsieur.'

At first he had thought that it might be a summons from the police to come to tell them about Belcastel. Instead, here was this news from another grave.

He took it into Passy village where sitting in a small, smoky café returned him so effectively to his time here that he imagined he saw Danièle drive past in a cab, wearing her blue hat! The one with osprey feathers! Her cheek was palely pressed against the glass. But she was in Belgium, so it could not be she. He had painted her features on to another face.

Why, with his mind so full of Cait, had he not imagined *her*? Poor Cait! Too bad Keogh had shirked telling her story to Adam's face. His presence would have been soothing. His healer's flair for drawing a sting was deft, and his assessing eye almost eccentrically cool.

'You,' he had told Adam once, 'think of girls as people with whom you might, but mustn't, go to bed. That thought breeds trouble.'

He himself, Keogh claimed, thought of them as likely to be more or less helpful with raffles and first aid. 'When you've played hide-and-seek with your sisters' friends from the age of six, you take a practical approach.'

Adam asked whether hide-and-seek had not led to the odd fumble? 'Where did you hide? In the schoolroom cupboard?'

'Fumbles are healthy. They teach you that girls are as manageable as your pony. When I'm ready I shall marry one who is neither a biter nor a bolter and has a little tin.'

'And – love?'

Keogh had shrugged. 'Think small, Adam. Even in politics quite small reforms can break cycles of outrage and despair. There's a big thought, so don't say I lack vision. Anyway I know you're really a practical chap. You ran Dr Blanche's hospital. Help us with ours.'

Which was how Adam had come to find himself teaching Cait and a straggle of other girls thought to be promising and recommended by their parish priests. 'We'll take things slowly,' Keogh had decided, and warned against expecting too much since, with regard to hygiene, the girls could have been living in the year dot. 'People who have had to carry water from the well are thrifty with it. They can't get used to the tap.'

This reminded Adam of the great water barrels which in his childhood had been carted from a nearby stream and on bright days leaked a silvery trail. The house now did have a tap and a water closet, but still no bathroom, only portable tubs which could be set up wherever one liked – preferably near a fire – and filled with water boiled on the kitchen range. Labour was cheap.

'Accuracy isn't Cait's strong point either,' Keogh went on. 'She measures medicines by the pinch.'

When asked why local ladies – those good at organizing

raffles – could not have taught her these things, he hedged. 'I suppose,' he admitted in the end, 'the quick way of saying it is that Cait has a bad name.'

Well, Adam now knew why.

Unknown to himself, Keogh's own name wasn't too good. Neighbours were unsettled by the energy he put into raising funds to start a fish-canning plant or organize co-operative creameries. Change, to owners of mouldering and encumbered estates, could mean only collapse.

'So you,' one of these had challenged, buttonholing Adam in the village street, 'work with the doctor? I'm told he thinks sharing in egg-production will teach us brotherly love. *Fraternité*, the French call it, don't they? Much good it did *them*!' And cackled at the century-old irony.

Adam was moved to wonder how much fraternity he would have found in the French parish he had once hoped to run. An old classmate, visiting him in Passy some time before, had amused the table with tales of the Breton one where he, as its *curé*, had had to take on the duties of a sage. Last winter, when the midwife broke her leg, he had been called upon to deliver a baby. How, Dr Blanche asked with professional interest, did that go? Not too badly, said the *curé*, thanks to advice from the local vet. Advice only, mark! Letting the vet do the job himself might have troubled his parishioners' faith.

'So what have *you* been up to?' he asked Adam who, being loath to say that he had possibly damaged two women, denied having been up to anything.

The question bothered him though. How, while in love with Danièle, had he become entangled with Cait? To be fair, the entangling had been mostly her doing – and Cait in hot pursuit was hard to thwart. At Christmas, for instance, when Keogh invited people in, engaged a fiddler and had bunting strung through what would soon be the women's ward in the new hospital, she had an avid gleam to her eye and kept pressing Adam to dance.

'People wouldn't like it,' he had to remind her, 'I am in mourning.'

'Ah yes!' She blushed.

She herself could not presume to mourn. That would have been an insult to Mrs Gould whose bid to make off with the piano must, since Keogh's disclosures, be seen in a different light.

Smoothing feathers ruffled in that wrangle had led Adam into a dalliance with Cait, and this, in turn, to some pique when he failed to follow it up. She had clearly thought he would when she turned up on his doorstep bearing a house-warming gift.

'Congratulations! You're in possession! Piano still here? Alleluia!' Then, seeing a photograph of his mother which he had hung in the drawing room, she had cried with mock aggression, 'At last! A friendly face!'

It was, both knew, remarkably like her own, and the perception, vivid with innuendo, made Adam wary. From then on he discouraged visits.

Then, just before leaving for Paris, he gave a dinner for a few neighbours and invited her. He did this on impulse, telling himself that there was safety in numbers and saw too late that the other guests – gentry and carriage folk – were surprised to see her sitting at table instead of waiting at it. Perhaps to discomfit them, she wore a startlingly elegant silk gown which was too low-cut for the occasion.

After dinner, her singing drew tributes. As she preened in her unsuitable dress, he recognized it as the one his mother was wearing in the photograph. Mrs Ross's husband – a boozy colonel – cried '*brava*!' and mumbled something about 'old Gary's fillies'. Cait was singing an encore when Keogh, who had driven her there, whispered to Adam that he had been called to a sick patient and must leave.

'Can you see Cait home?'

'Of course.'

But when the other guests had left, and Adam was making for the stables, she murmured, 'I could stay.'

'What about the maids?'

'I'll leave at first light.'

Naive? Or practised? He was tempted. 'Let's have a last brandy,' he compromised, 'for the road, then I'll drive you back. You're a lovely girl, but I can't promise you anything.'

After which disclaimer, he let the drink 'for the road' prevent their taking it. She had, after all, been warned.

'No need for promises,' she murmured. 'It's a safe time.'

***

How much, Adam now wondered, had become known about this? During Adam's visit, Bishop Tobin had seemed remarkably conversant with his affairs.

'I hear that you and Con Keogh,' Tobin had challenged, 'ran a nurses' training course! Busy bees the pair of ye! News travels fast in the wilds!' Delight at welcoming Adam had to be tempered by teasing. 'What do you think of my episcopal palace then?'

Smiling in self-mockery. The 'palace' was a roomy but shabby place which smelled of old, dampened tea-leaves – used for sweeping the floors – and equally damp red setter dogs. The dominant colour was mahogany. Tobin fussed pleasurably with wine, decanted two bottles, then asked whether Adam would keep pace with him if he opened a third or – why not? – a fourth? The occasion deserved to be toasted lavishly since, to a celibate, an old pupil's return could be like that of a lost son.

'So tell me about Keogh. I'd bet it was his idea that you charge trainees a fee! Six girls signed up, I'm told, whereas you'll need only the one or maybe two for your little hospital. But the scandal that might attach to a man teaching one woman would not attach to his teaching seven! Hence the training course! Very practical and Protestant! Thrifty too! Isn't it an odd thing that, though the sale of indulgences is said to have sparked off the Reformation, commerce is a Protestant speciality!'

'What have you against Keogh?' Adam asked.

'Ask what *he* has against us! *He* says we infect our flocks with Mohammedan fatalism. But *I* say he's the one fighting a holy war. Fear of Home Rule for Ireland puts the wind up chaps like him. They're afraid we'll take over. Hence the good works. Mark my words, when the Prods start those, it's war by other means. Onward Christian soldiers! It's good to have a Catholic like yourself working with him. Stake our claim!'

Talk had then turned to other things – *la douce France* and Tobin's scrambled memories of Latin love verse which, he claimed, Adam used to take from his shelves and read on the sly. Since Adam had no such recollection, they argued agreeably, quoted inaccurately and sat up so late that the warming pan in Adam's bed was stone-cold by the time he reached it, and the dawn chorus had begun. He shivered his way towards sleep and, on waking, found that the starched lace on his pillowcase had rubbed his neck raw, leaving marks which looked like love bites. He wondered if the ascetic bishop went around with these and unknowingly gave scandal to Protestants?

***

'Meuriot is uneasy at your visit. He thinks you'll have trouble with the law.'

'Should I stay somewhere else?'

'No. I like having him uneasy. Shows I'm still in control.'

Returning to the *maison de santé*, Adam had found Blanche alone with a cigar and joined him for a stroll. The day was still warm, and a smell of freshly clipped box hedges hung in the air. Beyond the river, the sun reddened the metalwork of the Eiffel Tower, from the top of which, according to Maupassant, God had proclaimed him his bastard. Poor Guy. His mother, Blanche confided, had put his beloved yacht up for sale! His *Bel-Ami*. No doubt she thought of him as dead. Well, he might soon be.

The doctor too was feeling his mortality. 'I'm seventy-two! It may be a race between myself and Guy.' And indeed he looked evanescent. His eyelashes had faded, and his facial hair was like blown foam. He began to speculate about the police inquiry and the *magistrat* who wanted to see Adam. A *pro forma* precaution? Probably. 'Politics interested them at first, but our poor friend had not been active lately and his and Father de Latour's plan to launch a newspaper could hardly be called subversive.' Latour, Blanche had heard, was going through some sort of crisis. His paper had lost money and was to fuse with one which had a different agenda. 'They say the pope made a few contributions, then stopped. God's vicar helps those who help themselves.' A shrug. It could have been predicted. Moderation didn't sell.

***

At table, there was some reminiscing about Guy's flashes of brilliance when he first came.

'It was the last flare of a dying lamp! You wouldn't,' Meuriot warned Adam, 'want to see him now. He has more and more accesses of blindness.'

'He who was so sharp!'

'He was a luminary!' Dr Grout, a fellow Norman, sighed loyally. 'In fact,' he reminded the others, 'he used to be able to see in the dark! He was a nyctalops.'

'And had keen vision for things which weren't there!'

They discussed the use writers made of hallucinations, and how Guy had stimulated his by ether and other drugs.

'First he took them for his migraines ...'

'... then for stimulus.'

In their experience, the doctors agreed, writing was itself a drug. It had been that for Balzac, whose house was not a stone's throw from this room, and for Nerval, who had been one of Blanche's patients until he hanged himself on a lamp post.

'Talking of not believing one's eyes,' said Meuriot, 'I had a surprise visit this afternoon. Madame d'Armaillé is in Paris. It was you she hoped to see,' he told Blanche, 'but she couldn't wait. She is here to see about letting her uncle's apartment.'

So – Adam felt faint – his had not been a hallucination at all! The lady with osprey feathers had been she! When Dr Grout murmured something in his ear, he failed to understand and answered at random.

***

Next day he went to see the magistrate, a man, magnified by a vast desk, who wanted to know the source of the monsignor's funds.

'Belgium,' Adam told him, 'or possibly the Congo. The veteran Zouaves whose donations came through Sauvigny earned money in three continents. Once the papal state collapsed, twenty-three years ago, their swords were for hire.'

The other man said nothing, so Adam felt he should qualify this.

'Mind, they were as likely to spend as to earn on these ventures. The monsignor thought them the least mercenary of mercenaries.'

The magistrate raised an eyebrow: one only, for a monocle was screwed into his other eye. It made him look exotic which, as the first Republican to confront Adam in an official capacity, was how Adam had expected him to look. He was civil though, and the interview was being conducted in a room with glazed bookshelves and soft armchairs.

'Would you say,' he asked, 'that the monsignor hoped to change the world?'

'*Monsieur le Juge*, his aim was to effect a reconciliation between the clergy and the Republic.'

'A sane goal!' The monocle flashed. Reflections from a yellow blotter gave it a ring of colour like a blackbird's eye.

Mindful of Blanche's anxieties, Adam observed that the line between sanity and folly could be hard to draw.

'And did the vicomte – a man viscerally opposed to the *ralliement* – expect his funds to be used to promote it? Might there have been a second, secret, very different plan? How can you be sure, Monsieur Gould, that you were fully in Belcastel's confidence?'

Adam said that, though he could not be sure that he knew *all* the monsignor's plans, he would have had an inkling of any practical ones.

'Mmm!' The monocle was removed and polished so that its gleam grew even more like that of a blackbird scouting for a worm. 'Did you know,' came an abrupt query, 'that his will leaves that money to you?'

'Dr Blanche told me.'

Cheated of his surprise, the magistrate pressed his lips together. 'It is a lot of money.'

'Oh, I doubt if he meant me to keep it. Leaving it to me was probably a provisional shift. In the end he must have meant it to go to a good cause.'

'There is evidence to the contrary, Monsieur Gould. This' – the magistrate produced a letter – 'is addressed to you, but, in the circumstances, we had to read it.'

Adam took the unfolded paper bearing a few lines penned in the monsignor's characteristically dashing script. The down strokes were as fat as pickets.

Dear Adam,
My advice is to use 'our' funds to do what private good you can.
Aspire modestly. Don't try to help any cause. Most overween.
Even Pope Leo overweens when he talks of making France
happy.

The more ambitious one's good intentions, the likelier, I have
come to think, they are to backfire. Keeping the money from the
madcap clutch of the quixotic Sauvigny is in itself a useful act.

Pray for me,
Belcastel

Looking up, Adam saw that the magistrate had his hand out for the letter.

'We have to keep it, Monsieur Gould. The case has ramifications. Keep us notified about any change of address.'

Adam handed it back and left. He wondered whether Belcastel had died in a state of despair.

On the outer stairway, he recognized a bony silhouette in a once-white cassock. It belonged to a morose-looking Latour, who seemed to have aged ten years and was as bent as the letter C. As they clasped hands, Adam said, 'I was thinking of poor Belcastel and took you for his ghost.'

The priest didn't smile. 'That is what I am,' he claimed, 'a kind of ghost going to see *le juge*! It sounds sinister, does it not?'

'It sounds like the *Dies Irae*!'

Latour nodded glumly. However, while labouring up some more stairs, he called back over his shoulder, 'Are you free on Saturday? Come and dine at the monastery. The food is bad, but we can exchange our news.' And on he trudged, raising stiff knees with visible difficulty.

***

Outside, a swollen river heaved along both sides of the Ile de la Cité. At the Pont Neuf the divided current licked the tops of the arches, then flowed together at the apex of the small *place* on the other side. Under a surface glitter, it was thick with mud. A drift of tawny ducklings dissolved in a blur, while a swan, magnifying itself, held its wings half-erect. In amused imitation, Adam thrust back his elbows, arched his chest and raced down the quay.

Crossing the Pont Royal to the Left Bank he found he was heading for the rue St Guillaume and the apartment of the vicomte de Sauvigny. High walls revealed the tips of trees whose flowers flew like pennants. Some had fallen. Galaxies of a bloom, whose name he didn't know, were being shattered. Spring's gaudy havoc raged unchecked.

He must see Danièle.

For half a year now he had been restraining himself, and restraint bred paradox. It recalled notions such as the one that the last shall be first. The Christian storyline laid the ground for romance.

He told himself that he needed to see her if only to say goodbye. She owed him that. He would not press – well, not hard – for more. But was reminded of the delirium that came from betting a hundred to one on the racetrack.

Every so often you had to nourish your soul's dream.

He wondered whether to lurk in her street. Wait? But a biting wind drove him to knock on her door and tell the unfamiliar manservant who opened it that he had a message from Dr Blanche for Madame d'Armaillé. The man put out a hand.

'There is no letter. I am to tell her by word of mouth.'

He wondered if she might guess that a message delivered like this might be from him. Maybe she had had him in mind when calling on Dr Blanche? She had, after all, turned up unannounced, therefore on impulse. And her impulse had touched off his.

He was shown into an anteroom where he stood for minutes. Then, behind him he heard a woman's voice.

'Monsieur Gould?' It was the maid, Félicité. 'What a turn-up!' Nodding and marvelling. 'Do you remember me?'

'Félicité?'

'That's right.' She looked at him assessingly and was clearly enjoying the moment. What happened now must depend on her. Sure enough, her next remark was, 'Madame won't see you if I say it's you.'

'How can I persuade you not to?' Laughing. A *douceur*, he thought and wondered how much.

'I am not looking for money.' Delicately, her upper lip twitched like a rabbit's. This, in someone so self-possessed, was touching. 'Not that I'd say "no" to it.'

Both smiled.

He produced some notes. Was it more sordid to bribe a maid, he wondered, or to refuse her?

She plucked a largish one from his hand. 'This is fair.' She folded his fingers over the rest. 'But you must promise not to upset her. It's easily done these days, so don't ask her questions or argue. She needs comforting. If you can do that, do. But only if she wants you to. Understood?'

'Yes.'

'Come then.' Opening a door, Félicité led him back across the hall where, he now noticed, boxes were piled on top of a large trunk. 'See,' she nodded at these. 'The place is to be let. We're leaving – supposed to leave in just over an hour. For Belgium. Her husband' s expecting her.'

'But then ...?'

'You might change her mind. Try! Luck is with you, Monsieur Adam, or you wouldn't be here now! Luck and Félicité. Don't let us down!' With a quick swoop, she caught his hand and slipped it inside her bodice next to her skin. 'That's to stiffen you! *Courage*, Monsieur Adam! Press her tenderly. Don't give her time to have scruples.' For seconds, her hand held his against the breast of which she was clearly proud. When he jerked his away, she whispered, 'Don't worry. This is part of the service. The secret part.'

By now they were at another door. Cautiously, she knocked, opened it, put her head around it, announced: 'A visitor for Madame,' motioned him in, then closed it behind him.

Danièle, seated at an escritoire, was shaking ink from her pen. She did not look up.

Adam spoke quickly: 'I had to see you.'

She got to her feet.

'We never said goodbye.'

She backed from the escritoire. 'You!'

'Yes.' He was standing just inside what he now saw was the vicomte's library. 'I shall leave if you want me to.'

Félicité would not have approved.

But then how could someone as set against scruples as Félicité guess that they could be bonding?

'Shall I go?'

She didn't answer.

Was Félicité listening on the other side of the door? Casting up her eyes at his lack of sense? Stroking her warm breasts and remembering the chill of his hand?

'Danièle, do you want me to leave?'

'No!' She walked into his arms.

He sighed. 'I'm ...'

Stopping his mouth with a finger, she took his wrist and drew him after her out of the door – Félicité, if she had been lingering, had gone – up the main stairs and into her bedroom.

What followed was not happiness.

Their first frantic bout of love-making was an inventory of body parts: here I, you, we are whole and together again! My cheek fits the hollow of your shoulder. Ah, and here's this! Yours. Mine? Ours.

'We're one!'

'Yes.'

Exultant. Possessive. Anxious. The second time they made love, he heard himself say – the weather seemed a calming topic – that in Ireland an unseasonably fine day was called 'a pet day' because there might not be another. When she took this for a description of their tryst, he regretted providing it.

How brief was the tryst to be? *Was* it a goodbye? How – he puzzled over Félicité's instructions – could he press Danièle while soothing her? She seemed as fevered as he.

So who here was thinking responsibly? And how dangerous was the duellist husband away in his rural retreat? Might her servants betray her? Félicité? No, but what of the man who had opened the door? He, Adam saw in hindsight, had a disturbingly insolent look. Viperish? Or was that thought self-important? Maybe the fellow's mind had not been on Adam at all?

Better keep delirium within bounds. Had a half hour gone by? Adam's watch was on a dressing table. He didn't want to be seen reaching for it.

Of course they could never be one or fused or even trusting! And yet he wished their skins would melt. He imagined being her Siamese twin. Sharing a heart and brain. Feeling at last and for the first time complete.

'Without you, I feel – amputated.' Instantly, without knowing why, he saw that that word was wrong.

'*What*?'

He felt her freeze.

'Adam, you're spoiling things!'

Her anger shocked him. 'May I not say ...?'

'Hush!'

'Very well, I'll hush – though words matter.'

'That's why they're dangerous – especially that one!'

It was like finding Eurydice and not being allowed to look at her. Like forgetting a vital password.

His view was tremulous, as if he were seeing a reflection in moving water or flawed glass. Touching her, he felt tomorrow's absence.

Danièle!

Maybe he should simply get up and leave? At the thought, desire flared and he started to make love to her again.

But she too had been thinking. 'Wait. I have a plan. I must talk to Félicité. There are two dressing-gowns in that wardrobe. Can you bring them here?'

He did. They were heavy silk and oriental. Whose? Her

uncle's? She looked magnified and male when she put on the long, masterly, exotic gown and told him that she had thought of a way to put off her return to Belgium. If she stole two nights from her conjugal life, could Adam spend them here with her?

Two nights! They seemed like an eternity.

When they were decorously gowned and seated in separate armchairs, she rang for Félicité and instructed her to send the manservant to Belgium with legal papers for Monsieur d'Armaillé to sign. Didier – this was the man's name – would find these in a drawer of the escritoire. There was money for his journey there too. Here. She handed over keys. He should leave at once and must tell his master that the lawyers wanted her to stay here until he had brought back the papers and they had reviewed them.

'Meanwhile send a telegram,' she told Félicité, 'to my husband. Tell him that I shan't be arriving as expected, but that Didier will and will explain everything. Sign it "Danièle with love".'

When Félicité left, Adam asked how reliable she was.

'Completely,' Danièle assured him, 'especially for a thing like this. She loves keeping secrets from Didier. He was in the Congo with my husband and *his* loyalties are to him, not me. He'll be back the day after tomorrow, and you must be gone by then.'

'Are you sure it will take so long? To and from Belgium?'

'It's not the train which takes time. It's travelling on into the hinterland. Bad roads. No roads. We have two nights. Then you must go.'

'For ever?' Already two nights seemed less long.

She told him that she could not hurt her husband. 'What I am enjoying with you, Adam, will give me the strength to renounce you.'

'Do you love him?'

'There are different sorts of love. Do you remember telling me once that by being gentle with the world you could make it gentler? Well, now I must make it gentle for Philibert. He deserves that. He's grown gentle himself.'

Gentle? Adam, who had been picturing the duellist as a heraldic beast – maimed but rampant – resented this metamorphosis. Was restoring the beast's conjugal status not enough? Must they also invite him into the haven of their dream? It was as if Brother Wolf, on being tamed by St Francis, had asked to join the monastery. What would Francis himself do? Wear a wolf skin and take to the woods?

'He never wrote to you!' Adam reminded wolfishly. 'Nor,' he reproached, 'did you write to me after I left. Not even to say goodbye! We might say that you "took French leave". For honourable reasons to be sure!' He knew he was bullying her.

'In French,' she reminded, 'we say of someone who left without taking leave that "he left like an Englishman".'

Still wolfish, he ignored this. 'Why *didn't* you write?'

Silence.

He read it to imply that he was wasting precious time on a quarrel – which was true. How, anyway – queried the tilt of her chin – *could* she have written in any meaningful way? What kind of letter could she have sent which would satisfy them both?

Absorbed by her imagined voice, he was confused to hear her real one echo it.

'If I wrote that I was unhappy, you would have been encouraged to hope the break was not final. But anything else would have hurt you.'

Had he *heard* her say those words? Or imagined them? Both. We *are* one, he thought. We have the same thoughts! And felt such a choking tenderness that, instead of surrendering to the pleasures of a quarrel – there was no time anyway for these – he made love to her again and then again, before and after eating a meal brought by Félicité, who had taken a cab to a restaurant to get the most delectable dishes available.

No need, she told the lovers, while laying these out on two card tables which she had covered with a creamy, damask cloth, no need at all in their case to choose food with aphrodisiac properties. She could tell. 'I'm remembering my time working for an older, foreign lady,' she told Adam carefully. 'Madame here is so innocent, she may not even get my meaning.'

Adam felt flattered, then, as he drifted into sleep, remembered that Félicité must have a repertoire of such remarks.

***

He awoke to find the place beside him empty. The shutters had been opened and, through the clotted darkness outside, a dim dawn was seeping like milk. Closing his eyes, he pulled the covers closer, only to hear a voice in his ear.

'Monsieur Adam!' Félicité was lighting a gas bracket. 'There's been an accident. We have to leave. I'm to take the keys to the lawyer. Madame has gone to the station. She had no time to talk to you and asked me to explain. We got a telegram saying that the master fell downstairs. She's demented with worry.'

'Fell downstairs?' Still befuddled by sleep, he saw Danièle's stockings dangling from the arm of a chair. So she can't have left, he thought foolishly. The stockings were grey silk embroidered with clocks. Two slippers, pointing in different directions, lay on the floor underneath.

Félicité, now folding things into a bag, spoke over her shoulder. 'It looks as though he fell just after getting *her* telegram, the one she got me to send, saying she was not coming home as planned. The accident must have happened before Didier got there to explain why. The master can be very moody if he's left alone.'

'Why,' Adam tried to collect his wits, 'could she not tell me this herself? Does she blame me? Does she think he ...'

'... tried to kill himself?' Félicité nodded.

'And that I'd be glad? Is that what she has against me?'

'I don't think she's thinking of your feelings, Monsieur Adam.'

***

Letting himself out through the garden, Adam caught a remembered glimpse of the manservant standing here in leafy starlight. Getting up to relieve himself, he had spotted Didier who should by then have been on his way to reassure Monsieur d'Armaillé that, though tediously delayed, his wife would soon be home. If something other than tedium had delayed her, it would be better for his master not to know. Yet there the fellow stood – unless Adam had dreamed him. Air slashed by slanting rain was starting to erase him and when Adam looked again he was gone.

***

But the worst dupery
Is that the price of ivory
Will be our bones!
Nos os
Will stay *au Congo*,
With no tombstones
To show
Where we lie
When we die,
Having sold
Our souls to Leopold!

There was ironic clapping, and the singer a priest whose skin had a sallow, tropical tinge – sat down, drank some wine and said, 'That's only one version of the railway builders' lament. It is always polyglot, but never the same. Singers improvise. Sometimes there are bits in Dutch or Danish. Here's a Latin bit:

So with fury,
King of vain cant,
Morituri
Te salutant.

'What never changes is the mood.'
    '*Le cafard*!'
    'Congo doldrums!'

'The natives' songs are more harrowing. They sing about *wanting* to die. They dread being forced to build the railway.'
    'Well, they wouldn't work if they weren't forced.'
    'But the methods ...'

'*If* one believes the rumours!'

'I heard that they sing about white savages. I hope they don't mean us.'

'I fear they do.'

'I mean *us*: the White Fathers!'

'I know.'

'Do you feel savage, Father Emile?'

'Yes, Father, I feel very savage when I learn that not long since nine hundred black railway workers died of disease in four months. That was nearly a fifth of those engaged in laying track.'

'It is a mercy poor Cardinal Lavigerie didn't live to see ...'

'Oh come, Father, one can't believe everything one hears. More myths than rubber come out of Africa.'

Saturday dinner was finishing in the White Fathers' refectory where talk was combustible and the food as bad as Latour had warned it would be. The Fathers, who had lost their battle to stay in the Congo Free State, spoke bitterly of how the Belgians who had replaced them closed their eyes to their country's atrocities. To be fair, they had little choice. Candour earned reprimands from Rome, where King Leopold had succeeded in presenting himself as a champion of Catholic civilization. Talking too openly could be risky. Some who *had*, murmured the singer, had come a cropper. The king's arm was long. Gossips' voices sank, but Adam caught the name d'Armaillé.

'Hadn't you heard?' Father de Latour poured brandy. 'Philibert d'Armaillé was amputated.' He gestured at his own legs. 'Below the knees. Has to be pushed about in a Bath-chair.'

'Amputated!' Reproach stirred in Adam's memory. 'I called

to see his wife,' he told Latour, 'at her uncle's place. She didn't mention that.'

'No?' Delicately, the priest's fingertips stroked his eyelids. 'Too painful, no doubt. So she's in town?'

'Not now. She left. It seems he's had a fresh accident.'

Latour nodded. 'Nobody recovers from that place. Survivors bring home their nightmares. The calvary goes on.'

Talk returned to tales from the jungle. The one about d'Armaillé was depressingly plausible.

'He talked too freely,' Latour murmured. 'Rumours in London newspapers were traced back to him.'

'Were they true?'

A shrug. D'Armaillé, Latour explained, had done well during the fighting phase of his time in the Congo and got rich without violating his conscience. Later, though, he had fallen foul of the king's Belgian rubber-collectors who, he learned from his black soldiers, were committing worse atrocities than the Arabs ever had. Children were being held to ransom so as to force their parents to harvest large quotas of rubber. This was slavery of a new kind. The stories were persistent; the men reporting them had fought for the Force Publique in the name of freedom, and their officers felt dishonoured. The FP was a small, old-style mercenary army whose hundred or so white officers had quite different relations with the natives from those of the rubber-collectors. When d'Armaillé's protests were ignored, he shared his indignation with friends who were about to leave the service and sail for home.

'You're saying he blew the gaff *on the king*?' Adam was taken aback. The news raised the spiritual stakes. It meant that d'Armaillé's wife loved him for his courage and his conscience.

Adam felt humiliated. What competition could he offer? Legs? Good God! He did not want to be loved – loved? – for those.

Hating himself, he tried not to imagine the shifts to which the couple must resort when making love. He could not restrain jealousy at the thought of the nobly menial tasks which she must perform for her husband.

'So he blew the gaff,' he asked again so as to rid his inflamed mind of these images.

'He tried,' said Latour. 'But who listened? King Leopold owns and greedily milks a vast, secret *domaine privé* in the Congo. Officially the Belgian state – which will one day inherit it – is unaware of what goes on there, so it suited no one to have ex-officers' friends publishing reports in foreign papers. Officers who were back in Europe were safe enough. But d'Armaillé, while still in the Congo, was set upon, shot in the legs and left in a remote location to die. By the time he was found, gangrene had set in.'

While the priest talked, Adam's mind wrestled with an image of a man in a Bath-chair bumping down a staircase. At what time had this happened? Perhaps while Félicité was warming the bought-in food?

Might the chair have fallen over? Skidded? Tossed him out?

'More brandy? You look green.' Latour was amused. 'See how much tougher than the laity we have to be.'

***

At another table Father Emile was discussing the case of a

priest he had known – perhaps now an ex-priest? – who, having knotted his alb around a large stone, used it to batter to death two drink-sodden rubber-collectors who had impaled a baby on a stake. Long after he had killed them, the novice executioner had kept frenziedly bashing their skulls until a porridge of pink brain emerged.

'When we found him,' said Father Emile, 'he was still bashing the ground with his wrapped stone. How is *he* ever going to forget what he did?'

Just perceptibly, Father de Latour shook his head. Don't worry, Adam read this to say, Father Emile himself will soon calm down.

Should that priest's act be considered a murder, Father Emile wanted to know. Note: he gave his victims no chance to repent and save themselves from hell. Which killing, he challenged, his or theirs, was the more evil? They, it could be argued, knew not what they did.

Just eight years ago, Father Emile went on, the powers at the Berlin Conference on African Affairs had pledged themselves to – he quoted, 'watch over the preservation of the native tribes and to care for the improvement of their moral and material well-being ...' Designated enemies then were the Islamic slavers whom the Force Publique had since defeated. Who now, did his listeners think, most threatened the native tribes' well-being?

There were contradictory replies. Some agreed about the need to speak out. Others said no, since if a new colonial power were to take over, it might be Protestant and even less benign. King Leopold was not typical of Catholic rulers.

Latour murmured in Adam's ear that the story about the

rubber-collectors was probably true. His own guess was that, to force the baby's parents to provide more rubber, they had threatened to kill it without at all intending to do so. Then, as if the threat had poisoned their minds, they carried it out.

Wondering whether his mind too was poisoned, Adam produced a parable. Imagine, he begged, a young woman in d'Armaillé's wife's situation. Suppose a man were in love with her. Would he be justified in rescuing her from a life of conjugal drudgery and the sins it must surely, in the long run, make her commit?

The dilemma failed to engage the priests' interest. Their attention had turned to the coming elections in which, Latour warned, the idea that Catholics should accept the Republic would split the conservative vote.

'The *ralliement*?' Adam was amazed. 'But surely you ...'

Latour raised a supplicatory hand.

'Weren't you its great supporter? Didn't you found a news-paper to promote it?'

Yes, the priest admitted. He had, but unwinnable struggles should not be pursued. 'That is why,' bending still closer to Adam's ear, 'the proper course for the man you mentioned is to stop tormenting Madame d'Armaillé and vanish from her life.'

***

Adam hated departures. In his seminary, it had been a truism that exile earned a special grace for French missionaries. Who, after all, would mind leaving some smut-blackened English town smelling of piss and herrings? Enterprising people left such places all the time to seek fortunes elsewhere, so how could the missionaries among them claim merit? But leaving France, and above all Paris, was like casting oneself from Eden.

He prolonged his goodbyes over several evenings: garrulous ones with Thady Quill, a glum one with old seminary friends, and a last, painful one with the Blanches, which began with a visit to a now chillingly 'animalized' Guy whose gaze met Adam's with wavering recognition and flashes of that false hope which can sometimes gleam in the eyes of neglected dogs. The day ended with Adam getting funereally drunk.

By then it was May. Paris was a carnival of sounds and smells; convivial chairs had been hauled onto pavements, and here *he* was, reluctantly heading home to where tricky duties awaited him. To prepare himself he pondered the ambiguities festering between Cait and himself and was still fretting over them while he sat in the mail-boat wondering whether he had taken advantage of her who, clearly, trusted people too easily.

'You don't owe me a thing,' she had said that last, rash evening, then stretched out on the hearthrug like a cat to show off the gown which she said his mother had given her when she was too pregnant to wear it and guessed that she would not have another chance to do so. It was too fine to throw away, so Cait's mother had wrapped it optimistically in tissue paper and kept it for Cait, who at the time must have been four years old and playing with mud pies. 'I've never worn it till now.' Proudly, she pressed his fingers against the silky stuff which slid like skin over her meek, muscular limbs.

'It is a lovely dress,' he admitted, 'it looks lovely on you.'

Then he had stoked up the fire and let himself be half

seduced, in spite of being in love with someone else, while his mother's photograph reflected flames and glinted like an icon. Later, he heard himself murmur endearments in his sleep. Cait, he realized, was what the French described as a *demi-vierge*.

When he awoke she was gone, the fire dead and the room freezing. She must have walked down the long muddy avenue in her silk dress. What if someone had seen her? Was she – he disliked himself for thinking this – aiming to 'set her cap' at him? The kitchen diction surfaced from his childhood and horrified by its meanness. Anyway, she must surely have been wearing a coat.

She had left a note saying – as if predicting his thought – that she would see him for supper that evening, 'with Keogh to chaperone us'.

He smiled, slid the note into his pocket and began inspecting the house's dilapidation, which yesterday's attempts to hide had made worse. Greenery had been recklessly nailed over damp patches, and removing it brought down plaster. Wondering whether the state of the roof would soak up all his cash, he scrambled onto it, found the slates slick with algae, and by the time he had had a bath prepared and washed off the muck collected up there, was too tired to join Cait and Keogh for dinner, so ate some left-overs and went to bed.

Next day Keogh took him aside. Cait, he said, felt crushed. She had roasted some lamb and asked *him* to bring wine, then the two had waited for Adam until the food was ruined. 'This may sound mad, but she thinks that on the evening before, when your guests had gone, you pretended to be asleep so as to make declarations of love to her. I'm not asking what you got up to, Adam, but she's very upset. Your guests snubbed her.'

Discomfited, Adam complained of her lack of judgement, and was told that if anyone lacked it, it was he. 'She's seven years younger than you and has never been further than Westport. You shouldn't have exposed her to gossip. Why ever did you invite her?'

'I didn't tell her to come wearing a ball gown and shock the county!'

'Did it occur to you,' Keogh's voice was cold, 'that she might *have* no other gown apart from what she wears for everyday? She didn't want to look like one of the parlourmaids.'

'I see.'

'She thinks of you as Frenchified and free. I wouldn't want the responsibility myself.' And Keogh, who always had many things in hand, raced off.

Meanwhile Cait was not at the hospital. She had, Adam was told, taken three days off to go to a funeral. *Three?* Yes, it was on an island and the tides were tricky. On asking whose the funeral was, he learned that it was that of a distant cousin of hers – who must, he supposed, be even more distantly related to himself. Living here was like wading through seaweed. Connections caught you in their toils.

The next day he left as he had always planned to do for Bishop J J's, and after that for Paris.

Now, returning after less than a month, he stood on the mail-boat deck, and sniffed air which smelled rustily of winter. Coming west felt like turning back the clock.

***

Kingstown by dusk. The scene was like a smudged pencil-drawing of waves, rocks, spray, greying palm trees and a teeming jetty. A jostle of nuns pressed down the gangway, followed by foreign visitors whose glossy riding boots hung like fruit from the vigorous stalk of a porter's arm. Home?

He thought of being brought here when small to greet his papa on returns from Westminster, then of the masses which His Grace John Joseph Tobin hoped would shorten the same papa's time in purgatory. When Adam, on his recent visit to Tobin, made a light remark about his father having a lot to purge, the bishop had pulled him up short. Gary Gould, he stated sternly, had been a good man, landlord and father.

'Good?' Adam was indignant. 'He threw me out.'

'No! He wanted you to stay. He even asked Kate, the English girl, to persuade you. Surely you remember?'

Adam didn't.

Wearied by his botched examination of conscience, he dozed off in the train and dreamed he was looking into the garden where Danièle's manservant had hidden to spy. On waking up, he remembered that he too, just before leaving Paris, had gone to stare up at her dark windows and been challenged by Félicité who opened one a crack.

'Oh it's Monsieur Adam. Neither Monsieur nor Madame are here. Wait, though, and I'll come down.'

Shivering in the kitchen, she stirred up embers, warmed cocoa and confirmed that on the night of Adam's visit Didier had indeed lingered to snoop instead of speeding to reassure his master.

'So I did see him?'

Yes, she confirmed, and if the master, on being left without news, had thrown himself into the stairwell, who but the ex-orderly was to blame? Not that Didier saw it like that. He believed it to be his duty to let d'Armaillé know what he had discovered about Madame! Félicité had tried to persuade him that this would further destroy the crippled man. But the orderly was prone to accesses of fury when there was no reasoning with him. So Adam had better keep away.

***

'It's hush-money. I don't believe Gary meant me to have it.' Cait clapped a hand to her mouth. She should not have called him 'Gary' – perhaps never *had* till now except in bed? 'Why wasn't it in the will, if what you say is true?'

Adam turned away his face. 'It *is* true,' he prevaricated. 'My Uncle Matthew has died' – this bit was true – '*his* remittances cease forthwith, and the capital goes to you. My father's will has a provision which now takes effect. You'll have enough to live on, but only just. The family was never generous with Matthew because of his gambling. Anyway, money's tight.'

'You're pensioning me off!'

'Pensioning? How old are you, Cait? Nineteen?' He laughed, then choked the laugh as he saw that the supposed bequest would nail her to the cross of her bad reputation. He had bungled his offer.

'It *is* Uncle Matthew's money.'

'But your father didn't leave it to me.'

'No,' Adam admitted. He asked: 'Did you hate him? Is that why you don't want the money?'

'Hate him? No! He was always a gentleman. I was fond of him.'

Adam had come straight from the train station to the hospital, where he found a note pinned to the door saying, 'Closed. Doctor away'. Keogh, Cait told him when she finally opened it, would be back in a week. She looked at him coldly. 'You never came to supper – or said goodbye.'

'I'm sorry. I'm sorry. Let me explain.'

But to explain would have involved tedious chat about roofs and funerals, so instead he found himself recklessly telling her about Danièle. To his surprise, this softened her, and in no time she was comforting him with tea as black as stout and saying that his friend was doing the right thing in sticking by her husband. Adam thought this conclusion hasty, but, remembering how saintly Cait had been with his appalling old father, supposed she had a right to her view.

After a while, she went out to the hospital hen-house, brought back eggs, soft-boiled them and made toast which she cut into 'soldiers' for dipping in the yolks.

'There's nothing else. Being alone, I didn't bother to buy in food.'

'It's a nursery meal,' he exclaimed, adding that his mother – her Cousin Ellen – used to feed it to him.

It was as her slow smile blossomed and expanded that, in his eagerness to make peace, he upset her all over again by inventing a legacy. Patching things up drew them, first into each other's arms, then into one of the ward beds, where they spent the night after she had put a fresh note on the outer door saying 'Repairs in progress.' He kept well back from the windows when she, whose presence here, unlike his, would not excite comment, went to buy provisions. Once a patient pounded so hard on the door that she had to open it and hand out the laudanum the fellow claimed to need for pain.

Coming back to bed, she slid cold hands into Adam's armpits and explained, 'If anyone is gravely ill, there's a doctor in the next town who'd help in a pinch. Otherwise, Dr Keogh says we're to carry on.'

'Does he now?'

'I don't think he meant what you mean.'

They laughed, though neither did Adam mean quite what she did, for he resisted her attempts to get him, as she put it, 'to go all the way' in his love-making. Had his father? He didn't want to find out. Perhaps the old man had been past it?

***

As though inventing a false legacy had conjured up a real one, a letter came from Belcastel's lawyers.

When Adam returned to his own house the next day, he picked the envelope from the hall table, then quickly put it down. On impulse and to put off knowing what it said, he told the manservant, Brady, whose eye struck him as quizzical, that he had just come from the station, had chosen to walk and would pick up his luggage later.

'It's such a lovely day,' he claimed, 'that I decided to enjoy it. I even picked some bluebells. See.' And he handed them over as though they might certify the truth of his lie which was triply inept since, as both the station master and the jarvey who had driven him to the hospital knew his movements, Brady must too. Adam remembered too late that, in places like this, all comings and goings were news – and lies about them ranked as a sensation. Cait's bad name could soon be as black as pitch.

The lawyer's letter informed Adam Aloysius Gould that he, unless a by now improbable challenge were to arise, would on a given date be entitled to the money held in the account opened in his name some time before. It was the equivalent of £30,000, a considerable sum, though once intended as a mere instalment of the far greater one needed to buy back Church property confiscated by the Italian State. French monarchists had hoped that this move would win papal support for their cause. But the cause was now moribund and, as Adam reminded himself, Belcastel had left word that the funds should be used for private purposes. Like Keogh's, his message was, 'Think small!'

To Adam though, the sum was vast. The roof, he thought! A decent carriage! A bathroom of the sort Guy would have liked! He burst out laughing, for the money's potential outstripped fancy! It would allow him, for instance, to engage a reliable steward, leave the task of running this place to him, then settle near where Danièle now lived and lay siege to her heart. He could rent, no *buy* a place deep in the Belgian woods – there must be woods! But this, he saw, was a fancy of the sort that poisoned minds. Think small, he scolded himself. Remember that the crippled Monsieur d'Armaillé has a right to his domestic peace. But the prospect of money coming elated him.

Ashamed of this covetousness, he tried to give it a gloss. Yesterday Cait had – pointedly? – mentioned a woman, distantly related to herself who, when the man whose concubine she had been died intestate, ended up working for his heirs for £12 a year! The heirs, Cait noted tartly, thought they were being charitable. Adam could change that woman's life without noticing the difference.

He could restart his father's racing stable and give his winnings to Keogh to do good with. Belcastel might even have approved, for 'social sins' – a newish term – had begun to interest him.

And of course something must be done for Cait.

Meanwhile the thought of stables sent Adam to inspect them properly as he had not yet done. They were in a depressing state, and one section looked as though tinkers had camped there. Clearly, Brady had been careless. There were signs of a fire having ravaged a couple of stalls. But maybe the damage went back years? Returning to the front of the house, Adam was taken aback on being greeted with martial music. The piano! Glimpsing Mrs Gould through the drawing room window, he saw that fun was being poked at him. Wasn't that the tune of *Ritorna vincitor*? He greeted her and when she noted that 'instruments need to be played', wondered for a stunned moment if the remark had an erotic thrust. Of course not! No! What a mad notion! It reminded him though that Cait, for all her professed eagerness to study the piano, had done nothing about it. Her whims were lazy – but how, having no social model at all, could she be anything else?

After drinking a glass of Madeira with Mrs Gould, he went upstairs and, to settle his nerves, brushed his hair with his father's ivory hairbrushes – Congo ivory? – then went to the wine cellar to find some claret to take back to Cait who was expecting him for supper. The wine must have been put down in a year when his father's horses were winning.

***

'Do you know where Keogh really is?' Cait was cooking blood pudding in an over-heated pan. On the windowsill a jar of flowers matched the yellow flare as grease briefly caught fire. 'Doing good works, didn't you say?'

She tipped food onto plates. Fumes alerted the hospital cat, which slid under her skirt, wound its soft self around her ankles and let its tail flick in and out of sight. 'He's staying with the Earl and Countess of Sligo with whom he is secretly in love. They do good works together. That, he told me, is why he may remain a bachelor.' Cait paused. '*I* had been telling him about us, so he wanted me to know that he understood about men and women.'

'Us?' Adam speared some half-burnt black pudding, cut the slightly repulsive object into roundels and smuggled them down to the cat. 'Am I,' he asked, 'to learn what you told him? And,' wiping grease from his hands, 'why?'

'Because he's a doctor.' she exhaled nervously. 'And I needed to know if you could have made me pregnant. This was in February.' A pause. 'After that first time, remember? What was frightening was that you were avoiding me. Then, when you invited me to that dinner, I risked it again – and of course he knew.'

'Knew?'

'Guessed that I was afraid.'

'Can't we be friends, Cait? Trust each other?'

She looked away. 'You're upset,' she informed the yellow flowers, 'because I told Keogh about us? But if I had turned to you instead, you'd have thought I was seeking more than friendship. And,' she turned and held his gaze, 'I knew there must be an impediment to that. As it turns out,' dropping a wry curtsy, 'the impediment is a married French woman.'

It was a day for reproaches.

He put his head in his hands, raised it, then silently and thoughtfully, drank two comforting glasses of claret. Was she an innocent, he wondered, or sly? Rural folk, he remembered, liked to juggle these roles. He had been careful not to make her pregnant. Indeed, for all he knew to the contrary, her hymen could be intact and what she feared was a virgin birth.

Neither of them spoke.

The poor girl, he realized, hoped I'd marry her. He had not eaten, and the wine was going to his head. Keogh's letter clearly carried more coded warnings than he had picked up. The prospect of tackling the meat she had put before him became intolerable.

Neither of them spoke. He pushed away his plate.

'I'm sorry,' he said. 'I'd better leave. We've given enough scandal without my spending another night here.' He told her about Brady's knowing looks. 'I'll call by in the morning.'

Only when he was alone on the unpaved, white road did pity filter into his mind. Her face reproached him in hindsight, and he remembered having seen her with that same stunned expression shortly after he first arrived. Then, too, it had been his fault. While he was living at Keogh's, he had taken to retelling some of Guy's stories to neighbours who dropped in after supper. They seemed to relish the entertainment, so he was taken aback when, one evening, Cait jumped up, declared it hateful and rushed out into the dark.

'Tonight's story upset her.' Keogh had seemed to be wondering whether to say more.

What Adam had retold was Guy's tale about a simple youth – he could have been one of that night's listeners – who, on his father's death, discovers that the old man had had a secret, illegitimate family. To avoid the impropriety of mentioning them in a will, a concubine and her small son had been left with no support. The father, however, relying on his elder son's good heart, had left a letter asking him to look after them discreetly. Dutifully, the youth makes their acquaintance, plays shyly with his small half-brother and gradually finds himself taking his father's place in the young woman's life. The story – Adam now saw – might be embarrassingly like Cait's private fantasy about what might happen to herself, who had also been a concubine.

'What upset her,' Keogh guessed, 'may have been the story's tolerance for compromise. I suppose that's French? It acknowledges opposing needs.' People like Cait, he noted, didn't do that. They hated holding contradictory ideas in their heads. 'It frightens them.'

'You'll tell me next that that's why Catholics tell lies?'

Keogh had laughed. 'Not, it seems, in France.'

Turning his mind to the present, Adam remembered what Cait had just told him about Keogh and wondered if *he* would wait patiently for his hopeless love for the Countess of Sligo to wane, then make a sensible marriage. Wasn't that too a compromise? Slow, sad, serial and rather smug? The Protestant way?

***

Going home, he slept badly, rose early, then took a short-cut back to the hospital. It led through wet fields full of nibbling rabbits, a greedy dazzle of spiders' webs and vegetation as tender as young lettuce. After scrambling through this, he had to scale a near-vertical cliff which crested some yards from the hospital front door. While doing this he was out of sight but within earshot of two people who seemed to have just met.

Cait's voice rang out above his head. She was teasing some-one – ah, it must be Bishop Tobin! – about his tall silk hat which gave him, she noted, added stature. Was this a formal visit, she asked playfully, and explained that she herself had just come from a farm, where she had got a jug of milk. 'It's still warm from the cow. Would Your Grace like a cupful?'

'Cait,' the bishop's voice was embarrassed. 'I'd best put my cards on the table. This is not a friendly visit.'

'Ah!'

'Reports have reached me of what is going on here, and the word they use is not friendly. It is "fornication".' Tobin's tone was mildly apologetic, as he explained that the scandal left him no choice. He must intervene.

'Why?' Cait's high-pitched fury struck the eavesdropping Adam as rightly intended for himself. The bishop, like a man passing a street fight, had been hit by mischance. Fornication, she scolded, was winked at when the gentry got up to it among themselves. No doubt her accusers' objection was to her look-ing above her station? Who were they anyway? If they were anonymous, why did His Lordship believe them?

Because, said the prelate, the most vicious accusations had come from her brothers. 'They say they'll kill you if you bring more shame on them.'

'More?'

'We know what they mean.'

Impatient to interrupt this, Adam sped along a goat track which zigzagged up the cliff. Skidding, his foot dislodged scree while he heard the bishop say that he didn't want to create bad blood in the village. The blood, Cait responded, was clearly already bad.

'No more so than in the rest of my diocese.'

'Your Grace lacks charity.'

'What My Grace lacks and cannot afford is tact. I must talk to Adam. Alone. For at least half an hour. I suppose he's inside?'

'Your scandalmongers mislead you.'

'But you *are* expecting him? Isn't that why you fetched milk?'

'Not at all. I myself, though Your Grace thinks me so sinful, do not drink penitentially black tea!'

Sounds of retreating shoe-leather signalled dudgeon, and a door banged. Gone. But not, Adam noted, before giving as good as she got. His papa – a polemicist famed at the hustings in his day – must have groomed her. So perhaps those two had been good for each other, after all? Clever old Gary and the sixteen-year-old Cait? Could they have been kindred spirits? And might Adam, even now, find in her the spirit of the man he had missed knowing when *he* was sixteen? Gary the shape-shifter.

Woa there, Adam! She misunderstands friendship. Keep in mind how dangerously her hopes rise! *Merde*!

She put him in mind of the bishop's red setter dogs: affectionate, silky creatures whose bright coats matched her hair colour and who always flung themselves on him with wet, lolling tongues. It was wise to stop play before these reached his face or the play – in Cait's case – was mistaken for a contract.

She behaved, it struck him, with the desperation of a much plainer woman – but perhaps, in this country, everyone had a desperate streak. Better not stay here, Adam.

Wondering, 'Am I heartless?' he cut across a last loop of goat track, grasped a root, hauled himself past a stretch of crumbling cliff and, like a pantomime demon, popped up by the bishop's knees.

'Adam! The very man I've been wanting to see!'

'I've been spying on Your Lordship! You've been playing God! Ejecting and rejecting! Casting out!'

Shaking steepled fingers, the bishop said, 'Let's go in and make tea. I should have asked her to leave the milk. And before you stop me, let me say what I came to say which is that you, who are so quick to condemn your father, are doing precisely what he did to your mother!'

'Just now the one tormenting Cait was you!'

'Adam, I had to. She risks coming a cropper – as happened to your mama. Which is why I am begging you to either love her or leave her. For good.'

The comparison roused unmanning feelings.

'Neither one of them,' said Tobin sadly, 'knew the world. But do you suppose either would listen to my advice? Women think celibates know nothing.'

'Where has she gone?'

'To the right place, I trust. Ah, you mean Cait? Flounced off. Are you going to give me that tea? To warm us.'

'Unfortunately, I have no time.' To change the subject, Adam plunged into an improvised account of why he must leave for France.

'But you've just come from there!'

'Yes, but I've had a disturbing letter.' And he told of the legacy which he might be accused of having schemed to acquire. This fear, as he dwelled on it, grew worryingly plausible. 'People may think me grasping,' he realized. 'Zouave donors certainly will.' He wondered why the nudge to his conscience had been so slow.

The bishop asked about legal impediments, and was told that these seemed to have been cleared up. Perhaps, though, the bequest had been hasty, even dishonourable? Adam could no longer think straight. It was Congo booty, so how give it back? A jungle clung to it.

'Greed,' the bishop reminded him, 'exists everywhere.'

Adam admitted this. '*Bel-Ami*, Guy's tale of an unscrupulous careerist, shows him using women to help make his way. I, without meaning to, may have used Belcastel.'

Visibly flummoxed by this new dilemma, Tobin had nothing to say.

'Not,' Adam confided, 'that I can be described as "enjoying" property.' This was true. His father's was proving a worry and a drain. Possessions had set up a need of more possessions and, without the monsignor's bequest, he could not preserve the status quo.

'By the way, I see you came here in your trap. So perhaps you can drive us to my place so that we may have our talk over lunch?' At home, Adam calculated, there would be less privacy, and it would be hard for Tobin to return to the thorny topic of Cait.

***

Sure enough, the prospect of cooking for a bishop threw the household into turmoil for, as Brady revealed, the cook was ill – which might mean drunk – and the only pudding on offer was two-day-old Caragheen Moss, a seaweed blancmange which Adam found repellent.

While maids scurried, Brady chivvied and the bishop repaired to the water closet, Adam spied a second envelope with a French postmark. Its return address was Thady Quill's, and the handwriting that of Thady's wife who wrote most of their letters. This one, though, must be a joint effort, for hyperbole throbbed through its prose – which bore news. Apparently, Monsieur d'Armaillé's manservant, Didier, had sought out the Quills to report that his master was in such despair over the distress which his condition was inflicting on his wife that Didier felt it to be his duty to reveal that she, having had a lover, deserved no better. Little could be done for the maimed man's body, but his mind, Didier argued, should surely be set at rest?

'It is my duty,' he insisted, 'to tell him. And I will once he's well enough to bear the blow.'

'If this happens,' warned the Quills, 'Monsieur d'Armaillé may want to fight a duel. That is how he always dealt with trouble, and Monsieur Didier thinks that doing it now would bring him relief. He says men in Bath-chairs can use pistols and that if his master were to challenge you, he, as the injured party, would have the right to fire first. He is still a crack shot.

'In the light of all this, Madame d'Armaillé should be got

out of the way. Perhaps you could ask Father Latour to arrange for her to stay a while in some discreet convent.

'*We* think that this visit to us may be taken as a challenge to you whose address we naturally refused to reveal. Such a proxy challenge, of course, needs no reply.'

Didn't it?

An inky postscript in English gave it as Thady's opinion that both master and man were off their heads, and that Adam would be wise to stay put a while longer in Ireland.

'But if you feel that matters should be resolved, come and stay with us,' urged Madame Quill in a PPS. 'You'll need to be with friends.'

Conjugal disagreement registered like a watermark. Madame Quill clearly felt that Danièle might need help.

So, Adam told himself, I really have to go!

***

A week later he was in Paris – not Belgium. Going there might be rash. He must find out.

'Monsieur d'Armaillé's old orderly came looking for you,' Father Latour told him. 'He went first to the *maison de santé*, but Blanche was away, so he came here and hung about until I agreed to see him. As your friend Quill had alerted us to the man's obsession, I considered it my duty to see if he was dangerous.'

'And concluded?'

'That he is. He put me in mind of animals – cats, for instance – whose movements body forth their brains. He is as focused as a knife!' Latour closed his eyes as if assessing an unpleasant image.

Didier's attachment to d'Armaillé, he had learned, was painfully close. 'He told me that he nurses him "like a mother".' The priest grimaced. 'Madame d'Armaillé may or may not be grateful.'

'When last we met,' Adam reminded him, 'you advised me to disappear from her life. What do you say now?'

Latour's response was blunt. 'Keep well out of sight if you care for her safety.'

Adam didn't argue.

'She's never alone,' Madame Quill warned when told of Latour's advice. Armies of aunts were said to be relaying each other so as to show solidarity, quash rumours and possibly restrain her.

'Are they afraid of her husband or' – Adam felt shy about asking this – 'me?'

'Possibly herself?' Madame Quill shrugged. 'We heard that they keep her semi-sedated.'

François Tassart, on dropping by to sell the last of Guy's clothes, had reported this. As a Belgian and a servant, he sometimes got news of the d'Armaillé household which he described as uneasy. Something – possibly violent – seemed set to happen.

'Why,' Thady reproached Adam, 'did you not take my advice and wait discreetly in Ireland?'

Ireland, Adam reminded him, was not discreet. It was secretive, which was different.

He was thinking of something Tobin had said at their recent lunch, after Brady removed the uneaten seaweed blancmange, and left them alone. While they lingered over coffee, the bishop's mood had darkened. Studying the dregs in his cup, he confided that the clergy were tormented by knowing what went on in places like this: things like incest, sexual slavery and betrayal. 'We don't just hear of them in the confessional,' he insisted. 'People pick on us when they need to get them off their chest and pass the burden on – usually when it's too late to help. Sometimes a family member is privy to a thing, or a doctor or magistrate stumbles on and helps cover it up. Because depravity must be hidden. Else people would despair. It's why we sometimes seem tyrannical.'

'Not you,' Adam had soothed

'No?' The bishop's smile was puzzled. 'I was too soft. You see, as the gentry here are mostly Protestant, a man like me could be as lonely as a lighthouse-keeper. Thanks to your parents, though, I had the run of this house and a mount for the hunt when I wanted one. So when your Papa divorced us all – your mother, you and me – my loss was personal. Mind, I pitied his case – the clash of duties – and cheered on his bid to find a compromise. But none proved workable. One was to get the girl – Kate, remember? – to wait till you were older and marry you. Her dowry could then be promised, a contract drawn up and money borrowed straight away on the strength of it to save his estate. Maybe that too was unworkable? Anyway, Gary gave it up.' Thoughtfully, Tobin poured himself the last of the coffee and said that he had come to see that Gary *wanted* both women. 'He hoped to import some of the shine of his London life to this place where money was tight and the air tarnished by shadows. He was a hybrid, you see. Like yourself and – God help us – me!' The bishop's laugh was glum.

Some time later, when chatting with Thady in Paris, it occurred to Adam to ask if he too was a hybrid.

'Divil a hybrid!' said Thady cheerfully, 'even if some call me "Monsieur Qui"!' And he pointed out that in Ireland he would be seen simply as a servant, whereas here, on the rue St Lazare, he was a businessman. An entrepreneur! 'That,' he told Adam, 'is why you are an exile, and I a settler. I,' he thumped his chest, 'have shaken the dirt of Ireland from off my feet!'

'Thady!' His wife called. 'Monsieur Didier is across the street watching our door. He must know you're here,' she told Adam. 'Maybe you'd as well see what he wants.'

***

'Monsieur Gould.' Teeth glistening, the ex-orderly held out a letter.

For a mad moment Adam thought it might be from Danièle. His glance slid over the extended hands, and he wondered whether they might make a lunge for him. But no. Men like this believed in ritual. Duels? Adam could have laughed. It was years since he had fired a gun and then only to kill rabbits.

'Is Madame d'Armaillé safe?'

'My master blames himself too much to let harm come to her.'

Adam took the letter. There was no envelope, just a sealed sheet of folded paper on which he couldn't get a purchase. His hand shook, and he turned away to hide it.

'It should be a challenge,' said the orderly, 'but, somehow, I don't think it is. Read it, sir, and see if I'm right.'

More theatre, thought Adam resentfully. He asked, 'Can you open this?'

Didier slid a tough, yellow fingernail under the sealing wax and levered it off. Still holding the letter, he said, 'My guess is that he's entrusting Madame's happiness to you lest something happen to himself.' Was there mockery in the small, lively eyes?

'Is this some trick?'

'*Mais non, Monsieur.*' Didier returned the letter.

Adam read:

Monsieur Gould,
You and I know enough about each other to dispense with beating about the bush.

My wife knows nothing about the proposal I am about to make. This means that, if you so choose, you may refuse without embarrassment. Nobody will ever know.

Glancing at the patently hawk-eyed Didier, Adam saw the absurdity of this. He read on.

The proposal is that you tell me whether, if I were to withdraw from her life, you would undertake to ensure her happiness.

'Well? I was right, wasn't I?'

Looking up, Adam caught the unwavering blast of Didier's curiosity.

'He must have told you.'

'No!' Didier spoke with satisfaction. 'But, you see, I know him. Even when he is not himself, I can tell what he will do.' Clearly the sort of knowledge which Bishop Tobin found painful exhilarated Didier. But then, Adam reflected, Tobin had the care of a diocese full of souls and Didier had only one.

He went back to the letter.

> *There is a villa where people like me are looked after and the company is as congenial as it can be for men in my condition. I would let her divorce me. Then she and you could marry.*
>
> *You may fear that I have a hostile aim, but I give you my word that I have not. To be sure, if we put this offer to my wife, she may refuse from pity or pride. This is a risk. My question is: shall we take it?*

Adam handed back the opened letter. 'Had you really not seen it?'

Didier shook his head and began to read slowly, mouthing the words like a child. 'Not a word about honour!' he noted. 'If he's tricking anyone, it's himself. What's your answer?' Opening his coat, he produced a writing case with pens and ink bottles and laid them on a convenient window sill. 'Just write "I accept" at the bottom of the letter and sign. Or,' insolently, 'the opposite.'

Ah, thought Adam, he needs something on paper! He asked, 'Are you contriving a plot against your mistress?'

The small eyes blinked. 'No need, Monsieur. I saw what you and she were up to when you thought I had gone off on a fool's errand.'

'But you have no proof.'

'Monsieur d'Armaillé asked for none. He knows what I saw.'

'Then he knows too that by lingering to spy on us, you left

him in such distress at his wife's absence that he flung himself downstairs. You are to blame for his injury – and are clearly jealous of her. If she comes to harm ...'

'Yes?' The man's tone was challenging.

'The police will know who to blame.'

Adam retreated to the Quills' flat.

***

'You're a magnet for madness. Do you think it's because you're so sane?'

In Thady Quill's mouth, that word could mean 'cowardly' or, at best, 'inert'.

It was now mid-July and Thady, having travelled to the seaside hotel where Adam had registered under a false name, was dispensing news. He had started with an account of Maupassant's funeral and of the eulogy delivered by Monsieur Zola, which Tassart had described in tearful detail to the Quills. A pity, Thady thought, that the man whose life attracted such praise had not been allowed to choose when to end it.

'"A bad passing"! Doesn't his name mean something like that?'

Adam dismissed a fear that this was a taunt. Thady could not know that he had failed Guy and might now be failing Danièle. No! That couldn't be true. After all, it was for her sake that he was lying low in Uncle Matthew's old bolt-hole and refraining from either visiting or writing to her.

What, though, if the husband's offer were sincere and Adam's restraint misjudged?

Inert? Cowardly?

On impulse, he told Thady that he had an errand to run, then slipped out to the post office and sent a telegram. It consisted of one word and was unsigned. If d'Armaillé had been waiting for that word, he would know who sent it.

Back in the hotel, Adam marvelled that he had not done this sooner. Solitude must have softened his brain during his stay here, where his only visitor was Thady Quill. Thady brought him letters and news, which meant that on his visits the tempo of Adam's life shifted from tedium to anxiety.

He didn't mind tedium – welcomed it, in fact, having fled here from Paris when the ex-orderly was spotted, once too often, stalking him in the breezy dusk, coat-tails flapping like a malevolent bird. To cap that, a letter had come from Félicité saying, 'While Monsieur is alive, Didier will do nothing daft!' It was worrying to learn that d'Armaillé's health was all that stood between daft dangers and Danièle. *She* did not write either, being watched too closely for letters to be smuggled out. Félicité had written hers in a post office in the nearest town. An admirer – Félicité could find one anywhere – had driven her there and back in his gig. Today again, there was a letter from her in Thady's bag. It advised Adam to bide his time and consider the following: Monsieur d'Armaillé seemed to be waiting for something and was behaving like a man in a trance. Didier had returned. Danièle was suffering from melancholia and might be becoming addicted to morphine. She sometimes mentioned Adam but in a dreamy, inconclusive way. Perhaps the sight of her husband sitting stoically in his Bath-chair had paralysed her.

'But you mustn't come,' emphasized Félicité, 'anywhere near

here. Not <u>yet</u>.' She underlined the words so forcefully that her pen pierced the paper.

Paralysis. Hypnosis! It was like a spell! Well, for better or worse, Adam's telegram would break it. Its single word was 'Yes.'

***

'Any move,' Thady approved when told of this, 'must be better than none. As it is, you're like three sleeping beauties!' And Thady, who had enjoyed a bottle of Saumur with his lunch, laughed with tipsy wisdom and poured himself some Calvados.

Next, fishing in his bag, he said he had letters from Ireland. 'Tell me first,' he paused, 'which of your two women you really want. I think I should know.'

Adam grimaced. 'Don't torment me. I'm half dead with need for Danièle.' Telling Thady that to lose her would be to lose a vital part of himself reminded him of how, when still ignorant of her husband's plight, he had described this same feeling to her as an 'amputation' – then been perplexed by her anger. 'May I?' Picking up the glass of Calvados, he drank, then grimaced again when the alcohol blazed in his mouth. 'The other day I stabbed my hand, just to feel something. See.' He showed the scar.

'What do you expect to be the result of your telegram?'

'Who knows?' Adam turned up his hands. 'Perhaps a gun will go off. I don't think Danièle will be the target. It's more likely to be me. Or some bystander.' With amusement, he saw Thady blench. 'Here.' He handed back the glass.

Thady raised it. "'May we be alive this time next year!' That's a modest old toast. So now,' he drained his glass, 'for the Irish news. Cait.'

'Oh God!'

Adam had managed – more or less – to put her from his mind, which was frantic with fears for Danièle. So how could he deal with Irish responsibilities? He could, perhaps, have mollified Cait by sending seaside postcards, but had feared that this must seem cavalier. Anything kinder, though, would fall into the dread category of 'raising hopes', a thing which, though he had never intended, he seemed repeatedly to have done. Cait was in some ways as baffling to him as a Congo native and as eager – guiltily he quashed the thought – to eat him. In their hinterland, where there were few people of her station, he must be the nearest she had come to finding her match. Unmatched, she risked becoming an outlandish figure, and children might soon be pelting her with stones.

'How is she?'

'She's mounting a demonstration,' Thady reported. 'She has been visiting her mountainy clan and returned with a son whom she calls after your father, while hinting that he may, instead, be yours.'

'How could she have a son?'

'Well, I'm told she put on weight last year and was away a lot, supposedly to help nurse an aunt. It seems that he looks about fifteen months old, a big bouncing fellow like the Christ child in the Italian picture that Bishop Tobin brought back from one of his trips – too big for a nativity, as the mothers in the congregation often remarked, but perfect for Cait's purposes. There's a letter here from the bish himself, who is no doubt furious. I haven't read it, but have sources of my own, as you may imagine. Brady for one.'

Adam felt reluctant to pick up either Tobin's letter or the one from Con Keogh, which was now emerging from Thady's bag.

Thady, noting this, informed him that Cait was back living in Keogh's hospital and had the child with her. Gary *Óg* she called him. Young Gary.

'Give me Keogh's letter.' Fumbling it open, Adam skimmed and took in its guess that Gary *Óg* could have been sired by one of Cait's cousins. She might not even be its mother. In her mind though, Con insisted, the child was a claim made flesh: her claim on Adam and his father. To her this would seem perfectly logical. After all, one way or another, the boy – who looked like them both – was of their blood.

'You've driven her mad, Adam,' Keogh reproached. 'And your friend the bishop is mad too. He thinks my charity to her is designed to disgrace his flock. The backwoods behaviour of Cait's relatives was tolerated as long as it remained in the backwoods, but ...'

Adam put the letters in his pocket.

'I sometimes think of her,' he told Thady, 'as a reincarnation of my mother.'

'Adam, you're mad! Cait is a ...'

'Don't say it.'

Adam felt his tongue swell. Anger, at words which might not have been in Thady's mind at all, gagged him. 'I must,' he thought, 'settle money on her.' By now he could do this, for Belcastel's funds had become available. 'She needs ...' He paused unhappily. What she needed was himself.

'Hold your horses, Adam,' Thady advised. 'Best send no more telegrams.'

Adam blushed. It had not occurred to him to send one to Ireland. The code which came so promptly to Thady's mind – his wife liked reading him sentimental novels – required that, gallantly and even at the cost of his own happiness, Adam should be Cait's saviour.

Thady, who did not in fact hold with the code, supposed Adam to need rescuing from it. 'I advise you,' he urged, 'to keep your feet on the ground. You must have other worldly friends. If you don't trust me, think what they might advise.'

Guy's name sprang to mind, and Adam wondered what *he* would have done. Given both women syphilis, perhaps?

Regretting the thought, he made an excuse and again slipped out to send a telegram. It was to Keogh, and its gist was that Keogh should calm any fears Cait might have of being abandoned. Adam, he should tell her, was coming to Ireland.

Back in the hotel, he and Thady talked late into the night, then staggered to their beds and slept till noon.

After lunch – a headachy affair, due to the previous evening's drinking – they moved to a porch to restore themselves with coffee then, in the interests of further head-clearing, agreed to take a walk up the coast.

However, as they marshalled hats and sticks, Adam looked out, saw a priest descend from a trap and recognized the habit of the White Fathers. Latour, he remembered, had his address. But this was not Latour. It was a young priest.

Thady had just been warning that if Adam made Cait his housekeeper, he must beware lest her relatives move in and help themselves to his property. 'Let her know,' he finished harshly, 'that if there's any sign of that, she'll be out on her ear, and themselves ahead of her.'

'Poor Cait!' The implacable hinterland voice roused pity.

'Are you really going to Ireland?'

'I must,' Adam realized, 'if only to let neighbours see that she has my moral support.'

***

Just then, however, the young priest walked in with news that changed everything.

He was Father Gérard, and Latour had sent him. Something appalling had happened to Monsieur d'Armaillé, so Latour himself had gone to comfort the widow.

'Widow?'

As Thady discreetly tiptoed away, Father Gérard reported that, late yesterday afternoon, Madame d'Armaillé, her maid and a muscular footman who always accompanied them on walks, had happened on a chilling scene.

In one of the family's favourite picnic spots, a rug had been spread, a trap drawn up and a pony tethered to a tree. On the rug was a wine-bucket with a half-full bottle of champagne, a picnic hamper, various oddments including cushions arranged to prop up the dead body of Monsieur d'Armaillé, the slumped, equally dead body of his ex-orderly, and a pistol. Each had been shot through the head: a clean, efficient job, said the priest, but, according to reports, there was no way of knowing which of the two had done it. No doubt the thing had been agreed between them, for they were close together and there was only one gun.

'Tied to the champagne bottle was a telegram consisting of one word.'

'Yes?'

'That was the word.' Father Gérard tripped over his tongue. '"Yes" was the message.'

'Christ!' Adam guessed that he must look alarmingly ill, for Thady, who had been hovering in the corridor, was now at his side, holding a glass of something strong to his lips and asking if there was anything he could do.

'You could go to the post office,' Adam told him, 'and send a telegram begging Con to tell Cait that I can't come after all. Tell him I'm sorry. He must look after her and if he is out of pocket, I'll reimburse him.'

After that he sank into a state where he felt nothing. Perhaps the feelings he might have felt had cancelled each other out? Guilt? Hope? Rousing himself, he became aware that Father Gérard was speaking urgently, that the sky outside was red, and that a man who looked like Guy was looking in. But of course it was Thady back from his errand and probably wearing one of Guy's overcoats.

Focusing on the priest's words, Adam grasped that he was being asked to let a year elapse before marrying Danièle. In the meantime, they could meet discreetly in an apartment in the home for old officers to which d'Armaillé had once thought of retiring.

'If he had,' explained Father Gérard, 'the plan would have been for his wife to visit him there whenever she chose, then slip upstairs to see you. Even now, we can make use of it. Appearances still need to be kept up. Father Latour is hoping to ensure that the double suicide can be presented as a mercy killing. That, of course, is a sin and a bad example to others, but the reality behind it is worse.'

'It *is*?'

'I'm afraid so.'

The real scandal, the priest explained, was not Adam's passion for a married woman. No. It was her husband's corrupt relations with his ex-orderly, which explained why the pair had gone to the Congo in the first place, then lingered there for so long.

'Didn't he have to go because of a duel? And didn't your brothers in religion send reports of his enjoying relations there with Arab women?'

'Pff!' Father Gérard's mournful exhalation blew away such smoke screens. 'My brothers in religion were bamboozled! The "women" may not have been women, and the duel – I believe it ended more bloodily than intended – may have been designed to earn a remission from a marriage of convenience! Alas Monsieur, reality is trickier than one thinks.' And, as the priest filled in his story, kaleidoscopes of strategies and devices fanned in his mind's eye and transferred themselves to Adam's. 'The destructive passion,' he insisted, 'was neither the wronged wife's nor yours. You were both victims.'

'Of unfortunate encounters? *Mauvais passants*?'

The priest sighed. 'We must pray that at the last they managed to repent.'

***

A year later Con Keogh, in Paris for Adam's wedding, brought news of Cait. She had settled into the gate-lodge where Adam and his mother had stayed just before their lives fell apart. Cait liked it though. Keogh, using Adam's money, had had it fixed up. He had had the big house fixed too and sent Cait to learn from one of the Earl of Sligo's stewards how to run an estate so that she might one day run Adam's. Within months, though, this hope foundered when the job proved beyond her. She hadn't the head for it, wrote his lordship's steward. Nor, perhaps, the heart.

'Well, thanks to you,' said Keogh, 'she doesn't need to work. When are you coming to visit us and see the improvements?'